Berkley Sensation Titles by Linda Winstead Jones

THE SUN WITCH
THE MOON WITCH
THE STAR WITCH

PRINCE OF MAGIC
PRINCE OF FIRE
PRINCE OF SWORDS

UNTOUCHABLE
22 NIGHTS
BRIDE BY COMMAND

Bride by Command

Linda Winstead Jones

BERKLEY SENSATION, NEW YORK

THE BERKLEY PUBLISHING GROUP
Published by the Penguin Group
Penguin Group (USA) Inc.
375 Hudson Street, New York, New York 10014, USA
Penguin Group (Canada), 90 Eglinton Avenue East, Suite 700, Toronto, Ontario M4P 2Y3, Canada
(a division of Pearson Penguin Canada Inc.)
Penguin Books Ltd., 80 Strand, London WC2R 0RL, England
Penguin Group Ireland, 25 St. Stephen's Green, Dublin 2, Ireland (a division of Penguin Books Ltd.)
Penguin Group (Australia), 250 Camberwell Road, Camberwell, Victoria 3124, Australia
(a division of Pearson Australia Group Pty. Ltd.)
Penguin Books India Pvt. Ltd., 11 Community Centre, Panchsheel Park, New Delhi—110 017, India
Penguin Group (NZ), 67 Apollo Drive, Rosedale, North Shore 0632, New Zealand
(a division of Pearson New Zealand Ltd.)
Penguin Books (South Africa) (Pty.) Ltd., 24 Sturdee Avenue, Rosebank, Johannesburg 2196,
South Africa

Penguin Books Ltd., Registered Offices: 80 Strand, London WC2R 0RL, England

This is a work of fiction. Names, characters, places, and incidents either are the product of the author's imagination or are used fictitiously, and any resemblance to actual persons, living or dead, business establishments, events, or locales is entirely coincidental. The publisher does not have any control over and does not assume any responsibility for author or third-party websites or their content.

BRIDE BY COMMAND

A Berkley Sensation Book / published by arrangement with the author

PRINTING HISTORY
Berkley Sensation mass-market edition / March 2009

Copyright © 2009 by Linda Winstead Jones.
Cover art by Daniel O'Leary.
Cover design by Lesley Worrell.
Interior text design by Kristin del Rosario.

ISBN: 978-0-425-22804-3

BERKLEY® SENSATION
Berkley Sensation Books are published by The Berkley Publishing Group,
a division of Penguin Group (USA) Inc.,
375 Hudson Street, New York, New York 10014.
BERKLEY® SENSATION and the "B" design are trademarks of Penguin Group (USA) Inc.

PRINTED IN THE UNITED STATES OF AMERICA

10 9 8 7 6 5 4 3 2 1

With special thanks to
Allison Brandau, Wendy McCurdy,
and Christine Zika.

Prologue

✳

The Columbyanan Palace in the Sixth Year of the
Reign of Emperor Nechtyn Jahn Calcus Sadwyn Beckyt
First Night of the Spring Festival

WHEN he had dismissed the last of his advisers, Jahn
gave a tired sigh and sat heavily in the crimson padded
chair which dominated one corner of his spacious and ornate bedchamber. There were times when he found peace
in this private room he called his own. The bed was large
and comfortable; the furnishings were finer than anything
he had known before coming to Arthes; there was a fire
whenever he wanted or needed one; and there was no
skimping when it came to the scented oils which burned
here and there, lighting the dimmer corners and adding a
sweet scent to the air. Here there were no demands made of
him. The demanding moments took place in the ballroom
or his suite of offices. This chamber, decorated in imperial
crimson and made as comfortable as any man could wish
for, was meant for pleasure and rest and rare peace.

But tonight Jahn could find no peace. What had he
done? In a fit of pique he had set in motion a ridiculous
contest which would end in his inevitable and unwelcome
marriage. Perhaps he would have a bit of fun along the
way, as he watched those around him scramble to make

this concept work, but would it be worth the trouble? He could just as easily have instructed any one of his ministers to choose a bride for him. They all had very strong ideas about which woman would make the best empress. The ladies were all talented or intelligent or beautiful or came from a fine bloodline which would strengthen his ties with a country or a tribe. It wasn't as if love or physical attraction would play any part in his decision, no matter how the game was played.

Being emperor had its advantages, and he was not ignorant of them. His word was law. Literally. If he wanted something, anything, all he had to do was ask and it was delivered to him. Loose women, his favorite type, cared only for pleasing him. He had his own army at his command. His days of indulging in physical labor and answering the commands of others were over.

And yet he could not have the simple luxury of falling in love before marriage. He could not choose to remain unwed, if such a lifestyle suited him. This extraordinary palace was often more a prison than a home, and there were days when he could almost feel the walls closing in on him, as they did now. Marriage and the resulting fatherhood would only imprison him more surely.

He was trapped.

Still sitting, Jahn began to unfasten his long, cumbersome robe. He was damned tired of crimson, especially on this night when he had set the wheels of change into motion. One word, and the sentinels who were positioned outside his door would fetch one or two of Jahn's favorite ladies, and they would make him forget that he was as much a prisoner as a ruler. They would make him forget everything. Melusina, perhaps, or Anrid. Just the thought of them made him grin. Melusina had a wonderful laugh that always made him smile, and Anrid possessed great, white breasts so soft he could happily fondle them for hours.

Once he was married, he would give them up, he supposed. He *could* keep all the women he desired. He *could* continue to live as if he were not a husband, as if he had no bonds, no boundaries. His marriage could, if he so chose, be approached as if it were for nothing more than politics and for the sake of producing a child. And once the empress caught a babe, he could banish her to some remote corner of the palace, bringing her out for holidays and social affairs and such, and resume his lascivious lifestyle.

But he would not. Jahn was determined that he would not become his father. No matter what his weaknesses might be, he was a good ruler who put the needs of the people first, always. He had not been trained all his life for this position, he had not been born and bred with politics in his mind and his heart. But he knew how to make people like him, when it was necessary, and he was good at surrounding himself with capable followers who did their jobs well and in the process made him look as if *he* were capable.

And unlike his father, once he was wed he would be faithful—even if it killed him.

Knowing his carefree days were numbered, Jahn found the energy to leap from his chair and rush to the door, blasted crimson robe halfway undone. He opened that door swiftly to reveal four sentinels whose duty was to keep their emperor safe. Jahn's eyes fell on Blane, a quiet and sensible and slightly rotund man who had been with him from the beginning.

"Melusina," he said sharply.

Blane nodded once and turned away.

"And Anrid," Jahn called after him. If his days were numbered, he might as well enjoy them all to the utmost.

LADY Morgana Ramsden had crept from her soft bed, escaped through her bedchamber window, and walked a relatively short distance from her fine home to hide in the shadows of the forest and watch the servants and villagers dance around the bonfire and celebrate the season of life, of fertility. Morgana had heard whispers that for some it was also a season of sexual awakening, of virile men and welcoming women, a celebration of pleasure given and taken, of life begun. Knowing how protective her stepfather was, it was no wonder she was not allowed to attend such a common celebration, that she had been forbidden even to observe the festivities from afar. What her stepfather didn't know wouldn't hurt him.

Morgana led a blessed life for the most part, a much easier life than those of the plainly dressed girls who danced around the fire and laughed out loud and flirted with brawny men. She watched in awe as a young woman with wild, dark hair all but pressed her large, round bosom in the face of a momentarily startled man and then danced away, laughing. The man recovered from his surprise quickly and followed, and he laughed, too. Any one of those girls would likely do anything to be in Morgana's position, and yet she often envied them their laughter and freedom.

She was so intent on watching the revelers she did not realize Tomas Glyn was behind her until he laid a hand on her shoulder. Instinctively Morgana gasped, threw off his hand, and spun about. Her fair hair whipped across her face, and even though she was relieved to see it was a lifelong family friend who had surprised her, she remained angry.

"You should not sneak up on a girl that way," she admonished. "You startled me. I would not wish to hurt you."

Tomas smiled widely. "You? Hurt me? Impossible."

"I might've been armed with a dagger or a small sword."

"Are you?" he asked, his tone friendly.

"No, of course not, but I *might've* been."

He moved a step closer. "A fine lady of your position should not be out here all alone. It is not fitting."

The back of her neck tingled; she did not like the way he looked at her. "I am not alone now."

"True enough." Tomas looked past her to watch the revelry she had so recently envied. The peasants were far enough away that they could not hear whispers from the forest over their laughter and song. "Look at them. Aren't they pathetic? Dancing around the fire and singing as if some god or goddess will bless them simply because they threw a party to see in the new season. I suppose they must take whatever small pleasures they can find, poor creatures."

Morgana did not think the villagers pathetic, not at all, but neither did she wish to argue. "You won't tell my stepfather that you saw me, will you?" she asked. "He has forbidden me to wander away from home on my own, and he would be livid if he knew I'd sneaked out at night. I shouldn't have disobeyed him, I know, but I did so want to see the celebration." In years past she had considered stealing away to watch one festivity or another, but this was the first time she'd dared to actually leave the house.

Tomas's eyes narrowed in obvious disapproval. "You should not defy Almund. He's been very good to you."

"Yes, he has."

Tomas could not accept that agreement and move on. He had to elaborate. "Almund gave you his name, raised you as his own, and even now he allows you to have more freedom than any woman should."

Morgana's chin came up. They had had this conversation before, too many times. "I suppose you are speaking of my unwillingness to marry?"

"Yes," Tomas said softly.

Before her death seven years earlier, Morgana's mother, the lovely Awel Ramsden, had made her husband, Almund, promise that he would not force their only child into taking a husband she did not love. Awel had been frantically insistent, in fact. Caught up in the emotion of the moment, the grieving husband had agreed to his wife's last request, and so far had stuck with that promise, even though he was openly weary of Morgana's constant refusals of offers. What Almund Ramsden did not know was that his wife had also begged her daughter not to give in to marriage until she discovered a love she could trust. Awel's first marriage, her short-lived union with Morgana's long-deceased father, had been an arranged one. Though Awel had never offered Morgana details, she had made it clear that to marry without love was a terrible mistake.

Real love was worth waiting for, Awel Ramsden had insisted fervently, not long before she took her last breath.

Morgana was taken by surprise when Tomas reached out and caressed her hair. He'd offered himself as husband more than once, and she'd always refused, just as she refused all others. Unlike her stepfather and the other men who no longer called upon her, Tomas displayed quite a lot of patience. He was persistent to a fault.

"Marry me," he said, not for the first time.

"No."

"I know you're uncertain about me, but if it's love you want, as so many women seem to do, then be assured that love will come, in time," he said. "Even if it does not, we can be great friends for a lifetime. Are the best of marriages not between friends?"

"My answer remains no." She did not know if the kind of love her mother had spoken of existed for her—it certainly had not shown itself thus far—but she did understand that she didn't love Tomas and never would.

In the darkness she could not see his face well. Shadows of the forest hid his expression from her. But she saw too well the tightening of his lips, the tic of his jaw. "Are you too good for me, Lady Morgana, is that it? Are you too pretty? Too rich? Too pure?"

"No! That's not it at all."

"Then what is your problem? Why do you constantly refuse me when I have done everything to win you to my side?" Tomas's frustration was clear in his voice and in the alarming balling of his fists.

Morgana instinctively stepped back, wondering if Tomas would catch her if she tried to escape. Of course he would. His legs were longer than hers, and he was not impeded by a heavy, cumbersome skirt.

He looked into her eyes, and something in his expression softened. "There's nothing to be afraid of," he said, and he reached out to boldly caress her breast with the tips of his fingers, much in the same casual way he had caressed her hair moments earlier. When Morgana stepped back once more, when she tried to move away from his touch, Tomas grabbed the fabric of her dark blue gown, chosen for this night so she could blend into the shadows, and forcefully pulled her to him. Stitches popped, fabric ripped, and Morgana felt a growing chill inside her, as a seed of fear took root in her heart.

"Stop," she whispered.

"I'll show you there's nothing to be afraid of," Tomas said, and then he grabbed her chin and with unkind fingers forced her face up. He planted his mouth over hers for what she supposed was meant to be a kiss which would sway her. As if his forcefulness would make her desire to take him as a husband! Morgana pursed her lips and tried to push him away, but he was too strong. The chill grew colder and larger. It reached deep, like shards of ice, as Tomas forced his tongue into her mouth.

She had never felt so cold, and the chill at the center of her being scared her almost as much as Tomas's insistent touch. "Stop right now or you will be sorry," Morgana said when she was able to turn her mouth from his and take a deep, ragged breath.

"I don't think so," Tomas said with confidence. "Until now I have been very tolerant of your quirks and demands. I have asked nicely, and I've waited for you to come to your senses. I'm not going to wait anymore. Almund has spoiled you, but I will not. I see now that tolerance is not what you need from a man. Perhaps you have simply been waiting for a man to take what he requires of you. You need a man to control you, a man to own you. I'm man enough to take what I want, Morgana. When I saw you slip out of your window, I knew this would be the night."

The chill inside Morgana grew, and seemed to move throughout her body, traveling through the blood in her veins. She was struck by the certainty that this chill was not normal. Something was very wrong. "You followed me?"

"You're mine," Tomas said in a threatening voice. "Stop fighting what is meant to be."

As with the others who had pursued her, what was "meant to be" was a partnership with the Ramsden family fortune and lands. One day her stepfather would be gone, and the house and the land would all be hers. It was an elegant, finely crafted house and there was a lot of land. Tomas was greedy like all the rest, not a friend at all. "Stop this while you can," Morgana said softly.

Maybe Tomas heard something he did not like in her voice, because for a moment he did stop. He went very still, but unfortunately that stillness did not last. He foolishly continued, clumsily lifting her skirt and poking at her with his fingers.

"Do you like that?" he asked.

"No," Morgana whispered, trying to contain the frostiness that made her feel as if her heart were literally made of ice. Her fingers tingled, and it seemed that the icy water flowing through her veins was cold as snow. Tomas's hand slipped between her legs, and he grabbed. It hurt; his rough touch terrified her. She tried to slip from his grasp; she slapped his hands and pushed against him, hoping to free herself from his hold on her and *run,* taking the chance that she could lose him in the dark shadows, but he held her tightly.

"You will like me well enough before I'm done. Relax, and you will like it very well."

Unable to escape, Morgana attempted to contain the iciness inside her, to push it down. She didn't understand the growing coldness which was coursing through her, but she knew instinctively that it was bad. No good could come of it. But the excitement of the moment, the danger, the rush of vulnerability and anger had awakened a dark power she did not wish to possess. There was no turning back. Still, she tried. She reached for calmness, for peace, and found only coldness. She delved deep inside herself for control and found only chaos. Never in her life had she experienced pure panic, a complete loss of control and peace, not until now.

"You will marry me, Morgana," Tomas said. "After tonight, you will have no choice. No other suitable man will have you once everyone knows we've become lovers beneath the moon of the First Night of the Spring Festival."

"There is no love in this, Tomas. Please stop."

He slapped her once and threw her to the ground, then quickly dropped to press his heavy body atop her. That was a terrible mistake, for with his violence he made it impossible for her to contain the horror he had awakened. What Morgana had so hoped to control was now unleashed, and there was no turning back. Tears stung her eyes, trailing down her cheeks and turning to ice that clung to her skin. Her body went rigid and a scream rose in her chest. She fought to contain that scream.

"You truly are cold," Tomas said as he reached down to unfasten his trousers so he could take by force what he considered to be his. "Cold to the bone. Cold skin, cold eyes . . . cold heart, I suspect. Stop fighting, Morgana. Relax. Do you not know that this is the season of carnal initiation? Never fear, woman, what I'm about to teach will warm you up quite well."

What she had attempted to still was unleashed, and Morgana screamed. The sound which was torn from her throat was foreign and frightening to her ears. Surely only a wounded animal would screech so.

Tomas backed away from her, falling to the side and rolling away, then coming up on his knees. "What the hell was that?"

He was no longer on top of her, no longer an immediate danger, but it was too late for her to stop what had begun as a simple chill. The unearthly coldness that had been building inside Morgana escaped from her body in one pulse, coloring a circle around her in blue and white light, and transforming everything within that circle—everything but Morgana herself—to crystal.

The grass, the fallen leaves, the trees, and Tomas—all clear and lifeless. Moonlight glimmered on what had once been life and was now cold, hard death. Lying on the ground in the midst of it all, Morgana reached out and touched what had once been a long blade of grass. It looked sharp but crumbled beneath her fingers, turning to dust without even marking her skin.

This should not be possible. It was wrong, unnatural, and wicked. What was she? What had she become? Was this destruction the result of a curse? Whatever the reason for her ghastly act, Morgana knew she had to escape before anyone found her here. She longed for the safety and warmth of home; she craved the heat of a fire in the hearth and a warm blanket and a locked door which would keep men like Tomas away from her.

As she stood, rising to her feet as carefully as possible, crystal grass and leaves beneath her feet broke into tiny pieces. The brittle crystal did not pierce her slippers or cut her feet. Instead, it simply crumbled into dust, more fragile than any ice or stone could ever be. Whatever substance all things in the path of her rage had become was unknown to her; it was not stone nor was it crystal.

For a moment she stared at what was left of Tomas. The statue before her looked like the man she knew had been sculpted of ice, down to the shape of his lips and the crease in his jacket and his halfway unfastened trousers. Moonlight gleamed on his frozen face; he looked so scared, as if in his last moment of life he'd realized what was happening, what he'd awakened, what a monster she was.

Morgana felt a surge of hope. If she had the power to transform everything in her path to this strange substance, perhaps she also had the power to undo it. A deep chill had preceded the burst of power. Perhaps warmth would turn Tomas to a man again. She reached out and touched his cold, hard face gently, hoping to give him some of the warmth which had returned to her. She leaned forward and blew a warm breath upon him, hoping all the while that he would become a man again.

Then she would run.

But Tomas did not transform; he remained a crystal statue in the shadows of the forest. A sob escaped Morgana's throat. Tomas was a bad person, a greedy man who was willing to take what he wanted if it was not offered to him, but that didn't mean he deserved to die this way. Was he entirely cold? Was there any life left in the form before her?

If only she had stayed in her room tonight, as her stepfather had ordered, Tomas would still be alive. Too soon Morgana heard the villagers approaching, their voices carrying sharply. She looked toward the bonfire and saw that at least half of the men there were headed her way. They had been drawn by her screech or the flash of light, and they could not find her here with what was left of Tomas. If they found her in the midst of destruction, they would know she was to blame—they would know she was cursed.

"I'm sorry," Morgana whispered, and then she ran, crystal grass and leaves crunching easily beneath her feet, until she left the circle of destruction she had created. Long before she reached her bedroom window, she heard the first villager's scream.

Chapter One

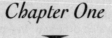

"IF I may be so bold as to say so once more, M'Lord Emperor, this is a very bad idea. A *very* bad idea." Blane was brave enough to attempt to look at Jahn as he spoke his mind, but their eyes did not quite meet. The sentinel seemed to stare at Jahn's forehead.

"No, you may not be so bold," Jahn said calmly. "And stop calling me M'Lord Emperor, and anything else that might give me away."

He should be annoyed with the sentinel for daring once again to speak out against such a brilliant plan, but the day was lovely and clear, the sky was a brilliant blue, and the road beneath the horses' hooves was even. Jahn wore a borrowed sentinel's green uniform which had seen better days, rather than the usual impeccably crafted crimson robe which had become his own uniform, of sorts. There was no crown upon his disheveled head. He had not shaved in more than three weeks.

He was much too happy to waste time chastising a man who was only trying to do his job.

"I have told you a hundred times to call me Devlyn

while we're carrying out our little charade," Jahn said without anger.

"It does not seem right, M'L . . . Devlyn."

"Devlyn was my name for many years longer than Jahn has been. You need not spit the name as if it tastes bitter."

Blane was indignant, in tone and in posture. "Still, it isn't right. You're the emperor! We should have a contingent of guards to watch over you. In truth, you should not be here at all. You're safer in the palace, where you can be properly guarded."

That was true enough, but there was more to life than safety. At least, there should be. "Would you deny a condemned man a few precious days of freedom?" Jahn asked.

"Marriage is hardly a condemnation," Blane argued.

"Are you married?" Odd that he did not know, as Blane was one of his favorite sentinels.

"Quite happily," Blane said with a lift of his chin. "I've been married to a wonderful woman for five years, now."

"No wonder you always look so well fed. Did you pick your bride all on your own?"

After a moment of silence, Blane's posture eased and he nodded. "I did."

"Well, then, you have an advantage over me."

After that, Blane remained silent.

They would reach the home of Lady Morgana Ramsden in the afternoon, by Blane's usually impeccable estimation. Of the six potential brides, she was one of two who lived close to Arthes. Since Jahn had never traveled in this particular direction and this route was not heavily traveled, they should be able to collect the woman in question and return to the palace without raising any suspicion. Jahn had met Almund Ramsden briefly, years earlier, but with his disguise—of which the beard was no small part—it was unlikely he'd be recognized. The entire excursion wouldn't take more than fourteen to sixteen days. Six of those days had already passed.

Jahn estimated he could remain out of the palace for

two weeks or a bit longer without raising any alarm. All was well in the country, except for the lack of an heir, a situation which seemed to terrify quite a few skittish followers. Those he called upon to keep things running smoothly continued to see to their duties in his absence, so the daily routine of government would not be disturbed. Before escaping from the palace Jahn had pleaded illness, something quite nasty and venomous that would keep all but a few loyal servants out of his bedroom. Those who cooperated with him in this charade would be well rewarded after his return. The others need never know.

And he would not only get out of the palace for a short while of blessed freedom, he would have the chance to see at least one of his potential wives up close long before he had to make his decision. Would she be a good and pleasant traveler or a pain in the ass? Most ladies of her type—rich and pampered—were a pain in the ass, but he supposed it was possible that he would be pleasantly surprised. After all, what woman would not be delighted at the prospect of being empress?

He would see Lady Morgana's real face in a situation where she had no idea he might one day be her husband. You could tell a lot about a person by the way they treated those beneath them; he had learned that quickly after he'd taken his position. If the lady was kind to the lowly sentinels who had been sent to escort her, along with whatever maids and chaperones accompanied her, then that would be a point or two in her favor.

If she was a demanding pain in the ass, he'd reveal himself as emperor, then reject her and send her home without a second thought. Eventually.

He rather wished he'd brought a woman with him, for companionship on the chilly nights when he slept on the hard ground as he had during his long-past days as a soldier. The happily married Blane might not like having a female along—he would probably find it unseemly—but he would not object. Brave or not, he would not dare. Lady Morgana would be sure to object, however, and if she ever made the connection between the humble bearded sentinel and the emperor, there would be hell to pay. With such women there was often hell to pay.

Why could he not simply marry Melusina or Anrid? Or both? Now, that was an idea. He did not love them, but they were pleasing in bed and undemanding, and they made him laugh even at the end of the longest day. Was that not enough to make a decent marriage? It was more than many men had.

In any case, he recognized that it was too late now to turn back and collect one or both of them, so he'd have to wait until he returned to the palace and made a "recovery" from his illness to enjoy the company of a woman or two in the short time he had left as a free man. Once he married, he would be faithful; like it or not, that was decided.

Fittingly enough, with that thought a gentle but cold rain began to fall.

MORGANA had been in a constant state of agitation for the past four weeks, since the unexpected message had arrived from the palace. That frenzy, on top of the distress connected with the events of the First Night of the Spring Festival, had her passing many a sleepless night—and her days were not much better. That was not good, not good at all. Her stomach was constantly in knots. She had a headache that would not go away. There were dark circles beneath her eyes, and her skin had little color. A slamming door or a dog's bark made her jump out of her skin, and when she did sleep, the dreams that came to her were so disturbing she woke more tired than when she'd fallen into her bed.

She was not suspected of causing Tomas's tragic fate. Who would suspect her? In the early days she had worried that perhaps someone had seen her slipping out of her window, or that Tomas had told one of his friends that he'd planned to see her that night. Her worries on those counts had been for nothing. The villagers and her stepfather, as well as Tomas's friends and family, had decided that poor Tomas had been lured into the forest by a traveling witch who'd seduced him—hence the undone britches—and then used black magic to turn him to glass, perhaps as part of dark sexual ritual.

Some of the first to arrive on the scene had made the mistake of trying to move the statue that had once been a man, and when they had done so, what Tomas had become in the wake of Morgana's anger had shattered into a thousand small pieces. All that was left of Tomas Glyn was a pile of ash his family had buried weeks ago.

Yes, a witch traveling through on the First Night of the Spring Festival made much more sense than even to consider the possibility that someone with such wicked power lived in their midst. Most chose to believe that whatever had transformed Tomas was now gone and would never return, but a few, a disturbing few, continued to question whether or not the monster who had killed one of their own was living among them or waiting nearby in the forest for another victim, hiding its dark powers until it chose to strike again. Morgana had become the fiend in a tale told to scare small children and skittish women—and men who might think to wander too far from home.

Now this. It was insulting that the emperor thought she'd agree to his inspection. Even if she had not decided—in the wake of the disaster with Tomas—never to marry, she'd be outraged. Her stepfather had refused to send a message of denial to the emperor, somehow thinking that he might be able to change her mind. Morgana planned simply to tell whatever official arrived to fetch her that she was not interested in the emperor's offer. Perhaps she would apologize for the wasted trip—or perhaps she would not.

Her stepfather continued to be stubborn. He insisted such an insult to the emperor would be unforgivable, and that she had been offered a great opportunity and should grab it gratefully. What about the insult to *her*? Did that count for nothing?

And now, to add to the insult, she discovered that her

planned escort was not to be a highly placed official at all, but instead, consisted of two common sentinels and whatever chaperone her stepfather might decide to send with the party—not that any party would be necessary, as she had no intention of leaving this house. Still, she did not even rate a highly placed escort! Not that she would agree to the ridiculous proposition if a minister or even a prince had come to collect her.

The sentinel who stood before her in the main room—pale-faced and squat, with his longish dark hair pulled back in a semi-neat braid—apparently realized the depth of her displeasure. He did not look her in the eye, and his fingers twitched often. No, he was not a man of influence and power. He took orders, he did not deliver them. Making him run back to the palace empty-handed would be easy enough.

It was the other one she was worried about.

The fair-haired, bearded sentinel was taller than his companion. He had intelligent eyes and, even though he was a common sentinel of low rank, a superior air. His long hair was worn loose, thick and straight and oddly streaked with different shades of blond. Above the untended beard, his cheekbones were high and well-shaped. He might be handsome beneath the beard, but perhaps he was one of those men who hid the fact that he had no chin with an abundance of facial hair. Why else would he sport a beard which seemed to be constructed of every color hair under the sun? Even from a distance she could see several shades of red, blond, and brown. Since he looked so annoyingly smug, she took some small pleasure from imagining that he had no chin at all.

"This is a once-in-a-lifetime opportunity," her stepfather said tersely. "Don't be stubborn."

Morgana responded as she always did. "You promised my mother that I would be allowed to choose my own husband."

"At that time, I did not realize you would be so blasted particular," he responded with apparent anger. His face turned red as he blustered. "You will soon be twenty-five years of age! The time for marrying and producing children will pass you by, and you must have children so all that I have created here will be passed on to family." There was a distant nephew, but he was less than bright and had no manners at all. To leave him the estate would be unacceptable.

Morgana could not tell her stepfather that she would never marry, because he would insist on knowing why she'd come to that decision, and she could not explain it to him. That broke her heart, since even though he was not her real father and she had sometimes been mulish in the past few years, he still considered her his daughter as surely as if he had sired her himself. Could he not see that they would have a pleasant life here, just the two of them? She could care for him in his old age. No one would rile or enrage her, not if her life was quiet and well-planned from day to day, so there would be no repeat of the disaster with Tomas. She and Almund could play cards and throw the occasional party, and if people thought she was odd, well, she could live with that.

Morgana knew she could not allow herself to relent, not even a little bit. What Tomas had brought to life in her could be activated again, by some other man who made demands or roused fear in her. For years she had waited for the true love her mother insisted was real, and now . . . now she knew she was not fit for any man or for any love.

She could not share her deepest fears with anyone, not even her stepfather. "Everyone who has been presented to me is either too old, too portly, too arrogant, or too stupid. From all I hear, the emperor is guilty of all four, except maybe the portly. Since I have never seen him, I can't say, but since he's well-known to be indiscriminately lascivious, I suspect he's guilty of gluttony as well."

The sentinel before her went impossibly paler, and she could swear his lower lip shook. The taller man who stood in the corner seemed to suppress a smile. Her stepfather placed a hand over his heart.

"Morgana, the words you speak will be repeated to the emperor by these fine sentinels."

"I do not care." She looked squarely at the dark-haired soldier before her, hardening her heart. "You may tell your emperor all that I have said, and you may also tell him that I refuse, refuse, *refuse* his ridiculous offer."

Both sentinels bowed crisply and turned away to exit the room. Her stepfather trembled with anger and balled his fists tightly. When the door had closed behind the two soldiers from Arthes, the man who had cared for her since the age of four turned on her. His face was truly and disturbingly red, and his hands trembled.

He screamed. He accused her of terrible things. None of them were as terrible as the act she had actually if accidentally done, but still, his words were hurtful. She was not horribly spoiled, and she *did* care about the feelings of others. She was *not* impossible, and in truth she was no pickier than any other woman of discrimination.

She was prepared to argue with Almund, to calm him down with sweet words, as she was usually able to do, but he did not seem to be in the mood for reason. So she told him the truth. Part of it, anyway. "I have decided that I shall never marry."

Almund's face turned red. "Ridiculous. You *will* marry." He shook his head once and then shouted, "I rescind my promise to your mother, here and now. I swear to God, Morgana, I will marry you to the next man who walks through that door, whether you like it or not!"

She did not get a chance to argue, as the door opened and the tall, fair-haired sentinel walked into the room. He looked briefly at Morgana and then turned his attention to Almund. "It just so happens that I'm in the market for a wife, and I suspect your daughter would do quite nicely."

JAHN had been standing in the entryway, waiting for Blane to return from the kitchen with food for the second half of the unsuccessful journey, when he'd heard Ramsden's words. Still annoyed by Lady Morgana's rejection, he had not been able to help himself, and now here he stood, facing a beautiful, arrogant woman and a stunned, angry man. Both of them were beautifully dressed, well-groomed, and filled with pride—not a hair or a thread out of place— and among the finest citizenry Columbyana had to offer. And they were completely at his mercy.

"You did swear to God," Jahn said when neither of the others responded. "The emperor, as well as the priests who counsel him, take such vows very seriously. The emperor and Father Braen will be very upset if they hear that you made such a vow and then rescinded it, as you verbally annulled your promise to your late wife."

"I . . . I lost my temper," Ramsden said in a lowered voice. He was not a tall man, nor did he have the slenderness of youth or the brawniness that came from physical labor. No, he was a gentleman who'd led a soft life. "I truly did not mean . . ."

"Then you should not have sworn before God," Jahn said, taking a few steps closer to Lady Morgana. "My needs are not cumbersome. I simply require someone to cook and clean and wash my uniforms," he explained as his eyes met hers. She had warm green eyes which were complemented by her golden hair, full lips, and a fine—if smallish for his taste—bosom. She looked tired and her face was too pale, but perhaps she was always a touch haggard. Being unrelentingly difficult was certainly tiring. She most definitely needed to be taken down a peg or two, and a bit of sun wouldn't hurt. "There will be some mending, I suppose." He fingered a frayed section of his shirtsleeve. "I can also give you those grandchildren you so desire. Lots of them." He gave the lady a wink.

"You were listening in on a private conversation," Ramsden snapped with indignation, pulling himself up to his full unimpressive height.

Jahn turned his head to glare at the older man. "I was in

the room when you mentioned heirs, and you were practically shouting at the time. I would have had to be deaf not to 'listen in,' as you put it."

Morgana and the old man began to speak at once, both of them making excuses. Still, Jahn was determined. Since becoming emperor he had learned not to back down. He had learned to stand his ground longer and more firmly than anyone else. He had learned to get what he wanted. Truth be told, he had always been able to get what he wanted. *Backing down* had never been his strong suit.

"I refuse," Morgana said haughtily, turning her face away from him and lifting her cute little chin in defiance. "Honestly, I don't know what would make you think I'd reject an emperor and then accept *you*."

"It would take many days for me to arrange for a priest to arrive to conduct the ceremony, and I'm sure you don't have many days," Ramsden said nervously. "The emperor will be awaiting your return. You do not want to make Emperor Jahn wait."

Jahn was not swayed. "In many parts of the country, all that is required for a common marriage is that the man and woman agree, or that the woman is given to the man by the head of household. Once they consummate the marriage, they are legally man and wife. There is no real need for a priest for those of us of a lower station."

"How dare you?" Morgana whispered. "I am not a slave or a possession to be given away."

Jahn stood tall. "Perhaps I should speak with your father alone." He waved his hand dismissively. "Go make yourself pretty for the travels ahead."

Morgana gasped, but when her stepfather nodded his head and told her everything would be all right, she fled from the room.

Ramsden seemed confident enough. Perhaps the rich man thought he could buy discretion and a bit of forgetfulness from a sentinel who had been in the right place at the right time and was looking to be rewarded for his good luck. A few gold coins, a small piece of land . . . what would he offer? Jahn didn't want to play the game long enough to find out.

When Morgana was gone from the room, Jahn turned his full attention to Almund. "Sir, you have not looked me fully in the face since I arrived. I realize that I am a lowly servant, and therefore not worthy of your attention, but I suggest you look at me now. Look me in the eye as you would an equal, if you please."

No matter what he wore, no matter how disheveled he appeared to be, he was emperor—and he had met this man once before, shortly after the coronation.

Almund grudgingly looked Jahn in the eye as directed, and almost instantly recognition colored his face and filled his eyes with fear. "Oh, My Lord Emperor." He bowed and then came up crisply. His entire body shook. "I'm so sorry you had to hear my daughter's tirade. She's spoiled horribly—yes, spoiled—and it's entirely my fault. All my fault. Naturally I did not recognize you in your clever disguise. Clever, very clever," he muttered. "I hope you were not offended."

"To hear that I'm old, fat, arrogant, indiscriminate, and what else? Oh, yes, stupid. Why should I be offended?"

Almund went pale, as he should. "Morgana is sometimes a difficult girl, but deep down she's very sweet."

Jahn did not bother to agree that Lady Morgana might be a saint, deep down. What he had seen of her was not at all sweet. She must keep that part of her personality well hidden and buried *very* deep. She needed to be taught a lesson in humility. The woman who had lived her entire pampered life getting anything and everything she desired needed to learn that life was not so easy. Lady Morgana should be pleased to be considered for the position of empress. She should be delighted that she had been given the opportunity to vie for a place in his bed. Before he was done with her, she would be.

"Here's what we're going to do."

* * *

MORGANA had returned to the main room expecting that she'd find her stepfather contrite over his lost temper and the sentinel gone, paid off in some profitable way. That had undoubtedly been his plan all along. He couldn't possibly want her as his wife! No, he'd been looking for a bit of profit, that was all.

Instead she had been unceremoniously given to the bearded sentinel as one might offer a stale loaf of bread to a beggar. One of the kitchen maids packed Morgana a very small bag that could not possibly contain more than a single change of clothes and a comb for her hair, and then she'd been tossed out on her ear in the company of two sentinels, including the one who claimed her as his wife.

She left her home with no retinue at all. No maid, no chaperone, not a single attendant.

Morgana worked very hard at controlling her anger. She buried her fear. In the not-so-distant past she had unwillingly tapped into an unknown power and taken the life of a man. She was certain she would never squash the guilt of taking a life, no matter what Tomas's intent had been on that night, and she certainly didn't want it to happen again, not even if the blasted sentinel who dared to claim her was at the center of her destruction. No, she would find another way out of this untenable situation.

As they rode toward Arthes, she kept herself cool and distant and separate from her emotions so the chill of destruction would not overtake her again, and yet she knew that if her passions were strong enough, if her insides roiled with fear or anger, it would. The sentinel—Jahn Devlyn, he said his name was—had not so much as touched her. Lucky for him. Angry as she was, she might be unable to contain the chill and its dark result if he pushed her any farther.

If he tried to force himself upon her, wrongly considering himself to be her husband, the night would end very badly. She didn't want to kill him; he likely didn't want to die.

At least her stepfather had supplied her with her own

horse, so she would not be forced to walk or, worse, ride with the sentinel. She had been saddened to see that on her departure Almund Ramsden had shown little emotion. No regret, no real sadness. He'd seemed worried, he was definitely a bit chastened—but he did not shed a single tear to see her ride off with a complete stranger. Perhaps she had pushed her luck too far. Perhaps he finally saw through her, catching a glimpse of the dark creature she had become. Did he see her as a monster? Did he somehow know what she hid?

As they rode onward, the sentinels spoke on occasion about where they might spend the night and how long the journey would take with a less experienced traveler along, and they discussed what the weather might be like in the days to come. For the most part they ignored her, and if not for the occasional glimpse, she might think she could simply turn back and they wouldn't miss her.

But now and then the sentinel who called himself Jahn turned to look at her with strong, determined eyes that told her too clearly that if she ran, he would come after her. And he'd catch her, too. And then where would she be? If he dared to bind her, if he was forceful with her, she would not be able to help what would surely happen next.

In more than twenty years she'd never gone far from the house where she'd lived. Why should she? Her mother and stepfather had cared for her dotingly. She'd been educated by the best tutors, visited by the finest dressmakers, entertained by poets and musicians who came through the area on a regular basis, and courted by men from near and far. Everything any woman could ask for had been given to her, and she'd never had to leave her home in order to have all she desired.

Looking back, Morgana wondered why she had been so protected. Had her mother known all along what her daughter was? What she would become? Was that why Morgana had been kept so close to home all her life? Had a loving mother hidden her only child from the world so there would be no opportunity for disaster? If that was the case, why had there been no warning? No hint of what was to come? No instruction?

Morgana watched as the landscape changed to one which was completely unfamiliar to her. There were no drastic changes, no dragons or pink trees or purple rivers, but still, the land was strange. She did not recognize the road nor the farms they passed. She did not know what would lie over the next hill. Most disturbingly, she did not know what would become of her. Was she truly destined to live her life washing this man's clothes and cooking his supper and—heaven forbid—giving birth to his children? Eventually silent tears did fall. She could not stop them.

Her "husband" ignored her tears. He did not even display a hint of sympathy or annoyance.

They stopped for the night at a pleasant enough campsite near the river. It was not yet dark, so Morgana had a chance to survey the area. An abundance of pink flowering bushes grew to one side of the site, alive and bright with the gifts of spring. The nearby water flowed fast and crystal clear, breaking over smooth rocks and staying well within its banks. The ground was hard and the land beyond looked harsh and unwelcoming.

The dark-haired one—Blane was his name, though she did not care what he called himself—took care of the animals. He was apparently responsible for caring for all three horses. He led the animals to the water, and then Jahn Devlyn turned to give Morgana his full attention. His full attention was enough to make any woman weak in the knees.

He crooked a finger at her, silently calling her to him.

Morgana held her ground, and the annoying man pursed his lips and called to her in an unnecessarily harsh voice. "Wife!"

Wife? Could he not even deign to use her name? Did she really want him to use her given name? Anything would be better than *wife*! "I will not be called like a dog," she said, not moving an inch toward him.

"Then how will you be called?" he responded.

Morgana pursed her lips. He should be intimidated by her. He should know his place! Most of all, he should've taken whatever bribe her stepfather had offered.

"I will not be called at all," she said calmly. "Not by *you*."

He surprised her by flashing a bright, joy-filled grin that showed too many teeth and far too much good humor. "That will make our marriage interesting, I suppose."

She pushed down the fear that threatened to choke her, wondering if—when—the dark chill of destruction might arise within her. "Surely you do not expect that we will actually remain married." She hadn't decided on a plan just yet, but she would. This man could be bought, somehow. Her stepfather would forgive her, eventually. Life as she knew it, as she had planned it to be, would continue.

Since she had refused to move toward Jahn Devlyn, he came to her, a sack of food taken from her own kitchen clutched in his hand. "You will come to like me, wife."

"I doubt that."

"I am not fat, nor arrogant, nor horribly old, and while I am no genius, I'm not a simpleton, either. I have my own rented room over a tavern in Arthes, so we will not have to share our home of wedded bliss with others. The room isn't much, but it will be ours. I have been told I don't snore too horribly." As he came nearer, she noticed that he had quite remarkable blue eyes. And then he tossed the sack of food at her. She did not attempt to catch the sack, so it fell at her feet.

The humor fled and Jahn's blue eyes went hard. "Slice the bread and cheese. Save enough for tomorrow's noon meal."

"I'm not a servant," she argued.

"No, you're a wife. Beyond that, you are an equal member of this traveling party. Blane is caring for the animals and fetching water. I will build a fire. You will prepare supper, which will be no chore as it requires only a bit of carving. Surely you're capable of that small task." He chose that moment to stroke his unattractive multicolored beard.

"I am going to be a terrible wife," Morgana said. "You should have taken whatever my stepfather offered you to let me be and forgotten the impulsive vow you overheard."

Jahn cocked his head and smiled again. "My darling wife, your stepfather offered me nothing. In truth, he seemed rather relieved to be rid of you."

Chapter Two

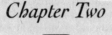

BY the time darkness fell, Jahn felt a bit sorry for his "wife" and a touch guilty about his role in this charade. Just a touch. Haughty as she attempted to be, the pretty and fragile blonde could not hide the fact that she was scared. He had never intended for this journey to be a nightmare for her. Just a lesson, of sorts, a test so that she could appreciate all she'd been offered, after she had a taste of an alternative life.

So, when Blane made his excuses, retreating to the woods to give them a moment of needed privacy, Jahn presented himself to Lady Morgana. She sat by the fire with her knees drawn up and her delicate chin resting on one of those knees. Her face looked paler than usual against the light blue of her dress and the firelight; her eyes had gone impossibly wide. She stared into the fire as if haunted by something she saw in the flames. Now and then she'd rock back and forth. That could not be a good sign.

"Just so you'll know," he said without emotion, "I do not expect to consummate this marriage during the journey."

She glanced up, her suddenly narrowed eyes displaying suspicion. "And why is that?" she asked coldly.

He smiled down at her. "With Blane around, it would be awkward." He considered making a joke about the other poor sentinel being jealous of the great size of his cock, but decided against it. The girl really was frightened, and perverse nature aside, he did not consider himself a spiteful man. "Besides, we should get to know one another first. It's not *necessary* that we get acquainted before making this marriage real, mind you. Many a couple has started their marital life together as total strangers. But as a gift to you, my bride, I will be patient."

Morgana narrowed her eyes. "We are not truly married until this godforsaken union is consummated, so please refrain from calling me your bride."

"Are you trying to change my mind about waiting?"

"No, just pointing out that you're going to have to stop calling me wife." She wrinkled her nose. "I am not your wife, I did not choose to be your wife, and every time you say the word I feel as if a million tiny irritating bugs are racing through my veins." For emphasis, he supposed, she shuddered.

She sounded as if she did not care for the binding state of marriage any more than he did. In his experience, all women longed for the bond and the security of marriage. They wanted someone to take care of them. Was Lady Morgana like him? Did she crave her freedom more than she longed for the tight bonds of a forever union and the security of marriage? That such a pretty and obviously pampered woman would turn her back on the acceptable and normally desired institution of marriage—as Morgana certainly had even before he'd come along—made her more interesting. He very much wanted to know why.

"Then what should I call you?" Jahn lowered himself to the ground, careful not to sit too close to the skittish woman.

"Lady Morgana," she said sharply. "Or even better, call

me nothing at all." The statement would've been quite cutting if her lower lip hadn't trembled.

"You may call me Jahn," he said, "or Sentinel Devlyn, if you prefer."

"Jahn is the emperor's name."

"It is common enough, and the only given name I have. If the emperor does not wish to share the name with me, he can choose one of his many others. Nechtyn has a nice ring, don't you think?" He had always thought that was the worst of the many names he'd been given at birth.

Lady Morgana turned her head and looked at him without fear. "You seem very confident that we will remain married, but I must tell you, you're very much mistaken. My stepfather might be angry with me now, and perhaps with some good reason, but I know he will change his mind and come for me, probably very soon. Maybe even tonight."

"I doubt that." Poor Ramsden would not dare to defy his emperor—though he had made Jahn promise that Morgana would not be mistreated in any way. Jahn knew very well what that meant, though the words had not been so blunt. Lady Morgana was to remain untouched.

"When he does come, will you let me go? Will you release me from this ridiculous, ill-advised, peasant union?" For the first time, there was a touch of hope in her voice, and even by firelight he saw the renewal of optimism in her eyes.

Jahn nodded. "If your father comes for you . . ."

"Stepfather," she corrected.

"If your *stepfather* comes for you and you wish to go, I will not attempt to stop you. We can call the marriage undone, and I will find another to take your place. Sooner or later."

She breathed a sigh of relief.

"I'm not such a bad person, you know," he said softly.

"I'm sure you're very pleasant, when you're not kidnapping unwilling brides."

"I did not kidnap you; you were given to me. On more than one occasion I've been told I'm quite charming, so I can imagine that eventually you will be willing enough."

Her spine straightened. "I will not," she said softly but with determination.

Jahn ignored her, smiling slightly as he leaned back on his hands. "I will call you Ana," he said. "Lady Morgana is too much of a mouthful. It's intimidating. Ana sounds like the name of a woman who is always sweet and easy and agreeable. It is the name of a woman who might give me many fat and healthy babies. Sons, of course, though I suppose after five or six boys I might agree to a daughter or two."

He expected an argument, as he had given her plenty of reason to disagree, but instead the lady said, in an emotionless voice, "My mother used to call me Ana, when she was feeling well and I had pleased her, or when she was just having a happy day."

"Then you will not mind if I do the same," he said.

"Until my stepfather comes to fetch me, you can call me whatever you like. I don't care."

As the days passed and Ramsden did not come for her, how would she react? Would she grow angry or despondent? Would she accept the situation she found herself in?

Jahn was of a mind that Lady Morgana should be humbled, that she should find some appreciation for her pampered situation, but he did not want her to be afraid. Her eyes and the way she stared into the fire spoke of fear even now, after he had told her he had no marital expectations of her at the moment. He had given Ramsden his word that there would be no taking advantage of this situation, so he had no choice. He couldn't very well tell Morgana that, however. It would ruin the game.

"I take good care of what is mine," he said in a lowered voice.

"I am not yours," she replied hotly.

She had been frightened enough for one night. "For now you are, like it or not, and while I call you wife, while you are in my care, no harm will come to you. You will not go hungry, and no man or beast will hurt you in any way."

She looked at him, perhaps less afraid than before. "What an odd man you are."

"Odd?"

"You do not know me at all, you have no valid reason to want me as your wife, and yet it is entirely thanks to you that we are here. You have offered me time, so I must assume that your interest is not entirely prurient, and now you offer what can only be called protection." Her brow furrowed. "Many men have wanted to take me as their bride, but all for the same reason."

"Your beauty?" he asked with a smile. "Or was it your abundant tenderness of personality and good cheer that called them to you?"

She did not take the bait. "It was my stepfather's land and the fact that he has no children of his own that called to them. Has it called to you, also? Do you wish to return to my home and take your place as next in line as master of the house?"

Maybe she was not so different from him, after all. To have lifelong bonds formed strictly for land or power or riches was somewhat sad. It was disillusioning, even to the most hard-hearted.

"I swear to you, Ana, I have no such desires," Jahn said honestly. "In fact, I can promise you that we will never live on the land you have just left behind, and I have no desire to be master of your stepfather's house. Arthes is my home, and it shall remain so."

She wrinkled her nose. "I'm not sure I believe you."

Since becoming emperor, Jahn had always realized that his choice of a life mate would be influenced by his position. Love and affection were not necessary; they might even become burdensome. Add to that the fact that he had always been easily bored where women were concerned, and the idea of such a shallow union intended to be for a lifetime was horrifying. This lovely lady's situation was no different from his own.

"Believe or not, it's the truth. I might not always embrace the truth, but I am not a stranger to it, either. I did not choose you for your stepfather's land, that I promise."

She relaxed a bit, and when Blane returned from the forest, their conversation died a natural death. Already Jahn was regretting his impulsive decision to bring her along in this way, but it was too late to turn back. Much too late.

RIKKA clapped her hands in girlish glee, though her girlish years were long gone. There were gentle wrinkles on her hands, and when she looked into a mirror these days, she saw evidence of the years that had passed so quickly and harshly. She was not yet fifty-five, but the need for vengeance she carried within her made her look older. Her hair, at least, remained beautiful. It had turned a soft, pearllike white years ago, and remained abundant and healthy.

"I've waited so long for the right opportunity, and this is it, I can feel the rightness in my bones. The girl the emperor chooses will be my way back into the palace, and once there, I can bring them all down." Not quickly. If she'd simply wanted to kill the emperor and his brother, she could've found a way to have it done long ago. No, death was not enough. They should suffer for what their father and their damned mother had done. They should know the pain Rikka herself had suffered. Not just pain, but heartache and humiliation.

Gyl, her friend, servant, wizard, and lover, did not seem so pleased. "I don't understand why you are so certain the emperor will choose a bride who will grant you access to the palace."

"I have my ways, you know that, darling." She gave him a tight smile.

He was not convinced. "Yes, you do have your ways, and so do I. But there are six chosen women, so we have heard, and there is no way to know that the new empress will be vulnerable to your charms, magical or otherwise."

Tempted as she was to tell him everything . . . she could not. "There are two girls among the six who will suit my plans well. Both are beautiful and born of an impressive bloodline, and both have secrets which make them vulnerable." Rikka looked away from Gyl's accusing eyes, hoping he would not see that she had secrets of her own. "Either of them will do. I have already made arrangements which will make the emperor's choice much easier." Eliminating the competition might not be subtle, but she refused to fail. Her plan was simple and foolproof. One of the two chosen girls would become empress. That girl would bear a child—the child of the emperor or of any other man, it did not matter—and when it was done, the empress would kill the emperor and, as mother of the heir, she would take control. With Rikka at her side, of course.

"How do you know the chosen one will do what you want?" Gyl asked, his voice too sharp for one who claimed to care for her. "Not everyone is willing to do anything for power."

"Blackmail is a wonderful thing," Rikka said calmly. "The two I have chosen both have secrets which will make them eminently agreeable to anything I suggest." Anything at all.

Gyl grabbed her by the shoulders, then took her chin in one large hand and forced her to look him in the eye. He was only two years younger than she, yet he looked a decade younger. His hair remained more brown than gray, though his temples were touched with bright silver. His eyes were bright and the same clear gray she had always known, and his face was only barely lined. It wasn't magic that added youth to his face, she knew, but his annoying lack of anger at what life had given him. In truth, his magical abilities were minimal. He was talented with simple potions and had on occasion created a charmed amulet or two, but he was more man than wizard. More lover than seer. There were more powerful magicians of worth in her life, but she would never find one more loyal than her Gyl.

Since being rescued from Level Thirteen, Rikka had called this well-designed and comfortable house in the forest of the Western Province home. She possessed riches and lands inherited from her father, and they were more than enough to see to all her needs. All but one.

"It is not too late," Gyl said in a gentle voice. "Let this madness end now. Cancel your orders and let the brothers be."

"I can't," she responded. "It's too late. Plans have been set into motion." As soon as her contacts in the palace had informed Rikka of the emperor's contest, it had been too late.

It was not fair that the sons of that bastard Sebestyen and his harlot should live in the palace and be happy when she could do neither. Rikka knew to her bones that she could not survive if the emperor and his brother continued to exist in such a charmed and effortless way. Their father and mother had made her suffer, and though she could not touch Sebestyen and Liane in death, she could and would destroy what they had made. Their sons. Their legacy.

"I love you," Gyl said, as he had so often in years past. "It's not too late for us. Forget your revenge and marry me. We'll move far away from Columbyana and everything here that hurts you, and we will begin again." He had been asking her to be his wife for almost twenty years. Her answer was always the same.

"I can't."

"You can." Gyl's hands dropped. "But you won't. When the twins are dead and you've had your revenge, then will you allow yourself some happiness?"

"Seeing them suffer and die will be happiness, love."

His spine straightened and his lips thinned. Gyl loved her, and he did as she asked, most of the time, but he did not care for her plan for revenge. There were moments when she was certain he did not believe she deserved her vengeance.

He started to walk away, and she grabbed his loose, dark blue sleeve to stop him. "Wait." Even though she always refused his offers of marriage, she did need Gyl. He was the only person in the world she truly trusted. The only one she knew would love her, no matter what. Her money had bought the soldiers—the mercenaries—who followed her orders, just as it had bought the jewels and fine dresses she wore and the servants who saw to her needs. A shared hatred and quest for power had brought others to her. She needed them all, but only Gyl cared.

"You don't understand what they did to me," she whispered, a hint of desperation in her voice.

"I understand very well," he replied. "It was a terrible injustice, but you have been clinging to that pain for too long."

Surely if she told him again he would understand. "I tried so hard to be a good wife, a good empress, but Sebestyen wouldn't let me. I tried to love him, I *did* love him, but it was not enough. He couldn't keep his hands off his whore, and when he grew tired of toying with me, he and that harlot Liane drugged me and threw me into a hole in the ground. They made me watch as they touched and smiled, and then they tossed me into Level Thirteen to die."

"But you did not die."

A part of her had died, but she could not make her lover see that. She couldn't even entirely explain it to herself. She was not the same wide-eyed innocent who had become Emperor Sebestyen's fourth empress. "No, I did not die. I lived so that one day I could deliver retribution. I lived so that I could deliver justice."

Again, Gyl touched her face. She loved it when he caressed her so, and she closed her eyes to revel in the sensation. "Living with hate has poisoned your soul, Rikka. We might've married long ago and had children of our own.

We might've made a new and beautiful life free of revenge and plots and blackmail. You wouldn't allow that to happen, because your revenge was more important to you than anything else in life. Why am I still here?" he asked with wonder in his voice. "I should've left you long ago, but I keep hoping you will see what your hate has done to you and you'll forsake it so we can start anew."

"Stay with me," she begged. He sounded as if he were actually thinking of leaving her. She couldn't bear to lose him, not when she was so close to the end, so close to all she desired. "Soon the worst of it will be over, and you and I can live in the palace in Arthes." It would be some time before the plan came to fruition, of course. A marriage, a baby, a murder . . . those parts of her scheme would take months, perhaps years, but they would happen. And she would be there to see it all, to orchestrate and savor each step. "Together we will have everything we've ever wanted."

"All I've ever wanted is you, Rikka," Gyl said.

That was nice to hear, it was very sweet; but for Rikka no man could ever be enough, not while her hatred for what had been done to her lived on. She burned with her old pain and humiliation. She dreamed of killing two people who were long dead.

Seeing their children disgraced and in the ground would be the next best thing.

MORGANA was pleasantly surprised to find herself relaxing somewhat as the days passed. One day became two, two days turned into three. She was concerned that her stepfather had not come for her yet, but it wasn't as if the sentinel who had claimed her insisted on consummating the marriage right away. He didn't even request that she do much work, though he did ask her to pitch in now and then. She did, glad to have an occasional chore, any chore, to take her mind off her situation.

Her pretty pale blue dress was already stained in a few

places and showing the wear of travel. Almund hadn't even given her time to choose proper traveling clothes! But at least he had allowed her to change into sturdy half boots instead of her usual slippers.

Perhaps, only perhaps, she had let go of some of her anger because Jahn had sworn he had no interest in the Ramsden lands and wealth. He could be lying, but somehow she did not think that was the case. Besides, it was best to keep control of her temper. Irritated as she was at the current state of affairs, she did not want her anger and frustration to lead her to yet another murder.

Annoyed as she was at the man and the situation, she had not once felt the growing icy cold that had preceded her flash of destruction just a few weeks ago. That surprised her a little, since she'd been alternately scared and angry and frustrated—as well as savoring recent moments of total relaxation and peace. Her emotions had been high on more than one occasion in days past, and yet she had not felt even a hint of a chill. Of course, Jahn hadn't physically confronted her, not even in the smallest way. If he tried to take her as Tomas had, would she lose control and let loose a burst of cold, icy death?

Even though she did not know him all that well, she didn't believe Jahn Devlyn was the kind of man who would do what Tomas had done. More than that, perhaps deep down some part of her realized she was in no danger while in his company, and that knowledge made it possible for her to keep her curse buried deep, where it could do no harm. Did something inside her recognize Jahn's promise to protect as real and true?

Jahn thought she was beautiful and would make a good wife. If only he knew that she had killed a man. She was a murderess. She had not planned or wanted to take a life, but she did not think those details mattered much, in the grand scheme of things. A man—a less-than-honorable man, to be sure, but a living being all the same—was dead, had died a horrible death, and it was her fault. She could not escape that fact.

They had stopped for an afternoon break, a needed rest for the horses and for themselves, and Morgana found herself standing on a small, green hill looking down at a pond of the clearest, stillest water she had ever seen. The sun reflected off the surface as if off glass, and the trees at the edge of the pond seemed to grow toward the water as if they longed to jump in but could not, as their roots held them at a distance.

She took a deep breath of cool, crisp air, and felt a rush of peace she did not ordinarily experience settle in her heart and her soul. How unexpected, that she should find any peace at all on this journey. Did distance from her crime make it possible for her to relax? Was she running away?

Jahn walked down the hill to the edge of the pond, and she watched as he washed his face, his hands disrupting the stillness of the water, sending ripples to the center of the large pond. She would not remain married, and she was still mightily annoyed at him for stealing her away from her home, but she had to admit he was nice-looking, odd beard aside. He was pleasant in personality, and he was strong and protective. Worse men might've taken advantage of her stepfather's heated vow, she supposed. If she were a peasant girl looking for a man to take care of her, he would do better than most. Much better.

Hadn't she, not too long ago, dreamed of being such a woman, a woman with no responsibilities? No expectations?

No curse.

If Jahn annoyed her greatly over one thing or another, would the curse rise up to take him? Would his protectiveness keep her at a distance from the type of situations which would make the destruction within her rise past all her defenses? She did not know, and that was another part of her curse, perhaps the worst part. She did not know what tomorrow would bring.

Face washed and waterskins refilled, Jahn climbed the hill to join her. Though in days past Morgana had often made it a point to avoid talking to him, to avoid coming face to face with him for a moment longer than was necessary, today she stood her ground. He had given her no reason to fear him, no reason to run. She realized, for the first time, that she had slept more since leaving home than she had since Tomas had died. With a blanket on the hard ground as her bed and the sky above, she had slept.

"How long before we reach Arthes?" she asked, searching desperately for some reason to speak to the man who called himself her husband.

"Four days, perhaps five," Jahn answered. "If the weather holds, I'd say four days will do it."

"What will we do if it rains?" she asked, looking up at the clear sky. Springtime could bring unstable weather.

Jahn grinned. "We will get wet."

"You said you would take care of me."

"Getting wet is hardly a danger, unless you're sickly and catch cold easily. Are you sickly, Ana?"

She should chastise him for calling her Ana, but did not. "No, I am not sickly. That doesn't mean I like getting wet."

"We don't always get what we want in life, now do we?"

"My current situation proves that well enough," she snapped.

His blue eyes twinkled, as if he actually liked making her angry. "It has always been my opinion that women rarely know what they really want. They might *think* . . ."

"You're not serious . . ."

Jahn winked at her, and something terrible happened. Morgana's heart skipped a beat. The man was maddening! He had that horrible beard and he'd kidnapped her—more or less—and he had no idea what women liked or wanted or needed. And for a moment, just a moment, she experienced what could only be called an intense liking for the infuriating man.

"You've got some color in your cheeks," he said, his smile fading. "The sun's been good for you, Ana."

She did not tell him that she suspected it hadn't been just the sun that added color to her cheeks.

With indignation, she turned her back to Jahn and stalked away. She'd taken only three steps before she realized she had nowhere to go.

DANYA pursed her lips toward the mirror and fluffed her dark hair. "I don't know why I can't go to Arthes and take up residence *now*," she whined.

Standing behind her, Danya's mother—still pretty, dark-haired Rheta Calliste—glowered. "It would not be fitting for you to seem too anxious. There are more than six weeks, still, before the emperor will make his choice, and the journey to Arthes will not take much more than eight or nine days."

Danya turned around and smiled gently at her mother. Frowning, or smiling too widely, caused unsightly wrinkles. Perhaps she was only twenty-two years of age, but she knew all about wrinkles. After all, she had four older sisters. "Mother, I might become empress. I might sit at the side of the most powerful man in all of Columbyana, I might give birth to the next emperor. Think of the jewels and the parties and the clothes. Think of the fine shoes! What woman would not be anxious about the possibilities?"

"Fine," Rheta said pragmatically. "Just don't make your excitement so clear for all to see. Every man, even an emperor, should have to work to gain the affection of his bride. You should display at least a modicum of indignation that you're to be inspected, that there are five other women in the . . . the contest." She whispered the final word, finding it distasteful.

Danya did not care how this reprieve had come about. She was going to escape! "That deputy minister of something or another has arrived to escort me, and he seems anxious enough to leave. Is it fair to make him wait while I dawdle?" True, the emperor's man had said she could take all the time she needed to prepare herself for the journey. She could make him wait a month, if she insisted that she needed more time to prepare. But no, she wanted to escape *now*.

"Yes," Rheta said succinctly. "Remember that one day that deputy minister and many others might answer to *your* orders. He can and will wait a few more days while you prepare yourself."

"Mother, I'm prepared!" Danya said impatiently. Oh, was she prepared! She could not wait to get out of this house.

"Well, let's not allow the emperor's servant to see your eagerness just yet, shall we?"

Danya could not tell her mother why she was so anxious to leave the only home she'd ever known. A part of her longed to tell everything, to cry and plead and confess, to lay her heart on the line and sob for what had been lost. But another part realized that this staid and proper lady she loved so much would not believe her. At the very least, she would not believe the details, and the details were very, very important.

Rheta would also be so disappointed and aggrieved— even if she did believe the tale in it entirety.

Danya's mother waved a well manicured hand. "Besides, all your sisters and their husbands are coming here for a lavish farewell dinner, three days from now. I had wanted the party to be a surprise, but it looks as though I'll have to tie you down to keep you from beginning the journey to Arthes for another three days."

A cold chill walked up Danya's spine, and in the mirror she could see that her face paled. She detested family gatherings.

"I would like to have my girls together one last time before you leave," Rheta said in a gentler voice. "It's difficult enough to see you go, and if the emperor chooses you and you remain in Arthes, then it will become even harder." A mother's expression was difficult to deny. "Please stay. Once the family party is done, you can race for Arthes and your destiny, if you'd like, though I think a few more days are not too much to ask."

Danya, unable to speak, nodded her head. She would stay for her mother's sake, but in truth the planned party was one more reason for her to run for Arthes as soon as possible.

And though she would not, could not, tell her mother, even if she was not chosen as the new empress, she would not return to this house and take up her position as the youngest and prettiest and, yes, silliest daughter of five. No, she wasn't ever coming back here, and for that reason she would allow her mother one last family gathering. There would not be another with Danya in attendance.

Chapter Three

JAHN could not help noticing that as they moved closer to Arthes, Morgana glanced over her shoulder more often. As the final days of their journey unfolded, she insisted on stopping frequently, then watching their trail for her step-father and those she believed he would surely send to collect her, once he realized he had been foolish to give her to a lowly sentinel—oath to God or not. Did she think that by stopping often she would give her stepfather the chance to catch up with them?

Ramsden did not come. He left his daughter in the emperor's care, for now. Arthes and a return to the life Jahn knew grew closer with every step. Pity. He did not want the easy days to end; he felt like he was just beginning to see the real Morgana Ramsden. Since her tears had stopped, traveling with the woman had been relatively pleasant. She was nice to look at, even when she was angry, and she had a sweet voice, though her words were rarely what any man would call sweet. He found her cutting comments bright and sometimes funny, and looked forward to what she had to say when he riled her. She was no longer as pale as she

had been when he'd met her, thanks to the sun and something else he did not dare attempt to understand. She was
more alive than she had been when he'd met her—more
vivid, perhaps.

The dishevelment caused by their days of travel only
made her look more fetching. Her once fine gown was
faded and beginning to fray here and there, and she couldn't
do much with her thick hair with only the single comb she
had found in her bag. At the moment the prim and proper
Lady Morgana who had denounced Emperor Jahn for his
gluttony and debauchery looked as if she had a touch of a
wild side. She usually hid that side well, he imagined, but
Jahn could see it in her eyes and in the set of her mouth. It
was simply more pronounced when her fine gown was
mussed and her hair was in disarray.

Perhaps he saw the hidden wildness in her because he
knew it in himself. She might be a better match for him
than he'd initially thought.

Still, in all these days she had not once said that she'd
been wrong to refuse the emperor's invitation. She had not
asked him to please, please, if he wouldn't mind too terribly, deliver her to the palace upon their arrival in the capital city, as she had made a grievous error.

They stopped while still in sight of the city, which
sprawled before them much different in style and shape
and sound than the countryside had been. Jahn was sorry
to see the journey end, sorry to see the palace rising before
them. Even more, he was oddly sorry to see the end of his
charade. He was certain he would know Lady Morgana
much more deeply if he had a few more days in which to
study and test her.

They should've taken a roundabout route, but it was too
late for that decision.

A tantalizing thought teased Jahn's wandering mind.
What would happen if he took his newly claimed wife,
changed his name once again, and fled for parts unknown?
What if he remained Jahn Devlyn, and spent a lifetime

making this woman his own? She would eventually make a fine wife for a simple man, and he would love to be a simple man once again.

Instead of fleeing, he took Blane aside and whispered in his ear. The sentinel was not happy about the turn of events, but as a loyal servant he would do what was asked. He certainly did not like what Jahn asked now, but he pursed his lips, nodded once, then mounted his horse and sped away for the city and his task.

Morgana was not pleased to see their chaperone go.

"What's this?" she asked.

"Blane is anxious to see his wife," Jahn explained. "He does not have the consideration for his horse that I have for ours. Tomorrow morning will be soon enough for us to enter the city."

Morgana glanced toward the brilliantly colored sunset. "Tomorrow?" she asked, her voice small as she no doubt remembered that Blane's presence was one of the reasons their "marriage" had not been consummated.

"Yes, do you mind?" he asked casually. "Can you bear one more night sleeping on the ground before I introduce you to your marriage bed?"

She straightened her spine and her eyes widened slightly. "Whatever you think is best. I would not wish to injure our horses by pressing onward too quickly or too soon."

No surprise there. He did not for one moment believe concern for the animals in their care made her agree to spend another night in such unaccustomed and rough conditions. "I believe you will be quite comfortable in your new home, though you might find it in need of a woman's touch."

"I can only imagine," she said dryly. "Where is your house located?"

Jahn laughed. "House? I have no house."

She blinked hard. "Then where do you live?"

"I told you early on, love, that I lease a room over one of the finest taverns in Arthes. Have you forgotten?" Had she even been listening? "Our room is near to the palace, which is handy, and only a few steps from the best ale in town, which is also very handy."

"I can't live over a tavern!"

"Of course you can," Jahn said smoothly.

Her eyes narrowed. "Do you drink very much?"

"When the spirit moves me, I suppose I do."

Her mouth pursed in obvious disapproval. "I will not have a drunkard husband."

Jahn was taken aback. Had she, or had she not, just referred to him as her husband? She was supposed to be horrified to find herself in this position; she was supposed to fervently wish for the opportunity she had so blithely dismissed only a few days ago.

"I will not have a woman tell me what I can and cannot do," Jahn responded tightly, "unless we are in bed, of course, and then I am quite amenable to direction." He did not give her a chance to respond to that. "Besides, a man must have a leisure pursuit of some sort, in order to shake off the stress of a long workday."

"Drinking to excess is not a leisure pursuit!" Morgana argued.

"Of course it is. There are not many diversions suitable for a man like me," Jahn said, shucking off his sentinel's vest and beginning to make himself comfortable for the long evening ahead. "Drinking, womanizing, gambling . . ."

"None of those are acceptable. What's wrong with woodworking or gardening or learning to play a musical instrument?"

Jahn looked at Morgana and grinned. "You're joking, right?"

"No husband of mine is going to drink, gamble, or womanize," she said.

Again with the "husband." Jahn leaned close, enjoying the glow of her skin and the light in her eyes as she argued with him. "Need I remind you, love, that I am not yet officially your husband?"

Instead of getting angry or haughty, she blushed and

turned her head to the side, breaking eye contact. "No, you need not remind me."

Interesting . . .

DANYA sat between her sister Hetta and her brother-in-law Bevan at the long dinner table on this last night in her childhood home. The small children, her innumerable nephews and nieces, had all been fed and put to bed early, thank the heavens. The family seemed quite proud of their ability to reproduce. Two of her sisters were pregnant once again, but were not so far along that they couldn't travel a short distance for an important family gathering.

All of them were excited about the prospect of having a sister in the Columbyanan palace. Danya had not yet told her sisters that if she was chosen empress, she would cut all ties with her family as soon as possible. Her father, who sat at the head of the table with a large ewer of wine, did not seem to be at all impressed or sad. As usual, he was quiet and without emotion. He had already drunk too much wine, and before the meal was finished, he'd be nodding off in his chair and everyone would ignore the embarrassment.

Logically, she realized her mother and her sisters had done nothing to earn her dislike. They simply reminded her of a life she wanted desperately to leave behind; they reminded her too sharply of her failings. Her fresh start should be entirely fresh!

The deputy minister of whatever, whose name she could not recall, sat at the other end of the table. The poor, unsuspecting man was positioned between Althea and Rodric, so he had her sympathy. The imperial man from Arthes was a quiet sort who wore his fair hair in a long, well-tended braid and often kept his eyes down. He revealed little in the way of emotion, even when his hostess insisted that he delay his departure to attend this gathering he so obviously did not wish to attend. To Danya's eyes, he looked quite young to be deputy minister of anything.

She'd always pictured ministers and deputies as old and either very thin or too well fed. This official escort was neither.

He did look slightly perturbed now, and she could not blame him. Rodric had a boring habit of telling the same stories over and over again, and Althea had a sharp and grating laugh.

The deputy minister of something could not be more irritated than Danya was. Her unsuspecting mother had put her directly across from the newest member of the family, Vida's husband, Ennis. If Ennis were seated anywhere else at the table, Danya would be able to completely ignore him. Instead, every time she lifted her head, she caught him staring at her. More than once she'd almost choked on her food, so now she only pushed it around on the plate, in order to stave off another embarrassment.

Why did he have to be here? Why, why, why? She should've refused the request for this one last gathering, but knowing that it was truly the last, she had been unable to deprive her mother. The matriarch of this house did so love having all her girls together.

Danya was certain her mother would get along well after she was gone. There were grandchildren to dote upon and grown daughters with whom she could share her wisdom of nearly sixty years. Her husband was tipsy only in the evening, so it wasn't as if she'd be without companionship. She would thrive when all her girls were on their own, each busy with her own familiy.

Everyone chattered, and as the night progressed, the volume grew unbearable. The four married sisters were all excited about Danya's opportunity, as if they themselves were the ones who had been chosen. Even Vida, naive, ignorant Vida, smiled happily and wished her youngest sister the best. The talk turned to shoes and gowns and jewels, naturally. What other concerns would an empress have?

Ennis remained silent, though he did raise his glass to her once, when their eyes inadvertently met.

Danya tried to keep her face impassive; she attempted

to participate at least minimally in the conversations around her, even when she gave them only half an ear. Soon the noise was too much to bear. Her facade was crumbling, it was about to fall away. She needed a moment, just a moment, to gather her wits, to shake off the pain and put on her prettiest and happiest face once again. She excused herself and left the table at an acceptable pace, running toward the doors which would open into the night only when she was out of sight of the others. A deep breath of air, a quiet moment, and she would be composed once more. An empress would need to be able to compose herself, no matter what the circumstances.

She could not imagine that there would be anything more trying than this, even when she was empress. Political intrigue would pale in comparison to her tumultuous life thus far.

Outdoors, all was silent and peaceful. The air on her face was wonderfully cool. Danya closed her eyes and took a deep breath and thought of Arthes. She imagined the wonder of the palace she had never seen and all the luxuries she would know when it was her home. She thought of escape, of forgetting the past, of starting anew in a finer, better place.

"I have never seen you look more beautiful."

Danya's eyes snapped open at the sound of that soft, deep, seductive voice. Ennis stood not two feet away, an empty smile she knew too well on his pretty face.

"What are you doing here?" she snapped.

"I have come to verify the safety and comfort of my favorite sister-in-law, who is soon to be empress."

"There is no guarantee that the emperor will choose me."

"How could he not?"

You didn't. The heartbreaking words she did not dare to say aloud shot through her brain in an oddly painful way. "You should return to your wife," she said coldly. *Your pregnant, blissfully ignorant wife.*

"I told Vida I was going to make sure you were well,

since you looked so pale all through dinner. I am ever the concerned brother-in-law." He bowed insolently before moving closer. His hand lifted slowly. He reached out as if he planned to touch her, and she slapped his hand away.

He laughed. "There was a time when you did not dismiss my attentions so quickly."

There was a time when I thought you loved me. "I'm smarter now than I was then," Danya said, proud that her voice remained calm. Inside, she was shaking. Somehow she imagined Ennis saw that inner tremble. He knew her too well. The man who had once been her lover knew her weaknesses, her dreams, her failures. He had made her tremble and shake and confess her undying love for him, and then he had chosen another.

"I'm sure the emperor will be pleased with you, Danya. You're one of those rare women who does so love the pleasure a man can give. If you scream for him as you screamed for me, he will think himself a master of the bedchamber. Of course, you and I will always know that he was not your first. A woman never forgets her first lover, the man who teaches her all about the pleasures of the body. I taught you well, didn't I? How about one more kiss, just a little something to remind us of what we no longer have?" Ennis asked, slowly moving his head toward hers, parting his lips, touching her shoulder.

Danya froze. This was what she wanted and feared, what she craved and despised. If Ennis had chosen her to be his wife, as she had been so certain he would, she would be happy and ignorant like Vida, and she would not be on her way to Arthes to vie for the position of empress. But he had not chosen her. He had made her love him, he had shown her pleasures that she had not known of before he'd seduced her, and then he had destroyed her with his rejection.

Before his lips touched hers, she said, "I gave birth to your child."

The words stopped Ennis cold. He came no closer; he did not move away.

"A boy, in case you care to know."

Ennis licked his lips. He paled, she could see that even in the dim moonlight. There were no questions or concerns about her well-being or that of his child. His cold words to her were "Who knows?"

Danya laughed without humor. "No need to fear, Ennis, I told no one. When I realized I was with child, you had already chosen Vida over me, so I saw no reason to inform you or anyone else of my condition. I told the family that I was going to visit my childhood friend Lyla for the summer, but instead I went to the coast, where I hid myself away for a few months, until the baby came." Now she felt the blood drain from her face. Why was she telling him this? He did not deserve to know, and the telling hurt more than the memory she tried so hard to bury. "I stayed with a midwife who promised to find a good home for your unwanted child. I sold some of the jewels my grandmother left me, and with the proceeds I paid her well. She cared for me as best she could. Still, your son came weeks too early, and he died within three days."

"Surely that is a blessing . . ."

Danya slapped Ennis with all her might. "Don't you dare say the death of our child was a *blessing.*"

He backed away, one hand over his offended cheek.

"Still want to kiss me?" she asked, surprised at the sharp bite in her words as an anger she had buried for too long rose to the surface. "Knowing what you did to me, do you still wish to touch me as if we were lovers?" She managed a tight smile that made her face feel as if it would crack. "Do you think I should tell Vida my sad tale? Should I tell them all the truth—here, tonight—before I leave home to begin my new life? I have always imagined that they would not believe me, that they would think I was telling a tale to stir up trouble or that I was the one who seduced you and was bitter that you chose Vida over me. But maybe that is not so. Vida knows you well, now, so perhaps she would believe."

Instead of cowering and begging her forgiveness, as he

should've, Ennis surged forward and clasped her throat in his hands. He pressed her against the wall, gripping too tight. She could barely breathe . . .

"You cannot tell Vida. You cannot tell anyone!" Ennis insisted. His fingers tightened, and Danya's throat closed. She quickly grew lightheaded, but she had the strength to reach up and grasp Ennis's steellike wrists to claw at the exposed flesh there. She couldn't make him ease his grip; she was too weak and he was too strong. Her vision dimmed, and fear grew. Was he trying to frighten her or to kill her? Danya raked her fingernails across Ennis's hands, but he did not budge. He squeezed harder; he was actually trying to strangle her.

"Release Lady Danya now," a calm voice interrupted, "or I will kill you."

Ennis dropped his hands, and Danya took a deep, ragged breath, thankful for the fresh air flowing into her lungs. She raised protective hands to her throat before looking up to the intruder who had very possibly saved her life. Ennis would do anything to keep his neat little world from falling apart. And fall apart it would, if people knew . . . if they believed . . .

"This is none of your business, Deputy . . ." Ennis stumbled over his words. He hadn't remembered the minister's name, either.

"Rainer," the tall man said, "Deputy Minister Angelo Rainer. And Lady Danya is most certainly my business, at the moment. It is my duty to deliver her to the emperor undamaged."

Ennis sneered. "It's too late for that, I'm afraid. This one is damaged to the pit of her soul, the lying, spiteful . . ."

The man who had once been Danya's lover said no more, as Rainer's hand shot out and brushed against Ennis's finely sculpted nose. The blow looked to be insignificant, no more than a graze, and yet Ennis let out a howl. His nose began to bleed. Rainer grabbed Ennis by the collar and dragged him toward the door to the house. "Dear me," Rainer said as he opened the door and shoved Ennis inside, "this poor clumsy man has taken a nasty fall in the dark. Do be careful, poor fellow." Ennis stumbled into the house, then tripped over his own feet and went sprawling.

Danya found herself smiling, though moments earlier she had thought such an expression to be impossible.

She stopped smiling when Deputy Minister Rainer turned his fierce gaze to her. "The delays are over, Lady Danya. I leave at first light. You can travel to Arthes with me, or I can send an escort back for you in a month's time."

"I will go with you," she said, more anxious than ever to escape from this house and its memories.

"Then don't be late," he commanded.

He turned gracefully to enter the house, but Danya stopped him with a whispered "Wait!"

Rainer turned, and she took a moment to really look at him for the first time. The blond hair was remarkably silky and full, the eyes were powerful and pale blue-gray, the features were masculine and very nicely shaped. How much had he heard? How much did he know? Were her secrets still safe? "I'm not sure I ever heard you say. Of what branch of the government are you deputy minister?"

He gave her a cold and impatient smile. "The Ministry of Magic."

MORGANA lay upon her blanket, staring at the stars. She should've gone to sleep long ago, but her mind continued to wander to what tomorrow would bring. A marriage bed. A room over a tavern. A husband she did not want. A husband who thought drink, women, and gambling were acceptable pastimes!

No, she understood well enough when he was teasing her, and he'd been teasing then. Not that he'd found any of her alternative suggestions acceptable.

She had been so certain her stepfather would've rescued her by now. He must be very angry to leave her in the company of a sentinel who claimed her as his wife as if they were peasants who had no option but to make marriage in the most primitive manner. Perhaps her refusal of the emperor had been the last straw for a man who was loyal to his ruler. Perhaps she should not have told him the truth, that she wished never to marry at all!

She had slept well on this journey, and she did feel oddly and unexpectedly safe. Did she want to be rescued? Did she truly wish to return to a house where she would always fear that someone would discover her secret?

Morgana knew that her mother had truly loved Almund, and that the kind man had more than accepted a fatherless little girl as his daughter. Still, there had been days when a younger Morgana had wished desperately to know her real father, the man who had died when she'd been two years old, too young to remember him. Awel Ramsden had refused to discuss her first husband, and so Morgana had always imagined that she'd loved him too much to bear his loss. Still, after her mother's insistence that Morgana should marry only for love, she'd wondered if perhaps the opposite had been true. Had that arranged marriage been so terrible?

Marriage to a sentinel; marriage to an emperor. Any sane woman would choose the emperor. Maybe it was not too late. This "marriage" had not been consummated, and the palace was right there, before them. Given a choice of a royal bedchamber and a room set above a cacophony of drunken men . . . what woman would not choose the palace?

"Jahn," she said, knowing by the sound of his breathing that he was not asleep, "what if I change my mind about marrying the emperor? I'm not saying that I *have* changed my mind, you understand," she added too quickly "just . . . exploring my options. There is no guarantee that he would choose me, of course, but perhaps I was being hasty when I dismissed the notion without giving it proper consideration."

Jahn sighed, and there was a short pause before he said, "Too late," his voice sleepy and perhaps even weary.

Her heart thumped too hard. "How can it be too late?"

"Blane will have delivered the message by now."

Morgana sat up. "What message?"

Jahn sighed. "The message that you refused the emperor's offer. You refused quite adamantly, as I remember. It did not occur to me that you might change your mind."

"You said Blane was rushing to his wife!" Morgana said shrilly.

Jahn rolled onto his back, his face now lit by the dying fire. The dim light created sharp shadows on a face which was becoming familiar to her. "Not until his duty as sentinel was done and the message was delivered. By now the emperor knows you have refused and Blane is happily ensconced in the arms of his loving wife."

"Oh." Knowing she would not be able to sleep for a while, Morgana pulled up her knees and rested her chin on them, drawing herself into a tight little ball. She would not be empress. Not that she wanted to be, but still, now that her options had been narrowed, she did not know what would become of her tomorrow. "Just as well. I don't suppose the emperor would take it kindly if I refused and then changed my mind."

"No, he would not take it well. He can be a bit testy, and if Blane also told him what you said about him being old and fat and stupid, well, I doubt you'd have much of a chance in the contest. Perhaps if you threw yourself at his feet and begged . . ."

"I will not beg!" Morgana snapped, and then she sighed tiredly. No, an emperor would not be pleased to hear that he'd been insulted.

"Would it be so bad?" Jahn asked softly.

"What?"

"To marry a simple man and live a simple life," he said. "To make a home with whatever of life's blessings come your way, to make your days with another always at your side, through thick and thin."

"My mother said I should wait for true love." Perhaps she should not speak to this man who claimed her about something so personal, but there was no one else and she needed to talk. "She said I should hold out for nothing less, and when I asked, she said that I would know love when it came. She said love was worth waiting for. But here I am at nearly twenty-five years of age and I have found no love. I have not once in my life looked into a man's face and known in my heart that he was the right one for me." Morgana's frustration came through in her voice. "What if she's right and there is one right man for me, and he's on the other side of the world and we never meet?"

Now fully awake, Jahn sat up. "Your mother's notions make no sense to me. I think marriage at its best is rather like being in the military."

"That is ludicrous," Morgana whispered.

"Is it? Two soldiers, side by side, together fighting whatever enemies come their way. Those enemies might be sickness or bad crops or more conventional foes, but still, if the bond is a strong one, then neither one would ever have to face those foes alone."

"I have never heard marriage described in quite that way," she said.

"Most women seem to think that marriage is love and laughter and flowers, jewels and pampering and a life made forever beautiful by the man upon whom they deign to shower their favors. Nothing is forever beautiful, I imagine. And I'm sure love is nice, while it lasts, but I suspect friendship and lust are preferable and longer lasting than something as indefinable as love."

She squirmed as he spoke of lust and love.

"Marriage has always been about business," Jahn continued. "A man alone, a woman alone, they cannot survive. Together, however . . ." He finished with a shrug of his broad shoulders.

She was most afraid of passions and turmoil calling her curse to the surface. The life Jahn spoke of seemed to be devoid of passion. In spite of her mother's insistence that Morgana demand love, was this simpler existence Jahn spoke of the kind of life she had been searching for? No love, no hate, no fury to call to the worst of her.

Since riding away from her home she had not had a moment's struggle with the newly discovered curse at the pit of her soul. She'd been angry and frightened at times, and she and Jahn had argued. But she'd never had to force down the chill that had once grown in her heart. Was it because, truly married or not, she was not alone in this trial? Was it because Jahn had so ardently promised that no harm would come to her?

"Perhaps I will see what life is like in your room above the tavern," she said, knowing that in truth she had no choice. She could not make her way alone in the city, and she could not return to a home where she was no longer wanted. Morgana felt as if her life had suddenly shifted. She was no longer the pampered daughter of the manor, pursued by wealthy young men and an emperor. She no longer had servants to see to her every need, or a doting stepfather to protect her. All she had was Jahn.

And strangely enough, she was not afraid.

"I am not ready to share your bed," she said quickly, forcing the words out. "We do not know one another well enough for . . . that."

"How long do you expect me to wait?" he asked softly.

"I don't know. Until I'm ready." *Until I'm sure.*

"Until you want me so badly you can't keep your hands from my body," he teased.

"Until I'm *ready*," she said more sharply, realizing that she might never want Jahn, not in the way of which he spoke. But if she decided to make a new life as a sentinel's wife, sex would be part of the bargain. Eventually. They would have to move forward with caution, to make sure she didn't turn her new husband into a statue of glass if he moved too fast, if he frightened or pushed her. Would this odd calm continue? Would the warmth which currently filled her keep the icy destruction at bay?

"We should move slowly," he said.

"Yes." Relief was evident in her voice.

"We have been man and wife, of sorts, for several days now," he said. "I have been very patient and will continue to be, but perhaps we could start things off with a kiss." He moved gently toward her.

"You want me to kiss you?" Her words were not quite a screech.

"Only if you would like to do so," he said. He stopped where he was, waiting for her to come to him, waiting for her to lay her lips on his. "I suspect you are a woman sweeter given freely than taken or coerced. You have married a patient man, Ana. I will not seduce you. I will not cajole you. Come to me in your own way, in your own time, and soon enough we will learn if we are well suited or not." He smiled in that charming way he had. "I suspect we will find ourselves very well suited, but I will not rush you."

For that patience alone, she could kiss him!

When Tomas had moved toward her on that horrible night, he had done so with force and anger, and her curse had arisen against her will. At this moment, with Jahn so close and yet not at all threatening, she felt no chill at all. Instead, she felt quite warm and content. How strange. No, not strange at all. Angry as she had been with this man who had claimed her, she'd never felt endangered. In fact, Jahn had done all he could to make her feel safe and protected. He had kind eyes, she admitted to herself.

"I don't suppose one kiss will matter much," she said. After all, she had shared short, sweet kisses with suitors before. This would be no different.

Jahn waited for her to move nearer, leaving the next step entirely in her hands. She scooted toward him and reached up to cup his head in her hand. He was a large man, and she was made more aware of that fact since they were so very close, closer than they had been before. Her hand seemed so small against the back of his head; he seemed to dwarf her when he was so near. Everything about him—his neck, his hands, his shoulders—was massive.

And still, she was not afraid.

She drew his mouth to hers, intent on giving him a quick, passionless first kiss.

The moment their mouths touched, she realized this would be like no other kiss. She felt the touch to her very core. It shook her, in ways she had never before been shaken. Heavens, he was so warm and wonderful and gentle, and inside she was aroused with turmoil. She did not suffer the rush of cold that preceded her deadly gift, but was washed with an infusion of heat and pleasure. She had never felt so blissfully connected to anyone. She had never before felt so much a part of something more than herself. Her mouth moved, his lips parted, and the heat they generated was remarkable.

She did not want the kiss to end. Her hands settled on his shoulders, and she shifted her body so they were closer together. His arms wrapped around her, and instead of being afraid, she welcomed those arms. She was sheltered here, not abused. She was a part of this embrace, not trapped within it. This was a proper kiss, unlike anything she had ever known.

Perhaps she fell into Jahn because without him she was truly alone in the world. Were they like two soldiers, as he'd suggested, taking on the world side by side? Could she approach marriage as if it were a pact between two strangers who needed one another? Reasons didn't matter as the heat the kiss generated grew deeper and hotter.

It was Jahn who abruptly ended the kiss, and as he drew away from her, she noted the dazed look in his eyes. The intensity of the kiss had surprised him, too. There was a touch of pain in his voice as he said, "If you wish this marriage to remain unconsummated, the kiss must end. Now."

Interesting as the kiss had been, she did not wish to rush headlong into a situation she did not entirely understand. In spite of her odd sensations of connection and safety, Jahn was still, in essence, a stranger, and she could not shake the certainty that part of her attraction to him was tied to the fact that with his help she was running away from what she'd done to Tomas. He was a part of her escape; he was a large part of the reason she felt safe to-night.

This common marriage was not entirely done until they shared a bed. Taking that step, giving herself to him, would mean the possibility of babies, it would mean a forever marriage. There would be no walking away from him once that deed was done. Now, when she could still taste him on her lips, she did not want to walk away. Tomorrow that might change.

"Your beard tickles," she said.

"Does it?" Jahn ran a hand across the offending facial hair.

"A little." Morgana squirmed. She should not waste precious time on unimportant details, not when her mind was spinning so. She gathered up all of her courage to ask, "Why did you choose me?" She did not move away from him, as she should, but remained close. She liked being so near. "Truly, Jahn, why me? Just because you overheard my father make his silly vow, that didn't mean you had to walk into the room and take advantage of the situation. Any unwed girl in Arthes would surely be glad to have you, and she'd likely be less trouble, too." Morgana was well aware that she was not the easiest woman in Columby-ana to live with. She could be demanding, and Jahn knew that too well, having witnessed her refusal of the emperor's offer and all that came with it. "Why me?"

"You're strong," he said. "I like that in a woman. Some men prefer a mouse who will dance to their tune, but I want a wife with backbone and stamina." He smoothed a strand of hair away from her face. "It does not hurt matters at all that you are the most beautiful woman I have ever seen."

She smiled. "And have you seen many?"

"Yes, I have. None holds a candle to you, Ana."

It was nice that he thought she was beautiful, but she was more impressed by his admiration of her strength. Beauty was not forever; strength was bone deep.

"You have your own beauty, you know," she said.

"Though I am anxious to see you without the beard. It's rather scraggly and scratchy, and it *does* tickle. You will shave it, won't you?"

"I suppose I might," he said warily. "One day."

She touched the beard with her fingertips. "You also have your own strength, and an abundance of gentleness, as well. I am glad for both."

Jahn frowned and backed away from her a little. "I did not expect you to be so accepting so soon," he said.

"Neither did I."

"What happened?" he asked gruffly.

Morgana stared into what remained of the fire. She wanted to tell Jahn what had led her to this point without telling too much. "On the First Night of the Spring Festival, I spied upon a bonfire where women from the village danced and laughed and flirted outrageously with the men who danced after them. For a moment, I was horribly envious." There were those at home who would be shocked to hear that she had been out and about on that night when Tomas had been murdered, but Jahn would never go back there and tell. This moment was just for them. What an odd thought that was! "Those women would not be bartered to the highest bidder; they were not chosen for their social standing or their family lands or the blood in their veins. They could choose a husband for the color of his hair or the brightness of his smile, if they wished."

"Hardly valid reasons . . ."

"But the point is, they could *choose*." She touched Jahn's face again, then pulled her hand away. It would not be wise to move too quickly. "Though I was surprised and a teeny bit dismayed when I first heard that Blane had already delivered my refusal to the emperor, I find I am not sorry that option has been removed. In fact, I'm not at all sorry. I'm glad it's done."

"You might be sorry tomorrow," Jahn said ominously. "An emperor and a palace are a lot to give up. As empress you would have jewels and so many gowns you could not count them all. You would have servants to see to your every need, fine chefs and ladies' maids. Is that not a tremendous sacrifice?"

"Not for the freedom to pick a man for myself."

"And will you pick me?" he asked, oddly solemn.

Morgana gave him a tired smile. Suddenly she felt sleep coming on, and she knew she would find good dreams and much-needed rest when she laid her head down once more. Jahn had said no harm would come to her while she was in his care, and she believed him. "Perhaps I will." Her smile widened. "Then again, perhaps not."

Chapter Four

✳

THE room Blane had arranged was barely suitable for a beggar, much less a lady like Morgana. Jahn felt a moment's guilt as he led her through the tavern—where no one recognized him in his disguise—and up the stairs to their new home. In the beginning he had planned to end the charade as soon as they reached Arthes, but along the way he'd changed his mind. He wasn't ready to give up whatever this was that they'd found. He wanted more.

Morgana surprised him by accepting the situation. He'd expected to be forced to carry her kicking and screaming up the stairs, then have to endure hours of indignant screeching before she finally pleaded with him to take her to the emperor and the pampered life she deserved. She was a spoiled, haughty girl who needed a lesson in the harshness of life, and this room he was forcing her to call home was rough, even by his standards.

Actually, it was no longer true that he thought her entirely spoiled and in need of a harsh lesson. He told himself that on occasion, to justify housing her in this rough place, but to be honest, she intrigued him. There was more to this woman than met the eye, and he was not ready to let her go. Not yet.

She did sigh as she glanced about the small room, which was awash in sunlight which shone through the uncovered window. The mattress was uncovered, too, though there were stained—but clean—sheets folded and lying upon a nearby table. In one corner there was a small, lopsided table which might be suitable for dining, and one unsteady chair. A wooden chest with no lid had been placed at the foot of the bed, storage for a sentinel's meager belongings. Blane had done his job well in creating the fantasy. The chest held a couple of ordinary weapons and a change of clothing, as well as implements for shaving and sharpening the blades.

There had been a time when Jahn would've considered the room more than adequate. He'd become spoiled himself, he supposed.

He'd make Morgana stay here only a day or two, and then either she'd beg to be taken to the palace to vie for the position of empress, or he'd give up and reveal himself to her. True, she had mentioned going to the emperor last night, but her sudden capitulation had been too easy, the result of a moment of fear rather than a true realization. One way or another, she would discover his true identity and she'd be relieved, or furious, or amused. He never knew what to expect from her. He had certainly not expected the kiss.

The kiss had been a mistake. He could not—would not—definitely *should not*—indulge in a physical relationship with Lady Morgana, no matter how tempting she might be. Not that she was likely to offer herself to him, even though she did seem oddly accepting of their "marriage." He would tell her the truth of who he was—one way or another—long before she decided to make this marriage of theirs the real thing.

As if she ever would.

"The room could use some work," she said as she walked to the window and looked down on the street. This was not the best part of the city, which was why there were, and would continue to be, four sentinels posted in the tavern below. Morgana would never know that she was being protected, but his most trusted soldiers would watch over her while she was a resident in this less-than-fine room.

Jahn thought of how she might react when she discovered his true identity, and he played the possibilities in his mind. He could imagine too well having Blane lead Morgana into an empty ballroom where he would be waiting for her, wearing his imperial robes and a heavy crown. He imagined her smile, her evident relief, in realizing that she was not married to a sentinel who had no ambitions beyond surviving from one day to the next and having an obedient wife to give him children. Perhaps she would laugh at her gullibility and his cleverness. Perhaps she would be so overjoyed that this inadequate room was not her home that she'd throw herself into his arms and claim another kiss.

What fantasy that was. Knowing Morgana as he did, Jahn suspected that when he revealed himself, she'd demand to be taken straight home. She would be furious.

"Don't be making too many changes," Jahn said roughly as he tossed his leather bag, which contained shaving implements he had not used on the journey as well as a single dirty shirt, onto the bed. "I like my room just as it is."

"It's my room now, too," Morgana argued. "Surely a few adjustments, perhaps a thorough cleaning and a bit of decorating . . ."

"We do not yet know that this will be your home, as the marriage has not yet been made eternal. Lie with me as a wife, and you can make all the changes you'd like." He smiled, knowing she would refuse his generous offer.

Morgana studied the room once more, with narrowed eyes. "I suppose it will do, for now." She gazed for a long moment at the single bed. "Where will you sleep?"

Jahn pointed to the bed she gazed upon. "Right there, as always. As you can see, it cants a bit to the right, but after sleeping on the road it's a welcome relief to settle my old bones on that mattress."

She pursed her lips for a moment, then asked, "Where will I sleep?"

Once again, Jahn pointed to the bed, "Beside me, unless you'd prefer the floor." He fully expected Morgana would choose the hard floor over sharing his bed, no matter how uncomfortable it might be. He wouldn't know for certain until nightfall, which was several hours away. "Well, I must go to the palace and report my return to Arthes."

Morgana's spine straightened and her face paled a little. "When will you be back?"

"I don't know," Jahn said, shrugging his shoulders. "A sentinel's life is uncertain. I serve at the emperor's pleasure."

Morgana made an unkind scoffing noise which originated in her throat. "The blasted emperor. He has other sentinels. Why does he need you so soon after your return?"

Jahn smiled. "I'm his favorite."

"Don't jest," she snapped. "I don't want to stay here by myself. I'm alone in a strange city, in a small, *dirty* room. Not so far below this room rough men are drinking and laughing. If you leave, who will protect me?"

Jahn removed a small dagger from his vest. "Here you are, love. Protection."

She paled again, and refused to take the weapon from him.

"No one will bother you, trust me on that," he said seriously. "You are safe here; I give you my word. I would not leave you here alone if I did not know that to be true."

"But . . ."

"Stay in this room, and I will return as soon as I can."

She wrinkled her nose, but seemed to accept the order and the promise.

"Blasted emperor," she said again. "It's quite obvious that I need you more than he does. What kind of emperor is he, anyway? A poor one, if you ask me."

"What is that supposed to mean?"

Morgana pursed her lips. "Arik fought for his throne. He earned it with blood and chivalry. Emperor Jahn simply walked into the palace and took his seat. He fought for nothing."

Jahn was taken aback. Was this what people thought of him? Did others think him worthless and undeserving? "He was a soldier in the war against Ciro."

"As were many others," Morgana replied. "What did he do that was so special that he was made emperor, except to have the luck to call an old, incompetent emperor father?"

"Many people think he's a fine man."

Morgana snorted and wrinkled her nose.

"We will continue this discussion later." Jahn left the room, closing the door solidly behind him. He waited in the hallway until he heard the latch fall into place. Morgana was locked inside.

He bounded down the stairs, strangely content even though Morgana had just called him a poor emperor. One of the sentinels on guard, the lanky Sorayo, met his emperor at the foot of the stairs. Jahn barely slowed down. "When she leaves, follow her. Do not allow her to see you, but keep her safe."

"You seem certain that she will leave," the sentinel said as he trailed Jahn to the door.

Jahn smiled. "Of course she will. I told her not to."

DANYA wondered how much the deputy minister of magic had heard before he'd bloodied Ennis's nose and issued his ultimatum. If he knew that this potential empress was not an innocent maid, if he knew that she had given birth to a child who had not lived, then he did not reveal his knowledge in his words or his actions.

Of course, he uttered few words, and his actions consisted of staying away from her and riding straight toward Arthes and the palace.

Danya wanted to be situated in that palace as soon as

possible. She wanted to make herself at home, study the palace and its residents, and make herself a part of life there so that the emperor would choose her when the time came. She would be pretty and agreeable. She would be the perfect empress.

And she would never go home. She would never again sit across the table from the man who had stolen her innocence and broken her heart.

When they stopped at midday, Danya handed her horse over to a sentinel who would care for it while she rested, and she walked toward a narrow stream which ran nearby. Her steps were slow and easy as she stretched her limbs and reacquainted herself with solid ground. She liked to ride, truly she did, but she had never been in the saddle for such long hours.

No pain was too sharp to keep her from reaching Arthes as quickly as possible. When her mother had suggested sending an elderly nurse along as chaperone, Danya had first balked and then refused. Instead of the nurse, her only chaperone was a young lady's maid, Fai, who rode at least as well as Danya. It was a further blessing that the maid was quiet and shy, so Danya did not feel compelled to carry on endless conversation during the travels. That maid, three sentinels, the deputy minister, and Danya herself made up their traveling party.

Taking care with the skirt of her riding outfit, Danya knelt by the stream and carried a handful of water to her overheated face. The splash felt wonderful, it invigorated her and steeled her resolve. So what if her rear end and her thighs hurt? Soon enough she would be living in luxury, and she would never know pain again.

If he chose her. If she was the one.

A rough voice whispered, "Do not look at me."

Instinctively, Danya's head snapped about, and she saw a hooded figure hiding at the edge of the trees behind her.

"I said, do not look!" The whisper was harsher this time, almost menacing.

Danya returned her gaze to the water. "There are four strong, armed men a short distance away, and if I scream . . ."

"I suggest you do not scream," the hooded man said softly. He did not move toward her, but remained in the shadows of the forest. "Just listen. If you wish to be empress, simply listen."

Danya's spine straightened. He had her attention. "I'm listening."

"Good." The single word washed over her like a breath of cold wind, and then the interloper continued. "What would you do to be empress, Lady Danya?"

She hesitated only a heartbeat. "Anything."

"I thought so. In my divinations I saw that to be true. You are desperate. You're hungry for power."

Divinations! If he spoke the truth, this was a powerful wizard who stood behind her, a seer . . . someone who could help her have all that she wanted. "Yes," Danya whispered.

"Would you truly do anything which was asked of you?"

"I would."

"Would you take a life?"

Again, Danya hesitated. "I don't know. I don't think so. Anything else. I would do *almost* anything."

"Almost is not enough," the hooded man whispered. "True power comes at a high price. Are you willing to pay that price?"

"Who are . . ." Danya began, but a hissing noise and another command not to look made her turn once more to the water, where her broken image reflected the sunlight.

"I know your secrets, Lady Danya. I have seen them in my dreams and divinations."

"I have no secrets," she said, foolishly hoping this man who obviously saw so much did not see too well into her.

"I see a lover who was not yours to claim," he said harshly, killing her hopes, "and as a result of your illicit affair, a child, a son you wrongly believe to be dead and buried."

A chill ran up Danya's spine. *Wrongly believe . . .* "My son came too soon, and he died."

"He did not. The witch who delivered him lied to you. She sold your baby to a childless couple who paid a high price for the son they could not produce. She did not wish to share her good fortune with you, and perhaps she actually thought it a kindness to make you believe the child was forever gone."

She had dreamed that it was true. The midwife had allowed Danya only a brief glimpse of her dead son, and then she'd administered a strong potion to take away a mother's pain of birth and loss. The potion had done more than ease Danya's heartache; it had made her sleep for two days. "I saw his grave."

"You saw a mound of dirt with nothing beneath but more dirt."

Danya wanted to believe this was true, that her child lived, that he had found a loving and safe home. He would be almost two years old, now . . .

"The emperor will never knowingly choose a wife who has such a sordid past, Lady Danya," the whisper continued. "But there are those of us who are pleased that you have the ability to produce a son. We would like you to do so again. We would like you to produce the future emperor."

"I would like that, too," she confessed.

"Would you?"

"Yes."

"Good." Again, the single word sounded inhuman. "We are also pleased that you have the strength and cunning to hide such a momentous event from all those around you. It is no small feat for a woman to take charge as you did. In the same circumstances many women would've panicked and done something stupid. Most women would have been lost, they would've cried and dragged a dozen innocent people into the circle of their drama, but not you. You handled the situation quite well and very discreetly."

"I had no choice."

"I suppose you didn't," he said with a hint of what sounded oddly like humor. "It is done, then. From now on, you are ours, Lady Danya. You will do what is asked of you, or you'll suffer the consequences."

"What consequences?" she asked. "What will you do to me if I don't cooperate?"

"We will not hurt you, that I swear."

Danya breathed a sigh of relief, but her relief did not last long. "But, we will tell the emperor about your liaison with your sister's husband and the resulting child, and then we will tell your family. Your mother will be heartbroken, I imagine, and your sister will likely not forgive you."

"It was not my fault! I did not know that Ennis was . . ." Danya argued in a heated voice.

The hooded man ignored her. "And while we will not hurt *you,* the same cannot be said for your son."

Danya's heart tried to burst through her chest, and she spun around to confront the monster who would threaten a child . . . but the hooded man was gone. From a short distance, from somewhere in the shadows, she heard a whispered, "They call him Ethyn."

Danya could not stop the tears that ran down her face as she dropped to her knees and absorbed all the information she had been given. Her child was alive. Alive and well, as long as she did what was asked of her. A part of her was filled with terror, but she did her best to push the terror away. These people, whoever they were, wanted the same things she did. They wanted her to be empress. They wanted her to have another son.

All that she desired would come at a high price, perhaps even requiring her to take a life. She didn't think she could do that; didn't think she could kill anyone.

But they would hurt Ethyn if she didn't do as they asked. Who would hurt a child? Danya remembered the hooded man's horrible whisper, and she didn't doubt that he was capable of anything. More tears ran down her face, and she hugged herself to try to rein in the sharp feelings that were tearing her apart. She had denied these emotions for so long that they felt fresh and raw. They tore at her insides.

A familiar voice interrupted her whirling thoughts. "Are you all right?" Rainer managed to sound genuinely concerned.

Danya lifted her head and looked at him as he neared. This was it. The choice had to be made now, at this moment. She could tell Deputy Minister Rainer about the hooded visitor and his threats, or she could prove that she had not been lying to herself when she'd said she'd do anything to become empress. She could ask this kind man for his help, or she could claim the position of empress—and save the life of the son she did not know, yet still loved.

"Of course I am not fine," she said sharply. "I'm sore from riding in the saddle for so long, and look at my hair!" She tossed back a tangled strand. "Is this any way for a potential empress to look? It is the first day of a long journey, and already I suffer."

Rainer's concerned expression turned cold. "I did offer to escort you by coach," he said.

Danya struggled to her feet. The deputy minister could've offered a hand of assistance, but he did not. "And double or triple the time of this journey?" she said. "No, thank you. I will deal with the pain and the assault on my appearance, but that does not mean I have to like it!"

"There is no need to rush," Rainer said coldly. "There are six weeks until the First Night of the Summer Festival, when the emperor will make his choice. You could choose comfort."

"I choose speed." She walked past him, head held high. When he was behind her, she allowed a few more tears to fall. If Rainer saw them, he would think the tears were brought about by her sore backside or her tangled hair or her bruised dignity. He would not know, could never know, that she had just taken a step which would further darken her already bruised soul.

MORGANA'S steps quickened as she found herself upon a stone pathway which ran between two tall buildings. The buildings blocked the sun, casting her in shadow and increasing the chill in her heart, a heart which beat much too fast. Someone was following her. At least two men, she was certain. They were roughly dressed and very large, and she was almost certain she'd seen them in the tavern as she'd made her escape.

Some escape. She had no coins and no skills with which to earn them. As she'd walked through the city, Morgana had had that truth hammered into her very soul. She did not know what she'd been thinking when it had occurred to her that she might actually remain married to a sentinel and live in such a common, coarse place. She did not belong here. She could not survive here, not alone. She had no place to go, no home but the one Jahn provided for her, no friends, no family, no one to turn to but the husband she did not want. She had nothing.

Many of these thoughts had come to her as she looked at the canted bed which dominated the room Jahn Devlyn called home. The choice to share that bed with a man who'd claimed her as his wife should not be made on a whim! She should not give in to her need for sanctuary so easily! Should she?

She walked through the marketplace where men and women sold food, fabrics, weapons, and anything else a city dweller might need. If she'd had a skill beyond turning those who threatened her into glass, she might've set up a booth of her own. Instead she wandered alone, feeling foolish for leaving the tavern and for thinking she could have any sort of marriage with a man simply because he was patient and a more than decent kisser. She was confused, she was scared . . . she was lost.

There was no choice but to return to the tavern. It was

while she scurried in that direction that she'd seen the two
men following her.

They could not hurt her, she knew that. If they tried,
her uncontrollable power would rise up and stop them. She
did not want to kill again. What if they just happened to
be on the same path she walked? What if it was coincidence that she'd seen them several times since leaving the
tavern?

What if it was not?

In trying to lose the men who followed her, Morgana got
turned around so she no longer knew where she was. The
path from the tavern to the market had been an easy one,
and she should've been able to find her way back without
any trouble. But she'd made a couple of turns just to see if
the men continued to follow. They had. And now she did
not know which way to go.

Morgana heard footsteps far behind her, and she felt the
ice at her center grow colder and stronger. In the weeks
since Tomas's death her curse had slept, but now it had
been awakened and she did not know how to stop what had
begun. She ran, and behind her the footsteps grew faster. If
she turned and lashed out, she would once again take a life.
She could feel it. The fear that had once before awakened
her curse was fed by the unfamiliarity of this place and the
helplessness of her situation.

At the corner she bravely looked back—and saw that it
was an unfamiliar man who was walking behind her, not
the heathens she had been so sure she'd spotted at the tavern. He did not look at all menacing.

Morgana leaned against the wall and relaxed, but for
some reason the chill at her heart did not abate. She was
lost, she was afraid . . . she was very possibly on the verge
of losing control and killing everything and everyone in
her path. If someone startled her, if she became more afraid
than she already was, would the burst of cold blue death
come again? Where was Jahn when she needed him so desperately?

Reaching for a calmness she very much needed, Morgana looked up at the palace rising at the western edge of the city. Suddenly she realized where she was. From the tavern she'd had a particular view of the palace, and she remembered well how close the plain building had been to the tallest, most magnificent edifice in the city.

Again she ran, this time with a destination in mind. Two turns, and she found herself on a street she remembered. The tavern was straight ahead. She lifted her skirt and increased her pace, longing for any sort of familiarity—longing, most of all, for Jahn Devlyn.

Morgana ran into the tavern and bolted for the stairs. The iciness in her heart grew. She was so afraid, so alone, so scared that it did not go away even now, when she knew she was not being followed. She was in no danger, and yet the curse continued to grow. What would happen when it burst? What if she did not find control and calm?

She glanced at the people in the tavern, roughly dressed men who watched her run but did not move from their tables. They were merely curious. Did they deserve to die for their curiosity? Of course not.

Morgana threw open the door to Jahn's room, and found the sentinel lying across the bed in a casual pose. His expression revealed a touch of annoyance and concern, but not much. "Where have you been?" he asked. "I told you to stay here until I returned."

Just looking at him made the chill start to fade, and she breathed deeply in relief. She remembered the heat of the kiss, the warmth he had sometimes roused just by smiling at her. Her gift of destruction was cold; Jahn was heat. She did not entirely understand, but she could not deny that he had a way of stopping the curse.

"Warm me," she commanded as she walked to the bed.

His eyebrows lifted in surprise. "What's this?"

"I'm cold," she said, not hesitating as she lay beside him on the bed. He had put the clean sheets over the mattress of this bed which had terrified her so. She knew now that there were much worse things in her world to be terrified of. "I'm cold to my very bones. Make me warm, please."

Almost grudgingly, Jahn wrapped his arms around her. She breathed deeply and rested her head against his shoulder. He ran one strong hand up and down her back in a comforting manner that made the ice in her heart melt away. "It is not a cold day, Ana," he said softly. "What has you so chilled?"

She could not tell him. She could never tell anyone! "I went for a walk and I got lost, and I was so afraid."

"You should've stayed here," he said, "as I told you."

"Yes, yes, I know," she admitted. "Men were following me."

Jahn's body stiffened. "Truly?"

"I think so," she confessed, no longer certain that her imagination hadn't been playing tricks on her.

The chill she'd experienced on that horrible night she would never forget had been out of control and powerful and terrifying. The warmth Jahn roused was just the opposite. It calmed her. The heat was a slow and familiar and pleasant sensation. She snuggled close to his warm chest and listened to his steady and strong heartbeat. She clutched at his shirt with chilly hands. Yes, she was getting warmer, but she was not warm enough. She wanted more heat; she wanted the ice at her core gone, once and for all, and only he could chase it away.

"Kiss me," she said, lifting her head to bring her lips close to Jahn's.

The surprise in his blue eyes was genuine. "What?"

Morgana smiled. "Kiss me. When you kiss me, I feel warm all over. I like that. I need it. My life is falling apart, and even though you are the cause of the turmoil, you are also the solution to my dilemma."

"What dilemma?"

She did not want to explain, not now, not ever. "Just kiss me."

He did, tentatively at first, then with passion. It was the unexpected passion that fed her heat, the fervor that chased away her curse. This warmth was marvelous. She drank it in; she savored it.

Jahn parted her lips with his and slipped the tip of his tongue into her mouth. It was as if a stream of fire whipped through her body, chasing away the last of the chill, the last of the fear. There was only warmth in this place, warmth and peace. She should tell him to stop now. He had done all that was necessary, after all. There was no longer any danger of her turning everything in her path to fragile crystal with a burst of cold she could not control.

And yet, she was no longer entirely in control, she recognized that very well. She was out of control in an entirely new way, but there was no danger here. There was simply desire and warmth and a longing for something more.

Jahn Devlyn was a husband she did not want. He had claimed her as if she were a horse up for auction, a lucky and convenient find. He did not know her; she did not know him. The life he offered was not what she'd dreamed of—it was more the stuff of nightmares. And yet, he had been the one to end the chill that was her curse. He was the one who had taken her from a home where she'd felt as if she were on the verge of being discovered as a monster. Would she trade the life of a pampered lady which was filled with terror and uncertainty for the simple life of a sentinel's wife where there was always someone to take away the curse? Would she trade ice and death for heat and life?

She loved Jahn's kiss. It was heartfelt and filled with promise. There was such heat in his mouth, in his body close to hers, and she felt like she was falling and melting and flying. She squirmed a bit, making herself more comfortable against him, pressing her body closer to his. So close, she could not help but feel his response to the kiss. That response pressed insistently against her.

Without a hint of a chill in her body, Morgana took her mouth from Jahn's. All her reservations were gone, wiped away by a kiss. "Make me your wife," she commanded, her voice husky and soft.

Jahn's eyes widened in surprise, she saw in the fading light. "What was that you said?"

"I have decided," she said, running her fingers through a strand of his oddly streaked hair. She wondered if their children would have his remarkable hair.

"You have decided what?" he asked numbly.

How specific did she have to be? Her husband had not struck her as dense until this moment. "I will be your wife; I will have your children. I choose to live in this room rather than to seek a place in the palace with the emperor."

"This is an important decision, Ana," he said, strangely uncooperative. "It should not be made while you are recovering from a frightening experience. We should wait awhile longer."

Jahn had no idea how frightening her experience had been. He didn't know that she had come close to destroying a portion of this city with her fear, or that he had been the one to save her.

Though Morgana had never lain with a man, she was not ignorant. She reached down and touched Jahn's straining trousers. "You cannot say that you do not want me."

"No, I cannot."

And she wanted him. She knew that now, as a flood of desire washed through her. She would not call it love, but if they were physically compatible, as they appeared to be, then was that not a fine start to a lifetime of marriage? She took his hand and led it to a breast which seemed oddly hungry for his touch. He did not pull his hand away, but caressed her through the fabric of her once lovely gown, a gown which was now travel-weary and faded.

She leaned into Jahn and placed her mouth on his neck, where he tasted warm and salty and male on her tongue. She'd never known anything like it, could not have imagined that she'd enjoy the taste of a man's skin so much. He moaned, and she was glad of it. Perhaps he felt as she did, that this was a good beginning to a strangely begun marriage. "Please," she whispered, "make me a wife. Warm my heart and soul. Take me, Jahn."

Jahn did not argue with her again, but instead slipped

his hand along her leg and up her skirt. He spread her legs, and she allowed him to do so. She trembled, as much with desire as with uncertainty, and when his fingers found her most intimate place, she gasped and lurched. What a magnificent feeling, and how unexpected. This must be the pleasure married women sometimes spoke of. This warmth must be the fulfillment of which they spoke. Why had she waited so long to claim it as her own?

Morgana had made her mother a promise that she would wait for love before marriage. But what was love, really? Intense wanting? Warmth to the pit of a soul? Safety? All this time, had she been waiting for Jahn? No other man had ever made her feel safe, or secure, or warm. Was he the man she had been longing for in the depths of her soul? Was he the promise Morgana had made to her mother?

Jahn stroked, and the newly found pleasure continued. He was so gentle, so easy . . . and yet this encounter was not easy at all. It was powerful, and she was quickly carried away by his touch. She subtly changed positions often, trying to get comfortable, but at her core Morgana was decidedly prickly—decidedly wanting and restless. If he kissed her deeper, if he touched her there, all would be well. She wanted more, so much more.

Soon enough Jahn would roll on top of her and fill her, but in spite of the fidgetiness, Morgana was in no hurry for that to happen. The sensation of falling and fidgeting was oddly exciting. She had always imagined the act of joining would be somewhat unpleasant and painful, but the more they kissed, the more she squirmed, the less she worried about the actual workings of the end of this encounter. She did not think having Jahn inside her would be unpleasant at all. It would be exciting and inevitable, and she could not wait to be his wife.

He moved. Ah, yes, this was it. He pushed her skirt higher and lifted her leg and placed his mouth on the back of her knee. She shuddered from the top of her head to her toes, the sensation was so great. Her body throbbed, and she wanted the end to this. She wanted him inside her.

He continued to kiss his way up her leg. It was totally unacceptable to have a man, even a husband, kissing her thigh while she trembled at his touch, and yet she did not once think of pushing him away. No, she would not do such a thing, not even when he trailed his tongue along her inner thigh, moving slowly and tasting her as if she were dessert on his personal buffet. Not even when his warm hands reached up to cup her rear end and pull her down the mattress, while his mouth traveled up.

He gently forced her legs farther apart, and then he kissed her there, where she was wet and needful, where she twitched and throbbed. Her breath would hardly come, her body seemed to have a will of its own as it moved in a gentle rhythm against Jahn's mouth. Something was happening, something was coming. Her hips moved faster and she dug her fingers into the sheets beneath her. Jahn's tongue flicked against her harder than before and Morgana felt awash in sensations she had never imagined. She moaned. Her back rose off the bed and she shook to the core of her being. The intense pleasure whipped through her body, heat and delight and an unexpected sensation of being a part of someone else, at least for this moment. She gasped as her body lurched and sensations she had never even imagined took control.

What she'd felt earlier, that warm pleasure, had been only a hint of what being a wife offered.

There was no trace of a chill remaining in her body, and hadn't been for quite some time. She was satisfied and content in a way she had never been before. She was boneless and shaking and happy . . .

And they were not yet done. Jahn had shown her pleasure and release but had not yet entered her body, as he would. Soon. Heaven above, she could not wait. As Jahn rose up, she touched his head. One of these days she would shave off his beard and see if he had a proper chin under there or not. Not that she cared . . .

"I have to go," he said, leaping from the bed as if he could not escape fast enough.

Much of Morgana's pleasure faded. "Why?"

"I'm needed at the palace. I came here only to check on you and tell you that I'll be working at night for a few days. You were not here, and now I have no time left for pleasurable activities." He did not sound at all pleased.

"When will you be back?"

"In the morning," he said.

"You're leaving me here alone?" she asked, caught between heretofore unknown satisfaction and disappointment.

Jahn sighed. "Not entirely. Some friends of mine will be in the tavern below when I am not here. No one will bother you. Did I not tell you that I would take care of you, that I would keep you safe?"

"You did." The truth dawned on her. "The men who were following me this afternoon, were they your friends?"

"Most likely," he mumbled.

And she had almost destroyed them. "You must not keep secrets from me, Jahn," she said softly. "That is not the way of a real marriage."

"A real marriage," he said. "You know, we haven't yet properly consummated our union. By the time I return you will likely have changed your mind and will be glad there was no time . . ."

"When you return, I will be waiting for you, husband," she said. She could not tell him why she had come to her decision, not without telling him everything. No secrets, she had said, but in this case she was certainly justified. He did not need to know. She did not want him to know.

Jahn must've been running late, because he left as if a demon were at his heels.

Chapter Five

THAT had not been in the plan. Jahn ran down the stairs, catching the eye of the senior sentinel on duty. At a nod, the man rose and hurried to meet his emperor.

Did these sentinels, like Morgana, consider him to be a poor emperor who had done nothing to earn his position? Did they see him as a wastrel, a worthless ruler, a lucky bastard? He did his best in the position he had fallen into, but in truth he had not done anything to earn his place in the palace. He was in power thanks to the blood in his veins and nothing more. Were his best efforts at proving worthy good enough?

"She does not leave the tavern tonight," Jahn said tersely as the sentinel neared.

"But, My Lord, if she . . ."

"I don't care if you have to physically restrain her, she will not leave!" Jahn snapped, his passions and fury roused on so many levels he did not dare to ponder them all. He was almost certain it had been his sentinels following Morgana this afternoon, but if he was wrong, if she was in danger thanks to his little game, he would never forgive himself. *Almost certain* was not good enough.

The sentinel bowed in compliance, and Jahn pushed his way into the early evening air, taking a deep breath and slowing his pace. Though he did not think anyone would recognize him in his current state of dress and dishevelment, one of the sentinels followed, an escort to the palace. That sentinel would return to the tavern as soon as Jahn was safely in his quarters, as it was clear Lady Morgana needed a full contingent of guards at all times.

Jahn mumbled to himself in a constant one-sided conversation. Anyone who saw him would likely take him for an insane beggar, between the beard and the mumbling. He did not care. Why had he not left the bed the moment Morgana had asked him to warm her? Why had he not refused her unexpected request, or come up with an excuse to leave the room, or—now here's a thought—why had he not told her the fucking truth?

No, no, they were now far past the time for his telling the truth without dire consequence. So much for his initial plan to make her grovel in appreciation of his position. So much for teaching her a lesson in humility and then sending her home. So much for taking her down a peg and making her appreciate the blessed life to which she'd been born. This amusement—for that was how it had begun, as a lark—had turned into so much more.

On the First Night of the Summer Festival—a mere six weeks away—he would have no choice but to choose Lady Morgana as his empress, he supposed. Now that he'd had his head up her skirt and had tasted her amazing response, now that he'd made her shudder and moan beneath him, he could hardly send her home as inadequate. Ramsden would have a valid grievance if he did so. At least he had not been foolish enough to find his own release inside her, tempted as he had been to give her all that she had asked for. No, that would never do.

Running up the palace stairs to his private chambers,

Jahn momentarily thought of calling Melusina or Anrid or both. Those lovely and willing and uncomplicated women would make him forget the lady he'd left lying in a tavern bed. They'd make the pain of his sacrifice go away, and for a while they would wipe clean his muddled mind. They would ease the throb, if not his conscience.

How could the most simple of entertaining plans go so terribly awry?

At the door to his bedchamber he ordered a sentinel to fetch his two favorite women, but before the young man had taken two steps, Jahn stopped him and rescinded the order. Tempted as he was to lose himself in the warmth of a willing and familiar woman, he could not do it. It wasn't right—he was no longer entirely free in that respect or any other. And to be honest, he had the sinking feeling no other woman would ease this particular ache.

After learning more than he'd wanted to know about his true past and his real father, Jahn's greatest fear had been becoming like the man who had so selfishly taken whatever he had desired, damn the cost to those around him. Perhaps in the end Sebestyen had loved his wife, Liane— Alix and Jahn's mother—but before he had loved her, he had stolen her from her family, broken her spirit, and ultimately broken her heart. He had owned her and he had degraded her. From all Jahn had heard, Sebestyen Beckyt had never been faithful to anyone or anything.

At this moment, Lady Morgana considered herself his wife. In a way she was. He had claimed her, after all, and she had succumbed.

When the door was closed behind him and he was finally alone, Jahn sank into a comfortable chair and dropped his head into his hands. Dear God, he was just like his father. His worst fears had come to pass. Though his intentions had not been entirely dishonorable, he had stolen Morgana away from her family, and he had done his best to break her spirit. Judging by the expression on her face as he'd left her lying in his bed, before it was all over, he was certain to break her heart.

After a cursory knock, Blane entered the room. "Minister Calvyno has been asking for you all day. He's quite insistent. Someone must've seen you on the stairway and told him where you are, because Calvyno is in the hallway and he says he's not leaving until he sees you."

"Give me a moment before you show him in." With a curse Jahn grabbed a blasted imperial robe and donned it, taking the time to remove only his sentinel's vest, then hiding the uniform under volumes of crimson. That small change would have to do for a long overdue meeting with his minister of foreign affairs.

Jahn had reclaimed his seat by the time Calvyno was shown into the room. The older man was pale and anxious, but that was not unusual. "You're feeling better, I pray?" he asked crisply.

"Much," Jahn said. "Thank you for your concern."

Calvyno nodded, then stared pointedly and with obvious disapproval. "The beard is . . . temporary?"

Jahn stroked the ever-growing length. "I like the beard. I'm thinking of keeping it for a while longer."

"I see," Calvyno said in obvious distress.

"Surely you're not here to discuss the state of my facial hair."

"No." Calvyno nodded, happy, as usual, to turn to business. "I have heard, through one of your most trusted sentinels, that those sent to fetch Lady Morgana Ramsden have returned with the message that she refused your offer."

Jahn sighed. So much for escaping his current troubles with mundane matters of state! Morgana was everywhere, it seemed. "Yes, she did." Blane was too efficient. Now that it seemed Morgana would be empress, after all, they would have to explain away her initial refusal and ultimate acceptance . . . but that problem could wait for another time. He searched his memory of the night when he had set this contest into motion. "Who was it that suggested Lady Morgana as a candidate?"

Calvyno wrinkled his long nose. "General Hydd, I believe. He's mentioned her name several times in the past few months, whenever the subject of a much-needed empress arose. He will be distressed to learn that she has declined. I believe he had great hopes for her."

General Hydd, Jahn's minister of defense, was a good and loyal soldier, a tested veteran of the battle with Ciro. Jahn found himself wondering how the general had come to recommend Morgana. Were they somehow related? Was Hydd friends with Almund Ramsden? The suggested women had all been hailed as the most beautiful or most gifted or most well connected. What had Hydd said about Morgana? He could not remember all the details of that night. Insistent voices had been talking too loudly and too fast and all at once.

Jahn knew that he could, with a minimum of effort, spread the word that Lady Morgana had changed her mind and would be participating in the contest. After all, women changed their minds all the time. No one would think twice about such a change of heart. But he said nothing. For now, he wanted Morgana all to himself. She was his, and he was not ready to give her up.

He could be a selfish bastard.

LONG past the time they'd stopped for the night, Rainer was certain something was wrong with Lady Danya Calliste. Something beyond the usual pettiness and silliness which seemed to be so much a part of her. She was beautiful, and annoyingly she drew his awareness more often than she should. But he did not like her, and fortunately, he did not have to like her in order to complete this task. Still, he was bothered by the change in her. Since they'd stopped that afternoon, she had not been the same.

Rainer possessed a healthy bit of magical abilities which had been inherited from his grandfather, much to the dismay of his down-to-earth farming parents. Reading minds and knowing the future were not among his talents, so he could not use his abilities now to discern what was wrong with Lady Danya. He could start a fire with a flick of his fingers; he could cause pain with the gentlest touch of his hand; he could grab the wind or rushing water and make it his own, for a short while; he could give pleasure with the same touch, slightly altered. Energy, his grandfather had said, was at the center of their powers, as it was at the center of all others'. Some who were gifted could control only one sort of energy or another, but Rainer could capture energy of many types and make it his own. Now and then he could read energy in a person, if it was very strong.

None of his talents would answer his questions about Lady Danya.

He shouldn't care. She was conceited, vain, and more than a little bit troublesome. He couldn't imagine the emperor choosing such a woman for the important position of empress, but he could be wrong. The others vying for the position might be just as bothersome, for all he knew. Still, they likely did not possess the same sort of sordid secrets.

Should he tell someone, anyone, what he'd overheard the night before their departure? The fact that she'd once been lovers with her brother-in-law was unsavory, but not particularly relevant. Still, it did speak to her character. Having met the man, however briefly, Rainer also thought Lady Danya's choice of a sexual partner showed a startling lapse in judgment.

Was that why she had taken to shedding silent tears as they traveled toward Arthes? Had she actually loved the unworthy man she'd left behind?

As the night wore on, and Lady Danya continued to sit by the fire rather than retiring to the small tent she shared with her maid, Rainer became more and more restless. He couldn't go to sleep and leave her in such a state. One of the three sentinels would be on watch at all times, but the woman was his responsibility. She was his assignment, his first as a deputy minister.

Her head snapped up as he walked toward her, and he was struck—not for the first time—by her incredible beauty. It was somehow wrong that a creation so flawless, so pleasing to the eye, could also be so bothersome. Perhaps it was a kind of balance in nature. The most beautiful insects and snakes were often the most deadly.

"We will depart very early in the morning," he said, his voice and his manner remaining detached. "You should get some sleep."

Lady Danya glanced at her tent and then at the shadowed forest beyond. "I'm not tired," she said, a touch of fear in her soft voice.

"Still . . ."

"I'll only toss and turn and disturb Fai's sleep."

"I'm sure you'll settle down quickly and find sleep, and your maid will never know of your unease. She was quite exhausted when she retired." Hours ago.

Why did he care if this challenging woman slept or not? Why did he care if she dozed and fell out of her saddle tomorrow after spending a sleepless night staring into the fire? All he had to do was deliver her to the palace. No one had mentioned the condition she was required to be in upon delivery.

Though he assumed it was implied that she be well cared for.

"You need your rest," he said.

"Have you ever done something truly horrible?" the lady asked, interrupting Rainer's gentle nudge toward retreat to her tent.

"I don't believe so, no," Rainer answered. With his talents he might've, but his grandfather had taught him that to use what God had given him for his own gain or amusement or power would be hideously wrong. "Have you? Is that why you cannot sleep?" Did she have a conscience that plagued her for giving a wife's gifts to her sister's husband?

"Not yet, no," she whispered, again looking to the forest.

What was she afraid of? Rainer did not wish to be intrigued, but he could not help but be curious.

"Is a horrible act performed for honorable reasons as

damning as one done out of evil, do you think?" she asked.

"I don't know. Can you be more specific?"

"No," she whispered. "I can't."

It was obvious that the woman had something troubling on her mind. Perhaps her concerns were more disquieting than the sore backside and mussed hair she'd complained about earlier in the day. "I should not do this," he said, sitting down beside her—not too close, given that she would one day perhaps be empress.

Her eyes narrowed. "Should not do *what*?" she asked with evident suspicion.

"Tell me what is bothering you," he said, "and I will swear to keep the knowledge here." He patted his heart, which beat steadily beneath the jacket of his best traveling outfit.

Lady Danya shook her head quickly and decisively.

Rainer sighed. "I believe I already know."

The woman glared at him, her eyes wide and terrified. "That's not possible, unless you have used your magic on me."

"I used no magic, Lady Danya, but I did overhear you and your brother-in-law speaking. You had improper relations with your sister's husband," he said bluntly, "and obviously the guilt weighs upon your heart."

"How much did you hear?" she asked sharply.

"Enough," he whispered.

With his well-meaning words he roused an anger in her, and that anger looked healthier upon her than her sadness had. Color flooded her cheeks and her dark eyes flashed. "I did not behave inappropriately with my sister's *husband*," she declared. "Yes, I was foolish enough to allow myself to be seduced, but Ennis and I became involved three years ago, *before* Ennis asked Vida to be his wife. I thought he was going to propose to me," she confessed, losing her anger and dropping her chin. "I thought he loved me." Tears ran down her cheeks and glistened in the firelight. "And now you will tell the emperor that I am a ruined woman and he will send me home long before the First Night of the Summer Festival."

"You were little more than a child three years ago," Rainer observed. In truth, she was young now. She was certainly too young to know such pain and guilt.

"Young and stupid," Lady Danya whispered.

"Young and naive," Rainer said. "I doubt you have ever been stupid."

She looked at him with suspicious eyes. "You sound almost as if you understand."

He did not know how anyone could've been duped by one such as Ennis, but she had been very young. He took a handkerchief from his pocket and offered it to the lady, who took it and quickly wiped the tears from her face. "You were duped by an immoral, conniving man, and if I had known the whole story of your shared past, he'd still have a bloodied nose."

"But that doesn't change the facts. I have given myself to another man. Once the emperor knows, he will not choose me." Her lips trembled and she clutched at the damp handkerchief. "I can't go home, Deputy Rainer. I can't sit across the table from Ennis for years and years to come, and pretend nothing ever happened. I can't smile at him for the sake of the family, when in my heart I despise him." She looked away from him. "Even more, I despise myself for being weak and foolish."

Rainer was surprised to find that he felt sympathy for the girl. "I told you any secrets you share with me tonight will be well kept. That has not changed."

Her eyes went wide. "You truly won't tell the emperor of my mistakes?"

Rainer smiled. "There's no reason. Emperor Jahn has made a few mistakes himself, or so I hear." Well, that decision was made. He would not reveal to anyone that Lady Danya had been seduced by an older man who had connived and tricked her out of her innocence. That long-ago past was not relevant. Perhaps now she would stop crying and moping about. It was likely she had a pleasant smile—though he'd never had occasion to see it.

"Thank you," she whispered, and in that moment, in the firelight and with an expression of true gratitude on her face, she was breathtaking. Rainer held his breath for a moment. The harshness he sometimes saw in her was entirely absent, though she was obviously still worried.

"Now, get some sleep," Rainer said, pushing himself to his feet. He could not afford to note the beauty of this woman who might one day be empress. She offered him the handkerchief, and he shook his head. "Keep it." Given her volatile state, she might need it more than he would.

Again she looked to the forest, and Rainer was struck by the certainty that even though she had poured out her heart to him, he did not know all of Lady Danya's secrets.

MORGANA prepared herself for Jahn's return, which would surely be soon. The sun was up, and he had been at the palace all night. He would surely be tired and in need of sleep, but first he would need some tending to.

His friends, who had remained in the tavern all night, had been remarkably amenable and helpful. All she had to do was open the door, and one or more of them came running to see what she required. A warm bath—which had once been hot—sat waiting, as did a morning meal of corn cakes and fruit and cider. One of the men had fetched her a broom and a feather duster, and she'd done what she could to clean the room—as much to expend her own pent-up energy as to prepare the place for Jahn.

All the while, she'd worn a strange smile on her face. It had come to her in shocking fashion, as she'd watched the day come to life as sunlight broke through the window, that for the first time in years, she was truly happy. There was no weight at all on her heart, no worry about what tomorrow would bring. How odd!

The sun had not been up very long when she heard a

familiar footstep on the stairs. She did not wait for Jahn to reach the door, but opened it herself and met her husband with a smile. "Good morning," she said. "Did you have a good night at work?"

He narrowed his eyes. "What have you done with Lady Morgana?"

"She is not here," Morgana said, "but Ana Devlyn is present."

Jahn shook his head and walked into the room, closing the door behind him. Down the stairs, his four friends watched with a great deal of interest, their heads lifted and their eyes bright.

"We must talk," Jahn said ominously.

"You should take a bath first," she said, "before the water cools any more than it already has." She picked up the razor she had just sharpened.

Jahn looked at the razor and his eyes widened. "What's this?"

"I am determined to discover if you have a proper chin or not."

"And if I don't?" he asked.

"Then I shall have to leave you for another man," she teased, "one who will produce children with strong, dominant chins that speak of fine character."

His eyes narrowed.

"I'm not serious," she said. "Can you not take a small joke?"

"Not about my chin," he responded. "It's a very sensitive subject."

She waggled the razor in his direction. "Take off those clothes and get in the bath," she ordered. "Once you're clean, we'll see about a shave and your morning meal."

He looked at the razor as he began to undress. "You leave me no choice."

As he took off his uniform, Morgana readied the soap and a cloth for scrubbing, implements which his friends had so obligingly collected for her. "What did you wish to talk about?" she asked, not feeling entirely comfortable looking directly at him as he shed his clothes, though she did take frequent peeks. Oh, he was fine! Lean and well-muscled, shaped as a man should be shaped, strong and quite lovely, in a masculine way.

"I'd like to know why you decided to remain married to me when, now that we are in Arthes, you have other options."

"Such as?" she queried.

"You could go to the emperor and beg his forgiveness for rejecting his offer."

"You said he would not accept an apology," she argued.

"I could be wrong," he muttered. "And I did suggest that you try begging."

"What other options do I have, in your opinion?"

"Surely a man such as Almund Ramsden has business connections in the city. You could seek them out, ask if you might stay with them for a while, and then send your father a letter begging for his forgiveness."

"All of your options include me begging for forgiveness," she said, wondering why she had not thought yesterday of searching for one of her stepfather's many friends in the city. Now it was too late; she did not care to go home.

"This is true," he said, stepping into the warm water.

Morgana glanced at her husband more boldly as he lowered himself into the bathwater. Though she had nothing to compare him to, he certainly seemed to be a fine specimen of a man. He was lean and well muscled, long limbed and obviously strong. And the length and hardness of his penis were extraordinary. Just that glimpse made her shudder in a place she had never before shuddered—until last night.

When he was seated, Morgana took the rag and dipped it into the water, then briskly ran it over the soap, making a generous lather. "If you must know, I have been thinking about some of the things you said."

"Such as?" he said, closing his eyes and allowing her to scrub his chest and shoulders.

"I rather like the idea of marriage being a partnership, rather than a love match."

"So, you do not love me?"

"Of course not!" She laughed a bit nervously. "How could I? We barely know one another."

"After last night I'd say we know one another very well," he whispered.

"Not really," she said thoughtfully. "What happened last night was lovely and pleasurable and I would like to continue, but is love really required for sexual pleasure?"

"No," he conceded rather quickly.

"And it's not as if you love me," she continued. He did not immediately agree. The hand which had been so gently washing his chest stopped in midstroke.

"No, no, of course not," he said, then added, "but I do like you quite a lot."

"And I like you," she said, resuming her chore of bathing her husband. "That's a wonderful way to start a life together, don't you think?"

"I suppose," he said grudgingly.

"Lean forward and I will scrub your back." He did as she asked, and she scrubbed the long, strong muscles as she spoke. "If we were in love, then there would be unreasonable expectations and fiery emotions and disappointments and the horrible possibility that we might one day fall out of love, which would be painful." Morgana took a deep breath. "Sadly, I have come to believe that my mother was wrong when she advised that I wait for love to come along. An emotionless, practical, well-planned life together, a union as if we were two soldiers going to war side by side, would suit us both very well." There, she'd said it. "With lots of sex, of course," she added. "I like the heat your touch arouses in me," she confessed, telling as much of the truth as she dared. "I like the warmth that settles within me when you hold me, when you make me tremble with wanting." That warmth might one day entirely chase away the seed of ice in her heart. Jahn might be able to end the curse which had caused Morgana to take a man's life, the curse which had, just a few weeks earlier, made her feel as if she had no choice but to live her life alone.

This bearded, simple, strong man might be the answer to all her prayers.

She rinsed the soap from his back and he reclined in the tub once again. "Let's make this marriage a real one," she said softly. "Make me hot again, Jahn." She knew that he wanted her; that was as evident this morning as it had been last night, so why did he hesitate to do what needed to be done? "I can be a good wife. I will be everything you want me to be."

Instead of making a similar declaration of his own, Jahn sighed tiredly. "You might change your mind about remaining married, and if it is too late . . ."

"I will not change my mind."

"Not so long ago you were determined not to be a sentinel's wife, if you will recall. I still don't understand how or why you changed your mind so quickly about that," he said, "so how can I believe that you will not change your mind again?"

"You do not need to understand; you only need to accept," she argued.

"But if you change your mind, you will hate me for taking advantage of you in such a vulnerable . . ."

"Oh, for goodness' sake!" Morgana stood, and Jahn looked almost relieved. She tossed the washcloth into the water, where it landed with a splash he ignored. Did he truly think she'd change her mind once it was too late to do so, or was he having second thoughts of his own? Did he think she had made her decision based on fear and loneliness? She would simply have to show him that she had no intention of changing her mind again. "I did not expect you to be so stubborn," she said as she began to unbutton her bodice.

"What are you . . ." Jahn began, pointing to her fumbling fingers.

Her hands shook, and the buttons were extremely uncooperative, and Jahn looked as if he were about to leave the bath and walk away. She had not expected that he would be so difficult to convince.

"Blast!" Morgana said angrily, dropping her hands and shaking them fiercely. Then, before Jahn had a chance to stand or she had a chance to change her mind, she stepped into the water and sat down, facing her husband. Her skirt was quickly soaked, and the fabric floated on the surface of the water and stuck to Jahn's chest and legs. She pushed the bulk of the fabric out of the way. "I am your wife, Jahn Devlyn, or will be very shortly. You claimed me, and now I claim you."

"You're saying these things only because I was the first man to offer you a woman's pleasure." His blue eyes, such a fine color, narrowed.

"No," she said with certainty. "Whatever this is, it began long before last night."

"This is such a terrible idea," he said softly, but when Morgana reached between their bodies and grasped his incredibly hard length, she was quite sure he did not think it was a terrible idea at all.

Morgana smiled as she boldly caressed and aroused her husband. The expression on his face was one of bliss and pain combined, of pleasure and surrender. This boldness, this need to take what she had decided she wanted, was so unlike her. At least, it was unlike the woman she had pretended to be for all her adult life. She had lived all her days caught up in what was expected of her. What her mother wanted her to be, what her stepfather wanted her to be . . . she had never stopped to ask herself what she wanted to be until Jahn had claimed her.

Not so long ago she'd been so sure that she was meant to be forever alone, that she could count on no one, and now it seemed that another—a very unexpected other—would be the one to save her.

As angry as she had been since Jahn had taken her from home, as hotly as she had argued with him, as helpless as she had felt . . . she had not sensed even a sliver of ice inside her until she'd made the mistake of leaving him. And now, instead of cold in her heart she felt a wonderful, growing heat.

JAHN had intended to return to this room and immediately tell Morgana of his true identity. She'd be angry, but perhaps she'd forgive him. Eventually. He was not foolish enough to tell her that he'd lied while she was standing there with a straight razor in her hand.

And now here he was, immersed in a cooling bath with the woman on top of him, bringing their bodies closer together, touching him with innocent and unskilled fingers that were more arousing than anything he'd ever felt until this moment.

He had come here with the best of intentions, but he was not a saint. Not by a long shot.

If he gave Morgana what she was asking for, his choice of empress would truly be made. After last night he already considered that to be so, but this took the matter a step further. He could not lie with one of the bridal candidates and then send her home rejected. He could not make her his wife in this primitive way and then take another by imperial law.

Not that he wanted another. Morgana would make a fine wife, for a sentinel or an emperor. She was strong, she was beautiful, and more—he liked her. He had not even expected that much when he'd begun his search for a bride. He liked her, he wanted her . . . and in an odd way she already felt like a wife.

The fact that she had her hand on his cock had a little something to do with that, he supposed.

"Are you sure?" he asked again.

Morgana rubbed her wet and mostly clothed body against his. "I am. I have never been more sure of anything."

She leaned toward him, and he latched his mouth onto her throat, and in that moment his decision was made. Her flesh tasted so sweet, and she clung to him so well. He had to have her, here and now. He could not wait to slip inside her wet heat and make her scream with pleasure, to ease the pain that had been plaguing him for days. No other would do, no one but this woman would suit. He wanted to feel Morgana's muscles clench around him and he wanted to find release inside her.

But he would not take her fast and hard. She deserved better for her first time. He slipped his hand under her soaked skirt and up her leg and touched her intimately, as she was touching him. He slipped a finger inside her heat, and she lurched, splashing water onto the floor and gasping in surprise and delight.

She was anxious and writhing, ready in many ways, but he did not rush. Instead he unbuttoned the bodice she had struggled with in her haste. Slowly, deliberately, he unfastened the tiny buttons that restrained her. He freed her breasts from the confines of the fabric, and he touched them. Such fine, firm breasts they were. He raked his fingers across hardened nipples, then tasted them both, one and then the other. She liked it. Again she gasped and lurched, and this time she grabbed at his hair and pulled him closer.

"Yes," she whispered hoarsely.

Jahn answered by suckling a nipple, pulling it deep into his mouth. Morgana held onto him, grasping the back of his head and pulling him to her. He was close, so close, to slipping inside her, but there was not enough room in this damned tub to take her properly.

If he was going to surrender to this maddening woman, if he was going to break all the promises he had made to himself last night and this morning, he wanted to do the deed properly.

He stood slowly, his arms around Morgana as he brought her with him.

"Don't stop," she whispered. "Please, don't stop."

"I won't," he said, yielding to the inevitable.

Her soaked gown would take precious minutes to remove from her body, and he would have nothing less than

Morgana spread beneath him naked as he himself was. He reached toward the small table, snatched up the straight razor with which she intended to shave his beard, and began to carefully cut the wet fabric. A seam here, a length there, he cautiously cut away all that stood between him and his empress. In moments, what had once been a fine gown fell to the floor, a heap of wet rags, and Morgana stood before him naked and wet and trembling. She did not tremble because she was cold or afraid, but because she wanted him.

Jahn had never seen Morgana like this, completely bare. No man had ever seen her this way, he knew. In appreciation he ran two admiring hands from her pale shoulders down trembling arms, reveling in the softness of her, in the vulnerable femininity that was such a contrast to his rough skin and hard strength. He touched her hips and her thighs and her bare ass while he leaned down and kissed the wet pulse at her graceful, long throat. Yes, she would make a very fine empress. From this moment on, she was empress. It was done. He had to be sure of that, he had to know it was right before this went any farther.

Without a doubt in his mind he laid her on the bed, spread her legs, and touched her. She was so ready for him, he could easily give her release with his hands and his mouth, as he had last night. But he wanted to feel her around him in a way he had never wanted anything else. He craved her release; he needed to feel her shake around him. He could—perhaps should—tell her who he was before he continued, but he did not. No one had ever accused him of being self-sacrificing or noble to a fault.

"Ana," he said gently.

"I'm sure!" she responded, revealing her frustration with her voice and in the way she pulled him toward her.

"This might hurt a little bit," he warned.

"I hurt now," she whispered. "Don't make me want you any more than I already do. Please, Jahn."

He spread her legs and pushed inside her gently, as gently as he could. She was tight and he was desperate for her, but he took his time. He rocked in a gentle motion; he introduced himself into her as easily and as tenderly as he knew how. There was relief and satisfaction in pushing inside her, there was a sense of rightness he had not expected.

Jahn felt as if he had waited a lifetime for her.

All the while he watched her face as she discovered new heights, new pleasures. When he broke through her maidenhead, she jerked a bit and uttered a quiet "Oh," but that was all. She did not hesitate to move her hips, to urge him deeper.

She closed her eyes, and together they fell into an easy swaying rhythm of joining and discovery and bliss. Jahn could see and feel her growing need, and his own was on the edge of his control. Every stroke was a wonder, every push took him deeper, took him closer to ecstasy.

Conscious thought faded, and there was just his body and Morgana's and the way they came together. There was a need here that went beyond any other he'd ever known, a union that was beyond a search for the pleasurable end.

Not that the end wasn't fine and right in itself.

He moved faster, and Morgana met him wave for wave. Her flesh and his met and mingled. She gasped; she grabbed for him and held on tight . . . and then she broke. She cried out softly and her hips rose against his to ask for more. She shook beneath and around him, and Jahn drove deep and found his own release as she rippled around him. Yes, this was ecstasy. This was the only paradise he would ever know.

He collapsed atop her and then rolled to the side, so as not to crush her. She was so small, compared to him. She was woman to his man; gentleness to his harsh need . . . brutal honesty to his deception.

She rolled into him, warm and soft and accepting. "That was very nice," she whispered.

"Nice?" he asked, resting his hand in her mussed hair.

She laughed. It was a pleasing sound. When he'd met her he had not imagined she had such a wonderful laugh.

No, he had seen only her demands, her abrasiveness, her insults. He had not seen the real woman beneath those defenses. He had not bothered to look.

"What shall I say if 'nice' is not acceptable?" she asked.

"You are a fabulous lover. I did not know such sensations existed. I want you again and again and again," she said, her voice filled with the new wonder she had found. She lifted up and looked down at him. No, that was not love in her eyes, but she was very pleased.

As was he.

"We're truly married now, are we not?" she asked.

"Yes, Ana," he said, losing a large portion of his own satisfaction as he imagined how she would react once she knew the truth. "We are truly married."

Chapter Six

✳

KRISTO Stoyan stood very still and watched from a distance as Lady Danya picked at her food. It had been four days since he'd made his "offer" to her and she'd accepted. He'd trailed her since, watching closely and wondering if she would lose the stomach for what had to be done and confess all that she knew to the man who escorted her. She had not, lucky for her and for all those who traveled with her.

Tonight he would leave this path, satisfied—thanks to the girl's compliance—that she was truly an ally in this endeavor. But first, he did need to offer her a word of encouragement.

He didn't have to wait long before Lady Danya slipped into the woods, entering the dense brush not far from where Kristo stood. She didn't like the forest much, not after having met him there, but she also did not wish to see to personal matters too near the sentinels and the attentive blond man of higher rank. She was shy even in front of her servant. Yes, she would rather face him again than embarrass or display herself immodestly before inferiors.

And she would see him again, sooner than she'd like.

If he were so inclined, he could wait until she'd tossed up her skirts so he could catch her in a delicate and embarrassing moment, but he had no time for such amusements—and no attraction to one such as Lady Danya, who was pretty of face and body but weak at the pit of her soul. Kristo liked his women strong and as determined as he himself was; he wanted an equal beneath him, not an inferior. Lady Danya was not strong, not in any sense which mattered to him, even though he'd assured her otherwise. Panic alone had gifted her with the courage to successfully conceal her pregnancy and the birth of her child. Pride and embarrassment had driven her to leave home to have her baby.

Kristo pulled his hood more securely over his face. Like the long robe he wore, the hood was too large. The dark fabric of both swallowed him, making the proportions of his face and body impossible to discern. He did not think this meek woman would dare to look at him too closely, but just in case she was so bold, he made sure his face was lost in deep shadows. Eventually she would know him well enough, but not tonight.

"I'm always watching you," he whispered.

The lady jumped and squealed, and she twisted as if she planned to turn and face him. Kristo slapped a fast and strong stilling hand on her shoulder, in case her eyes were so sharp they could see his features even here in the darkness.

"What do you want?" she asked, gazing away from him as he desired. She shook. That was good.

"We are allies; are we not? Might allies not meet and discuss their plans?" He wished he could look upon her face so he could see the fear there, but that would mean taking the chance that she would see his own. She had too much weakness within her, and he did not yet trust her; not until she was in too deep to find her way out. "I wish only to reassure you that Ethyn is doing well. He is adjusting to his new home."

"New home?" she asked.

"After the witch who sold him and the couple who bought the boy from her died so tragically, he had no one. He had to go somewhere; did he not? Would you have him sleep in the gutter?"

"They all died? Was there an epidemic in the village? Ethyn isn't sick, is he?" For a moment a mother's concern overrode her fear. He would remember that. Her love for the child she had given birth to was her weakest aspect.

"I have never been called an epidemic before, not to my knowledge, but I suppose you could say they all fell victim to the same scourge."

Her shaking subsided. She was now practically frozen. "You killed them," she whispered.

"Yes, I did. I needed Ethyn to get to you, so I took him. Those three were the only ones who knew the truth of his origins, and of me. What choice did I have?"

Her spine steeled for a moment. "How do I know you're not lying about everything?" she asked. "For all I know my son is truly dead and has been for a very long time. Somehow you found out about what happened and you spun a tale to make me do what you want."

Kristo moved in and placed his mouth close to Lady Danya's fine, pale ear. His breath felt like a winter's wind on her skin. "Ethyn has his father's hair, but your eyes. If he were to stand between the two of you, no one would doubt that he was the result of your liaison. He is a pretty child, looking almost like a girl with those long lashes and rosy cheeks." She was holding her breath now. "The child has a red birthmark here." Kristo stabbed her in the side with one forceful finger, making her flinch and stifle a cry of pain. "Do you recall that birthmark?"

"Yes," she whispered.

Smelling salt and sadness, he reached up and around to feel the fall of warm tears on a flawless white cheek. "Betray me, tell anyone of our meeting, and I will kill the boy and deposit his body upon your sister's doorstep, with a long note of explanation."

"He's just a child!" she protested.

"Children die just as easily as grown men and women do. Easier, in fact. They're very fragile."

She was shaking again, more fiercely than before.

"You I won't kill, if you betray me," he whispered, his mouth close to her ear again. "You I will sell as your son was sold, but not to a simpleminded couple who long for a child of their own. No, if you do not do exactly as I say, I will sell you into sheer misery."

"Lady Danya?" a concerned voice called from not far enough away. It was that damned blond man who possessed some sort of magic. "Is everything all right?"

"Tell him you are fine," Kristo ordered in a harsh whisper. "And make him believe it."

Lady Danya took a deep breath and then called out in a reasonably calm voice, "I'm fine. Can't a woman have a moment alone? Don't come into the woods!" She sounded quite alarmed at the prospect.

"I won't," the interfering man assured her in a steady voice. "You've been in there awhile and I was concerned." He sounded sadly deflated and rejected.

"Don't be!" she snapped, taking her anger out on an innocent man.

Kristo had not been certain about Lady Danya, secrets or no. He would much prefer the other—had all but demanded the other—but unfortunately the girl he preferred had gone missing. Lady Morgana Ramsden had refused the offer from the emperor and disappeared, running off with some common man, or so he heard. Kristo had not seen that possibility, not in his dreams or trances or imaginings. He could not see her well, not in the way he saw most. Try as he might, he could not locate her; he could not see her clearly even in the deepest recesses of his mind. She was too far away, and she was not weak of mind like this one. Soon he would see all, somehow. He still wanted Lady Morgana in the position of empress. This one seemed willing and capable enough, and she would do well enough if the other was not found, but oh—he did want to see Lady

Morgana in the palace, whether he could touch her mind well or not.

Lady Danya he saw quite well, inside and out. She was frightened and selfish and desperate. She was shallow, easy to understand and manipulate. It could very well be her desperation which would benefit them most; it might be her desperation which would bring down an empire.

"Do not cross me," Kristo whispered, and then he leaned down and placed his cold lips on Lady Danya's neck. She felt like fire to him, and he knew that on her flesh his lips would sting like ice. He held her in place while he allowed his lips to linger. He was not drawn to her—she was not strong enough to entice him—but he did enjoy the fear she emitted as he held her. She did not know what he would do, what he would demand. She only knew she could not refuse him anything.

He released her and whispered, "Don't look at me, Lady Danya."

"I won't," she whispered, terrified and unaware that he was backing silently into the woodland which offered him cover.

It was time for him to go. There was so much to be done, so very much. First and foremost—where was Lady Morgana?

STRANGELY enough, married life—which she had fought against all her adult life—agreed with Morgana. The room she called home for the time being was inadequate by any standard. She now had only one dress to call her own, since Jahn had reduced the other to rags in a moment of impatience. She had not complained as he'd cut it off her and she would not complain now, but the yellow dress which had been packed for her as she'd left home was not her favorite. And yet she wore a smile more often than not, and she looked forward to the end of each day in a way she never had before.

Though she had tried on several occasions during the

past four days, using all her newly discovered wiles, she still had not convinced her husband to shave off that awful beard, which was mostly light brown but also sported every color of hair under the sun, including a few disturbing streaks of bright red. When Jahn was working at the palace, guarding the emperor who had once asked her to vie for the position of empress, she missed him in a deep and unexpected way. He felt so much like family. Yes, he belonged to her in a soul-deep way.

When he'd claimed her she'd been so incensed, so horrified. Now she was grateful that he had been there on that day, that he had heard her stepfather's vow and taken advantage of it.

At least Jahn was no longer working at night, as he had at first, but was gone for several hours during the day. Then, when his workday was done, he was here in this room to share a bed with her. To share so much with her! Perhaps her life was not as she'd ever imagined, but since falling into Jahn's care she had never lacked for food or drink, and thanks to his friends, whatever she expressed a desire for was presented to her. Tea. A hot bath. Curtains for the uncovered window. A new pillow. Somehow, they always managed to obtain what she asked for, and though none of it was of the quality she had come to expect from life, everything was more than adequate. She had all she needed, and more. Sex was a wonder to her, and every night Jahn showed her something new. She craved him. That was not the same as love, she knew, but what she felt was deep and undeniable. There was a connection she had not expected. It was the sex and more that brought them together so well. He was a friend, and she had not had a true friend in a long time.

Her mother had been wrong, sad to say. It was not love she'd waited for but friendship. Companionship. Trust.

At this rate there would be a child soon enough, and then they would be forced to find better accommodations. Though this room had become more than tolerable, it was not fit for a child.

Jahn's touch, his presence, his protection continued to keep the curse at bay, and there were moments when she wondered if it might be gone for good. Perhaps what had happened on that horrible night had not been a curse at all, but an isolated incident that would never repeat. She could almost make herself believe that what had happened had nothing to do with her at all, if not for the chill she'd felt when she'd run away from this room and had found herself on the streets, thinking she was being followed. Like it or not, she could not deny that the destruction had come from within her.

There were rare times when she felt as if she should tell Jahn everything. These impossible feelings usually arose after sex, while she was lying naked in his arms. The fabulous sensation of belonging she had never dreamed of experiencing weakened her somewhat. Jahn's imagined response was what stopped her. How would a man who served the emperor react to the news that his wife was a murderer? What would he think of the fact that when she was afraid or angry, she exploded and destroyed everything and everyone in her path? Since that afternoon when she'd so foolishly left the tavern on her own, she had not experienced even a sliver of ice in her veins.

Maybe she was cured. Maybe she would never have to fight off the curse again. If that was the case, then why should she tell anyone anything? It wasn't as if Jahn didn't have secrets of his own. He did. Several times in the past few days he had started a conversation with an ominous "I have something to tell you" that quickly turned into a pursuit much more pleasurable than talk. If what he wanted to divulge was important, he'd say it sooner or later.

As she had on more than one occasion, she met him at the door with the straight razor in her hand. She was determined to see what was hidden beneath all that horrid facial hair!

"Not again," Jahn said as he came through the door, unfastening his belt and the sword hanging there with nimble fingers. "I like my beard. It's very manly, don't you think?"

With the hand that did not hold a blade, Morgana pointed to a raw spot on her chin. "Beard burn," she said simply. "From this morning. Your lips are wonderfully soft, but that bristle is not. Shave off the beard or you will have to go kissless."

"Kissless," he repeated.

"Yes." She sighed dramatically. "You cannot expect me to live forever with a rash on my face."

"Why not? You're still pleasing to look upon."

"It hurts, Jahn," she replied with a laugh.

He looked surprised. "Truly?"

"Truly."

"Oh." He wrapped his arms around her and pulled her close, but he did not attempt to kiss her. Just as well, since she was prepared to turn her head and refuse him—for a little while, at least. "I missed you today." There was truth in his words, and they warmed her heart.

"I missed you, too."

"Palace life is tedious without you. The palace itself is dull compared to this small room with you in it."

"Are you trying to sweet-talk me into giving you a kiss?" she teased.

"Of course not. Though it is quite nice, kissing is not strictly necessary."

"I beg your pardon?" Kissing had quickly become necessary for *her*.

She recognized the fire in his eyes and he smiled down at her; she knew this expression well. He wanted her. "I can please you quite well without our lips ever touching."

"I'm sure you can, but that's not the point . . ."

"Is it not?" Jahn spun her about and lifted her skirt with talented hands, stroking her thighs a bit and then letting his strong hands rest on her bare hips. He pulled her against him, and his hard length pressed against her backside. Morgana felt a thrill of excitement, as she always did when

Jahn touched her. She closed her eyes and savored the way
he held her, they way they fit together so well.

"We don't even need to be face-to-face. You don't have
to study my offending beard and wonder whether or not
there's a proper chin beneath." He guided her to the window, their steps small and in unison, and she looked down
upon the people who walked on the street, all of them in a
hurry to be somewhere. She didn't want to be anywhere but
here.

"I'm sure I will love your chin, even if it is puny," she
said.

Jahn did not join her in teasing. "Grab the windowsill,"
he whispered.

She did as he asked.

"Bend forward."

She did, thankful for the window coverings Jahn's clever
sentinel friends had managed to obtain. The fabric was
gauzy, but it did offer some semblance of privacy.

Hand still beneath her yellow skirt, Jahn reached around
and found her most sensitive and sensual spot. He stroked,
and she was immediately wet. He slipped a finger inside
her, and she almost found release then and there. She held
on, yearning for more but not wanting this to be over so
quickly.

He stroked her slowly with fingers that had learned her
well, knowing how and where to touch her to keep alive
this remarkable feeling of standing on the edge. It was like
flying, and she half expected her feet to leave the ground at
any moment. There was nothing cold about her when Jahn
held her, not inside or out. He kissed the back of her neck
and his fingers danced. He aroused her gently until she
craved more; she craved all of him. Morgana trembled
and held her breath; she moved demandingly against his
stroke.

And then he was inside her, just a little bit, pushing into
her dampness while he continued to arouse with his fingers. The afternoon sun hit her face through the curtains.

Jahn was relentless. He was in her and all around her, he was *everywhere*, fingers moving against her as he pushed deeper inside and held himself there for a moment before resuming the slow, rhythmic movement.

Life went on around them, outside the window, beneath their plain wooden floor, and yet there was nothing else in her world but this. A joining. A search for pleasure. A marriage, the way a marriage was meant to be.

Morgana arched her back and took him deeper; she fell into a primitive rhythm that guided her body and wiped every thought from her mind. Every thought but Jahn and the way he felt inside her. She began to tremble, to glide back to meet his thrust, to move faster and with demand, and then she shattered. As she trembled, she felt his hot release. He trembled as deeply as she did. Did he feel as if he could fly?

A thought teased her brain, words lingered on her lips, but she quickly pushed them aside. This was not love, it was the warmth of sexual fulfillment. They were soldiers, she and Jahn, taking on life together in the best way they knew how. They were partners in all ways, and that did not require an element so fleeting and insubstantial and indefinable as love. If they found a remarkable physical connection along the way, that was just an additional and extraordinarily pleasurable—and lucky—benefit.

"See?" he said in a gruff voice, lowering his head to kiss her neck. "No kissing necessary."

"You're kissing me now," she argued weakly.

"Not on the mouth."

"Stop that," she ordered with a laugh. "I said no kissing. I did not specify mouth only."

"What a shame," he said, turning her about and touching her lips with tender fingers and then lowering those fingers to her breasts to tease her tender nipples through the fabric of her plain yellow frock. Thank goodness the fabric was a thin one, as that allowed her to feel his caress very well. "I rather thought you liked my kisses."

"I do, but . . ."

And then his gentle fingertips were on the raw place on her cheek. "Does it really hurt?"

"A little," she confessed.

"I did not intend to hurt you," he said with a fierce honesty.

"I know."

"I would rather hurt myself."

"You are a good husband," she said with a smile.

"I take care of that which is mine."

"You do." She rose up and kissed his throat, allowing her lips to linger.

"I thought you said no kissing."

"I don't have a beard. I may kiss as I please." She teased his throat with the tip of her tongue. "You taste so good."

Jahn held her close and sighed. "I relent. How could I not? Have you ever shaved a man?"

"Of course not!" she answered indignantly.

He took her face in his hands, and she felt so small and yet so wonderfully safe.

"You watch," he said. "I'll do the shaving."

THE beard had made a nice addition to his disguise in weeks past, for traveling and for the short trips to and from the palace. He truly did not care about proving to Morgana that he *did* have a chin beneath it. But the rough and wiry hair scraped her delicate skin, and for that reason it had to go.

Jahn sat before a cloudy and cracked mirror and cut away the longest strands, then lathered his face well. Not so long ago he had marched into the room intent on telling Morgana the truth and found her standing there with this very blade in her hand. Many times since then he had approached her, determined to tell all, but she always managed to distract him and they ended up engaged in more pleasurable pursuits than confession. Now it was too late, by his way of thinking. She would be furious when she found out he'd lied to her.

He didn't have much time. There was little more than five weeks left before the First Night of the Summer Festival.

Jahn had decided that without question, Morgana would make a fine empress. She had all the qualities any man—or country—could ask for. Not only would she make a suitable empress, she made him happy. They were compatible. Good fortune had been with him when he'd decided to go north in his venture from the palace and his structured life as emperor. He had run from the palace and the inevitability of marriage, and in the end had found a true wife.

He could not wait to give Morgana the gifts she deserved, to dress her in crimson and drape jewels around her pretty throat.

She watched closely as he shaved—he could feel her eyes on him—and he pondered what might happen in the weeks until the Summer Festival began. He could be totally honest with her here and now and give up these pleasing moments, or he could pretend to be Jahn Devlyn, sentinel and husband, until the last possible moment. He would, of course, choose Morgana as his empress when the proper time came. That had been decided the moment they had taken up residence in this room as man and wife. As it was very possible that she would be carrying his child by then, she couldn't refuse him.

She would not be happy, though, not for a while. He'd likely have to pay for his insincerity for weeks after a proper wedding ceremony. Morgana would eventually forgive him. He caught her eye in the foggy mirror. Wouldn't she? When she found that she would have everything she might ever desire in addition to this fine partnership, when he gave her jewels and fine gowns and flowers and scented oils, she would be glad that he was the emperor and not a poor sentinel.

That all sounded very well in his mind. In truth, he

could not be sure that she would ever forgive him. Pity. He liked this alliance; he enjoyed coming home to this small, rough room. At the moment it truly was home, a home such as he had never known. He was happier here, warmer, more content than he had ever been in the palace.

Jahn was not ready to say that he might love Morgana, but he was definitely feeling something unusual and unexpected. Women had pleased him before. Women had thrown themselves at his feet and begged for his favor. Even before he'd become emperor, he had not lacked for the adoration of the opposite sex.

And yet, he had never felt anything more than gratitude toward them for what they offered. Gratitude and an entirely physical yearning for their fascinating bodies. He had never wished to protect any one of them with his life; he had never been delighted to see them smile. He had never longed to open a door and catch a glimpse of a woman who was truly glad to see him. He had certainly never been afraid of losing a woman's affections.

When he told Morgana the truth, his newfound happiness was going to go away in the blink of an eye, and he was not ready to give it up. Not yet. Her affections could not be replaced.

When Jahn was clean shaven for the first time in more than a month, he turned about. Morgana very naturally and easily perched on his lap. She was light as a feather, delicate and fragile. His eyes fell on the red spot on her chin. He had not seen it in the darkness of this early morning, when he'd left her lying satisfied and returning to sleep. He would not hurt her again.

She smiled. "You have a lovely chin," she said, touching the body part in question with loving fingers. "It's not at all weak or misshapen. Why did you hide it beneath that awful beard?"

"My beard was not awful."

Morgana nodded gently. "Yes, dear, it was most dreadful." She studied his entire face. "You are unexpectedly handsome," she said, moving her hand from his chin to his cheek. "There is a strong beauty about you. You're lovely."

"I am not *lovely*," he argued without heat. "Whoever heard of a lovely sentinel? A man can only be handsome or manly or, in rare circumstances, attractive, though such a word should be reserved for those less-than-masculine men who prance about in lace and pointy-toed shoes and douse themselves in sweet perfumes."

Morgana laughed, as he had intended. "Like the emperor?"

Jahn's good humor died quickly. "Has someone accused the emperor of prancing about?"

"No, but he is that type of man, isn't he?"

"No," Jahn said decisively. "The emperor is as manly as I am."

Morgana sighed. "I doubt that very much."

Now would be the perfect opportunity to say, "Here I am. Surprise, love, you've claimed the emperor as your husband. Won't you be happy to move from this small room to a fine suite of rooms in the palace?" But he said nothing, because he knew Morgana felt as he did. This room was home. She was happy here, as he was. The truth would ruin everything for a long while, perhaps forever.

She leaned forward. "You may kiss me now," she said sweetly, and he happily obliged.

DANYA had thought her first glimpse of the palace in Arthes would be wondrous and filled with gladness and hope for the future, but after eight long days of travel she looked upon the fascinating structure as if it were a cold prison. What would the cold, hooded man insist that she do in order to save herself and her son? Would he really expect her to kill? Yes, she imagined he would.

She would be empress as she had hoped, but there would be no gladness in winning that position. As they rode toward the tall palace, Danya felt as if she were being pulled into a dark, swirling hole from which there would be no escape. As if the hooded man were still standing behind her, she felt a brush of icy wind that chilled her neck where he had touched her with his lips. That touch had been wicked—she had felt the evil of it to her bones—and the coldness was a reminder that he was always watching. Somehow, some way, he was with her.

"Vile bastard," she whispered with heartfelt venom.

"What's that?" Rainer guided his horse nearer to hers.

The deputy minister was an odd man, disdainful and caring at the same time, curious and relentless, kind and cold—no, not cold, distant. Set apart. Cautious. She still carried the handkerchief he had given her, for some reason she could not fathom. Usually it was tucked into her modest bodice, but on occasion, when no one was watching, she took it out and clutched the linen in her hand.

"I was simply mumbling about my joy at being out of this saddle at last," she said, putting her own distance in the words even though her heart was pounding and she longed to tell him everything and ask for his help. In her heart she knew that there was no help for her. If she said anything, if she confessed all her sins—as she had confessed a small portion on one pleasant night of their journey—the hooded man would know. Perhaps Deputy Rainer did possess magic enough to make a snake like Ennis run, but the hooded man would be different. The hooded man would cut down this loyal and kind and pleasant man without a second thought. She owed Rainer nothing—well, little—but she could do him the favor of pushing him out of the sucking danger that was her life. "I want a hot bath straight away," she said in her most petulant voice. "And proper tea with a hot meal, all served upon the emperor's finest dinnerware. I would like to see a dressmaker first thing in the morning. The provincial gowns I have brought from home will not do, not at all." She spoke as if she were already empress, issuing demands.

"I will see to it," Rainer said with a nod of his head. His fair hair was so fine that the strands that had escaped his braid caught the wind and danced a bit.

"No," she said sharply, "you will not. Your job is done." She sighed tiredly. "Honestly, if I do not ever again see anyone to remind me of this dreadful journey, I'll be quite content. I'll require a servant, of course. A woman with some years of experience in the palace will do nicely." She looked back at Fai, who had been exhausted by the journey. The girl deserved better than to be drawn into the world Danya was about to create. She deserved better than to be dragged into a firestorm she did not understand. "There is one last thing you can do for me. Find a room for Fai for the night, and then arrange an escort for her in the morning. I want her on her way at first light."

Rainer looked confused. "I believe she intends to remain here and serve you."

"Perhaps she does," Danya said crisply, "but I do not intend to keep her. I prefer a maid who has some experience with palace life, a well-trained woman who can serve in Fai's place *and* in yours. Otherwise, how am I to acclimate myself quickly to this new place?"

Women usually didn't like Danya, and with a stranger she would not run the danger of confessing too much in a moment of weakness, as she would with Rainer or even Fai. One look into Rainer's pale and piercing eyes, and she might collapse and tell him everything. He had made himself too accessible in days past, too understanding and compassionate and strong. She could easily confess to him, and for her weakness her son would die.

Ethyn, nearly two years old, with his mother's eyes and his father's hair, was depending on her.

"I demand that a proper servant report to me immediately. Do not make me wait."

"As you wish," Rainer said distantly, and there was such distaste in his voice that Danya knew her job had been done well.

Chapter Seven

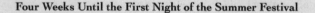

Four Weeks Until the First Night of the Summer Festival

MORGANA settled into an agreeable routine of wedded bliss, and the days flew past too quickly. She did what she could with the room which was her home for the moment, and planned for even better days to come. Though she had never been particularly interested in the arts involved in making a home, she did find herself spending hours mending her torn blue dress—a tedious task—and turning this plain room into a better place.

Jahn worked very hard, he was a fine and loyal sentinel, but surely he could do more with his life and livelihood. He was intelligent and strong, but not particularly driven to succeed.

When they had children, that lack of drive would surely change. They would need more when their family grew. More room, more food, more furnishings. They could always return to her childhood home, where with grandchildren to appease her stepfather, forgiveness would be offered, along with all the comforts one could imagine. But not only had Jahn declared to her that Arthes was his home and always would be, Morgana found she did not want to go back to the site of her former self. She had killed there. She had taken a life and she'd lied to protect herself. For a short but torturous while she'd lived in fear that someone, anyone, would discover her curse. Since so unwillingly leaving her home in Jahn's company she had known little fear—and signs of her curse had remained dampened, showing a hint of its existence only when she'd been so foolish as to think of running away from the inevitable. No, there would be no returning to the place she had once called home. She and Jahn would make a go of it here, in Arthes. This was home now.

She could help to improve their situation, she was sure of it, though she was not yet sure how. Looking from the window and occasionally venturing into the tavern below or onto the nearby streets—with Jahn's friends as escort, of course—she had seen women working as diligently as men. They sewed and cleaned and cooked for others, but Morgana did not fool herself into thinking she was talented enough at those womanly arts to call them a profession. Some of the women she saw on the streets obviously performed other wifely duties for coin—it was clear by their shocking dress and their outrageous manner what they were willing to do—but Morgana would not even consider earning a living in that way. She shuddered at the thought, and felt a rush of pity for the women who did not know what she had found in her marriage.

It was too pretty a day to remain inside, so as she had often in days past, she walked the stone streets of Arthes and soaked up the sun, watching people pass by, listening to their laughter, and wondering all the while what she could do to improve her circumstances. She was always drawn to the children at play when she passed them. Their laughter was infectious, and it touched her heart. One day she would have her own children, Jahn's children. Together they would create a family. She had never dreamed of such simple pleasures until she'd discovered them here.

Jahn's friends, eight of them who were always around in groups of four, were incredibly attentive. They must be very good friends to be so relentlessly dedicated to a woman they barely knew. The men didn't talk much to her, but they were always close and considerate. She had argued more than once that she hardly needed so many men to keep her safe, even in a bustling city like Arthes, but Jahn insisted. They were all sentinels like Jahn, she knew, but in their hours spent guarding her they wore plain, non-descript clothes. They were always armed.

Iann, who was one of the more talkative of the lot, increased his pace until he was walking beside her. "If you don't mind me asking," he began almost shyly, "how do you get your hair to be so smooth and silky?"

She looked up at him in surprise, and her step faltered.

Iann's eyes went wide and he offered a meaty hand of support. "For my wife, you see," he explained. When it was clear Morgana was steady on her feet, he dropped his hand. "She's a pretty enough lass and sweet as honey, but her hair is always wiry and tangled as that of the stray dog that begs for food out back of the tavern."

Morgana laughed, but not for long. She had seen the stray dog. "I use egg yolks in my hair, when I can." Which had not been often lately, since she and Jahn ate most of the eggs they could afford to purchase. "But some hair types require rose water or specially made oils."

"Oh," Iann mumbled. "I thought maybe there was one womanly trick which would work for all, and no one had told my Emilia. Her mother died when she was very young, so . . ." He shrugged his shoulders. "It was a silly idea, though I suppose she could try the egg yolks a time or two and see if it makes a difference."

Morgana's spine straightened as an idea came to her. The women who sold their baked goods were experienced cooks. Those who worked as seamstresses were talented with a needle and thread. Those who sold their bodies . . . well, she didn't want to ponder their expertise. What did she know? She knew pampering. She knew beauty. "Have your Emilia come to see me tomorrow afternoon," she said thoughtfully, "and I'll see what I can do."

"Truly?" Iann said, beaming.

"Truly," she responded, wondering if she had finally found a way to improve her financial situation.

The conversation ended abruptly as an uproar commenced at the end of the street. In an immediate and smooth maneuver, the four men who accompanied Morgana surrounded her, instinctively placing their bodies between her and danger. She heard a sharp shout from the direction of the palace, then a bloodcurdling scream.

Her head snapped around. Jahn was there, in the palace. "What's happening?" she asked.

Iann and the others turned her about and they all rushed back toward the tavern. One of the men—the stout Maril—left them, rushing toward the excitement. Whatever had occurred was already over, or else for some dire reason had gone silent. There were no more screams, no more jostling of crowds and shouts of alarm.

As they reached the tavern door, Maril returned to them with a scowl on his face. "Some drunkard attempted to molest one of the"—he glanced sheepishly at Morgana—"one of the, uh, *ladies* who resides in the palace. A sentinel was nearby and tried to stop him, and took a knife to the gut for his trouble."

Morgana felt the blood drain from her face. She went cold all over, and inside, deep inside where she had been warm for weeks, a sliver of ice formed. "Jahn," she whispered, "was it Jahn?"

"Oh, no, My Lady," Maril said confidently. "Surely not."

"Then who was it?" she asked.

"I don't know, but . . ."

"Then you cannot be certain it was not my husband!"

Iann stammered. "My Lady, I assure you it could not be . . ."

"How?" she asked sharply. "How can you be sure?"

The men looked at one another with puzzled expressions, and more than one shrug was used in an attempt at silent communication.

Morgana entered the tavern and sat on the first bench she came to, feeling as if her knees would buckle beneath her. Her stomach was in knots, and the chill remained—though it did not grow to a dangerous level. She fought to keep the coldness which terrified her buried deep.

She would not survive without Jahn. In her mind she saw him walking through their door after a long day in the palace. She could feel his arms around her, hear his laughter, taste the sharp saltiness of his skin. She felt the loss of the children she would never bear if some senseless act of violence had taken him from her; she felt the loss of her newfound happiness, and realized exactly what this sharp pain meant. The truth was unexpected and horrible.

She loved Jahn. What other name could one put to such a heartwrenching reaction to the possibility of loss? What else was she to call the certainty that she could not exist without him? If she were widowed, there were other husbands to be had, if she so desired, but she did not want another husband. She wanted Jahn. She could not lose him.

Morgana looked at Maril. "Bring him to me or take me there."

"My Lady?" he asked, raising his eyebrows.

"I must see my husband," she said staunchly. "Here or in the palace," she added. "I don't care where, but I must see him *now*."

It was Iann who backed toward the tavern door. The place was deserted but for the five of them at this time of day. Even the tavern owner was absent. "I will fetch your husband for you, My Lady," Iann said. "You look a mite peaked to be up and about at the moment."

"Hurry," she ordered, and then she added a softer, oddly wrenching "Please."

KRISTO entered the house without knocking and moved silently through the large and lavishly furnished rooms. Long ago he had learned to move upon any landscape without making a sound, even one as unnatural as this. Though it was no longer necessary, he continued to wear the oversize robe and the hood which concealed him. He enjoyed the anonymity of his chosen costume; he liked the reaction he caused upon first sight.

Lady Rikka was here, he knew it. She was so energized with hatred that she was always easy to locate in his mind; easy to read and understand. Even though they did not always agree on the way they might have all they wanted, he could not have asked for a better partner in his endeavor.

He slipped into a narrow hallway and followed the highly trained senses which told him Rikka was in the back parlor she so preferred. This house always smelled of musky oils, and the windows were rarely opened more than a crack, even on a mild and sunny day like today. Like him, the lady who had once been empress belonged in darkness; she thrived upon shadow.

When he opened the door to the back parlor, he found the woman he had come to see peering through the narrow opening in thickly opulent draperies. Elegant as always, she was dressed in an elaborate but drab and dark gray gown which hugged her appealing figure. She was waiting for someone. Not him, though. She would not be happy to see him, he imagined. Even those who needed and relied upon him were not entirely comfortable in his presence, not even their man in the palace, a skittish man Kristo had met with just two nights ago.

That traitor had his agenda. Everyone involved in the scheme had his individual plan and desire. What they had in common was that what they desired would begin with the emperor's downfall.

Rikka needed him, just as she needed their man in the palace and the mercenaries and assassins she had purchased, but she did not like him. Why should she? Why should anyone? Kristo had never wasted time trying to earn the affections of others.

He walked closer to Rikka, soundless as always. Even the movement of his loose robe was without the gentlest swish or snap. When he was upon her, he whispered, "Who are you waiting for?"

Rikka jumped and spun around, as he had known she would, gasping for air in surprise. "You frightened me," she said, a pale hand placed over a cold heart.

"I do apologize."

She scoffed at that, knowing him too well.

"Who are you waiting for?"

"Gyl," she said.

Her lover Gyl, the weak and infatuated wizard who had thus far kept Lady Rikka from falling entirely into darkness.

"I have news," Kristo said, pushing his hood so that it fell limply to his back. Rikka had seen his face before; she did not seem to mind looking upon it.

Many women who did not know Kristo found his face pleasing. It was almost entirely unlined, in spite of his years, and the features were equal in proportion. His eyes were a striking gray, and his hair was a healthy chestnut which leaned to red in the sun. With the magic which ruled his life and his heart he could maintain the illusion of youth. What mattered in this life but illusion?

Youthful or not, he did not have a pleasant smile. A genuine smile was something no human could properly feign, so he did not bother to attempt to do so unless he was truly amused. Still, those who did not look too closely might think him handsome.

His touch always gave him away, though, proving that, appearance aside, he was not pleasant at all.

"Lady Danya is with us," he said. "She fell as easily as I knew she would."

"And the other?" Rikka asked anxiously.

"Gone, for the moment." A frown crossed his face. He would find her, eventually, but it was annoying that Lady Morgana had altered his plans with her disappearance. "I will locate her before it's too late."

"You still prefer her to Danya," Rikka said.

"I do."

"Why?"

She did not need to know his secrets, she did not need to understand his deepest desires. He doubted he knew all of hers, after all. "Morgana has a strength the other does not. We can use that strength very well, when the time comes."

"If you find her."

"When I find her."

Rikka fidgeted, working her fingers. "I don't care which one it is, as long as this plan works."

"It will work," Kristo said confidently. "Sebestyen's sons will be disgraced and then dead, and you and I will be in the palace, ruling from behind the skirts of a woman we own and a babe who will wear the crown for as long as we deem proper."

Rikka shook her head. "So much could go wrong before we find ourselves there."

"Nothing will go wrong."

"You can't know that. Even you don't see *everything* that is to be."

Kristo grabbed her chin and made her look him in the eye. She did not flinch at his cold touch the way other women did.

Lady Rikka, former empress, had almost been lost. There had been a time, not so long ago, that she'd been on the verge of letting her pain go and building a new life with the pathetic magician who loved her in spite of all her faults. Kristo had fed her hate. He had stoked the fire of her rage with maddening patience, and she was almost entirely his, now. As long as she had doubts about what was to be, there was a chance she would fall to Gyl's side and give up her plans for vengeance. A small chance, but one he did not wish to take.

Even if he did not have plans of his own, he would crave the chaos Rikka's vengeance would bring.

"Take off your clothes," he commanded, his words emotionless.

Rikka's eyebrows lifted slightly. "I'm expecting Gyl."

Kristo lifted his hands and glanced around the small parlor. "He is not here now, and I am needful."

She did not capitulate easily; she never did. "I told you the last time you were here, we can't continue to . . ."

"You've said those very words more often than I can recall, but you never mean them. I give you something your boring magician cannot, and you crave me. Don't deny that craving, Rikka, not when you know I see inside you so well." Kristo unfastened the ties at the throat of his robe and whipped the garment over his head. Beneath it, he wore nothing.

Rikka would deny him for a moment or two, as she always did, but she truly liked his body, lean and tough as it was. She even liked the chill he offered her, though she had never admitted as much aloud. Not yet, at least.

"Put your robe on!" she demanded.

Kristo smiled. "No. I will remain naked"—he looked down—"and aroused until you give me what I want."

She sighed as if put upon, even as her heartbeat increased in speed and her cheeks flushed. "Put on your clothes and we'll adjourn to one of the bedchambers."

"No. I want you here and now. I am not a patient man, as you know well."

"No, you are not at all patient." Rikka glanced at his penis and the flush of her cheeks deepened. She was so entranced and lustful she practically licked her lips. "Fine!" she snapped, gathering handfuls of dark fabric and carefully lifting the volumes of fabric that made up her skirt. "Let's just get this over with."

"No," Kristo said sharply. "If I wanted nothing more than a quick, mindless poke, I would've paid one of the many loose or bribable women I passed on my journey here. I have waited for you, and I want this done properly. I wish to see all of you, every inch. Now, Rikka. Naked."

He saw the tremble his command aroused, and he knew it was not fear that made her shake. The coldness that repulsed other women appealed to Rikka. The darkness that made other women shudder aroused her. She undressed as quickly as was possible, given the complicated nature of her gown. There were buttons and ties and ornaments. He might've helped her to speed things along, but he much preferred watching. As she removed her clothing, she cast an occasional glance toward the door he had closed behind him or the window she had been looking out of. Kristo knew where her mind had taken her, and he did not want her distracted.

"Your Gyl has been delayed and will be late," he said impatiently. "Stop dithering."

Rikka met his gaze, foolishly trusting his word. She stripped the last of her fine garments away, shaking in anticipation and craving what only he could give her. Yes, she was almost entirely his.

When she had done as he asked and removed all of her clothing, casting her dark gown to the floor without care and kicking her slippers aside, he instructed her to sit on the edge of the desk where she wrote genteel notes and venomous poems and plans of revenge. A sliver of sun shot across her body, which was slender and attractive, if not as firm and perfect as Lady Danya's. Kristo did not care about physical perfection; inside, Rikka was perfect for him. Soon she would be as dark and as lost as he. Already she teetered on the edge of a darkness so deep it could not be cast aside.

"Touch me," he demanded, and she took his hard length and stroked with hot hands.

"It is like ice," she whispered.

"You are like fire," he countered, parting her thighs and poking her with two cold fingers. She gasped and jerked toward him.

"There will be a full moon tonight," he said as he teased her. "And on the next full moon, one lunar cycle away, we will see the beginnings of what we most desire."

She sighed, her satisfaction brought about by a combination of his words and his touch.

"The twins will fall," he whispered. "And you will be there to see it."

"Yes," she whispered.

"From their graves, Sebestyen and Liane will scream in horror. They will know the peace of afterlife no more."

Rikka smiled. Yes, she was almost as dark as he was.

"You want me very badly, don't you?" he asked. "Not only for my help in your endeavor but also for my body, which is unlike any other."

"No," she said, writhing against him in a gentle rhythm. "I succumb to you only because you command it and I need your assistance to have my revenge."

"Lies," he said. "Speak the truth, Rikka. Deep within, you desire that which only I can give you." He teased her with his fingers and she responded. He lowered his head and kissed her breasts with cold lips; he ran an icy tongue across her heated, pebbled nipples. "I see so much, you cannot hide. You should know that by now. Lie to the world if you must, but tell me the truth now, Rikka. Tell me what you want. Tell me in real words that have not been made pretty. Tell me, Rikka, or you cannot have it."

He stood tall and she looked him in the eyes, bolder than any woman had ever been. "Fine, you vile bastard. I want your icy cock inside me."

"Why?"

She did not answer, but licked her lips and stroked his length with hot fingers. Her body trembled. Rikka had become a woman who took little pleasure in life, other than her need for revenge. Perhaps she saw her desire for him as a weakness. Perhaps it was.

"Why?" he asked again.

Her answer came pouring out in a quick, breathless voice. "I have never experienced anything like it. I have never experienced any release to compare to the orgasm that shakes me when I have your cold body deep inside mine. The sensations are beyond pain or pleasure, beyond ordinary sexual relations, beyond anything I have ever known or imagined. Sometimes when you fuck me, I think you will melt or I will freeze, but it's not like that, it's not like that at all."

"No, it is not," he said softly, raising one hand to grasp a warm and giving breast. She writhed and gasped in response. "So, you truly do want me?"

"Yes," she whispered, eyes closed as she moved her hips closer to him.

"You need me, don't you, Rikka? You need something no one but I can give you."

"Dammit, Kristo, do it!" she commanded.

Kristo smiled as he guided himself into her intense heat. She gasped in sheer delight, she rocked against him, and while he watched that place where they came together, marveling at the sight of his body joining with hers, he grabbed her head and turned it toward the door, where her lover stood watching, gape-mouthed and white-faced, as he had been for several minutes.

"Oh," Rikka said, trying for a fraction of a second to scoot away from Kristo, to uncouple and undo what had been done.

He grabbed her hips and pulled her onto him, hard. When he was buried deep inside her, she did not fight to get away. Instead she moaned and pushed her hips toward his. She surrendered.

"Tell your old friend Gyl that you do not need him anymore," Kristo whispered.

"I . . . I . . ." Rikka muttered helplessly.

"Tell him he has been replaced, in all ways."

"I can't," Rikka whispered.

"Look at him," Kristo commanded. "Look your poor Gyl in the eye and tell him there is nothing left of the woman he once loved. Nothing left," he whispered. "Nothing at all."

Rikka turned her head, and for a moment she looked almost lost. She was aching and confused.

Kristo moved gently in and out of the woman before him. "We don't need him," he whispered, his words so soft they were for her alone. "Those who hurt you will be punished, and only I can give you what you want. Vengeance will be ours. Blood will be ours. No one will ever again treat you as if you are less than nothing, and if they dare, we will cut them down as we will cut down the seed of those who abused you." He was moving faster now, and so was she. He pounded against and into her, and she gasped in pleasure. Gyl was all but forgotten, and Kristo knew he had won when Rikka looked toward the doorway without cowering. Her confusion was gone.

"Go," she said breathlessly, her eyelids heavy with desire and her cheeks flushed with pleasure. She was beautiful at that moment, perhaps as beautiful as she had ever been. "I don't need you anymore."

Gyl remained silent and motionless, stunned beyond words at the sight he had found upon his return to this house he'd called home for a very long time. The first sign of life was a tear which ran rapidly down one cheek.

"Do you really wish to *watch*?" Rikka asked harshly. "Fine, then," she said breathlessly, as her completion drew near. "Watch, if you must."

She shattered, crying out and grasping Kristo with hot arms as she pressed herself against him so he was deeper, so his chill touched a hot part of her he had not touched until now. She grasped his hair and held on as she shook violently, as she whimpered and shattered, beyond all control. Soon she went limp but Kristo continued to move in and out with an almost tranquil rhythm. Completion never came quickly for him. More often than not he didn't finish at all, but he liked the heat, now and then. He craved that heat the way other men craved release.

Flushed and sated, Rikka glanced toward the doorway where Gyl had so recently stood. The man she had once called lover was gone.

"You won't see Gyl again," Kristo said evenly. "He's gone from your life. I see that truth very clearly."

Rikka's voice was cold as she said, "Just as well. I should've ridded myself of him years ago. He was weak, much weaker than you and I."

This dark and evil woman Kristo had shaped from a sad girl into the monster she was today was now entirely his.

She would do anything for her revenge; she would do anything to bring the chaos he craved. With that knowledge Kristo passed beyond an edge he so rarely found, and he discovered unparalleled release inside the woman who would help him bring a country and its people to ruin.

JAHN kept his head down as he rushed toward the tavern and Morgana. Iann insisted that she was quite upset at the news of violence in the palace and had commanded that someone fetch her husband. The sentinels were not in an enviable situation. They were obliged to obey Morgana's commands without letting her know that she was—or soon would be—empress. They had to protect and obey her without allowing her to realize just how diligently they pursued that calling.

The excitement had been nothing of concern, to be honest, though one sentinel had been wounded. The wound was not a serious one, thank goodness. One of Melusina's admirers had attempted to accost her as she'd left the palace, and she'd screamed. Melusina had quite a scream, when it suited her, and she was not happy these days. She and Anrid were feeling put upon and ignored. He needed to get them both out of the palace before he moved Morgana in, but he couldn't very well put them out on the streets. No, they needed husbands who would care for them properly. Unfortunately, neither was inclined to take a husband.

Jahn stepped into the tavern and Morgana was there, watching the door and waiting for him. She all but threw herself into his arms, clutching at him desperately while she fought to regain her breath. She did not cry, but seemed to be on the verge of tears. He hated tears. Didn't all men? Nothing made him feel more helpless.

"You're cold," he said, leading Morgana toward the stairway while his sentinels watched silently.

"I know," Morgana whispered. "What would I do without you to warm me?"

With his arm around her, he led her up the stairway. "You will never have to know."

The words were meant to be reassuring, but they only stirred Morgana up more. "How can you be so sure of that? What if the palace is attacked? What if you're killed protecting the emperor?" She snorted as he guided her into their room. "Why should he have your protection? Isn't he capable of protecting himself? Useless excuse for a . . ." She stopped and took a deep breath. "What if we have children? What would I do if something happened to you? Your life for his would be a poor trade. You're worth a hundred of Emperor Jahn!"

"How can you be so sure of that? You've never met the man."

Morgana looked him in the eye, and he could see the fear there. She cared more than she'd intended when they'd begun this marriage. So did he, to be honest.

"No, but I know you, Jahn," she said, her voice somewhat calmer. "You're smart and dedicated, and you're capable of making your livelihood in many ways. Soldiering is a dangerous profession, and there are so many profitable trades you could take up. Will you always be a sentinel?"

"No," he answered honestly.

She closed her eyes and took a deep breath. "Good," she whispered. Finally, a hint of a smile teased her lips. "I'm going to help," she said.

"Help with what?" Jahn asked, immediately suspicious.

"If I can earn a bit of coin myself, then you'll be able to leave your position in the palace all the sooner."

He did not like the sound of that. "And how do you intend to do this?"

"Beauty," she said, the word slowly and easily falling from fine lips. "It's all I know, after all. Hair, skin, fragrance. I will have to start small, with a few well-chosen consultations, but in time I should be able to build quite a clientele." She touched his cheek with loving fingers. "Every woman wishes to be more beautiful, and I can help."

"I don't like this idea at all," Jahn said in a lowered voice.

"Why not?"

He could not very well tell her that it was unheard of for an empress to seek employment. "I want you here, at all times, waiting for my return."

"That's silly," she said.

"It is not. And when there are children . . ."

"We can deal with that when the time comes," she argued. "Until then, my efforts will only make life more comfortable for our family." She leaned into him, no longer chilled, no longer shaking.

"You were a lady of privilege who wanted for nothing when I met you, and now you speak of seeking employment," Jahn said, only slightly testy. "You have been pampered all your life, and now you speak of pampering others. I don't like it." He could not say so, but even though their life here was a lie, it wounded his pride that his wife should want for anything.

And Morgana was his wife, in every way. Contest aside, there could be no other empress but this one. If he could do it without causing a diplomatic nightmare, he would call the contest to an end today and declare this woman his wife. He wanted everyone to know.

"There is something else I should tell you," Morgana said, and a note of trepidation in her voice warned him. "You won't like it either, I imagine, but I can only be honest with you."

He did wish she would not speak so often of honesty . . .

She looked him in the eye. "I love you. It was not my intention," she added quickly. "I truly did believe, for a while, that friendship and lust would be enough. But my mother was right. Love is worth waiting for. I know it's not what you planned or wanted, but it has come to pass that I do love you. If I doubted my feelings at all, when I thought you might be dead or wounded, I could doubt no more. I love you, and . . ."

"Ana . . ."

"Don't try to argue with me. We can still be soldiers fighting through life together; we can still have the friend-ship and physical compatibility that brought us together. There's just this little . . . complication."

"Ana . . ."

"I know it's not what we planned, and you might be a bit upset with me, but I couldn't go on without telling you . . ."

Jahn laid a silencing finger over her mouth. "Ana," he began once again, "stop blathering. I love you, too."

She sighed, and it was as if she emitted a rush of warmth that cut through him. "So, what are we going to do?"

Jahn picked Morgana up and took the two steps that separated them from the bed. He dropped her onto the mattress, where she bounced and laughed. "We're going to do what people in love do, and we're going to do it well and often."

And the truth could wait awhile longer.

Chapter Eight

✳

WHEN she'd taken up residence in the palace six days earlier, Danya had been upset that she'd not been immediately introduced to the emperor. With effort, she had decided to push her displeasure aside. Soon enough she would meet and charm the man who was destined to be her husband. In a matter of a one short month she would be empress, no matter how high the price might be.

Until then she would smile as best she could and graciously accept the welcome of ministers and deputies and their wives. So far she sensed they did not really like her at all, but were cordial to her just in case she did win the emperor's contest.

On a couple of occasions she had seen the emperor very briefly, but he did not seem interested in meeting her. He didn't care about getting to know her. She was no different from the other women who graced his dining hall or his gardens. It wasn't easy to contain her ire and her anxiousness. She was particularly unhappy when someone appeared at a function in a gown too much like her own, or when someone dared to mention the others who might be empress. Her life here should be perfect, it should be without pain or challenge. And yet it was not.

Living constantly on edge did not agree with Danya, who had never been one to hold her tongue. She had, on one occasion, told a general's daughter that her lavender gown made her look plump and sallow, and she'd sent back a stew that tasted as if someone had pissed it in—she told the serving girl as much—and then insisted upon a plate of properly cooked quail while those around her ate the offending stew. She had only told the truth, as she'd seen it. Of course the general's daughter had friends in the palace and they turned against her, as did the insulted cook and a few serving girls who thought she was too demanding and ungrateful.

Danya convinced herself that she did not care what others thought, and when an opportunity to be blunt came along, she usually took it. Criticizing someone's clothing or hairstyle or food seemed such a small matter, given all that was happening in her life. Sometimes it made her feel better to let out the anger that was building up inside her. Without an outlet of some sort she would explode! When she was empress, the palace residents would all be cordial to her, whether they liked her or not.

She had settled into her lovely suite of rooms, where she kept a personal distance from the servants who saw to all her needs and where she cried each night when she was alone and the rooms were dark. Deputy Rainer's handkerchief was put to good use. A few of the maids and housekeepers had attempted to be friendly in those early days, but Danya quickly cut them down and put them in their place. She could have no friends here; to befriend her was dangerous.

Danya memorized names of other palace residents and visitors, and tried to discern who might be an ally and who might be a foe. Very quickly she put them all into the category of foe, at least for now, which gave her more freedom to allow her tongue free rein. No one here could be her friend, not now, not ever.

Deputy Minister Rainer kept his distance, and she was glad of it. Now and then she caught him watching her from a distance when they dined in the same large hall or when there was a social gathering to which they both had been invited, but she never acknowledged him and he did not approach. What good could come of it? He saw too much; he knew her too well. He already knew too many of her secrets, and that could be dangerous. If it was in her power, she would send him away as she had sent Fai back home, but it was not in her power to be rid of him. Not yet.

Day and night Danya waited anxiously for the hooded man to reveal himself as he most certainly would, sooner or later. On the twisting stairwell she walked every day; in a crowded room of strangers where she grew ever distant; in her chambers. Alone or in a crowd, she felt safe nowhere, at no time. She waited for his instructions, whatever they might be. She dreamed of a child, her child, and wondered if he was truly safe in the hands of those who would align themselves with one such as the hooded man. Did they feed him well and teach him songs and stories? Did they tuck him in each night and keep him safe from harm? God in heaven, had the hooded man's cold breath ever touched her son?

Preparing for yet another torturous meal with yet more strangers, Danya sat before a mirror in her chambers. She looked older than she had before leaving home, as if the touch of the hooded man's cold breath had stolen years from her life. No, it was not his breath that had stolen color from her cheeks and years from her life. The terrible promise she had made sucked the life from her body. A promise of darkness, a promise of death, a promise of betrayal.

Help from the hooded man and his people aside, no emperor would choose a woman who looked so pale and haggard as his bride. Danya closed her eyes and dipped her head. She breathed deeply and thought of her son, a sweet little boy called Ethyn, a child she did not know. She thought of having him here with her, when her promise to the hooded man was done. She willed herself to be beauti-

ful, to be alluring, to be perfect so that no man could resist
her, not even an emperor who had many women to choose
from.

When she lifted her head and looked again, it did seem
that she was prettier than before. She attempted a smile,
which frightened her, as it was all teeth and no joy.

There was more than one way into a man's heart, she
knew. Deputy Rainer had done as she'd asked and sent a
dressmaker to her almost immediately. Danya had insisted
that the bodices of her new gowns be cut low to show attributes other than her smile and her rosy cheeks. She'd
had a number of frocks made since coming here, and all
were cut to show her body to best advantage. The colors
were bright, the waists were small, and the necklines were
low and tight, so that an abundance of pale, soft flesh was
pushed up and out. If she had to seduce the emperor before
the First Night of the Summer Festival, and then insist that
since he had ruined her, he was obliged to marry her, she
would do so. Ennis, snake that he was, had taught her to
please a man. He had shown her tricks she could do with
her mouth and her tongue, he had taught her to bring him
to the edge and back again, insisting all the while that he
loved her. Her body was her only weapon, and she would
use it if she had to.

If she was going to sell herself body and soul, she might
as well look like the whore she had become. Thinking herself still too pale, Danya reached for a container of rouge to
brighten her cheeks.

This was war, after all, and her son's life was the prize.

MORGANA was shocked by how quickly and completely
her business venture succeeded. Iann's wife was well
pleased at the results of her consultation, and she recommended Morgana to a friend. Word spread, and in the past
four days the tavern had been busy morning and early afternoon with Morgana's business. She'd thought the tavern

owner would be annoyed with her, but he wouldn't even accept payment when she offered him a percentage of what she earned. True, it might be difficult to decide how to divide the length of lace or the pretty vase she'd accepted in lieu of coins, but much of what she took in came in the form of silver and gold. Instead of being grateful, the tavern owner simply growled and threw up his hands in what seemed to be despair, though his words were always kind enough. Like Jahn's friends, the owner of the tavern was wonderfully accommodating.

Most of the problems presented to her were simple enough to solve. A specially formulated lotion for dry hands or feet; a potion concocted of ingredients from the kitchen for a woman's newly discovered wrinkles; an oil or a treatment for the hair. Her mother's teachings all came back to her as she solved one problem after another.

Though she had found no solution for the poor woman with the warts. That concern was beyond her capabilities.

The two ladies who entered the tavern on this particularly warm and lovely afternoon did not look at all like Morgana's usual clientele. Their gowns were made of much finer fabrics than she had seen thus far, and they were also cut shockingly low. Morgana was certain she had never seen breasts displayed in such a blatant and voluptuous way. One woman's bosom seemed to be about to spill over the top of her gown; the other's looked more likely to burst forth in an explosion of flesh that would very likely take out someone's eye, if they happened to be standing too close. Their hairstyles were lavishly complicated, and they both wore too much rouge and a heavy application of dark eyeliner.

Morgana could not help but notice that the women had a different sort of effect on Jahn's friends than had the other women who'd visited. Iann paled considerably, and the others put their heads together and whispered in what appeared to be excitement and concern. It was probably the profusion of breasts that excited them. Men were quite sensitive in that regard.

"This is ridiculous," the fair-haired woman with spillage whispered loudly.

"We have to do something!" the dark-haired woman who looked burstable responded. "He wants to marry us off!" She looked at Morgana with narrowed, suspicious eyes. "Are you Ana Devlyn?" she asked.

"I am," Morgana responded. "And you are?"

"Anrid," the darker woman said crisply, not bothering with a last name.

"I'm Melusina," the pouting blonde added.

"I've heard you can work wonders with beauty creams and hair tonics and such." Anrid lifted her chin, almost as if daring Morgana to agree that she might need such things as beauty creams and tonics.

"I know a bit about such matters," Morgana answered. "Is there anything in particular you are concerned about?" She knew what she would do to these two unfortunately clad women if given a free hand, but she couldn't be sure what they wanted, and she did not wish to insult them. Bad taste aside, they obviously came from a well-to-do family. Those fabrics were quite expensive, and their shoes were remarkable. Were the jewels there real? Bejeweled shoes were not the norm, not in the world in which a sentinel's wife lived. Someone wanted to marry them off. A father, perhaps? A beleaguered brother?

"Make us irresistible again," Melusina said.

"To whom do you wish to be irresistible?" Morgana asked.

Both women looked at her as if she were daft. Finally Anrid said, "You have not been in Arthes long, I take it."

"A few weeks," Morgana admitted.

"Well, Melusina and I are the emperor's favorites."

"His favorite . . ." Morgana began.

"His favorite *companions*," Melusina supplied delicately, and then she stuck out her lower lip. "At least we were, until he decided to take a bride. Now he's determined to be proper even though he's not yet married. He does not call for us anymore. As far as we can tell, he's saving himself for his wedding night, as if he were a simpering virgin."

Morgana didn't argue that she saw nothing wrong with that. In fact, her estimation of the emperor rose a bit—and at the same time it plummeted. These crude, painted women were his favorites?

Anrid added, "He has even suggested to one of his advisers that we marry and move out of the palace. Can you imagine?"

"How can he resist these?" Melusina wailed, grabbing her breasts and hefting them in her hands as if they were melons at the market. "How can he wish to give them away to another man?" She shook her large breasts with each heated word, as if for emphasis.

Morgana was very glad that she didn't have to worry about the emperor's loose women and whether or not they remained in the palace after he chose a bride. He wouldn't be the first emperor to keep a wife as well as women intended solely for pleasure. She was so relieved that she did not have to concern herself with such unpleasant matters! Refusing to participate in his ridiculous contest was the best decision she'd ever made—for many reasons. "I have found marriage not to be so terrible," Morgana said with absolute honesty.

"You have not had the privilege of living in the palace as one of the emperor's favorite playthings," Anrid said hotly, "so your situation can hardly be compared to ours." She sighed. "We were adored, and now he wants to cast us off. He will likely choose old men for us to marry—old, doddering, wealthy men who will squeeze our boobs too hard and never be able to play all night and into the morning, as the emperor used to do."

Morgana looked at the women's faces, trying to see beyond the unnatural color and the profusion of breasts. "You could choose your own husbands, I imagine," she said. Both women were very attractive. Some might even call them beautiful, but dressed and made up as they were, it was difficult to tell. Not all men would be pleased to take

the emperor's castoffs, but there were those who might find
it an honor.

"We would rather woo the emperor back into our beds,"
Melusina said.

Morgana did not care if the emperor kept lovers or not.
It was wrong, but he was not *her* emperor, after all. "Are
you willing to allow me to make considerable changes to
your appearance?"

"Yes," both women said in unison.

"Will you trust me?"

"We'll try anything," Anrid said desperately.

Morgana nodded, and the women stepped forward.

"Devlyn," Melusina said in an offhand manner, "that is
your man's name?"

"Yes," Morgana answered, holding her breath.

Both women shrugged their shoulders, and Anrid said,
"Never heard of him."

Morgana let out a long, relieved breath. Thank God!

THREE weeks and three days remained until the First
Night of the Summer Festival when Jahn received word
that Lady Verity of Mirham had died in a horrible riding
accident while on her way to the palace to be considered.
He could not help but be dismayed. If he had not put this
ridiculous contest into motion, then Lady Verity would
still be alive. On top of everything else, he now had an innocent woman's death on his head.

Why could he not have met Morgana in some normal
way? Perhaps General Hydd, who had suggested her,
could've invited Morgana and her father to court, where
she could be presented. Would their feelings have grown as
rapidly in that situation as they had in the workings of a
lie? Would he still have his empress? He could not know—
would never know. And still he mourned Lady Verity and
cursed his foolishness.

Jahn dismissed the deputy minister who delivered the
bad news, and did his best to return to business. His days

were caught up in endless details. A drought in the Southern Province was already causing problems with the crops there. A land dispute to the north was getting out of hand. Settlers near the mountains to the north swore the shape-shifting Caradon and Anwyn were trying to force them away from land which had always been sacred and untouched.

General Hydd wanted to send soldiers north to handle both problems. Then again, the minister of defense was always ready for a fight. Jahn preferred diplomacy, which his general had declared a waste of time.

Father Braen had insisted upon having time with the emperor on this afternoon, so that plans for the wedding ceremony could be made. Everyone had his own ideas about what, how, and who . . . and none of them asked the emperor what he wanted. Jahn didn't think it was because they didn't care, but rather because they felt so strongly about their own opinions. There could be no other way.

As soon as Father Braen left, Blane burst into the room.

"My Lord," Blane said, bowing deeply and then casting a glance back to make sure they were alone. "It seems that your wife has two new clients on this afternoon."

Jahn grimaced. "She has new clients every afternoon, does she not?"

"Yes, but these clients are"—Blane stopped and swallowed hard—"Melusina and Anrid."

All his other concerns faded as for one terrible moment Jahn saw his neat plan, his marriage, his *life* falling apart before his eyes.

RIKKA felt oddly calm as that time which she had so longed for drew closer. Gyl was gone, and days after his departure she found she was incapable of mourning the loss of what she'd once known with him. He had been a weakness, and with Kristo's help she'd finally rid herself of him, as she'd always known she must.

Kristo shared her bed when it suited him, and she found completion in his arms to be sharp and wonderful and sensational . . . and entirely devoid of emotion. What he offered her was physical release without the complication of an emotional component; he gave her pleasure without the demands of love. He did not ask her to change who she was or what she wanted, as Gyl had done. She liked it, more than she'd thought she would. Gyl's demands had been draining, and had become more so in the past few years as he'd attempted to change her, to make her release her anger. The anger within her was so much a part of who she had become, she not only didn't want to let it go—she was incapable of living without it.

After that one episode in her parlor, when Gyl had watched, Kristo did not find completion himself, not one time. Instead he examined her like a hawk as she enjoyed his cold touch, he studied her responses and seemed pleased when she found release—but not pleased enough to give anything of himself in return.

She didn't care. What he did to her felt good, it made the long days of waiting a little less long. He amused her; he distracted her; he entertained her as she waited for the right time to travel to the palace to see the end to the scheme she had planned and executed. That time was coming soon.

Cold bastard or not, Kristo was going to deliver to Rikka the revenge she had longed for since the day she'd crawled out of Level Thirteen.

When Kristo joined her in the parlor on a rainy afternoon, Rikka wondered what sort of mood he would be in today. He'd spent hours in meditation lately, trying to locate the missing bridal candidate with his formidable magical powers. She was somewhat shocked that he had not yet been able to do so. Kristo saw so many secrets in his powerful mind—he knew so much of what had been and what was yet to be. And yet, he could not find one small, insignificant girl.

Thank goodness the other one was already theirs. Rikka

didn't know why Kristo preferred Lady Morgana, and she didn't care. Lady Danya had proven to be quite malleable. She would do well enough.

When he burst into the parlor in a near rage, she knew he had tried again to find the Ramsden girl and once again had failed. Kristo was a man unaccustomed to failure. It did not agree with him at all. Most women—men, too—would be rightly frightened of Kristo in a rage, but Rikka simply watched him and admired his masculine form and his formidable power and his hypnotic eyes. She could not ask for a better partner in her quest.

"Nothing?" she prodded.

He looked directly at her, and she could swear she felt a chill even with a distance between them. "I think she is already in Arthes."

"You *think*?"

"Yes. I believe that she is there, somewhere."

"Arthes is a large city," Rikka said. "Your uncertain belief that she is there *somewhere* is not particularly helpful."

"Don't you think I know that?" Kristo shouted.

Rikka was not afraid of him, not as others were. He would shout and perhaps break a few things, and then he would strip her naked and with his cold body he would make her scream before leaving her shaking and spent while he departed from her unfulfilled. There were worse ways to spend an afternoon.

The angrier he was, the more fiercely he would take her. Rikka liked fierce. "Why is she different?" She took a step toward her lover and fellow conspirator.

"I'm too close to her, I suppose," he admitted, his voice lowered but his eyes no less brutal. "It is harder for me to see those who are near to me." His eyes bored through her. "There was a time when I could see into you very well, but lately I see almost nothing."

Rikka smiled. "Because you love me?"

That got a grin out of Kristo. Rikka shuddered. The

man should not smile. The expression did not agree with him at all. "I love no one," he said, "but we have shared a physical closeness that clouds my knowledge."

"Did you once share such a closeness with Lady Morgana?" Rikka asked. "Is that why you do not see her well?"

Kristo laughed loudly. It was a sound Rikka had never heard before and would be very happy never to hear again. His laugh grated like broken glass. "No, but I did fuck her mother a time or two." He looked Rikka in the eye. "Lady Morgana is my daughter."

HIS time of bliss was almost over. Jahn realized that too well. If he was not very careful, it would end very badly.

When Morgana had begun helping women with their beauty concerns, he had considered it a hobby which would keep her occupied while he tended to business in the palace. The pastime was harmless enough. That supposition had changed abruptly. Learning that his former mistresses had called upon his wife that very afternoon was more than a little disturbing. He'd had to wait for word that they were gone before he could even think about returning to the tavern! He was always careful not to be seen and recognized, but this was ridiculous. Morgana's business was no longer a harmless hobby; it was a potential disaster waiting to explode in his face.

Morgana was obviously quite pleased with herself as she welcomed him home. After seeing Melusina and Anrid in the palace staircase as he'd made his way from one home to another, Jahn understood why. In a single afternoon, in a matter of hours, she had transformed them from painted ladies to pretty girls. She had, with a few small changes and a few large ones, given the women a touch of elegance they had never before known. Their faces had been scrubbed clean, and looked younger and softer. Their hair had been arranged simply, also taking years from their appearance. Though not primly styled, their clothing was no longer shocking. How had Morgana gotten them new gowns so quickly? The woman was a marvel.

Melusina and Anrid had been quite pleased with his surprised expression, even though he had not stopped to speak to them. He could not help but wonder what, besides the concerns of beauty and fashion, the three women had talked about during their long afternoon.

When Jahn walked into the room he now called home, Morgana kissed him well, a welcoming ritual he always began to crave long before it was time for him to return to this simple, false life he had created for himself. She loved him now, when she did not know who he was. Would she love him tomorrow?

"I have news," Jahn said, giving Morgana a wide smile. "In the morning we're moving into the palace."

Her bright smile faded and she paled considerably. "I don't want to move into the palace. I like it here."

So did he, though he could not tell her how much. Jahn placed a hand on Morgana's cheek. "My friends have been missed at the palace, and some of them have hardly seen their families in the past few weeks because they're so often here. I cannot continue to ask them to make that sacrifice. In the palace I can see that you are safe with a much smaller contingent of guards."

It was tedious to leave the palace dressed as an emperor and guarded by an entourage, duck into one private place or another and change clothes, then make his way to the tavern as another sort of man, but tediousness would not make him change this routine. Keeping Morgana in the dark a bit longer—that was what motivated him.

"Do I really need . . ."

"Yes," Jahn said sharply, not giving her a chance to finish her question. "You are precious to me, and I will not leave you unguarded."

"Other women are not escorted about town by four armed guards," she argued.

"Other women are not my wife," Jahn replied.

"During the daylight hours I see many of them out and about unaccompanied."

"The last time you were out unaccompanied, you were frightened."

"Needlessly so, since I didn't know you had your friends following me. I can take care of myself."

"There is no need, not as long as I take care of you."

Her expression softened. "You make it so difficult to argue with you. What about my business?" she asked. "Will I be able to work here still, or will there be a place for me in the palace?"

Jahn took a deep breath. She was not going to like this change, he suspected. "For now, I have made arrangements for you to work for the palace laundress. The pay will be much better than what you're bringing in with your little venture, and . . ."

He knew he was in trouble when her eyes went hard. "My little venture?"

"I'm not saying you can't earn some money of your own." For now, when she was ignorant of her true position . . . "It's just . . ."

"My little venture?" she said again.

Obviously that was a poor choice of words on his part. "I want you to be happy," he said. "More than once you have wondered aloud what we'll do when we have children. You're right; you have been right all along. We cannot raise our sons and daughters in a small room over a tavern; we cannot make a home for a family here." He gave her a smile and tried to picture the Level Seven room he had in mind. No one used that level much anymore, as it had once been the home of witches and wizards and less-than-wholesome magic, and many palace residents were a mite suspicious. He could do with that entire level as he pleased. "There is a room there that is at least three times as large as this one, and the emperor has promised it to me."

Her expression softened. "Three times?"

"Perhaps four." There might be a greater risk that his

charade would be discovered, as he would now be leading his double life and changing his costume within the palace, but at least his wife would not be swapping stories with the women who had once shared his bed! Melusina and Anrid wouldn't be caught dead near the laundry. Besides, he intended to have them both out of the palace as soon as possible. Could he get them out before he moved Morgana in?

The First Night of the Summer Festival was fast approaching. Three weeks and three days to go. He could maintain his charade until then, if he did not break down and confess the truth in a moment of weakness.

"The furnishings there are palace castoffs, but still they will be much nicer than these," he promised. "If we can make a happy home here, imagine what we can do in the palace, with more room and a proper bed and a sturdy table and chairs." He leaned into her and lowered his voice. "It will be very quiet at night, without the drunken voices of tavern patrons invading your sleep."

"I like the sound of that," she said, her voice kinder. Gentler.

He breathed a sigh of relief, even though he knew he was digging his own grave with each lie, and that grave got deeper with each passing day that he allowed the lies to continue. If he were a better man, he would tell her the truth here and now, even if she had just met his former mistresses. No, this was the worst of times for such a confession.

"We will move in the morning," he said as he backed Morgana toward the waiting bed.

"So soon?"

"I see no reason to delay," he said, raking his nose across her neck where it turned to shoulder. She was wearing the blue dress she had so carefully repaired. He would not cut it off her again, not until he could tell her the truth of her place in this world and gift her with a dozen more suitable frocks. "You smell so good, and you are so warm."

"You warm me," she whispered. "You always have."

"Is that why you love me?"

She answered with a touch of humor in her voice. "Perhaps."

He took his time removing her best dress, which had seen much wear since he'd taken her from her home. Yes, soon he would dress her in fine gowns and bathe her in jewels. He would feed her well and she would sleep on the softest, most luxurious bed imaginable. She would want for nothing.

All she had to do was forgive him.

Chapter Nine

"WE leave tomorrow for Arthes," Kristo said, his eyes on Rikka's face. She was not the prettiest woman he had ever known, and she was far from the youngest, but she was the most wonderfully broken. Inside, where it counted most, she had never been complete. She had never been happy, not even as a child. He sensed that she hadn't enjoyed sex at all until he'd come along. Her cheeks flushed in the aftermath of an orgasm that had made her scream, her face lit up even more at the news that her plans were about to come together.

"The women, the foolishly hopeful brides we did not choose, are they dead?" she asked breathlessly. "Can you see that are all four are dead?"

She was naked beneath him, and unlike other women she did not cringe at the touch of his cold skin. In fact, she liked it very much. He could even run his hands across her flesh without making her flinch. He touched her as she questioned the outcome of her plans. "Dead or out of the picture."

Her smile faded. "They are not all *dead*?"

"No."

Rikka's short-lived contentment fled. "Who failed me, Kristo?"

"Many failed you, but the result is that which you desire. You will have all that you want."

Though he did not see Rikka's future well since they had become lovers, he did get a sudden flash of knowledge which warned him that she might not live to see all that she had planned come to pass. If he cared more for her, he might fight to learn the details, he might warn her to be cautious in days to come, but he did neither. She was a diversion along the way to the total chaos he craved; she was the impetus which would eventually put his daughter and grandson into a position of great power—and Kristo would be there beside them, guiding and teaching.

Kristo had sensed at Morgana's birth that his daughter had inherited some of his gifts, but they had been weak and he'd been disappointed by her gender and her frailty. If he'd cared to take her under his wing and nurture her long ago, perhaps she'd be more powerful now. At that time in his life he'd been too busy developing his own magic to bother with that of a child. He'd neglected Morgana and her gift over the years, and she was not well taught in that regard. His grandson would be taught from birth; he would see to it himself. He would not fail his grandson as he'd failed his daughter. Allowing Morgana's mother to take her away had been a mistake, the biggest of Kristo's life.

All his life, having power only made him want more and more and more. Morgana's mother, the only woman he had ever taken as a true wife, had never understood that. She'd wanted him to be happy with what they had; she'd wanted him to be a loving husband and father, much as Gyl had wanted Rikka to be satisfied with being a loving wife.

Which reminded him . . .

"Gyl tried to come back this afternoon," he said, rubbing his cold, hard body against hers and stealing even more of her heat.

"Did he?"

Was there a touch of longing in her voice? Did this broken woman still yearn for something only her ineffectual wizard could give her? "Yes. He came to rescue you, I think, or to kidnap you. I suspect he thought those two actions would be one and the same."

"I trust you sent him away."

"No. I killed him."

Rikka tried to hide her reaction, but he felt her body lurch, just a little.

"I turned him to stone as he foolishly lunged for me with a knife. You have never seen me use that power, but perhaps one day you will. It's quite remarkable."

"Where is he? Am I to have a statue of Gyl frozen in midattack in my garden?" she snapped.

"Of course not," Kristo said. He touched her hip with his cold hand, he grabbed her flesh hard, and this time she did flinch. "I shattered the stone figure and spread what was left of it across the western fields. If I had left Gyl's remains intact, there would always be the possibility that someone might possess the magic to bring him back again. We can't have that, now can we?"

"No," she whispered.

"You mourn him," he said, amused by her reaction.

"I do not," she argued, but there were tears in her eyes, and she suddenly looked old. She wore every one of her years on a hardened face.

"Tomorrow," he said. "Tomorrow we leave here and you start a new life where all you desire, all you deserve, will be given to you. When Sebestyen's sons are dead and you rule Columbyana, all the sacrifices you've made will seem small."

"Yes," she whispered, eyes closed, and for a moment it seemed she was every bit as cold as he.

DANYA had been expecting the hooded man to surprise her at any time, and she still jumped and pulled away when, as she approached her suite of rooms for the evening, she felt the unexpected weight of a hand on her shoulder. She jerked away and spun around, to find Deputy Minister Rainer standing there. She should've known. The hand which had touched her had been a warm one.

"You should not sneak up on a woman," Danya snapped, annoyed that he had been so easily able to do so.

"I did not intend to startle you," he said, bowing slightly.

They were entirely alone in a Level Five hallway, just outside the door which led to her chambers. She could've— and perhaps should've—demanded that an escort be provided for her at all times when she was not locked away in her rooms, but not only did she prefer to be alone, she knew it was safer for all that she not bring anyone too close.

She'd avoided Rainer all this time for a good reason— many good reasons, in fact. There was a kindness in his eyes that made her feel weak; he knew too much; there was something about the way he looked at her that made her want to break down and tell him everything.

"Well, you did startle me. What do you want?"

He cocked his head to one side, studying her critically and much too closely. Eyes such a pure gray-blue they rivaled a winter sky bored through her. "I want to know what has happened to you," he said simply.

"Nothing has happened. I am as I have always been."

"No," he said simply. "That is not so, not at all. I should've realized something was wrong when you sent Fai away and tried to do the same to me. But I did not see, not until tonight as I watched you eat your supper—or rather, as I watched you *not* eat your supper."

Danya lifted her chin and hardened her eyes. "How was I supposed to eat that swill? When I'm empress, the food around here will be better prepared and presented. It's quite clear that at this time no one has proper control over the kitchen."

Her insults should send him running, but of course they did not. "The food was fine. More than fine. In fact, it was quite tasty."

"It was . . ."

Rainer did not allow her to finish. "And this gown." He shook his head. "The revealing dresses you've taken to wearing and the paint on your face, they are not you."

"Earlier this evening I was pale and needed some color, and the gown is very well made and fashionable." She lifted her chin. "Most men would find this revealing dress, as you call it, quite charming. I find it peculiar that you do not. Don't you like women, Deputy Rainer? If you do like women at all, I suppose you prefer them meek and genteel, quiet ladies who simply take whatever it is you have to give without ever daring to question your superiority."

"You're not fooling me, Lady Danya," Rainer responded gently. "Something is horribly wrong. Tell me."

She held her breath and fought back the tears that threatened. Why did he continue to be kind to her when she had been so unkind to him and to others? Why did he care what troubled her? Did he know, did he have even a clue, that a dark, cold man had taken control of her life by taking control of her son? "You go too far," she said. "When I'm empress, I will have you stripped of your position and sent away; I will have you banned from the palace."

He smiled gently. "If you continue to insult all those around you, you will never be empress." He reached out and gently rearranged a tendril of hair which had fallen and touched her cheek. "And if you were half as tough as you pretend to be, you would have threatened to take my head rather than simply sending me away."

She opened her mouth to do just that, but instead of speaking, as she'd intended, a sob escaped. She clapped her hand over her mouth and tried to undo the damage, but it was too late. Tears slipped down her cheeks—large, fat tears she usually reserved for private moments. What if the hooded man or one of his cohorts saw her weakness? What if they saw her break down in front of this annoyingly persistent man? No one could see; she could not allow it.

Danya opened the door to her chambers and ran inside. She did not invite Rainer in, but neither did she shut him out, and after a moment he followed her. She wanted to send him away, to order him out of her sight, but instead she fell against him and sobbed like a brokenhearted child.

Everything she had been holding inside her broke free, and she grasped at Rainer's shirtsleeve with desperate fingers as she cried hysterically. Eventually the tears and the shaking subsided, and she became aware that he was holding her as certainly as she was holding him.

She had been waiting for the ground to open up and swallow her, but Rainer made her feel safe for the first time since she'd met the hooded man, since she'd accepted his offer and condemned herself and all those around her.

"Tell me what is wrong," he whispered.

"I can't." The tears stopped, but she did not move away. She grasped his sleeve as she had when she'd sobbed, needing him, needing this. "Can you just hold me for a little while? A few minutes." An hour, a day . . . forever. Usually she had only a square of linen to remind her of him; to have him here was much better. She liked it.

"I am here for as long as you need me." Rainer stroked her hair, he rubbed his hand along her back. He soothed her. He held her.

After a while Danya's panic, her weak episode of terror, faded away. Rainer, sensing that she was calmer now, stopped soothing her with his hands. He'd expect sex now, she imagined. As a favor for his comfort, he would expect her to spread her legs and offer him relief of another sort. Heaven help her, at this moment she could think of much worse ways to pass the long hours of a dark night. Would he be as kind a lover as he was a man?

But Angelo Rainer was a man of surprises. He set her back, kissed her forehead, and promised that they would speak again when she felt stronger. "Tomorrow," he said, that single word a promise that assured her that, like it or not, she was no longer alone.

And then he left her standing there in her fine bedchamber, without issuing a single demand or request, without naming a price for his comfort. And for the first time in a very long time, Danya felt as if she were not forlorn and completely lost.

MORGANA loved the room Jahn had arranged. It was much more spacious and better furnished than the tavern room, and it had recently been given a good cleaning by someone other than herself. Though her home was still just one chamber, this one was wonderfully large. Two heavy wooden dividers were set up to create small, private areas which might as well be separate rooms. The bed was large and soft and did not sag or cant to one side, and it was embellished with a silky blue coverlet and a number of pillows. She'd had no idea a sentinel could live in rooms so fine! It was not true of all sentinels, she knew; there was not room in the palace for every soldier to have such quarters, and she hadn't heard or seen anyone else on this level. Maybe Jahn truly was a favorite of the emperor, or perhaps he'd been given some sort of advancement or reward.

She didn't like the climb up the winding stone stairway, but she supposed she would get accustomed to it in time. Level Seven was three flights of stairs from the ground level, Level Ten. There were two levels below the ground floor, and the top of the palace—which was rarely used these days—was Level One. In the old days, when Emperor Jahn's father had ruled, that had been his domain.

There had been a working lift in those days, too. No emperor would want to climb all those stairs on a regular basis.

Morgana and Jahn had been living in the palace for two days, and she'd spent that time getting accustomed to the place, putting her own touches on the room she now called home. She still saw his friends on occasion, but not in the groups of four she was accustomed to. Usually they were in pairs. She missed her walks through town, and seeing the women who had become her friends and customers, but in time she would resume those pleasurable activities.

On more than one occasion she had explored Level Seven, which seemed not to be used by anyone but her and her husband. Iann said this level had once been the realm of witches and wizards, and so no one wished to live here. They were worried, he said, about lingering magics. He dismissed their unease as silly, and Morgana tried to do the same. She had certainly felt no lingering magic!

Jahn had gone to work early in the morning, just after sunrise. He was currently guarding the emperor on a lower level. The emperor and his closest advisers claimed all of Level Nine and Level Eight, so he did not have far to go. Someone would collect her when it was time for her to start work in the laundry, Jahn had told her as he gave her the plain shift she would wear when she worked. She hated to give up her new business, and had finally decided that perhaps it wasn't necessary to abandon her calling entirely. She'd meet women in the laundry and the kitchen, she supposed, and like all women they would want to be more beautiful for their husbands and beaus. There was no reason why she couldn't continue her work in the palace. If no one else cared to live on Level Seven, which seemed silly to her, maybe she could clean and make over one of the unused rooms and conduct her business from there. Surely the emperor would not mind.

Standing before a window which offered her a much finer view than the tavern had afforded, Morgana placed a hand over her stomach and let her mind wander. It was too soon to be sure, and she would not say a word to Jahn until she was certain, but she had begun to think that their first child was already growing inside her. Her breasts were tender and a bit swollen, and by her count she should've begun her monthly flow more than a week ago—not that she'd always been regular in that regard. She had not been ill, as many women were in the early stages, but perhaps it was too soon for that.

Her life had changed so dramatically in such a short period of time, it was startling and sometimes difficult to believe. At this moment Morgana was glad her stepfather had lost his temper and made that angry vow, and she was glad Jahn had overheard it and taken advantage of the situation. She was glad to have two worn and mended dresses to her name, glad to have love, glad to have even the possibility of a child in her mind and her heart. For a while she had considered herself cursed. Now she could truly believe that she was blessed.

Perhaps she would find happiness in this Arthes palace after all, though not in the way the emperor or her stepfather had intended. That thought made her smile. Life could be filled with such unexpected and pleasant surprises!

All too soon, there was an impatient knock on her door. Morgana rushed to answer, determined to make the most of whatever this day might bring. She found a sour older woman standing in the hallway, and her greeting was harshly spoken.

"I hope you don't expect me to collect you every day."

"No, madam, of course not," Morgana said sweetly. "My husband made the arrangements. I'm afraid he tends to be overprotective."

At this, the woman's expression softened. "He's a fine man, then."

"Do you know him? Jahn Devlyn?" Morgana asked as she stepped into the hallway and closed the door to the chamber behind her.

"Can't say that I do, but there are many sentinels who make their way in this palace and I have met only a few of them. Most are not as caring as your man seems to be, but they are soldiers, after all." She glanced down the long, deserted hallway. "Yours is the first sentinel I know to have residence in the palace."

"I'm Ana," Morgana said as she rushed to keep step with the taller woman who moved toward the stairwell as if on a mission. "Ana Devlyn."

"I'm Natesa," the older woman said, "Nattie to those who work for me and to my friends." She cast a suspicious glance Morgana's way. "You don't look like a particularly hearty worker, Ana. Ever washed a tub of sheets?"

"No, madam," Morgana said.

"How are you at mending?"

"Fair enough, I think," Morgana responded as she made quick work of the stairway.

"We'll start you there, then. There's always lots of mending to keep us busy."

Morgana smiled. She was married, possibly with child, and about to start a new career as a laundress. And she could not remember ever being happier. A tickle ran up her spine, and for a moment, just a moment, she wondered if that tickle was a warning of some sort. Perfect happiness did not last.

She pushed that morbid thought aside. There was nothing at all wrong with wallowing in her good fortune!

RIKKA did not want to stop, not even for the sake of their horses. If they ran these animals to death, they could be replaced. Arthes and the palace awaited her; the end of her careful planning and scheming awaited.

But Kristo insisted on caring for the horses, and so they rested while the sun was high in the sky.

Rikka paced impatiently while her companion saw to the animals. He spoke to them more kindly than he spoke to her, even when he was inside her. Not that she'd ever wished for or expected kindness from Kristo. Unwillingly, she thought of Gyl and his years of gentleness and love, but she pushed those useless thoughts aside. The death of her former lover was simply another price she'd had to pay for her revenge.

Kristo's head came up, hinting that he heard or sensed something. A few moments later Rikka heard the sound of a horse's hooves on the road they should be traveling. They were not alone on the road to Arthes; she had never expected that they would be. Travelers made their way to the capital city and back again on a regular basis. The question was, would this traveler bring trouble? Kristo did not look particularly pleased as the sound of the rider grew louder and closer.

When Rikka saw the rider, she immediately recognized him as one of her own. The long silver hair was as unmistakable as the slender but strong frame.

"That's Cayse Trinity. He works for me." Trinity was her most deadly and trusted assassin, a man who could never die, a man who considered it his privilege to send those whose time had come to their reward, whatever that reward might be. Kristo insisted that some of the potential brides Rikka had ordered killed had survived, but Rikka suspected Lady Leyla had not been among those who'd escaped death. She smiled at the ageless silver-haired man as he dismounted and stalked toward her.

He didn't look happy. Perhaps he had gone to her house looking for the second payment for his services, and was annoyed that he'd found her gone and had to track her down in order to get paid. No, he was not at all happy. Rikka's smile faded. Was he talking to himself?

Kristo shouted, but it was too late. In a movement almost too quick for the eye to follow, Trinity drew his knife and thrust it into Rikka's stomach. The entire long, sharp blade was inside her, having pierced her elegant black dress and cut her insides to ribbons. Blood bloomed quickly but she did not fall, as Trinity held her up with one arm and the knife itself.

"You did not tell me she was a witch," Trinity whispered. "You should've told me. Everything is ruined, now. Everything."

Kristo pulled Trinity away from Rikka. The blade left her body and she dropped hard, having no control over her damaged body. The life was draining from her; she felt it. And yet she did possess the awareness to see that Kristo did to Trinity what he said he had done to Gyl. He directed one hand in the direction of the assassin, he pointed a slender finger, and in an instant the man and the ground around him turned into a dark green stone shot with what looked to be veins of crystal. She drew up her feet, afraid that she'd be caught up in the transformation and she, too, would turn to stone.

With Trinity taken care of, Kristo turned to Rikka. He looked annoyed at the turn of events, but not particularly displeased. And why should he be? She'd never fooled herself into believing that she meant anything to him.

"I would've stopped him sooner if you hadn't insisted that he was your man."

"He moved too fast," Rikka said, looking down at the damage that had been done. "Am I dying?"

"Yes," Kristo said without emotion. "Not quickly, but you will be dead by nightfall." He turned to look at the statue in annoyance, then muttered, "Shut up."

"I didn't say anything," Rikka said weakly.

"No, but he did. The bastard still lives in there, and I can hear his thoughts. That's never happened before."

"Trinity is . . . immortal," Rikka said, gasping as speaking became more difficult. Her vision swam.

"Truly? We'll see about that." Kristo smiled, searching the ground for a moment and then bending down to pick up a sturdy limb which had fallen from a nearby tree. He hefted the limb in his hands before swinging it with all his might at the stone statue which had once been Rikka's most trusted assassin. The wood splintered, but there was no damage to the assassin. None at all. Kristo swung again and again. He battered Trinity's hard form until there wasn't much left of the tree limb but splinters. The stone was unaffected.

Rikka could wish, a little, that Kristo's anger had something to do with the fact that Trinity had killed her, but she knew better. He was simply irritated that his plans had to be altered to suit the new situation. He would no longer have her to lead him into the palace—not that she doubted he could find his own way in.

In frustration, Kristo kicked the stone figure Trinity had become. The statue fell to the ground with a thud, but did not break.

"Interesting," Kristo said as he studied the fallen Trinity. "He should've shattered right away, and now it actually looks as if his fingers are beginning to turn back to flesh. Slowly and quite painfully, I'm happy to say." He turned to face Rikka and dropped to his haunches beside her.

"He would have slit your throat, but he intended to torture you for some wrong you did to him. Something about a witch."

Lady Leyla.

"He was so intent on you, I don't think he ever saw me, not until it was too late."

Rikka looked up at the cold man who had more power than any other she had ever known. "You can save me."

"Perhaps I could, if I had the time, but alas, Arthes and my destiny call," he said in an offhand manner. "I do wish I could stay, as there is much still to be decided. Will you still be living when your assassin regains the use of his body? Will he have the chance to torture you, as he plans, or will you disappoint him by dying before he can take his knife to you again? He will be so annoyed if he wakes and finds you already dead." Kristo glanced back at the fallen man. "Oh, look, one hand is almost flesh again. How extraordinary. Usually those I turn to stone go to pieces quite easily. Like your Gyl. One good tap and he fell into more pieces than I could possibly count. Of course, like the others I have killed in that manner, he was already dead. At least, I think so. Do you think being shattered in such a way would be painful if there was, in fact, any life remaining?"

Tears filled Rikka's eyes.

"If you have any romantic notion that Gyl will be awaiting you in the afterlife, I would set it aside. Knowing you both, I am quite certain that you're headed to two different segments of the Land of the Dead. You might see me where you're going, one of these days." He patted her cheek. "No time soon, I hope."

Rikka cut her eyes to the side and saw that Trinity was indeed changing. Most of his body remained stone, but his hands flexed and she saw a bit of silver hair flowing across the ground and catching the wind.

The loss of blood had weakened Rikka. If Kristo would help her onto her horse and take her to Arthes for proper medical care, she might be saved. He would not take her anywhere, of course. She had doomed herself the moment she'd chosen him over Gyl; she knew that now. Gyl would've moved heaven and earth to save her; Kristo cared for no one but himself. She should not be surprised. It wasn't as if he had ever made secret of that fact.

"You could help me," she said.

"There is no time, My Lady," Kristo said without a care. "Arthes awaits. Besides, it would be cruel to rob your assassin of his revenge. According to the ramblings of his maddened mind, he seems to be most deserving of it." He grinned. "I have always been a great supporter of revenge, as you well know." He stood and brushed the dirt from his robe. "I do wish I could wait to see what happens next. Will you bleed to death before Trinity can exact his revenge? Will he find the satisfaction he seeks when he regains the use of his immortal body?"

Rikka licked her lips, suddenly and completely afraid. "Kill me," she whispered weakly. "It is the least you can do after all we've meant to one another."

Again, he smiled. "Lady Rikka, I do hope I never misled you. You mean nothing to me. Nothing at all."

Kristo left her lying there and collected not only his horse but hers as well. He did not attempt to collect Trinity's horse, which remained loyally nearby. Rikka tried to call him back to her but could not. She could only watch him ride away, taking the road to Arthes, finishing the journey she had begun so long ago.

When she was alone, she looked again at Trinity. His arms were flesh again, as was a portion of his legs. His face and torso remained stone, and he could not move much. Neither could she. With every drop of blood she shed, she grew weaker and closer to death.

The race was on.

*   *   *

EVEN though Jahn missed their small room over the tavern, living in the palace had its advantages. Tonight, when the rain fell and lightning lit the sky, he did not have to run through the storm to get to Morgana. He did not have to protect her gift, which might be ruined by even one raindrop.

"Do you like it?" He held up the gown he'd had made for her, a simple and elegant frock of a dark blue fabric that draped as softly as Morgana's hair. There were no embellishments, no beads or feathers or gems. This gown was, like the woman who was meant to wear it, flawlessly elegant.

After another long day in the laundry, Morgana was tired. He wanted her to be busy; he wanted her to work if that was what she wanted to do, yet he hated to see her weary. Her eyes lit up at her first sight of the gown, and then she shook her head. "It's too expensive, I'm sure. You should return it."

"I can't," Jahn said, draping the gown across one of the dining chairs. "I bought it from a man who'd taken it in trade from another man whose wife didn't like the color. It was a real steal, I tell you. It cost almost nothing."

"Really?" Again, there was a light in her eyes.

He should've waited until he revealed his true identity before giving her lavish gifts, but she deserved so much more than he had given her so far. One gown was surely not too much.

Jahn sat on the other dining chair, near the one which now held the blue gown, and with a little encouragement Morgana joined him, perching on his knee. Perhaps he should be less entranced by her than he'd been when he'd first claimed her, but he was not. If anything, he wanted her more than ever. He began to unbutton her yellow dress.

"You should try the new dress on," he said, "to see if it fits."

"I've never had anything quite that color," she said, looking at him, not the gown.

"It will shimmer against your skin," he said, kissing her bare shoulder as he pushed the yellow sleeve down.

Without warning Morgana laughed out loud. "And where will I wear this fine shimmering dress? To the laundry? Perhaps to the market?"

Jahn did not laugh as he continued undressing her. "You will wear it for me, love."

As he worked at the fastenings on her yellow gown, she pushed off his vest, then moved to his trousers to work on the ties there.

"Why are you undressing me?" he teased. "I don't plan to try on any dress."

"Neither do I." She straddled him. "Not until much later."

AS he had for several previous nights, Rainer waited outside the door. The maids who always saw to her at night were gone, their job done. It wasn't as if any of them remained any longer than was necessary. When Danya was certain no one was about, she invited him in. Since that first evening there had been no more crying jags, no more breakdowns, and he had never again asked her what was wrong or criticized her dress or makeup.

But he was there. In the secrecy of her room they talked about little things that had no meaning. What foods they liked, what season of the year was their favorite and why, which of the ministers' daughters had the funniest laugh or the most bizarre fashion sense. And so on. He told her to call him Angelo, his given name, and sometimes she did. In public they never spoke. Deputy Rainer might nod to her in the dining hall, and she might do the same in his direction, but this friendship with Angelo—if that's indeed what it was—was private. It was as secret as her deal with the hooded man.

Danya kept expecting Angelo to make demands, but he

did not. He asked nothing of her. On occasion he'd kiss her on the forehead before he left her alone for the night, and on other occasions he simply bowed to her formally, as if she were already empress and he was her loyal servant.

Beyond this room, nothing had changed. Danya continued to assert herself with the palace residents. She continued to demand to be treated well, to demand only the best from all those around her. If she had truly thought to seduce the emperor, she'd been disappointed, since he was rarely about—and she'd had no time at all alone with him. That was just as well. The hooded man promised she'd be empress, so she left that chore to him.

She waited. She waited for the hooded man's demands and the return of her son. And for a few precious nights, Angelo Rainer helped her to find and hold onto a bit of sanity, and for that she loved him. A little.

Chapter Ten

✳

Two Weeks Until the First Night of the Summer Festival

MORGANA carried her midday meal—a large slice of bread with cheese and fruit, all wrapped in a square linen napkin, and a big mug of cider—outside the laundry room to sit and eat. It was too pretty a day to stay indoors. She wanted to breathe in the fresh air, and seeing the newly washed sheets whipping in the wind was somehow soothing. None of the other girls joined her on her outdoor excursion. In the early days she had hoped they might be interested in her beauty consulting business, but she'd quickly learned that they had other concerns. When they had the time to converse, they spoke of babies and grown children, of sewing and cooking, and, in Natties's case, of the aches and pains that came with age.

Morgana enjoyed having a little time to herself, so she often stepped outside to eat alone. As was usual, one of Jahn's friends happened along. Today it was Blane. She was not as naive as her husband seemed to think she was. Every day she ran into someone who insisted on walking with her to and from the laundry. Every day that she chose to eat outdoors, one of his friends happened by. Jahn was as protective as ever, and had asked these men to keep an eye on her when he could not. She might chastise him for being overly protective, but since his concern only proved that he cared, she did not.

"Hello, Blane," she said cheerfully.

He nodded to her, respectful and a little shy.

"Would you join me?" She held out her napkin, showing him her meal. "There's more here than I can possibly eat."

"No thank you, My Lady," he said with a crisp bow. "I have already eaten."

She smiled at him and patted the ground beside her. "Sit with me, then, if you have the time. And stop calling me 'My Lady.'"

He sighed at that request. After a moment's hesitation he did sit, a few feet away. "How is the, uh, laundry?" he asked.

"Never ending," Morgana said as she broke off a piece of bread and popped it into her mouth. "Tedious. Necessary." She shrugged her shoulders. "It certainly doesn't make for interesting conversation. How is your lovely wife?" She'd met Blane's lady once, when he'd brought her to the tavern for a bit of advice on a rash on her shoulder. She was a nice woman, and as shy as Blane himself was.

"She is very well. The cream you suggested worked wonders."

"Lovely to hear." She looked Blane in the eye. "Where is Jahn today?"

Blane turned slightly red. "With the emperor, of course."

"Of course." Morgana had often wondered why Jahn's friends could find the time to walk with her and visit over lunch while he could not. She also wondered how he had arranged lodging in the palace, a favor which was not shared with the others sentinels. She'd thought he'd been teasing when he'd said he was the emperor's favorite, but perhaps there was more to his job than he'd let on.

Blane did not stay with her for very long. He waited until she had almost finished her meal, then he surveyed the quiet, walled area filled with lines of sheets and crimson robes drying in the sun above a carpet of green grass. He said goodbye and went back in the same direction he'd come from.

Morgana rose from her seat on the ground and brushed a few crumbs from the linen shift she wore for working in the laundry. Before she could return to the laundry room for an afternoon of mending, a slightly shrill familiar voice called her name.

"I thought that was you." Two well-dressed ladies rushed toward Morgana as fast as their pointy-toed slippers would allow. "See, Anrid, I told you it was the sentinel's wife. Ana, isn't it?" Melusina asked.

"Yes," Morgana answered, happy to see that they continued to take her advice. Though there was no way to disguise their large bosoms, at least those attributes were now more covered than not. Neither of them wore face paint, and their hairstyles were simple and flattering. "Are you here to see the emperor?"

Anrid snorted, and Melusina shook her head. "No. We've come to collect a few belongings we left behind when we moved out."

"You no longer live in the palace?"

"No," Anrid answered. "The emperor found us husbands and made us leave."

If he planned to marry in a few days, that was likely a very good idea!

"Brothers," Melusina said. "They're both involved in trade." She stuck out her hand to display a huge red ring. "My husband, Haydon, deals in gems, many of them from the Turi Mountains. He trades in only the finest."

Anrid added, "My Jarold is in fabrics." She plucked at the sleeve of her elegant and tasteful frock. "I have never been so well dressed."

"So, it's going well?" Morgana asked.

The women looked at one another, and their expressions softened. "Yes," they answered as one.

"I did not expect to like being married," Melusina said. "But Haydon is handsome and sweet and generous, and I do not have to share him." She smiled. "He rather adores me."

"Jarold was very quiet in the early days," Anrid revealed, "but he's coming around." She, too, smiled. "He's coming around quite nicely. When we are alone, he isn't shy at all."

"I'm happy for you," Morgana said.

"We wanted to thank you," Melusina said. "Our husbands are well respected businessmen who would never have approved of our former manner of dress and adornment." She leaned in. "They know of our former positions here, of course, but they also think we're fine, well-bred ladies. Most of the time."

Nattie called, and Morgana turned to the open door. "It was lovely to see you. I'm glad to hear your lives are going well."

"We should visit one evening!" Anrid suggested.

"Certainly," Morgana said. Strangely enough, she had more in common with these women than she did with those she worked alongside. "Jahn and I are living on Level Seven."

The women looked at one another. "The witches' level?" Anrid said.

"There are no witches left on Level Seven," Morgana said. "Unless I am a witch!"

The women laughed, and Nattie called again—with less patience than before. Morgana waved and hurried back to her mending.

DANYA finally had a chance to get close to the emperor, just before dinner was to be served. He never ate with the rest of the palace residents. She supposed he was afraid of being poisoned. He did, however, make frequent and all-too-brief appearances. Usually she was unable to get near. Tonight, she was determined to make her way to his side.

They barely knew one another! The hooded man's assurances aside, how was the emperor supposed to know to choose her if they had never spent any time together?

She made her way toward the tall, crimson-clad man. He was handsome enough, she would give him that much, and he wore his smallish gold crown well, as if it were as much a part of him as the oddly streaked hair. A minister's chubby wife stepped in front of Danya, and almost without thinking, Danya elbowed the woman aside and placed herself before the emperor.

"My Lord Emperor," she said, curtseying and thrusting her bosom forward so he would be sure to appreciate the wares she had gone to so much trouble to show. "I do hope you will be joining us for dinner this evening."

He stared at her strangely, with an air that seemed to her almost like pity. Pity and annoyance. "I'm afraid I will not be able to do so, Lady Danya."

She looked him in the eye, determined to evoke something other than pity. "I was so hoping we could get to know one another better, before the First Night arrives."

"I will see what I can do to clear my schedule," he said in a tone of voice that screamed of dismissal. There were others waiting to speak to him, others clamoring for his time. Danya did not step aside.

She tried to imagine seducing the emperor, either before or after the night came for him to make his decision. She tried to picture herself kissing this powerful man, stripping for him, opening herself for him in all ways . . . and she could not. When she imagined giving all of herself to any man, she saw only Angelo Rainer. This was a disaster.

Danya curtseyed again and stepped aside. After returning to her assigned table she barely ate her dinner, and she was quite sure she managed to insult all those sitting around her, though later she would not remember precisely what she said. Something about the deputy minister's daughter eating too much and threatening to burst out of her ordinary little frock, and perhaps something else about a man laughing too harshly and gratingly. Rainer was not here tonight; he often ate alone, before or after they met to talk and she allowed herself to relax in his company.

She left before anyone else at her table had finished their meal, hurrying for her room. Angelo would be there, she imagined, or else he would join her very soon. He always waited for the maids to finish their jobs for the day, and since Danya had told the servants that she did not need help getting ready for bed, they finished their work early. They put out water and soap; they turned down the sheets on her bed; they lit the oil lamps and the fire . . . and then they left her alone.

Though she had enjoyed Angelo's company in the past few days, she finally realized she had to let him go, too. He was too close. She should've been able to make the emperor aware of her intentions, to concentrate completely on him, and instead she had seen only Angelo!

He was waiting in her anteroom on this night, and when she slammed the door to her bedchamber, he joined her. He looked glad to see her, happy for this short time they had together.

"You again," she said, walking with purpose toward the fireplace as if she needed the heat on this warm night, holding out her hands to suck up the warmth of the flame.

He walked up behind her. "Yes, me again," he said calmly. "What's wrong?"

"Nothing is wrong." She turned to face him, even though she did not relish the idea of looking at his face while she did what had to be done. "I spoke to the emperor tonight."

Finely shaped eyebrows arched slightly. "Did you?"

"Yes. I don't think he likes me very much."

"You have not given him reason, have you?"

"No. I was hoping that perhaps you could help me gain entrance to his bedchamber before he makes his decision." She smiled. "I know of only one way to sway the emperor, and I can hardly do it in a crowded dining hall."

Angelo's face fell. "Danya, you can't . . ."

Danya thought of her son, she thought of the hooded man and felt his chill upon her neck. She silently chastised herself for allowing Angelo Rainer to get so close that he clouded her reason. "I will do whatever I have to do to become empress," she interrupted. "If you can't help me, then get out."

"Danya . . ."

"I thought if I pretended to be nice to you, you might help me, but I can see that's not going to happen. Just leave, and don't come back. I don't need your help to do what has to be done. I will find my own way into the emperor's bedchamber."

By the firelight, she could see Angelo's face change. It fell; it was filled with disappointment and hurt and perhaps even a touch of hate. No, not hate. Angelo Rainer did not hate, not the way she did. All the more reason to let him go. To *make* him go. "Get out."

He bowed crisply and did as she commanded.

Ten Days Until the First Night of the Summer Festival

JAHN glared at an angry Minister Calvyno. This was a disaster of major proportions. He did not believe that his brother, Alix, was capable of what he'd been accused of . . . No, that was not entirely true. Jahn knew full well that there was a part of Alix which was capable of anything, but the younger twin had always had such control over his volatile emotions and his deeply seated anger.

Lady Verity of Mirham dead in an accident, and now this. His contest had turned decidedly fatal, and he could not allow himself to believe that it was coincidence that two of his potential brides were dead.

"The foreigners from Claennis are being entertained," Calvyno said, "but I do not expect them to remain charitable for very long. They want justice, as do the Tryfynians."

One of the potential brides had been murdered, ostensibly by Alix, and everyone expected Jahn to handle the matter immediately. Until he knew more, there was nothing he could do. He would have to hear from Alix's own mouth that he'd done murder before he would believe.

Jahn had thought rejecting a princess and a few well-bred ladies would be the worst of his problems, but that was not to be the case. The very real possibility of war between Tryfyn and Columbyana now existed, and Jahn did not want to be an emperor who led his country into battle. General Hydd would be pleased to have the opportunity to enter a time of warfare once again, but that was not what Jahn wanted for Columbyana. War was sometimes necessary, but if it could be avoided, he would do so. He certainly didn't want to go to war over a misunderstanding.

He refused to condemn his brother on the word of a handful of hotheaded men looking for revenge. "See that the foreign guards are well entertained." Jahn looked at Calvyno, free to speak his mind when they were alone. "Keep them intoxicated and well laid." That should buy a few days, at least. "Tell the Tryfynians that I am studying the matter and will meet with them when I've come to a decision." Where was Alix? Jahn could not come to a decision until he knew what had happened on the trip from Tryfyn.

Calvyno was a fine, loyal minister, one who did not hesitate to speak his mind. That was a trait Jahn respected—but it wasn't always convenient. "My Lord, you have been too often absent in weeks past. I sometimes look for you late at night and you are nowhere to be found."

"I've been ill," Jahn said halfheartedly.

Calvyno bowed. "There are a mere ten days until the start of the Summer Festival, and we will have much to do in those days. This new turn of events makes it imperative that you be *present*. I'm glad to see you looking well and hope that if I look for you on any evening in the near future, I'll find you where you are supposed to be."

"Yes, yes," Jahn said with a wave of his hand. "You will

find me." Arrangements would have to be made for some-one to fetch him if the minister of foreign affairs came calling.

The harried minister left the imperial office properly reassured. When Jahn was alone, he sat in a large chair and dropped his head into his hands. In the beginning he had imagined studying an eager gathering of beautiful, appro-priate women, weeding out those whose appearance did not please him, asking questions to discover who among them might have some intelligence, studying their smiles to see who among them was amiable, and then choosing. The worst part of that scenario, of course, was sending away the rejects.

He had never imagined this. Two women were dead, and he could not help but grieve, knowing that if he had not called them here, they would be alive and well in their homes. The one potential bride in residence—Lady Danya—had been annoying the other ladies of the palace with her arrogance and her coldness, and on the few occa-sions he had been in her company, he had not found her to be at all suitable or pleasant. Another, his own Ana, had already been chosen, though she remained ignorant of that fact. She had been taken into his bed, and by the laws of many in the country was already empress. What of the other two? How had his simple plan gone so wrong?

It was a frightening possibility, but Jahn had to ask him-self if it was possible that all the brides were in danger. Even Morgana.

ON this particular day Morgana had stabbed her fingers more times than she could count. Her stomach roiled, just a little bit. She was hungry. She needed a nap. A pretty young girl, one of Nattie's nieces, also saw to the mending, and four others washed. Morgana drew a drop of blood, and it fell upon the linen shift she wore. The shift was plain and quite unattractive, but she was happy to have it. At least she would not ruin either of her own everyday dresses in this work, not even if Nattie set her to scrubbing sheets and stained shirts.

Would she ever have the opportunity to wear the beautiful gown Jahn had bought for her? At this rate, it was unlikely. If she was with child, as she suspected, she might outgrow the gown in a matter of weeks. It was still too early to be sure, and she would not say anything to Jahn until she was positive.

Offering beauty advice was so much more fun than mending. Extra earnings aside, she would have to talk to Jahn about this new employment. It was hideously tedious. Seeing Melusina and Anrid the other day, recognizing the amazing changes in their appearance and in their lives, made her long to do something more than mend crimson robes and linen shirts.

A rakish-looking man with a beautiful woman in tow rushed into the room from outdoors. No one else paid him much mind, but Morgana's head snapped up at the intrusion. She felt unusually queasy, and the hint of illness made her cranky. "You're not supposed to come in this way," she said, annoyed that the couple was having so much fun while she was forced to mend an endless pile of clothing.

The dark-haired man who looked more than a little unscrupulous glared at her, and Morgana immediately regretted speaking.

"Do you not know who this is, girl?" Nattie asked. "This is Prince Alixandyr. He comes and goes as he pleases."

Must be nice . . . Before Morgana had an opportunity to apologize, Nattie continued. "Forgive her, m'lord. She's new."

"How was I to know he's a prince?" Morgana asked. "He doesn't look like much to me," she whispered in a voice that carried more than she intended. Jahn was worth a hundred of this ne'er-do-well prince, she would imagine.

Nattie studied Prince Alixandyr with a more critical eye. "You do look a mite rough, m'lord."

The prince smiled tiredly at Nattie and ignored Morgana altogether. Just as well. "I've had a trying journey and want only to rest for a while before I resume my duties. A few days of complete privacy away from prying eyes and questions are all that I need, and for that to happen, no one can know I'm home. Can I rely on your silence?" He looked about the room. "I ask for discretion from all of you, if you please."

"How about discretion, a tub of hot water, and a warm meal?" Nattie asked. "I think I can even scrounge up some of your favorite sweet bread."

Without warning the prince hugged Nattie, who squealed in surprise and blushed like a girl. He then kissed her cheek. "I would be forever grateful."

Nattie tried to look proper as the prince withdrew, and Morgana could not help but smile. Perhaps the prince was not such a bad sort after all. A wearying bit of traveling might explain his rough appearance.

"I've never known you to be so gregarious, m'lord," Nattie said with a smile. Then she glanced at the prince's companion. "Would you like discretion, water, and food for two, m'lord?"

"I would."

"You'll have it," Nattie assured her prince.

When the prince and his woman were gone, Nattie looked at every woman in the room with calculating eyes. "Not a one of you will say a word to anyone about who you saw here today. The prince has asked for discretion, and he will get it. Is that understood?"

Everyone nodded, even Morgana. Still, she had to wonder if anyone would care overly much about the return of Prince Alixandyr and a woman who was obviously to him what Melusina and Anrid had once been to the emperor. Princes were even less worthy than emperors.

And his woman had *no* need of Morgana's beauty advice.

* * *

JAHN made use of hidden passages to travel from one level to another on the occasions when there were many palace residents about, using the stairway between Level Eight and Level Seven. All the while, on the public stairway or the hidden, he wondered if he could pull off this charade much longer. He dreaded Morgana's reaction to the truth, hated even more knowing she was going to be so angry she might never forgive him. Love or no, the string of lies had gotten out of hand.

Not all was lies. He did love her; she did love him. He had never expected to find love in this contest, but he could not deny that was what he'd discovered with Morgana. Could he keep it? Did she love him enough to forgive all that he had done?

After learning of Princess Edlyn's death, he should've immediately collected Morgana from the laundry, told her the truth, and locked her away until she forgave him. The murder of a princess who might have many enemies and a tragic riding accident might have nothing at all in common, but he could not be certain of that until he had proof.

He could not pretend that nothing had changed, and he could not continue to hide from his responsibilities for many hours of the day, as he had in weeks past. An emperor did not work sunup to sundown like a blacksmith or a cobbler, but was on call to his ministers and his people at all hours of the day and night. With these newest developments, he knew he could no longer continue to live another, simpler life after the sun set.

Jahn waited for Morgana's return in the room he had claimed for them, anxious to see her after a long day of meetings with his ministers. He needed to see her, he needed the respite he always found in her company.

He didn't relish the idea of sending three unwanted women home when he took Morgana as his bride, any more than he looked forward to smoothing the waters with the king of Tryfyn or sending his condolences to Lady Verity's family. He had no choice. When he'd begun this foolish contest, it had seemed like a lark. That was no longer true, as he found himself planning a lifetime with one special woman who was like no other.

The door opened and Morgana stepped into the room, bidding a sweet and tired farewell to Iann, who, at Jahn's instruction, had "accidentally" run into her as she left the laundry, as one sentinel or another did every day. Ignorant of her status or not, Morgana was empress, and she deserved an escort. From now on, a single man could not suffice. How would he explain that away?

She smiled brightly when she saw him, even though her eyes were tired. Perhaps allowing her to work, as she'd said she wanted to do, was a mistake. An empress should have nothing to do but to make herself pretty and entertain if it pleased her and love her emperor. Morgana should be waited upon night and day . . . and she would be, very soon.

She walked into his arms and melted there, seeking comfort as he held her, sighing deeply.

"You're tired."

"I am," she responded.

"Tomorrow you will not go to the laundry," Jahn insisted. It was no small concern that two of the bridal candidates were dead. One had been an accident and one an assassination, but that did not make Morgana seem any less fragile to him.

She laughed lightly. "I will not quit because I have had a few long days. We will need the extra money when the babies start to come."

Babies. Jahn's heart leapt at the thought. There would be babies, of course, and he would not be at all surprised if Morgana was carrying an heir very soon. If she was not already with child. The production of an heir was important; it was the reason for this bridal contest. And yet, it was also secondary to what he had found.

"I've been given a raise in my salary," he said. "We'll

have everything we need, and you will not have to work at all."

"Why did you get a raise in your salary?"

He was tired of the lies, tired of spinning one story after another. "There are some things I cannot tell you," he said. "Not yet. Just trust me in this. Let me take care of you."

"I knew you were special to someone other than me," she teased, and then Morgana rose up onto her toes and kissed him, and they shared the kiss of a man and woman who knew one another well. It was the kiss of lovers and partners, of friends and companions, of man and wife.

The way she undressed him was gentle and insistent, and he took great care with removing her plain linen shift. They came together in a way that was inevitable and important, and he was able to temporarily dismiss all the problems of a country, all the pains of his mistakes.

His flesh against hers, as they fell into the bed they shared, was a simple pleasure he had never before paid much mind. Morgana was different from other women. She was his. His wife. His empress. The last and only woman he would ever love.

"I am no longer tired," she said as she kissed his throat and her hands roamed wonderfully. "There was a moment this evening when I thought I would have to ask Iann to carry me up the stairs, I was so weary, and yet now I feel a burst of new energy. My heart swells and my body sings, all because you hold me. You are magical," she whispered into his ear. "Your magic has changed my life. How did I ever live without you?"

How did I ever live without you? Those words seemed more important and heartfelt than the oft-repeated "I love you." The words touched Jahn in a way he had not expected, and in another way they hurt. He did not deserve Morgana's love, not yet. He would, though. He would earn her love again and again, if he had to.

He lost himself inside her, in a way he had come to need as much as air to breathe and water to drink. There was pleasure and more; there was joining and joy and shared release.

They lay entwined for a while, breathing hard and barely moving, before Jahn spoke. "I swore to you that I would protect that which is mine," he said.

"You did." Morgana ran her hand up his bare back, seeking connection even now.

"I promise you now that you will never want for anything in this life. I will give you all that any woman might possibly desire, and you will never again think to seek employment of any kind. You will be my wife and the mother of my children. That is all the employment you will ever need."

"I only wanted to help . . ."

"I will provide; you will make our home. Wherever it might be," he added, wondering how she would like their quarters on Level Eight when he introduced them to her. They were much finer than this room, and were worlds away from a rustic room over a tavern, a room which had become their first happy home.

As Morgana fell asleep in his arms, Jahn wondered . . . How forgiving was his empress? Was their love enough to overcome what he had done?

KRISTO traveled well into the night, putting as many miles as possible between himself and the mercenaries he'd met with earlier in the day. They were ready for whatever might happen—Rikka had prepared them for every contingency.

As it had in days past, his mind went to Lady Rikka, former empress and broken female. She would be dead by now, one way or another. Had she bled to death or had her assassin Trinity been able to exact his revenge? He did not know, and frankly did not care. Kristo was more concerned with what lay ahead than he was with what lay behind. Rikka was dead, and that was all that mattered. He would miss her hatred and her bitter need for vengeance, but it wasn't as if he needed her. She'd done her part, and she'd done it very well.

When he saw the palace rising in the moonlight, he smiled as he realized, for the first time, that his daughter was there. Not just in Arthes, not miles away waiting to be found, but in the palace itself. The knowledge came to him in a burst, clear and real and indisputable. He had worried for nothing. Lady Danya could be disposed of or dismissed, and Kristo would make his daughter empress and his grandson emperor. Emperor Jahn had done his best to keep peace, to amuse and pacify the people of his country, to keep the people happy and safe. What Kristo wanted, what his grandson would want, would be quite the opposite.

Absolute power awaited.

Without Rikka's well-known name and political connections, gaining entrance to the palace would be a bit trickier for Kristo than he'd planned, but he did have Lady Danya to help him. The girl would do whatever he asked. There was no reason to tell her, just yet, that she wouldn't be needed to fill the position of empress after all.

RAINER positioned himself not too far from Lady Danya's room, hiding in an alcove while she made her way down the wide hallway to retire for the evening.

She looked older and more tired with every passing day. A face which had once been beautiful was turning haggard and lined, as if she were being drained from the inside by something dark and ugly. The woman he saw treat everyone with disregard and disdain was not the woman he had come to know on the long journey from her home to Arthes, and on evenings spent talking and sometimes crying here in this palace—before she had callously dismissed him from her life.

Something was wrong. He should not care what bothered Lady Danya. She would make a totally unsuitable empress in so many ways. She was not pure of body or of heart, and she had not only *not* charmed the residents of the palace, she'd blatantly made enemies of many of them and simply annoyed the rest. If not for the tears she'd shed against his chest, if not for the handful of late-night conversations which revealed to him the real woman, he might think her cold and simply unpleasant, but something was wrong. Something was eating her alive from the inside out.

He should not care what it was, but he did. Danya was more than she revealed to others, and she had touched his heart. After she closed her chamber door, Rainer exited the alcove and sat on the cold stone floor to lean against the wall, taking a position where he could see the door to her bedchamber. It was going to be a long night, but he could not leave her alone. Even if she did not know he was here . . . he would watch over her, the only way he knew how.

JAHN was not happy to be called away in the middle of the night, but it wasn't as if he could sleep. When Morgana had awakened and he'd ordered a large, hot meal delivered to their chambers, she had eaten ravenously and spoken with vigor about her day, almost halfheartedly mentioning that she'd seen Prince Alixandyr and a woman slip into the palace in secret. She was not supposed to tell anyone that she'd seen the prince, but that didn't include her husband, she argued. She could not be expected to keep secrets from him.

The prince was a rather rough-looking fellow, to hear her tell it.

So, Alix was here somewhere, and he did not want anyone to know. Not yet.

When Calvyno asked—through Blane—for a late-night meeting, not too long after Morgana had fallen asleep, Jahn did not argue that the minister could wait until morning. It wasn't as if he could sleep. He took the hidden stairway from an adjoining room on the all but deserted Level Seven to his chambers on Level Eight, and with Calvyno and Father Braen discussed the choice which was still—or so they thought—to be made. With Princess Edlyn, the natural choice in their opinions, murdered, the young Lady Verity victim of a terrible accident, and the acceptable Lady Morgana refusing the invitation, the field had been narrowed to three. Lady Danya, whom no one considered acceptable, and two potential brides who had not yet arrived: Lady Belavalari and Lady Leyla.

Jahn nodded often and tried to pay attention to their arguments for Belavalari and Leyla, should either of these women actually arrive. He was tempted to tell them that the new empress slept in this very palace—well loved, possibly with child, and ignorant of her position—but he did not. He would not tell them, or anyone else, before he informed Morgana of her good fortune. Would she consider her position good fortune? Or would she despise him for all the lies?

They left him in a foul mood as he pondered the days ahead. He paced, he sat and stewed in his own confusion and anger, and he cursed—at times quite loudly.

When there was a knock at his door, he was not surprised. Had Alix come to tell him he was home? Had Morgana found him?

Was someone else dead?

He was surprised to hear that his visitor was a "gift" from the king of Tryfyn, a woman, according to the sentinel. Jahn did not rise from his chair as he directed the nighttime caller to enter. He had no use for any woman other than Morgana, but this one might know something of Alix, and of the murder of Princess Edlyn. Perhaps she knew the truth.

"King Bhaltair sent you?" he asked.

"Yes." The woman who walked into the room, as the sentinel closed the door behind her, was undeniably gorgeous and sensuous. She also matched Morgana's quick but detailed description of the woman who had arrived this afternoon with Alix.

Jahn maintained his calm, at least outwardly. "I have heard a distressing rumor that Princess Edlyn was murdered."

"I'm afraid that is true." She had a lovely and strange accent.

"I also heard that my brother, Prince Alixandyr, did the killing."

"That is not true."

The sheer force of the relief that struck Jahn was strong. The death of a princess was a terrible thing, but to think that his own brother had done the deed was more than he could bear. He had no reason to believe this woman over those who accused Alix, but he did. "Thank the gods. I knew he couldn't do such a thing, but I have received word from more than one quarter that he did this unspeakable deed. Where is he? Do you know?"

The woman hesitated a moment, and then she shook her head. She was not a very good liar.

"You are Sanura, correct?" he asked.

"I am. You have heard of me?"

"The sentinel who just yesterday delivered word of the princess's death told me that Alix escaped with a blue woman named Sanura. Though you are no longer blue, you do match the rest of his rather vivid description." Yes, she was strikingly beautiful and sensuous, very much the goddess she had been described. "There are also at least two Tryfynian soldiers in Arthes who insist upon taking Alix's head, as well as two very insistent wild men in residence who are adamant about killing Alix for touching you."

"Paki and Kontar are here?" she asked.

"Yes. We've been doing our best to keep them occupied, but they remain quite insistent on killing my brother." Women and drink would occupy them only for so long, he imagined. "I cannot allow that to happen."

"Don't hurt them." Sanura took a step toward him. Dressed seductively, bold in her actions . . . was she here to seduce him? "They're only doing their duty."

A few months ago he would have gladly allowed this

woman to seduce him, but no more. "To protect you," he said.

"Yes."

"Where is Alix?" he asked again.

"I told you, I do not know."

"I don't believe you."

Sanura stopped while she was still a few feet away. "You know," she whispered.

"I know what?" Jahn snapped impatiently.

Her eyes lit up. "You know about Alix's struggle. At least—you suspect that something is not right with him."

Jahn fought to keep his face expressionless. "Don't be ridiculous."

"The shadows, the dark battle, the tight control . . ."

Unable to remain seated any longer, Jahn placed both hands on the arms of his chair and stood slowly. "You don't have any idea what you're talking about."

"I know too well, I'm sad to say," Sanura said. "For years a darkness has lived within Alix, wishing to rise and take power, to take control. His determination has kept that darkness deep within until I unknowingly unleashed that which Alix has fought all these years. What you do not know, what I have just come to understand, is that both parts, he who fought and he who tried to rise, are one and the same. Alix was fractured, but he is fractured no more."

"So you do know where he is."

"Yes." Sanura reached into the folded fabric across her midsection and pulled out a dagger. "I came here to murder you."

Jahn knew there were those in the palace who had expected betrayal from the prince, had perhaps even desired it, for a long time. He had even known that there were dark moments when Alix had desired as much himself. "Did he send you?"

"No," Sanura said emphatically. "He plans to do the assassination himself, but I cannot allow that to happen. He will never recover from such a dark deed."

"Neither will I, I imagine," Jahn said, hurt beyond belief to know that it had come to this. He pointed to the dagger. "What made you think you could kill me with *that*?"

"My plan was simple. I would get close to you, promising all that I was meant to give, and when you were lost in desire, I would stab you through the heart."

"Ouch." Jahn laid a hand over his heart. "Lucky for me I have enough womanly trouble at the moment and would not let you get so close."

Sanura tossed the knife onto the bed. "I am responsible for the change in Alix, though it was unknowing. I would never hurt him, never." She looked boldly at Jahn, unflinching. "I love him."

"Enough to commit murder in his name?"

She glanced at her weapon, which was now out of reach. Did she so soon regret tossing it aside?

"Apparently not," she said.

"So, what now?" Jahn asked, losing what little was left of his patience. "Less than three months ago I set in motion a silly contest for the position of empress, and at this moment two of the candidates are dead, killed en route by accident or malicious intent; my brother is wanted dead by two burly, saber-wielding madmen and more than a handful of Tryfynian soldiers; Alix appears to have lost the battle he's fought for so long; and I . . ."

"You?" Sanura prodded.

Jahn shook his head. "My own problems matter little, at the moment. Where is Alix? Is there any way to save him from this?" He tiredly ran a hand through his hair. "As if you would know."

"But I do know," Sanura said. She stepped closer, and for a moment he wondered if she had hidden another knife in her form-fitting clothing. "You love Alix, and so do I. Together we can save him. Will you help me, My Lord Emperor?"

After a moment of deliberation he asked, "What do you need?"

Sanura sighed. "Time, m'lord. I need time."

"There are ten days remaining until the first night of the Summer Festival, ten short days until I will be obligated to make my choice." Not even this woman, an unexpected ally, needed to know that his choice had already been made. "Will that be enough time?"

"I hope so, m'lord. With all my heart, I hope so."

Chapter Eleven

MORGANA woke with the sun, ready to face another dull and trying day in the palace laundry in spite of Jahn's insistence that her time there was done. He'd said those things last night only because he didn't like to see her tired. Her husband, however, had other ideas. He said he was due some time off, and he planned to spend the next few days with her. She argued with him, but just a little bit. In truth, she liked the idea of being nothing more than his wife and eventually mother to his children. They would get by, just as other sentinels and their families did.

It was strange that he'd been given a raise in pay and a holiday at the same time, but she would not complain. She liked the idea of having Jahn to herself for a few days, and she did not for one minute question how they would spend that time. Food would be delivered to their door. They would spend most of that time without clothing, she suspected. They would laugh and love and plan for the future, and she would tell him again how much he meant to her.

Over a lavish breakfast which had been delivered by a grumpy Iann, Jahn asked her how she wanted to spend her leisure time—when he was not available to entertain her. Did she wish for paper and pen so she could write poetry? Did she wish to take up painting? What about needlework? She punched him playfully in the arm when he had the nerve to mention needlework, after her days spent mending clothes. She didn't care if she never saw a needle again as long as she lived!

She wanted to tell him that she thought she might be with child, but she still wasn't sure. She would be so horribly disappointed if she wasn't, and so would Jahn, if she knew him at all. There was no reason to risk causing him pain. She would share the news when she was certain. Still, she found herself asking, as she reached for a piece of fruit, "Jahn, will we continue to live in this room once we have children?"

He looked taken aback. "Are you . . ."

"Not to my knowing, but I have been thinking . . . it's bound to happen soon."

"I don't think we will still be here when the time comes."

"Why not?"

"Things change," he said cryptically. "I do promise you that you and our children will be well taken care of, always."

"I never doubted that."

Morgana smoothly moved into his lap. "I don't want to live here when we have children," she said. "I want a small house with a garden, and a grassy place where the children can play in the sunshine. I want my own kitchen, and I will learn to cook and to do my own laundry. I don't want sentinels outside my door at all hours of the night and day, or an escort every time I go to the market." She smiled. "I will be the mistress of my own house, our own palace, no matter how small it might be. I don't want to share our lives and our home with an emperor who once dared to command me to present myself for his inspection." She huffed in indignation at the memory.

"We did just get here," Jahn argued, and he looked

slightly pained, a bit annoyed. Did he not want the same things she did?

"And we don't have to move out immediately, but"—she draped her arms around his neck—"think about it."

"I love you, Ana."

"And I love you," she said, still surprised by how easily the words she had never even dreamed to speak came to her.

She was perfectly, completely happy with this life she had never known was possible for her. Her curse was warmed and gone; her husband loved her; she would give him a child—and then more, in years to come. She no longer thought concealing her curse to be a lie, since it was gone. Entirely, wonderfully gone.

DANYA had not been awake very long when there was a knock on her door. She answered sharply, and one of the many servants who saw to her needs walked into the room.

The girl did not smile. No one did, not at Danya. "My Lady, your uncle has come calling. He insists on seeing you right away."

"My uncle?" Danya asked impatiently.

"He says you should be expecting his arrival," the girl said.

Danya felt a chill walk up her spine. It was him. It was the hooded man, come to demand her alliance in return for her son's safety. He was here to give her what she wanted, the position of empress, and at the same time offer safety to the child she'd believed buried long ago. There would be a price, though. He had been very clear about that part of the bargain.

"Should I show him in?" the girl asked, when Danya did not immediately respond.

"Yes," Danya said in an emotionless voice. "Have my uncle escorted to the anteroom and inform him that I will join him shortly."

She needed to dress, to make herself pretty, to steel her spine. Meeting the cold hooded man again would not be an easy task.

"For Ethyn," Danya whispered when the maid was gone.

She took her time getting ready, even though she knew the hooded man would not count patience among his qualities. More than once her mind went to Angelo and the way he had comforted her without expecting any comfort in return. She thought about the solace he had offered, and how his brief but precious friendship might've saved her sanity. It had been a weakness to claim that easy time with him. More than once she had thought about telling him everything and asking for his help, but that wasn't possible. Not only would such a weakness endanger Ethyn's life, it would also endanger Angelo's. It was best to let go of silly notions of being saved and concentrate on pleasing the cold man she had made her ally. And still, she tucked his handkerchief into her bodice, and it gave her strength.

When she was prepared, physically and mentally, Danya made the short trip from her bedchamber to the adjoining room, where she might have taken visitors if she had made a point of making friends. She had never seen the hooded man's face, and at first she did not think the ordinary-looking man sitting upon the sparest chair in her anteroom could possibly be the monster she knew. Perhaps this was someone who worked with the hooded man, someone who did his bidding as she did. And then her visitor lifted his head and his eyes met hers, and she almost fainted from the rush of evil that emanated from him. Reddish brown hair and pleasant appearance aside, there was no mistake that this was the hooded man.

"You test my patience," he said crisply.

"An empress is allowed to make others wait for her. Even you," Danya said more bravely than she'd imagined she could.

The man smiled, and Danya trembled. "What am I to call you?" she asked, adding in an insolent tone, "Uncle."

"Uncle Kristo," he said, rising slowly. Standing, he did not seem so small. "Kristo Stoyan, your mother's younger brother, if anyone asks. And yes, that is my real name, in case you're wondering. I expect you will make the proper introductions as soon as possible. It is only right that a representative of your family be here when you're chosen empress, after all."

"How is Ethyn?" she asked.

"Well, at last report," Kristo Stoyan responded.

"When I am empress, you will have him brought to me?" She should not reveal such longing, she should not let this horrible man know how she felt, but she could not help herself. She wanted to touch Ethyn's cheek and hear his heartbeat against her ear and make him laugh. She wanted to hold him in her arms. Any sacrifice was worthwhile if it meant he would be safe.

"Yes. But first, we have business to tend to," Kristo said as he took a terrifying step toward Danya. "There is a lady in the palace I must speak to most urgently. Her name is Lady Morgana Ramsden."

"She's the one who refused the emperor's offer, is she not?"

"Yes, she has apparently refused, but she's here in the palace. Somewhere," he added in a less than tolerant voice.

"What are you going to do to her?"

"Trust me, you do not want to know."

"I haven't met Lady Morgana," Danya said honestly. "I had no idea she was here in the palace." She wondered where the lady, her competition, might be. Lady Morgana had not made herself known at any of the palace functions or meals, and everyone had been talking about how she'd refused the emperor's summons, so if she was here, there would be gossip. "I don't believe she's here at all."

Kristo didn't like that answer. "If I find out you're lying to me . . ."

"I have promised to do anything to save my son, and I will keep my end of the bargain," Danya said. "That has not changed. I don't care what you do to Lady Morgana in order to get her out of our way." Her heart leapt. "What does she look like?"

Kristo furrowed his brow. "I'm not sure. Blonde like her mother, I think. Pretty, certainly, given her parentage."

"I hate to tell you this, but pretty and blonde does not narrow the field much. The palace is filled with ministers' wives and daughters and more distant relatives, as well as a number of women who seem to be here strictly for more pleasurable pursuits. If the woman you seek is not using her real name . . ."

"Why would she not use her real name?" Kristo snapped.

"I don't know! But if she refused the emperor and yet is, for some reason, here, it makes some sense, does it not?"

He smiled at her, and she wished he had not. "Of course. You're very clever, Lady Danya."

"Empresses should be clever, don't you think?"

She turned her back on him so she would not have to witness that awful grin for a moment longer, and that was a mistake. He crept up on her soundlessly, and before she could prepare herself, he placed a stilling hand on her shoulder. "You're prettier than you were when I saw you last," he whispered, his breath on her neck as cold as she remembered.

She knew that was not true.

His hand snaked over her shoulder, and icy fingers brushed the swell of her bosom. If those fingers dipped beneath the fabric, they would touch the plain linen of Angelo's handkerchief. "I imagine you're missing your lover by now. It's been a long time for you, hasn't it?"

Danya gathered every ounce of strength she possessed to step away from the cold man. "Don't touch me," she commanded, taking him by surprise. She turned to face him. "We have a common purpose, and I will do what you ask in order to win the position of empress. But you are not to touch me again, is that understood?"

He seemed amused by her command. "If that is what you wish. However, if ever you change your mind . . ."

"I will not."

He gave her an exaggerated bow. "At your service, My Lady, in whatever manner you choose. Or don't." When he looked her squarely in the face again, his eyes were stone cold. "Demand that I be given quarters in the palace until the Summer Festival arrives and the emperor makes his choice. Introduce me to everyone you know as your beloved Uncle Kristo." His hand snapped up and he grasped her throat, much as Ennis had once done. Angelo wasn't here to save her this time; she'd sent him away. "And find Lady Morgana."

IT was easy enough to pretend to be away from the palace, in order to give Sanura the time she required. Even with all that needed to be done, those who served the emperor would believe that he'd gone on an extended hunting trip. Jahn was not at all opposed to the idea of spending a few more days as nothing more than Morgana's husband. They could laugh, they could sleep and make love. The scene was warmly domestic and ordinary and he loved it, for the short amount of time it actually lasted.

Late in the afternoon they were interrupted by a knock on the door of their Level Seven bedchamber. Blane was apologetic, but Minister Calvyno insisted that Jahn's presence was necessary, and the savvy minister, having seen the emperor's favorite sentinels on duty, rather than out of the palace with the man they so loyally served, knew something was afoot.

Jahn's annoyance at being called from his bedchamber and his wife to deal with matters of his station changed to alarm when he heard the news. Lady Verity of Mirham was alive, but she had barely survived an attempt on her life—an attempt made by the man Jahn had sent to collect her.

First Princess Edlyn and now this. His initial seemingly unnecessary concern was validated. Someone was killing, or was attempting to kill, the bridal candidates. Jahn saw that those responsible for the murder attempt were imprisoned. The idiots had believed themselves successful and were living in the palace, eating and drinking and enjoying the life of those blessed to be in the court. Sentinels were sent south and east to meet and warn those who had not yet returned—if they had survived thus far.

Minister Calvyno was most distressed that Lady Verity had chosen to leave the palace as the intended bride of the sentinel who had saved her life, but Jahn cared nothing for that detail. There was now one less woman to send away rejected, when the time came.

At this rate, Lady Danya would be the only woman rejected! He would not be sorry to see her leave. Neither would anyone else, from all that he saw and heard. She was an unpleasant and inappropriate woman, but he had not sensed evil in her. Still, was it possible that she was somehow involved in the misfortune of her competition?

It was late in the evening before he was able to climb the stairs to Level Seven and Morgana, whom he'd left alone for too many hours after his promise that they would have some time alone. Jahn had changed from the emperor's crimson robes to the green uniform which he wore in his disguise as a common sentinel and husband. He was leading two lives, one filled with power and responsibility, the other simpler and happier. Could he combine the two well when the time came? Would Morgana accept him as emperor as she had accepted him as sentinel?

There were two sentinels at Morgana's doorway on this night, two guards who snapped to attention when Jahn appeared with two other sentinels behind him. The stairwell had been deserted, as the palace was quiet this late at night. Morgana would be asleep, he supposed. He wondered if he should wake her.

As he reached for the door latch, Iann said, in an ominously lowered voice, "My Lord, your lady has visitors. You might wish to wait until they depart."

"At this hour? Who . . ." Before he could finish, a familiar laugh drifted through the doorway. "Melusina?" he asked, horrified.

"And the other, Mistress Anrid," Iann said. "Apparently they have sought out your lady for more beauty advice with which to impress their new husbands."

"Collect me when they're gone." Jahn turned on his heel to escape, but it was too late. A woman's voice sounded closer on the other side of the door, and the latch clicked as it was turned. The door opened, and a seductive voice called a delighted, "My Lord Emperor, how lovely! Have you come here looking for us?" With that Anrid grasped Jahn's shirtsleeve and pulled him into the room.

EVEN though they had discussed visiting just a few days earlier, Morgana had been surprised when Melusina and Anrid had shown up at her door. They were newly married and happier than they'd thought they'd be with their husbands, and they were also anxious for more beauty and fashion help from Ana Devlyn.

Strangely enough, Morgana had enjoyed their company more and more as the night wore on. Perhaps these ladies were very different from her, but she liked them. They were bright and funny, and they laughed well and often. Without the low-cut bodices and face paint which had once marked them as loose women, they looked like many of the ladies Morgana had known throughout her life—though these two were much more open and honest about their lives. In fact, they were honest to a fault.

Morgana could not be so open. She really didn't want to share with these two what she and her husband did when they were alone. Comparing sizes—length and girth—of penises, as well as staying power and special erotic tricks, was a conversation Morgana did not participate in. She could not help but listen, though.

When Anrid heard whispers outside the door, late at night, she jumped from the edge of the bed and ran. "I'd like a look at this husband of yours," she said, as she opened the door and then gasped in surprise. "My Lord Emperor, how lovely! Have you come here looking for us?" She reached into the hallway and pulled Jahn inside.

Morgana sat on the opposite edge of the bed and Melusina remained in the chair by the window.

"If you've come looking for us, My Lord, you're much too late," Melusina said almost coolly. "You've married us off and we are no longer available for late-night parties of your sort."

"We should be faithful for at least a few months, don't you think?" Anrid said as Jahn shook free of her grasp.

"Perhaps come fall he will be tired of his empress and we will be tired of our husbands, and then we can renew our relationships," Melusina suggested.

Morgana stood. What kind of joke was this? Had she misheard Anrid's greeting? "I thought you didn't know Jahn."

"Your Jahn Devlyn, no," Anrid said, "But this is . . ."

Jahn interrupted her tersely, his eyes never leaving Morgana. "That's enough. Go. Your husbands will be missing you, I imagine."

"Still determined to be faithful, I see," Melusina said as she stood. "How annoying and . . ."

"Don't you see, it's him!" Anrid said. "They are one and the same, that Jahn and *this* Jahn. Oh, my, I did not expect this at all."

"Go!" Jahn commanded in a stern voice Morgana had never heard before.

Melusina and Anrid scurried toward the door, which remained open. Jahn turned to his friend Iann. "See that they are escorted from the palace and taken safely home. They should not be out so late."

"Yes, My Lord," Iann said, and then the sentinel blushed as he looked at Morgana.

A tiny sliver of ice formed around Morgana's heart as the door closed behind Melusina and Anrid.

"Why did he call you, My Lord?" she asked, though in

her heart she knew. She should've known all along, but she had allowed herself to remain blind. "Why did Anrid call you *emperor*?"

"Ana, I have tried to tell you a thousand times . . ."

"Jahn," she whispered. "A common enough name, as you said. A name you share with the emperor." *They are one and the same, that Jahn and* this *Jahn.*

The men who were always so accommodating were not Jahn's friends, they were his sentinels. His servants.

Melusina and Anrid, who had been so happy to see Jahn even though they had always said they knew of no Jahn Devlyn in the palace, apparently knew him very well.

The escort she always had to and from the laundry was no accident.

They had been given these fine quarters in the palace, though it was clear none of the other sentinels had such privileges.

The way her stepfather had sent her away, even that made sense, if he knew exactly to whom he'd been giving his daughter.

An iciness grew, shooting through her midsection. It swelled at an alarming rate, even faster than on the night she had taken a life. One moment there was a seed of ice, the next she was consumed by it. It took over her heart, her breath, it raced through her veins. She did not know how to stop what had taken hold of her; she did not know if she could. "You are Emperor Jahn," she said.

"Yes, but . . ."

"Dressed like a sentinel, having a bit of fun, enjoying a charade before you settle down to a life of wedded bliss."

"In the beginning I did not intend . . ."

"Get out," she said, as calmly as possible.

"Let me explain."

There was no time for explanations. She couldn't stop what had begun. The curse she'd thought gone had been quiet for a long time, but it would be quiet no more. She could not control it; she could not stop what was coming.

Heavens, even her eyes felt cold. "No, get out of this room. Get out now!" she screamed.

"Iann," she cried, "get him out of here, or I'm going to kill him!"

The door burst open and four sentinels rushed in. They were friends, hers and his, or so she had thought. Perhaps they liked her, perhaps they liked and obeyed Jahn, but their first obligation was to protect him.

"My Lord, perhaps we should . . ." Blane began.

"No, Lady Morgana and I need to talk about his now."

So, she was Lady Morgana once more, no longer Ana Devlyn. The charade was over. Morgana knew she did not have much time. Angry as she was, confused and hurt and furious, it would be impossible to contain the destruction much longer. "I need a few minutes alone," she said desperately. "Just a few minutes. Then we can talk."

"All right," Jahn said suspiciously.

"Don't come in until I tell you it's safe to do so," she said. He could not be here when she unleashed her anger, as she would in a matter of heartbeats. One. Two. Three . . .

"Ana," Jahn said, and then he looked into her eyes and took a step back. What did he see there? Did he finally see who she truly was?

Morgana waited until the door was closed behind Jahn and his sentinels, and then she let loose a scream. A pulse of blue energy followed, as her fury was released, and in that heartbeat the home she had found in this palace turned to glass. A large portion of the bed and everything upon it; the chair where one of her husband's former lovers had been sitting not so long ago; a wooden chest filled with what little she owned; the carpet beneath her feet. The icy glass climbed the walls but did not touch the ceiling. Instead, the transformation took stone and pictures to a certain point and then stopped, like moss growing up the side of a tree. All here was cold and fragile and destroyed.

Tears ran down her face, and they were cold. Her heart still felt cold, even though she had released her destruction.

How could she have been so foolish as to think it was gone?
She took a step toward the door, and beneath her feet what
had once been a fine rug crumbled to dust.

She ruined everything she touched.

She could not stay here.

FOR hours, Kristo had been lying in the small bed in the
insufficient chamber Danya had arranged for him. He
didn't sleep much, never had, but tonight his mind was
busy with plans for the days to come. Morgana was here;
he knew it. Felt it. He needed it to be so. But where was
she?

A shriek from a distance teased his ears, and he smiled.
A burst of cold energy from somewhere below froze his
heart in the same way another man's might be warmed.

He sat up, laughing in delight. Not only was his daughter here in the palace, as he had seen, but she was apparently angry at something or someone. The power he had
neglected had grown strong on its own, and tonight, as he
searched for her, she'd unleashed it. Now that he'd sensed
her power in such a strong way, she'd be easier to find. She
was as good as his.

"Don't worry, dear," Kristo said as he reclined once
more upon his hard bed and crossed his arms over his
chest. "Daddy's here, and he's coming to save you."

Chapter Twelve

JAHN stood in the hallway, four wide-eyed sentinels watching him closely to see what he would do next. They were determined—duty-bound, in fact—to protect him, but none of them had ever thought they'd have to protect him from Morgana.

The inhuman shriek that broke so sharply through the heavy wooden door and the stone walls made him cringe. In all his imaginings of how his wife might react to the truth, he had never even considered this. The strange thump and crackling sound that followed made him reach for the door handle, but Blane's quick hand stopped him.

"We should wait a moment, My Lord," Blane said in a lowered voice. "We should wait for her word, as she said."

Jahn did not want to wait, and yet . . . he was afraid of what he might find on the other side of the door. The shriek had been Morgana's, and yet it had not. That unearthly sound had been as alarming as the chill he had seen in her eyes when she'd ordered him from the room. The eyes he loved had gone paler than ever before, and were a blue gray. In that instant they had looked as if they were sculpted of ice.

"Morgana!" he called, throwing off Blane's stilling hand.

He was answered with a strained "You can come in now, if you must."

Jahn pushed the heavy door open. Not an easy task, as something impeded its swing. As the bottom of the door moved inward, the clear crystal which grew in and on the floor crumbled to dust and fell away with a strange crinkling sound that sent shivers down his spine.

Behind him, one of the sentinels whispered a vile swear word that even Jahn would not repeat. Men accustomed to battle, some who had fought monsters, stepped away from the scene before them—they stepped away from Morgana.

She stood, unchanged, in the center of a room that had been transformed. She was pale hair and sunny dress and warm skin at the center of a circle of iciness. A profusion of crystal surrounded her. Bluish and clear and unnatural, it covered the floor, climbed up the walls, and possessed the furnishings. Jahn walked into the room and the substance beneath his boots crumbled. What appeared to be hard crystal fell to dust beneath his step.

At his command, the sentinels remained in the hallway. He did not have to tell them more than once.

"Ana," he said gently, studying her eyes to see, with relief, that they were once again the warm green he knew so well. "What happened?"

"I thought it was gone," she said, as tears fell down her cheeks. "I thought you had chased the curse away, but instead it was only sleeping, and your lies brought it back." Anger grew in her eyes, eyes which remained green and warm. "Did you enjoy your little charade, My Lord Emperor?" She gave him an exaggerated curtsey.

"It wasn't like that," he said, as the crystal-like substance crunched beneath his feet.

"I refused your offer and insulted you, and you made

me pay. You got your revenge. I suppose I should've expected as much." There was a flash of iciness in her eyes, but it did not remain. "The game is over, My Lord Emperor. Please, send me home. I am suitably and regrettably humbled, as you no doubt intended."

Jahn stopped while he was still several feet from his wife. "You *are* home."

Morgana laughed. She laughed harshly and cried at the same time. "I am *not*. I'm a plaything like your friends Melusina and Anrid once were, nothing more."

"You are my wife," Jahn argued.

She looked him bravely in the eye. "No, I am not. Our common marriage, which was sufficient for a sentinel, is not at all binding for an emperor. You knew that all along."

"We will have a proper ceremony . . ."

"We will not."

"Ana . . ."

She shook a finger at him, and for a moment he wondered if ice wouldn't fly from that fingertip. "Do *not* call me Ana. You lost that right the moment the game you played was over."

"It's not a game!" Jahn argued.

Morgana crossed her arms over her chest and cocked her head to one side. "Is it not, *Jahn Devlyn*?"

"Perhaps the charade began as a sort of amusement, but I fell . . ."

"Don't say it," Morgana commanded. "Don't you dare. Love cannot be built on nothing but lies, and everything we have is false. You lied about who you are." She waved one hand at the destruction around her, and then—for emphasis, he supposed—she slapped her hand against the bed behind her. The bedcovers and the pillows fell to dust just as the crystal beneath his boots had. A portion of the bed remained, but it was damaged beyond repair, only half of what it once had been. Her blue dresses, one pale and old, the other dark and all but unworn, had been hanging on a room divider, and like everything else they were crystallized, their form forever changed. "I lied about who I am, too, though in another way. Tell me, My Lord, can you have a wife, an empress, who has the power to turn your allies and your enemies to dust when she loses her temper?"

"We will find a way to undo what has been done to you."

"Nothing has been done to me!" she shouted. "This is who I am! This is the woman I thought I had left behind when you claimed me, but I was wrong!" She walked past him, headed for the door and the waiting sentinels, who backed away as she approached them. "I cannot remain here a moment longer. I'm leaving tonight," she said softly.

Jahn grabbed her arm and pulled her back to him. "You're not going anywhere." One bridal candidate was dead, and another had barely escaped a murder attempt. Morgana wasn't safe, not until they knew who was behind the violence and stopped them. As if he would be willing to let her go even if he believed her to be safe.

Morgana glared up at him. "How do you know I won't turn you to dust here and now?" she asked quietly, no doubt trying to hide her threat from the sentinels.

"Your eyes are green," he said, unafraid.

"Aren't they always?" Morgana snapped.

"No," Jahn said. "They turned to an icy blue gray before I left the room at your instruction."

"That doesn't mean . . ."

"You won't hurt me," he said, alarmed by the coolness of her flesh and the horror in her eyes. Was that horror for his lies or for what she'd done here—for what she still might do?

"You don't know that." Morgana tried to escape his hold, but she could not. She stared at his chest and pulled on her arm for a moment, then stopped and leaned into him. "I hate you," she whispered.

"No, you don't."

"You played with my life and made me love you, you pretended to be someone you're not, and you made me be someone I'm not, and none of it was real. My mother was wrong. Love is horrid, and no woman should wish for it, much less wait for it to come to her. Love will break your heart and soul, if you let it."

Jahn grabbed her chin and forced her to look at him.

"Checking to see if they're still green?" she snapped.

"No, I just want to make sure you hear me well," Jahn said. "I love you. You're my wife, my *empress*. I don't understand what just happened, but we'll find a way to fix it. We'll find a way to fix it all."

"Hear me well," Morgana said coldly. "I can't love a man who lies to me for sport. I am not your wife or your empress." Her eyes filled with tears. "And I can't be fixed. Let me go."

She asked for the one thing he could not give her. "No."

Jahn kissed Morgana's cool forehead and left her standing in the middle of the ruined chamber. He ordered the sentinels to guard her room. She was not to leave, nor was she to have any visitors.

He locked her in the room they had shared, and as the bolt clicked into place, he waited for another unearthly shriek. Instead, all he heard was the deepest, darkest silence he had ever experienced.

WHEN she was alone, Morgana dropped to the floor, her legs too weak to bear her weight any longer. She hid her face in her skirt for what felt like a long while, hiding from the destruction around her, trying to still the furious beating of her heart.

It had been foolish of her to think the curse was gone. The curse which had made her believe she had to hide from everyone and everything had just been sleeping, waiting for a rush of anger to unleash it, waiting for betrayal to bring it all back in a fast, unstoppable wave. At least she hadn't killed anyone this time. If she had, it would've been Jahn, and even though she truly did hate him at this moment, she didn't want to see him dead. She just wanted to be far, far away from him and his lies.

Tidbit after tidbit fell together in her muddled mind, and with each realization she gasped or sobbed. Her stepfather had surely known, when he'd sent her away, that Jahn Devlyn was no sentinel. No wonder he had not come after her!

Melusina and Anrid, women she had come to consider friends, had been Jahn's paramours, back in the days when they'd been painted ladies in tight clothing that barely contained their wares. She imagined that when Jahn spent time with them, they wore no clothing at all. Morgana lifted her head slowly. It wasn't as though she'd thought Jahn to be an untried virgin, but no woman wanted to meet her husband's former lovers, nor did she wish to know that his taste had been so questionable. It gave her some solace to know that he had sent the women away when they'd come to Arthes as man and wife, that he had told them he planned to be a faithful husband, but that solace was not enough to wipe away the picture in her mind. The tricks they spoke of, the way they had longed for the emperor and a return of his attentions . . . she did not want to know that they had been speaking of her husband all along.

No wonder his "friends" the sentinels had been so accommodating; no wonder he'd been able to obtain housing in the palace. She'd thought those men were her friends, too, and she'd lost them in an instant, just as she had lost her husband. Had they laughed at her for her foolishness? Had they been kind to her only because it was required of them?

But worst of all, the very worst, was knowing how well and how completely Jahn had lied to her. There had been many opportunities for him to tell her the truth, if he hadn't been lying once again when he'd told her that he did indeed love her. If he'd fallen in love with her along the way, he could've confessed everything and asked for her forgiveness. No, she had been sport for a bored emperor. She had been his amusement, no different from Melusina and Anrid and who knows how many others! Thank goodness she had not told him of her recent suspicions. He would never let her go if he believed the next emperor of Columbyana was growing inside her.

Morgana ran a hand across the stone floor. The cold crystal there disintegrated where she touched it, but solid stone remained beneath. The same would be true of the walls, she imagined, and of the door. Only a portion of the bed had fallen to dust. When Tomas had died, she hadn't stayed behind to study the destruction around him, other than to watch a blade of grass turn to dust. She did recall that Tomas had been solid crystal. He had been changed through and through. Were humans more vulnerable than stone and wood? Was her curse *intended* to take human life, or had Tomas suffered more before he'd been the cause, the subject, of her cold attack?

"I don't want to be a killer," she whispered. "I want to be a wife and a mother, I want to be a friend. I want to be a woman men don't shy away from in fear."

But she was not that woman. Morgana looked at the locked door, wondering how long it would be before she found a way to escape this all-but-deserted level of the palace. Again she sobbed as a new thought came to her. Apparently there was once again a witch on Level Seven.

She could not be empress, and she couldn't love a man who would betray her as Jahn had. Could she use her unwanted powers to escape without hurting anyone? Could her curse somehow become her salvation? Jahn had taught her that life could be more than she'd ever imagined it to be. He had shown her aspects of herself that she had never known existed. She was strong. She was capable. She had learned to live very well beyond the home she had always known, and she could, and would, learn to live without Jahn.

JAHN did not know Angelo Rainer, the relatively new deputy in the Ministry of Magic, very well, but he had come highly recommended and certainly seemed stable enough. "Stable" among wizards and witches was a rare trait, Jahn had found. It was as if their abilities ate away at their brains and their souls. It took great strength to maintain stability when there were powers and unearthly gifts at one's fingertips.

Rainer was obviously surprised to be called before the emperor, especially at such an early hour. Still, he was well put together, clean and clear-eyed and well dressed. His long, straight hair, which was fairer even than Morgana's, was caught in a neat braid.

Jahn was in no mood to do other than get straight to business. "Did you encounter any trouble on your journey to the palace with Lady Danya?"

Rainer blinked. "Trouble other than the lady herself?"

On another day, Jahn might've smiled at that comment. "Any attacks on your party? Any strange incidents or accidents?"

"No, My Lord," Rainer said solemnly.

So, either there was no conspiracy, or Rainer's traveling party had gotten lucky, or Lady Danya had a hand in the violence which was taking place. Having met her briefly, but not briefly enough, Jahn could see that as a real possibility. "What do you think of Lady Danya?"

Rainer hesitated, and Jahn read people well enough to know that whatever the man said next was going to be carefully measured and likely not entirely true, though he also doubted it would be a lie. Finally the younger man said, "She is very beautiful."

"That's hardly a comment on the character of a woman who might one day be empress. Would she make a good empress, do you think?" Jahn did not intend for anyone other than Morgana to fill that position, but he was interested in the answer, nonetheless.

Rainer sighed, and then he answered, "No, My Lord, I do not."

"Care to elaborate?"

Rainer glanced at the sentinels who stood nearby, and realizing the man's predicament, Jahn directed the soldiers into the hallway so he and the deputy could be alone for a moment. After the door had closed behind Blane, Rainer spoke.

"I believe Lady Danya is much more fragile than she appears, My Lord. In my opinion she does not have the stamina nor the wisdom to be empress. She is more girl than woman, and yes, it does not help matters that she has managed to alienate everyone she's met since coming here."

Jahn saw something he understood in the young man's eyes and words. "Yet you like her."

Rainer bowed crisply. "My Lord, I would not dare to care inappropriately for a woman intended for the emperor."

"Good answer," Jahn said softly. "Not that I believe you."

Rainer rose and met Jahn's gaze, but he did not say anything further.

Jahn had a good sense about people, and he liked Rainer. He also instinctively trusted the man. "As far as most of the residents of the palace are concerned, I am on a hunting trip and will be away for several more days."

"I will not reveal otherwise," Rainer said crisply.

"No, I suspect you won't." Jahn stood and walked toward the deputy. How much could he trust this man? He could not handle what needed to be done alone, he knew that much. He did not have magic, he did not understand the training and the temptations involved. This man did. Though Rainer had not displayed his powers, he would not be in his current position if Jahn didn't understand very well what he could do. "There is something else I need from you," Jahn said in a lowered voice.

"Anything, My Lord Emperor."

"It requires the most ardent discretion."

"Of course." Rainer bowed again, as Jahn drew close.

He did not know what to do with Morgana. He loved her still, always would, and he intended to keep her as his wife. But he didn't know how to save her, how to keep her . . .

how to help rein in her considerable power. It was quite obvious to him, after a long, sleepless night of remembering every word he and Morgana had exchanged and searching his mind for answers, that his wife did not have control of her destructive power. All those times when she had asked him to warm her, she'd been chasing away her unwanted power in the only way she knew how.

Jahn looked into Rainer's eyes, man to man. "Help me."

MORGANA had remained compliant and silent as sentinels she had once considered friends, men who now looked at her as if they expected her to sprout another head at any moment, delivered food, fine clothing, and even new furnishings to her chamber. She ate some of the food, for the sake of her baby in case there truly was one, and she sat in the plush chair which was placed by the window, a replacement for the chair she had turned to dust. She refused to wear the elaborate gown that was delivered. She preferred her ordinary, worn yellow dress, the only garment she could call her own after last night's destruction of so much in this very room. If Jahn thought he could buy her forgiveness with silk, then he did not know her at all.

Did she know him? Was anything he had said or done real?

It was Blane and Iann who came into her room to clean up the dusty remains of her anger. They scooped and swept, and Iann shuddered as he touched a footstool and it fell apart. Neither of them looked her in the eye. This was what she had to look forward to, if she stayed here. Fear. Her own fear that she would kill someone, as well as the fear of others.

None of these men would ever look at her the same way again. She'd lost them as surely as she'd lost Jahn.

She was surprised when a visitor was announced, and even more surprised when a young, attractive man walked into her chamber and gave her a small but genuine smile.

"How do you do?" he said formally. "My name is Deputy Angelo Rainer, and I'm a representative from the Ministry of Magic. I'm told you're Ana Devlyn?"

"That name will do, I suppose," Morgana answered, not bothering to rise from her chair. Why was he here? To arrest her? To recruit her? To interrogate her about her power and where it came from? If that was the case, he'd be very disappointed. There was only one way to find out why he was here. "What do you want?"

Deputy Rainer walked bravely, and perhaps foolishly, closer to Morgana. He studied her eyes and her folded hands, and then he extended his own hand, which fluttered close to her face but did not quite touch her. He muttered a few times, sputtering words like "remarkable" and "unusual," as well as a few less easily decipherable hums.

Morgana was quite annoyed at the man's demeanor. He studied her as if she were a two-headed cat! "I will ask you again," she said sharply, "what do you want?"

"At the emperor's request, I am here to teach you how to harness your abilities."

Morgana's heart leapt. She was tempted to send Deputy Rainer away, to kick him out of her prison room and send the ornate gown she refused to wear with him. But the words he spoke generated something she had not experienced since the moment Jahn had left her last night. "Is that possible?"

"I believe so, yes. No," Rainer said more forcefully, "I am *certain* it's possible. All abilities are ours to capture and use. Powers which some call unnatural but which are completely natural to those who have them are simply different types of energy. You own your power. It does not own you."

"But it does," she whispered. Her curse had ruled her life since the moment she'd killed Tomas.

"Not for long, Mistress Ana," Rainer said confidently. "Give me your hand, if you please." With that he offered his hand, which was well-shaped and long-fingered, and a little pale.

"If you had seen what I could do, you would not offer your hand so easily," Morgana said, as she left his hand hanging there, untouched.

"I am not afraid," Rainer said gently.

"Perhaps you should be."

The hand remained, solid and unmoving, and Rainer said again, "I am not afraid."

AFTER last night's triumphant moment when Kristo had been so certain his daughter was near, he'd felt nothing more of her presence. Still, he was sure she was here. So close. So damned close!

Danya looked as if she'd been drained of life, she was so pale. There were circles beneath her eyes, and she was skittish. There were moments when she looked horribly delicate, as if she were about to break in two. He'd thought her to be a bit stronger than this, but her secrets were beginning to weigh upon her.

Time to test her, to see if she could be at all useful. With Rikka dead, he could use another ally. Besides, until Morgana was in his hands, Danya remained the only choice for empress. He would not have all that he wanted, if that was the case, but he could and would use every power he had over Danya to get what he wanted most of all.

All Kristo needed was a child. He would prefer that child to be his own blood, his own grandson, but if necessary, Danya's offspring would serve. If the child was as malleable as the mother, he would serve quite well.

"I want you to kill Deputy Rainer," Kristo said without preamble, as he closed the door to Danya's chamber behind him and confronted her. She was alone, as he had known she would be, and was dressed for the day in one of her new, inappropriately seductive gowns. This one was made of a dark, bloodred fabric, much too close to imperial crimson to be proper. The neckline was cut so low that if she sneezed, her nipples would likely be revealed, and the waist was caught up tight to show how tiny her figure was.

She had used artificial color to give life to her cheeks, and to be honest, looked no more appealing than the cheapest village prostitute.

She went impossibly whiter as Kristo made his demand. "Why?"

"He watches you too closely; he knows too much." And Kristo didn't like the way Rainer had looked at him in the dining hall. The deputy's restrained abilities apparently included a sensitivity to magics which could reveal Kristo's powers much too soon.

"He knows nothing!"

"Then kill him simply because I order you to do so," Kristo said. "You know who will suffer if you do not do as I command."

Danya swayed on her feet. "How? How am I to kill a man in this palace, an important man in the emperor's service, and not get caught?"

"That's your concern, not mine. Women seem to prefer poison over messier methods of disposal, perhaps because they are so often the ones who have to clean the messes more violent actions leave behind." He walked toward her, silent and smiling, and when he was very near, he reached out and raked his fingers across the exposed swell of her bosom. "It would be quite difficult to get blood out of such a fine fabric, and I suspect it might never wash off your delicate skin."

"Don't touch me," she whispered, not for the first time.

Kristo allowed his hand to drop. "You will do as I direct." He did not like the way Rainer looked at Danya, the way the man had remained close even though Lady Danya was not at all pleasant these days. Murder likely wasn't necessary, but Rainer was one of the men who would not be welcome in the new order. Besides, he enjoyed the idea of testing how far his ally would go. What would she do to save her son? Would she kill the emperor when asked to do so?

"Of course."

"You will kill him tonight," Rainer said.

Danya's eyes snapped up and she glared at him. "I need more time! You expect me to plot and carry out a murder without implicating myself in less than one day? Where will I get the poison you spoke of? I will never become empress if I'm caught, and then where will you be?" She pursed her lips and her tired eyes narrowed. "You need me," she said, perhaps realizing the truth of those words for the first time. "If not, you wouldn't be here. You would not have taken Ethyn and bothered to blackmail me if you didn't, for some reason, need *me*."

He would need her only until she produced a child and named Uncle Kristo its guardian. And if he found Morgana before the First Night of the Summer Festival, he would not need Danya at all. And yet he answered with an almost friendly "Of course I need you."

That admission gave her a new confidence. "I'll need a few days to plan."

"Rainer must be dead before the emperor chooses you."

After a moment's hesitation, Danya nodded, and then she ordered her "uncle" from her presence.

Kristo didn't like that new boldness in the woman he controlled. He didn't like it at all.

Chapter Thirteen

JAHN didn't bother to change into a sentinel's uniform as he rushed up the stairs to Level Seven, two loyal guards directly behind him. What was the point? Morgana knew who he was, so disguises were no longer necessary.

Almost everyone else in the palace was at supper, so he and his men had the stairway to themselves, as they had planned. Maintaining the fantasy that the emperor was on a hunting trip was difficult when he had no choice but to meet with a handful of his staff to deal with the newest crisis, but he would do what he could to give Sanura the time she needed.

The two people he loved most in the world, his wife and his brother, both had reason to take his life—and both had threatened to do so. How had he gone, in a matter of days, from being happier than he could remember to this low point in his life?

Rainer had reported that Morgana's powers were most definitely controllable, but as they had been ignored for years, it would not be an easy task. She had agreed, through Rainer, to remain in the palace while she took his instruction, but she made it clear that, agreement or not, she considered herself a prisoner.

She would remain under constant guard, in case she changed her mind about staying in the palace until her instruction was done. He wouldn't lose her, not like this. When she calmed down, she'd forgive him. Wouldn't she?

Morgana had not agreed to see her husband. Since discovering his true identity, she did not even admit to anyone that she had a husband. Jahn was determined that he would change her mind, even if it meant facing a cold-eyed, powerful witch every night until she came to her senses. He would imprison her here for as long as it took to convince her that she was empress and he would have no other. When she calmed down—*if* she calmed down—she would see reason.

The chamber they had shared for a short while had been transformed once again. The remains of Morgana's anger had been taken away, the dust cleared, the broken and destroyed furnishings replaced. What was most changed, however, was Morgana herself, a much-too-solemn woman who sat by the window. She hadn't donned one of the three very nice gowns he'd had delivered to her room today, but wore the yellow frock which was now no more than a faded, patched rag. Her hair was drawn back in a simple twist, as she sometimes wore it when working, and though he had sent more than one pair of fine slippers to her today, she continued to wear the battered walking boots she'd had on her feet when she'd left home.

It was her face which had changed, her face and the set of her shoulders and the almost visible wall she had built around herself which made her look different than she had just yesterday. The eyes which glared at him were blessedly green.

"What are you doing here?" she asked sharply.

"I live here."

"No, you don't," she said softly.

Jahn stepped deeper into the room, determined not to

give up so easily. "Did you not like the new gowns I had delivered to you?"

"Not particularly," she said crisply.

"Tomorrow I will try to choose more wisely. Is there a particular style or color or fabric you prefer?"

"Do you think you can buy your way out of your lies with clothing and shoes?" she asked, not rising from her chair to greet him or to push him back.

He would prefer anger to this calm, cold acceptance. He wanted her to rail against him so he could argue with her and make her see reason. "You can have anything you want, Ana," he said, perhaps a bit desperately.

She glanced down at her lap and shook her head. "You can't give me what I want. And don't call me Ana. I am Lady Morgana Ramsden, and I have not changed my mind about participating in your ridiculous contest. When the time comes, you will have to choose another as your empress."

"I will not," he said testily.

She looked up at him. "Then you will remain unwed," she responded in that maddeningly easy voice.

"How can you be so calm?" he asked, losing his temper—the last thing he'd intended to do.

"I must remain calm. You saw what happens when I lose my temper, when I let my emotions take form and fly from my body." Her eyes bored into him. "Why do you think I was so determined to remain unwed?"

"You said you promised your mother you would wait for love."

She blushed. "That was long ago, when I was a girl foolish enough to believe in the kind of love my mother spoke of. Later in my life I thought more practically. I knew all along a husband, any husband, would eventually rouse the worst in me." Those warm green eyes softened. "I was wrong to think you were different."

"You were not . . ."

She very quickly changed the subject. "The tutor you

sent to me, Angelo Rainer, says I must learn to contain my emotions before I can learn to control my curse. I can't do that with you here, My Lord Emperor."

"I'm still Jahn to you," he argued, hating the sound of such a formal address coming from her mouth.

"No, you're not," she whispered. "The Jahn I thought I knew does not exist. He was a fantasy, a dream, a *lie*." A spark of a chill flashed in her eyes, and she closed them quickly and muttered a few words he could not discern. "Please, My Lord Emperor, go. Leave me be. Allow me to learn to control my curse and live my life far from any who would bring it to the surface again." Her hands balled into fists. "Just . . . leave me alone!"

"I can't."

"I don't want you," Morgana said coldly. "You are everything I *do not want* in a man."

"That's too bad. I'm yours whether you want me or not." He reached for something, anything, to hold onto Morgana. "What if there's a child?"

"Emperors have produced bastards before," she said with maddening composure.

Jahn could not suppress his flash of anger. He was prepared to grovel, to cajole, to charm, but it was clear that Morgana was not ready to forgive him. Not yet. He backed toward the door. "Do you remember how I told you, on our first night together, that I take care of my own?"

"Of course."

"That was not a lie. I will take care of you. Learn what you need to learn from Deputy Rainer, Lady Morgana. And while you're learning, take time to look into your heart and remember what we shared. Yes, there were lies, but what we had went far beyond any falsehood I could arrange. We had love. We can have it again." Again he was reminded of his father, a man he did not wish to become. "And if you cannot forgive me, if you can't find love again, then I will let you go." With that he left her, the knowledge that her forgiveness was not forthcoming gnawing at his insides.

* * *

RAINER was surprised when, after ignoring him for days, Lady Danya sought him out after a fine evening meal shared with countless other palace residents in the Level Nine dining hall. He'd been ready to retire early, after an unexpectedly long day, and then he'd looked across the room and there was Danya, walking toward him with her dark eyes all but pinned to his face. She looked determined and tired; scared and alone; desperate and beautiful. Heaven above, he never knew what to expect from her.

The tight smile she forced as she came near caught him off guard. "Deputy Rainer," she said, as sweetly as she could manage. Not unexpectedly, others in the area fled.

"My Lady." Rainer gave her a brief but suitable bow. He was sworn to secrecy and could tell no one, especially not Danya, but after meeting Morgana, he found it impossible to imagine that the emperor would choose any other as his bride. Love had a particular energy that he could not help but absorb when the emperor spoke of the woman who considered herself cursed. It was almost certain that in a few days Danya would be rejected and sent home—whether Lady Morgana had her unwanted powers under control or not.

He could almost feel sorry for Danya, who wanted to be empress so badly it had turned her into a wicked person he did not recognize as the woman he had escorted here.

"It's a lovely evening," she said. "Would you walk outdoors with me? The emperor has a beautiful garden and there are many flowers in bloom."

Rainer blinked in surprise. After a few relatively pleasant days of what might be called friendship, she had dismissed him as beneath her, as a pest, as an unwanted nuisance. Now she invited him on an evening walk in the emperor's garden? What did she want from him? He was quite sure she wanted something.

"If you would like, of course." He offered her his arm, in an entirely acceptable manner, and she took it. When she touched him, he felt the almost imperceptible tremor that went bone deep. She was terrified, of someone or something. As they left the dining hall, he felt numerous eyes on his back. They would be the subject of malicious gossip, he imagined. He didn't care.

One level down from the dining hall were the ground floor and the rear exit which led to the emperor's garden. A few oil lamps burned there, for security purposes more than to illuminate the popular garden. He and Danya walked down a narrow stone path, and she did seem to admire the flowering plants they walked past. He said nothing; neither did she. They walked in complete silence until they reached the far edge of the garden.

Danya stopped near the tall stone wall that surrounded the palace grounds and turned to face him. "I suppose you're wondering why I asked you to walk with me, after our last unpleasant encounter."

"Yes," Rainer said simply.

Danya looked up as if studying the stars. "I'm sorry about that. To be honest, I realized that I liked you more than I should. We would spend time together and I'd find myself thinking . . . thoughts I should not allow." She looked him in the eye. "You are my only friend here, Rainer, and I have missed you."

"You might have more friends if you did not make an effort to be difficult," he said bluntly. "Since coming to the palace you've been demanding and often unkind."

Finely shaped eyebrows arched. "That's rather bold of you to say."

"Friends tell the truth," he responded.

Her lower lip trembled, and he could not tell if that reaction to his comment was an act or not. Was she vulnerable or manipulative? A lost little girl or an ambitious bitch? There had been a time when he'd thought he understood her, but lately—lately he could not be sure.

"What do you want from me, Danya?"

"I want you to be my friend again, and maybe"—she

glanced to the side coyly—"maybe you can be more than a friend." She took his hand and pulled him into darker shadows, and there she threw herself at him and planted a cold kiss on his lips.

Rainer tasted the desperation he'd seen on Danya's face earlier in the evening. He felt the pounding of her heart, the tremor of her lips. After a moment her lips parted and she slipped her tongue into his mouth, practiced and arousing. A hand grasped at his shirt and she pressed her body closer to his.

In the early days he'd found Danya extraordinarily physically attractive. During their private evenings she'd seemed a different woman, a woman he could care for— not at all the woman she had become. On more than one occasion he had dreamed of kissing her, but this was not the kiss he wanted. He didn't want to be the man she turned to for solace when she was despondent and forlorn.

Rainer took his mouth from hers. "We can't do this."

"I thought you liked me," she whispered.

So did I. "You are a bridal candidate," he said, even though he could not imagine that she would win the position.

"Yes, but the emperor's marriage will be one of politics and convenience," Danya argued. "Doesn't a woman deserve more? Don't I deserve love and passion in my life, even if I win the emperor's hand?"

"Don't you believe that you can find love and passion in an arranged marriage?"

"No," she whispered. "Is there someone else? Do you love another?"

"No."

"Then love me, for a while," Danya said seductively. She boldly placed a hand over the evidence that he was not unmoved by her offers or her kiss. She stroked, fingers firm and practiced, palm warm.

Rainer closed his eyes and allowed his mind and his will to drift. The emperor wasn't going to marry Danya, he knew that. It wasn't as if he would be taking advantage of a future empress, and it wasn't as if he hadn't imagined this very scenario a time or two.

But he would be taking advantage. He grabbed Danya's wrist and gently pulled her hand away from his body. "I will be your friend without the promise of anything more," he said.

"I know," she whispered, sounding defeated and dejected.

He wanted her to be neither. He wanted her to be happy, to be free. His ability to sense energy told him that she was not at all free, not inside or out. He didn't understand— wasn't sure he or anyone else could. When the emperor's contest was over and Danya knew she would not be empress, perhaps they could explore something more. But for now, for tonight . . . "We will take things slowly, you and I," he said.

"But why . . ."

"Slowly, Danya," he insisted, and then he kissed her.

This kiss was different from the first. This kiss was slower, and it was full of promise. There was no desperation, no grasping, no surging tongues. Not yet. The kiss was warm and gentle, two mouths barely touching, two mouths learning one another. Danya's lips barely parted and Rainer's did the same. She held her breath; her heartbeat slowed. They leaned into one another gently, sharing a breath, stealing a moment in time. When it was done, she swayed on her feet and he had to steady her.

The energy that rolled off her body was different from what he'd felt before. The desperation was gone. No, not gone but dampened, at least for the moment.

"I've never been kissed like that before," she said.

Rainer took her arm and led her back toward the palace. "Good."

DANYA was almost lightheaded as she allowed Rainer to lead her back to the level of the palace where her quarters were located. When she was empress, she would be on a lower level and would not have to climb so much, but tonight she did not mind. The tedious climb meant Rainer remained with her longer. She did not want to let him go. Still, she said good night long before she reached her door, just in case Kristo was in her chambers waiting for her, as he sometimes was. She did not want her "uncle" anywhere near Angelo.

The deputy minister of magic confused her. He was a man like any other, and she had offered him anything he might desire. He could've tossed up her skirt and taken her in the garden, and she would not have uttered a word of protest as he took what every man wanted from a woman. He'd been hard; he desired her well enough—and yet he had taken nothing. He had done nothing more than to offer her a kiss like no other she had ever known, sweet and arousing and deep in ways she could not explain.

When the door to her chamber was closed behind her, Danya leaned against it and sighed. She did not want to kill Rainer. She wanted to hold him, to kiss him again, to see him smile. She did not want to rid the world of one of its truly good men! What a waste that would be.

"I have your poison."

Danya's eyes snapped open as Kristo stepped from the shadows. From his hand there swung a small leather bag which bulged with something deadly. Something which would end Rainer's life and save the life of her child.

"I won't need it right away," she said, keeping her back to the door.

"Why not?"

"Before I can get Rainer to eat from my hand, he must trust me," she snapped impatiently. "At the moment he does not."

The deadly bag continued to swing from a cold hand. "You play with your child's life," Kristo teased.

Realizing that she had some power in this relationship helped Danya to be less afraid of the cold man than she had once been, and still she trembled. "You won't hurt Ethyn," she whispered. "You still need me." She bravely took a step away from the door and toward Kristo. To cower with her back to the wall only made her appear weak. "The plan has changed. Rather than killing Rainer, I'm going to bring him over to my side."

"He's annoyingly and unerringly good," Kristo said. "How could you possibly . . ."

"Sex," she said boldly. "He wants me, and I am more than willing to give him all that he wants."

Kristo's eyebrows arched in amusement. "You cannot wait for your wedding night, Empress Danya? You're so needful you'll turn to another man mere days before you're to take your vows?"

She smiled, though it took great effort. "I know what you want from me, *Uncle* Kristo. You want a child. You want the next emperor at your command. When we first met, you said as much. You told me that you and those you worked with were pleased that I had the ability to produce a son." She wondered if there truly were others, or if he had lied. Perhaps he was just one lonely, evil man, working alone. No, someone had to be watching over Ethyn. "If I have two men at my service, then the event you most desire is doubly likely to happen soon." She looked Kristo in the eye, glad at this moment that her chamber was dimly lit. "The emperor's father had several wives and was wed to one or another for many years before he produced an heir. What if Emperor Jahn is like his father? What if you have to wait years for the child you want? Rainer is fair-haired like the emperor, so if the child looks like the man who sired him, no matter who that man might be, then all will be well."

"You have given this some thought."

More than he would ever know. "Rainer has magic, you know. Wouldn't it be nice if the child inherited some of his father's abilities?"

"I suppose."

"Emperor Jahn is only a man," she said with disdain. "He possesses no magic, nothing to offer his offspring. It might actually be best if I'm with child when I wed the emperor."

"Perhaps that child should be mine."

Danya held her chin high, hiding her revulsion. "That's not going to happen. Touch me, and this alliance is over." She'd made sacrifices and she would make more, but she would not allow this man to get near her.

"You're quite confident."

She glared at the cold man. His name was Kristo, she called him uncle for the sake of others, and yet she often thought of him as the hooded man. He should live that way, always in shadow. She had to reach deep to remind herself that he needed her, that she was not entirely at his mercy. "You will get your child and I will get mine. You will have control of the next emperor of Columbyana, and I will have Ethyn. Rainer remains alive." She reached out and snatched the leather bag from Kristo's hand. "Until he has served his purpose."

MORGANA listened diligently to Rainer's teachings. Her curse was simply a form of energy, he said again and again. It was no different from breath or dance, laughter or tears. Control was not only possible, he insisted, it was necessary.

For this morning's lesson they had traveled a short distance away from the palace, to a western field. She and her tutor were not alone; Jahn would never allow that. Six sentinels had accompanied them to the field, and though they remained at a distance, they encircled her in a protective—or imprisoning—manner. Six men, all armed and solemn! You would think she was an enemy of the state, the way she was guarded.

At least Jahn himself was not here, watching her lessons and trying in vain to convince her that his lies were not unforgivable.

Still wearing the faded yellow dress she had worn when she'd been Ana Devlyn, Morgana faced the large, empty space before her, where trees and grasses grew wild, and the gentle wind whipped them all about in a rhythm that had a song of its own. The sun shone, and she drank in the rays that reminded her of freedom and better days—days when she had not known of her curse, and later days when she'd traveled with a lying, no-good, conniving emperor who had made her believe he could keep the curse at bay.

Now she knew it would never be at bay. She had to learn how to control her curse—her *abilities,* Rainer called them—or else she would have no sort of life at all. Not here, not elsewhere. If she did not learn control, she would forever be a prisoner of her cur . . . of her abilities.

All morning they had worked on finding and identifying and claiming the root of her power. The icy energy was not beyond her control. It was a part of her—a gift, he said. Next had been finding how best to direct that energy. It was not enough to harness the beast, she had to know how to steer it. They had found her right hand worked best. All that remained was for her abilities to be tested.

"Find the cold center of the power," Rainer instructed.

"But I'm not angry or scared," Morgana argued.

"That doesn't matter. The power is always there, and you must learn to hold it, or else it will hold you."

Morgana closed her eyes. Cold. She did know, and had told Rainer, that the destruction began with a sliver of ice at the core of her being. She had worked to deny that sliver, so it was difficult to call to it now. She did not want to search out that chill; she wanted to send it away!

If she could not send it away, she would learn control. She had not been able to learn it for herself, and did not want to stay here so near to Jahn, but for the child that might be within her, she would do whatever was necessary. Her child deserved better than a mother who was constantly afraid of who—or what—she was.

"Find the sliver and contain it," Rainer said. "Capture it; make it your own."

Just as Jahn had done to her . . . Captured. Owned. Released.

There it was, that sliver of cold. Instead of pushing it away, as she had attempted to do in the past, Morgana mentally wrapped her hand around that sliver of ice. She felt the power. She claimed it.

"See that one red flower?" Rainer asked.

Morgana followed his gesture and saw the single red flower among the pink. It was taller and brighter and more beautiful than all the rest. "Yes," she said. "I see it."

"Freeze that flower but leave all those around it untouched."

"I can't . . ."

"Try," he said gently.

Morgana stared at the red flower for a long time, while Rainer remained silent and patient. She acknowledged the power inside her, rather than trying to push it away, and so it did not explode; it did not overtake her. Eventually she lifted her right hand, as Rainer had taught her to do, and directed her cold power toward that one red flower.

There was a burst similar to the two she had experienced in the past, but instead of encircling her, the blue burst of energy flew forward in a sweeping motion. Her aim was off, and she crystallized not the one red flower but a dozen or so to the left.

"Very good," Rainer said proudly.

Morgana turned to see that her tutor had retreated to a spot several feet behind her. "Very good? I missed, and you were so worried, you moved well out of the line of fire."

He smiled. "I am no fool, My Lady," he responded. "Your power is a mighty one, and you do not yet have complete control."

No, but in a mere two days she had found, at last, some control. That little bit of mastery gave her hope.

"You're tired," he said.

"I am," she admitted. She had never been one for sleeping during the day, but at the moment she desperately wanted a nap. "Control is exhausting."

His smile was wide and bright, and Morgana wondered

why she could not have fallen in love with such a sweet, uncomplicated man as this. Why did she continue to love a man who had deceived and humiliated her?

Love or no love, she was not going to stay here. She would not marry the emperor! No matter what Jahn said, he could not make her take vows. She glanced behind her at the stalwart guard, as she and Rainer returned to the palace. And one day . . . one day his guard would falter, and when it did, she'd make her escape. She couldn't wait for Jahn to let her go, as he said he would.

Well beyond the green-clad guards, another contingent sat on horseback. Most of them were dressed in green, as were her sentinels, but at the center there sat one man in crimson, one man with flowing fair hair who sat on his horse and watched her from a distance. He did not approach, he did not ride away. He simply watched.

For a weak moment she wished he were close enough that she could see his face, and then she pushed the weakness away. That was not the man she knew, the man she had come to love. He was a stranger.

KRISTO was called to the window of his too-small room by a power he knew well. It drew him there, it sang to him the way sex or love or laughter sang to other people. He watched for a long while before he finally saw her. His daughter, walking beside a familiar man who really should be dead by now, moved closer to the palace with each step, and with each step Kristo felt the power more clearly. The man who accompanied her and the guards who walked behind and beside her didn't feel it, not the way he did. If they sensed even a drop of the power Kristo sensed, they would run for their lives.

He smiled. Morgana looked like her mother, but was stronger than that woman had been. Dressed like a beggar woman and wearing her hair in a simple twist, his daughter walked with the confidence of a lady. Of an empress. He should've stolen her away years ago, and might've if he'd known their paths would lead them here.

Once Rainer and Morgana were out of sight, once they were in the palace itself, Kristo ran from his chamber with great speed. He headed for the stairway and scampered down. Down and down and down, hoping he was not too slow. Sure enough, he passed the couple just before they reached Level Seven and entered the hallway there. He could not get close, as a contingent of guards was on her tail, but he saw her at last.

Rainer glanced to the side, recognizing Kristo as his lady friend's uncle. Knowing the man's powers of perception, Kristo had gone to great lengths to keep his distance, but they had dined in the same hall, smoked in the same gathering rooms. Morgana paid Kristo no mind at all, even though he looked her squarely in the eye and bowed with great respect. She had been hidden from him for a very long time, but being so close to her changed everything. Now that he saw inside her, he knew his plans had not been for nothing.

His daughter was powerful, she was a prisoner, she was angry—and she was already carrying the next emperor of Columbyana in her taut, flat belly.

Level Seven, that was where she'd been imprisoned. Now that Kristo knew exactly where Morgana was, they would not remain apart for much longer.

Chapter Fourteen

SHE should've expected the emperor to be persistent, Morgana thought as she once again stared down the man who foolishly claimed to be her husband. Jahn had always been stubborn, no matter who he was or pretended to be.

Well, she could be stubborn, too.

There were now untouched jewels mixed in with the un-worn shoes and gowns she'd set aside, rejected as they'd arrived. All the gifts had been delivered by the few senti-nels who knew—at least to some degree—who she was. The men who had been guarding her for many weeks—for nearly the past two months!—had known all along that their "friend" Jahn was indeed their emperor. They hadn't been doing him a favor, they'd been following orders! Mor-gana was displeased with them all. Their lies didn't sting the way Jahn's did, but still, they were lies.

"I knew you would be angry when you found out the truth," Jahn said calmly. "But you cannot remain angry forever."

She glared at him, trying to ignore the fact that he looked so imposing and handsome in his crimson imperial robes. He did not have a crown upon his head, but he could have, she supposed. His hair was worn loose today, as it had been yesterday, those differing shades of blond and brown mingling in an interesting way, and his jaw was so smooth she knew he had just shaved. For her? He knew how she hated his beard, and he did have a very nice jaw-line and cheekbones . . .

She should not find him at all handsome or appealing. He was a snake!

"Actually, I can remain angry as long as I'd like," she said coolly. "I can remain angry for years, I imagine. Maybe even forever."

Jahn stalked to the window and stared out of it as if there were something to see. "Deputy Rainer tells me your lessons are going quite well," he said.

"I suppose that's true," Morgana said without emotion, even though her insides were roiling. Her instructions must be going better than she'd imagined, since she did not at this moment feel even a sliver of ice, even though she was furious with Jahn.

"Rainer says that with practice you'll soon have complete control of your . . . your . . ." Jahn sounded like he was going to choke on his own words.

"My power to destroy everything in the path of my fear or anger," Morgana supplied without stammering. "My curse. My magical abilities. I imagine no matter what you call my unusual capability, it isn't exactly what you're looking for in an empress."

Jahn turned to face her again, and she wished he had not. Emperor or not, lies or not, this was the man she had learned to rely on, to need with all her heart. This was the man who had warmed her, who had made her hope and made her believe that the curse could be buried. This was the man she had fallen in love with. He looked devastated; she had never seen him so sad.

"I don't care what you can do or what you can't do," he said softly. "You're my wife. My choice has nothing to do with any damned magical abilities. I love you," he insisted.

"I never would've touched you if I hadn't known you were the woman I'd spend my life with."

If she was not careful, she would forgive him, she would agree to be his empress, and what good could come of that? She didn't want to live a life built upon a lie. She didn't want to look at him every day and wonder if—when—he would lie to her again. She had not truly trusted many people in her lifetime, and to live forever with the possibility of betrayal was unthinkable.

Besides, Jahn did not need an empress who had killed and would likely kill again. He did not need to share the burden of the murder she would always have to hide. It was best to push him away from her, as far and as completely as possible. "Never would've touched me, eh? I suppose that's what you said to your good friends Melusina and Anrid."

He went a little pale.

"It's not that I expected the emperor to live the life of a monk," she continued, letting her anger run a bit loose, "but no woman wants to sit down and listen to her supposed husband's mistresses go on about how talented or fun-loving or . . ."

"I did not touch either of them or any other woman once I claimed you," Jahn interrupted. "Say what you will, but I have been, and will always be, a faithful husband."

Morgana fought to remain calm. "I'm sure the woman you choose to be empress will be glad to hear that. There are just a few days until the First Night of the Summer Festival, when your choice must be made. Will you two be married right away? Will it be a large ceremony or something small, with only a few family members and friends in attendance? I'm sure your bride will be lovely, no matter what sort of ceremony you choose to have."

Jahn's jaw hardened. So did his eyes. She was not the only one capable of losing her temper. "I am already married."

Morgana took a brave step toward him, knowing it would not be good for her to get too near. She was vulnerable to him, still. "You're not married, and you know it. What's good enough for Jahn Devlyn, sentinel, means *nothing* to an emperor. A claim on a whim and a shared bed might be enough for peasants to call themselves married, but it's certainly not sufficient for the ruler of a country." She felt a sliver of ice in her heart but was easily able to restrain it, as Rainer had taught her. "You had your fun, My Lord Emperor. Now release me."

"Never," Jahn said as he stalked toward the door.

Her heart thudded too hard, but the ice there did not threaten to break loose. "You did say you'd let me go," she reminded him.

"Perhaps I was hasty in making that statement."

"So, I'm to be a prisoner here for the rest of my life?"

"If that's what it takes," Jahn snapped as he opened the door.

"You wouldn't dare!" she cried.

Jahn glanced over his shoulder, and she saw pure frustration on his face. "Watch me." The door slammed behind him, and Morgana soon sank into her chair. She could not stay here much longer; she was already too close to forgiving the man who had broken her will and her heart, and that would never do.

KRISTO had taken his time studying the comings and goings on Level Seven. For two days he'd watched and planned and waited with great patience. Once, in the early morning hours, he'd traveled well beyond the palace walls to meet once more with the small army Rikka had assembled.

He'd also managed to claim a few minutes of General Hydd's precious time. The general was one of those remarkable people who would do anything for what they believed to be right, no matter what that might be. Hydd believed Emperor Jahn to be ineffective, he was convinced that Jahn was making Columbyana weak, and so he was willing to lead a revolution which would oust the emperor in favor of a leadership which was not afraid of war. No, that was not quite right. He was working to put in place a leadership which would openly favor war and the spoils it would bring. If all went well, Hydd would lead the new army, at least for a while. Eventually he would be a hindrance, Kristo supposed, but for now he was necessary for leading the initial attack, if it was required, and for reorganizing the army once Jahn was dead.

Though he did not say so aloud, Hydd was hoping for an early attack. He wanted to see the new order begun. Since Morgana was already with child, that might be possible.

Rikka's army was a sad collection of misfits, but they were deadly misfits who would do anything for the coin she'd promised. Some preferred the violence and the power of their mercenary profession, but most were in this game simply for riches. None of them questioned Kristo's word that Lady Rikka was dead and that he and Hydd were now in charge of the operation. They were loyal to whoever paid them.

With his head down so his sometimes startling eyes were well hidden, Kristo walked toward Morgana's door with a wooden tray held steady in both hands. Upon that tray sat a pot of tea and a plate of sweet cakes, as well as a pretty red-gemmed necklace Kristo had stolen from an intoxicated minister's wife the night before. As he expected, one of two sentinels met him in front of the door they guarded.

"From the emperor," Kristo whispered.

"I'll take it in," the stout sentinel said, reaching for the tray.

Kristo's grip remained firm. "The emperor also asked that I deliver a message. Privately," he added in a whispering voice. He could turn both these sentinels to stone and continue with his plan without this deception, but he did not want to show his hand so soon, nor did he wish to expend the sort of energy it would take to turn two men to stone. Transforming one man was tiring; transforming two was draining; more than that—a trial. Still, if it was necessary, he would do so.

The sentinels looked at one another briefly, then the fat one nodded his head. "All right," the man said, as he knocked briefly and then opened the door. Kristo got a closer look at his daughter, who sat in a chair by the window. She wore the same ragged yellow dress he had seen her in so often of late, though there were finer gowns tossed about the room, on room dividers and wooden chests. The girl was stubborn, like her father.

She was drawing, passing the time as many fine ladies did, with pencils and paper. Did she draw flowers and birds, as a genteel girl might do? Or were her subjects more powerful and unusual? He wanted to see. Perhaps he would.

Morgana looked very much like her mother, but she had quite a bit of his strength. That was good. She would need that strength in the days to come. Kristo stepped into the room. His daughter was annoyed to be disturbed.

"From the emperor," Kristo said, as the sentinel closed the door behind him.

"I want nothing from the emperor," Morgana said, barely glancing his way as she made an angry swipe with her pencil. Not flowers, he would guess.

He'd always had difficulty reaching for and knowing what was in his daughter's heart and mind. He could not sense her from a distance, not as he could so many others. He could not see clearly into her past or her future. Their blood ties meant she was too close for him to see clearly. Her strength also held him back. It was always easier to read the minds of the weak and spineless. Morgana was neither.

Even with her blood ties and strength, she could not hide her anger from him. Nor could she hide the life inside her, the son who would change everything. Standing so near to her at last, he also saw death. Death at her hand, death like that which he himself delivered on occasion.

Kristo placed the tray on a small table. "I have waited a

very long time to meet you, Lady Morgana." His use of her name drew her attention, and she finally looked at him. Kristo met her strong gaze with one of his own. "Do you recognize me?"

She shook her head and settled her paper in her lap. "No. I'm certain we have never met."

"But we have. You were two years old when last I saw you." Kristo stepped nearer his daughter, glancing down at her drawing. No, she did not draw anything so simple as flowers. An angel filled the page, wings spread and powerful, gaze stern and not at all heavenly. There was power in that angelic drawing. "Your eyes had just turned from baby blue to a green much like your mother's, and your hair was even fairer than it is now. I swear, it was nearly white."

"How do you . . ." she began, but Kristo was not ready to stop talking. Not yet.

"Your mother left me because I refused to give up my magic. She took you, and she walked away. I could've gone after you, I suppose, but I had better things to do with my time: I honed my skills, I tended the raw magic I had been given at birth, and I searched for more talents which could be learned. A family at that time in my life was just a distraction from what was truly important to me. It wasn't as if your mother and I loved each other, after all. Our marriage had been arranged for us, and compliant children that we were, we simply did as we were told." He smiled. "She regretted that decision many times, or so she told me in those months before she left. She said you would never have any man forced upon you, and yet now here we are and you are imprisoned by a man who dares to claim you. Your mother would not be pleased."

Morgana had gone pale, so pale he was afraid she might faint. As she was still seated that would not be disastrous.

"You are my daughter, Morgana," he said, as if she did not already understand. "We share a gift, you and I, and we also share a purpose."

"I have no purpose," she said, and Kristo could not help

but note that her voice was very much like her mother's, in accent and in tone.

"But you do, daughter," Kristo said as he moved nearer the chair where his child, the next empress of Columbyana, the mother of the next emperor, a killer like him, sat. "Together you and I can claim a country and we can make the man who hurt you pay dearly for all that he has done."

THEIR walks in the garden had become a nightly event, but tonight a soft rain fell. Danya and Angelo stood at the doorway which led into the garden and watched the gentle raindrops wash over the plants and flowers.

Danya knew she would miss their walks when this part of her life was over. She would miss Angelo's deep, calm voice, his steadiness, his friendship, and his undemanding kiss that had the power to rock her to her toes. While they'd walked she'd found herself opening up to him, sharing stories of her youth as she had in those days before she'd forced him from her life, laughing in ways she had not thought to laugh in years. She found herself holding his hand without ulterior motive and leaning into him when the nights began to turn cool.

In the past two days she had done her best to gently seduce Angelo, but he was not giving in as he should. He would kiss her and then put her gently aside, or else he would ignore her blatant offers of anything he might desire from her and say good night. She knew he wanted her, so why was he being so obstinate?

"We could go back to my chambers," she said as the continuing rain made their evening ritual impossible. He would likely refuse her, but she had to try. Kristo would know if she did not even attempt to set their plan into motion. He was already annoyed that she had not yet managed to seduce Angelo and perhaps get herself with a fair-haired, magically gifted child, and he very much wanted this man who could sense certain kinds of energy dead before he saw too much of Uncle Kristo.

To her surprise, Angelo accepted her offer, and they climbed the stairs together.

Danya's heart beat so hard she thought it might come through her chest, and the pounding didn't subside when Angelo took her hand in his. Maybe her reasons for taking him as a lover were less than pure, but that did not mean she didn't want him. Ennis was the only man she had ever known in an intimate way, and though he had aroused her, he had not always been kind. He had not loved her. The emperor barely knew her, and he did not like her at all— not that she'd given him reason to like her.

In any case, Angelo was her only chance to have sex with a man who truly cared for her. This was the closest she would ever come to love, she supposed. That was why her heart pounded.

She did not lead Angelo into the anteroom, which would have been proper for guests, but instead guided him into the main chamber where her bed waited. A maid or two had already been in to prepare the room for the night. Bowls of scented oil burned, giving off gentle light and filling the room with a sweet scent. A small fire burned in the fireplace, and the coverlet of her bed had been turned back, exposing soft pillows and exquisite sheets. A large bowl of warm water and a washcloth had been put out so she could wash her face before bed. A decanter of wine and a single glass had been placed by the bed, since lately she had not been able to sleep without taking a glass or two.

Danya didn't waste times playing games or being coy, but turned and kissed Angelo in the way she had learned to kiss at his instruction. Softly, with emotion and gentleness and promise. She kissed him like a butterfly, rather than like a raven. She brushed her lips across his and waited for him to respond, instead of attacking him with anguished passion, as she had a few days earlier.

Angelo moaned gently against her mouth, returned the passion of her kiss, and then drew away. He did not wish to pull away from her; he did not wish to be apart. He wanted her.

Danya began to work loose the ribbons and hooks and eyes which held her low-cut fine gown together. The fabric was a startling purple that shimmered when she moved, and it showed her figure well. The garment had been meant to seduce an emperor, but it worked just as well for this man who—noble or not—often stole glances at her exposed cleavage. As she undressed, she kept her eyes on Angelo, who did not attempt to stop her, as she had thought he might. Instead, he watched with hunger in his eyes. He watched until she was standing before him in nothing more than an undershift made of a thin fabric which did nothing to hide her body.

"Have you decided to withdraw from the race for empress?" he asked, his gaze raking up and down her body.

"No. I intend to be empress in a few days. That doesn't mean I don't want you." She licked her suddenly dry lips. "I do want you, Angelo. We've been coming to this moment since the night you bloodied Ennis's nose," she said. "We've been headed here, *hurtling* here, to this bed, since the day we met."

"You would invite me into your bed and then turn around and take another man as your husband," he said.

"Yes."

"You would give yourself away, offer yourself without compunction, without love."

The word made her heart leap. "I didn't say I don't love you." The truth of the words was painful as it sank in. She did love this kind man who deserved so much more than anything she could ever give him. She did love this man who looked at her now as if he were disillusioned.

"Why do you not ask for more?" he whispered.

"I am asking for everything you have to give." Frustration was clear in her voice.

Angelo shook his head slowly. "No, you're not asking for much at all. You give yourself away too easily, Danya. To Ennis, to the emperor's command, to me . . . Why do you not demand more? You're beautiful, and you're smarter and stronger than you allow anyone to see. And yet you demean yourself more often than not. You don't demand respect or love when you should, you just grasp for whatever you think you can take from life, as if what you desire might disappear in an instant if you don't snatch it up in your greedy hands. I have tried to see into your heart, but in truth I don't understand you at all. You have a good heart, but it is so wrapped up in desperation that it has been blinded. Your heart has been hidden for so long you don't . . ."

"You don't know me," she snapped. "You don't have any idea why I do the things I do."

"Then tell me," he said, moving close and wrapping his arms around her. "Something is very wrong, I know that's true, and yet you hide the truth from me the way you hide everything else. I want very much to share this bed, or another, with you, but not until you're entirely mine. I won't share you, Danya; I will never share you. When you're mine, only mine . . ."

"I can't be yours!" Danya said, her mouth all but buried against his warm chest.

"When you're mine," Angelo said again in a calmer voice, "then we will share everything."

Danya felt like she was falling apart, literally crumbling to pieces in this man's arms. "If you don't love me, if you don't become my lover, he'll make me kill you." She shuddered. "I've done what I can to keep you alive, but if we're not together, he'll know. He knows everything," she whispered, and then she grabbed Angelo and held on tight.

"Who?" he asked sharply. "Who do you think could make you kill me?"

Danya sobbed, and the truth broke loose. "The monster who has stolen my son."

LONG after the man who'd claimed to be her father had left her, Morgana stood silent and still at the window which overlooked the western fields. The moon shone on fields wet with the evening rain, alive with the coming of summer.

She wished that she could dismiss the awful man as an impostor and a liar, but he knew too much. The man who called himself Kristo Stoyan knew why Morgana's mother had been so insistent that her daughter be allowed to choose her own husband. He knew about the power Morgana had never wanted, and somehow—some way—he even realized that she'd killed a man with her anger. He hadn't threatened outright to tell others about the death, but the threat had been there, gently undeniable.

He also said that if she continued to work on control, as she had in days past, she would soon find other powers which would serve her well. Apparently Kristo could sometimes peek into the minds of others. Strong-willed people were tougher to read, he said, as were those who were close to him—like her. He saw flashes of the past and the future, and used his knowledge to his own advantage.

She was so glad Kristo had not been able to reach into her mind. He would not have liked what he found there.

He'd been anxious to tell her more about the power they shared, and Morgana had listened carefully—and she hadn't liked what she'd heard. If she embraced the power and allowed it to come to its full strength, he'd said, she would one day be as cold as he was. Instead of a sliver at her core, she could be filled with the power and no one would be able to stop her.

All her life Morgana had wondered and even dreamed about her real father, a man she'd been told was dead. She'd imagined how much better her life would've been if he'd lived, how much he would've loved her, how close she would've felt to him. He would've loved her unconditionally, he would not have made her do things she did not wish to do. Childish fantasies of a father she'd never known had taken root in her mind, and she'd not put them away as she grew to adulthood, as she should've.

She'd always made a point of calling the man who'd

raised her *step*father, as if she could not allow herself to think of him as a real parent, as if her real father would've been better, as if he would've loved her more.

And now she knew without doubt that Almund Ramsden was her father in every way that counted. He'd loved her, cared for her, demanded that she behave like a lady and learn all she could. And in the end he'd given her to an emperor.

He would never have asked of her what Kristo asked.

Sensing her anger and disappointment with Jahn, realizing that she was a prisoner here, knowing that she had blood on her hands—and yet not sensing her regret, an emotion he apparently could not understand—Kristo believed the two of them shared a need for vengeance. Morgana had allowed him to continue to believe that as he'd laid out his plans. To deny him would only make him take immediate action, and she knew what kind of action he would take. Kristo would turn Jahn to stone without a second thought, and she could not allow that to happen. He would turn the sentinels who guarded her to stone, and though she had been angry with them since learning the truth, they were still her friends.

She had not forgiven Jahn, but neither did she hate him. Hate was a poison; talking to Kristo for just a few minutes had proved that to her. She did not want to become like her real father—she didn't want to let hate rule her life.

Understanding what kind of man he was, she'd allowed Kristo to believe that she was willing and even anxious to go along with his plan. Any other choice would lead to disaster. It would lead to immediate madness.

The child she had only suspected grew inside her was indeed real, if Kristo and his magic were correct. It was a boy, he said, an emperor who would share their powers. After she had held them in for so long, fighting for control as the day grew long, tears leaked from Morgana's eyes. She did not want her child to share in her curse—she did not want him to struggle as she had.

She placed a hand over her stomach, fingers splayed.

No, her child would not struggle. He would be taught from an early age how to control the abilities which were a part of his birthright, just as becoming emperor was his birthright. He would be loved and cared for, always; he would be warm, not cold.

But first, Morgana had to find a way to save her child's father from the plans Kristo had set into motion.

Chapter Fifteen

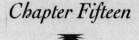

IN spite of Jahn's promise to Sanura to remain out of sight until the First Night of the Summer Festival, keeping his presence in the palace a secret turned out to be impossible. A message from Alix had found its way to Jahn, and he could not ignore it.

Jahn waited in the ballroom for the appointed meeting with his brother, and he was not alone. Two Tryfynian soldiers, as well as the two guards from Claennis, anxiously watched the main entrance. All four of them were incensed by real or imagined wrongs, and anxious to do battle with Alix the moment they saw him.

There were armed sentinels in the hallway outside that door, sentinels who would charge in at Jahn's command. But at Alix's request there were none in the ballroom. The prince apparently wanted privacy for whatever he had to say on this night.

Jahn paid little attention to the massive main doorway the others watched so diligently, fully expecting his brother to join them by way of the hidden stairway which would allow him to move through the palace with some secrecy.

Sure enough, after a short wait the inconspicuous doorway which was built into the wall at the back corner of the ballroom opened almost silently, and Alix appeared, his companion at his side.

Sanura, the woman Jahn had spoken with just a few days earlier, was now painted a lovely shade of blue. The blue cosmetic clung to her skin quite naturally. Though Jahn had heard that this was sometimes the case, he was still taken aback at the sight.

"Interesting," he said as he took a moment to study the woman. He then turned his consideration to his brother, who looked rougher and decidedly more menacing than Jahn could ever remember. Alix had always been so careful with his appearance, so fastidious, so unerringly noble, but tonight he displayed a wild side which was unknown to Jahn. With others in attendance, now was not the time to comment on the changes he saw in his brother. "We are all here, just as you commanded. I understand you and I have some business to discuss, but why are these other men present?" Surely Alix knew that these men wanted him dead. They had all threatened to kill him, and if their claims were truthful, they had some right.

Alix ignored Jahn and guided his blue woman toward the others. Both Tryfynian soldiers placed their hands on their swords, ready to fight the man they blamed for the death of their princess. Sanura's guards looked as if they were anxious to rush Alix and take his head here and now, but they did not. Not for the first time, Jahn acknowledged that being emperor had its advantages. Bloodthirsty as they were, these men were afraid to act in his presence—and with good reason. No emperor would stand back and allow a man to take his twin's life.

"We'll take care of the easy tasks first," Alix said, walking toward the Tryfynians. He didn't seem at all worried about the swords. Perhaps he knew, as Jahn did, that violence in this room would be incredibly foolish.

"You morons," Alix said darkly, a dangerous timbre Jahn was not accustomed to hearing in his voice. "I did not kill Princess Edlyn. She was an annoying little twit and I won't miss her, but I did not kill her. It was Tari, who did the deed at Vyrn's insistence. I suspect the same person who attempted to have Lady Verity murdered also planned the princess's murder, as well as arranging the scene to make it look as if Sanura and I were guilty." He glanced back, and his eyes caught Jahn's. "Someone does not wish my brother to marry, or so it appears. Since only one potential bride has arrived, I would suggest that the others have had challenges and accidents, and perhaps even more deaths, along the way." He turned away, once again glaring at the Tryfynians. "Besides, if I'd wanted the princess dead, I could have arranged some method of death which would not have pointed directly at me. I'm not an idiot."

The Tryfynian soldiers looked suitably humbled, their air of righteous indignation diminished. The hands on the grips of their swords fell away as they recognized the truth of Alix's words. Jahn had not believed his brother capable of murder, but still, he felt a rush of relief at hearing the words from Alix's own mouth.

Alix turned to the men who claimed to be Sanura's protectors. "I understand and appreciate that when you tried to kill me, you were only doing your duty," he said, "but you must realize that you are no longer in Claennis, and you cannot murder a man for innocently touching a woman."

"Innocently?" one of the guards shouted.

"In theory," Alix said, "it doesn't matter. Blue on a man's skin means death, unless he is the one, the only one, who possesses Sanura."

"That is correct."

Alix reached out and quickly ran his hand across Sanura's arm, and then he raked the blue stain from his hand onto his bare chest. When that was done, he moved quickly, perhaps realizing how the foreign men would react. With lightning-fast moves he disarmed one guard and then the other, tossing the weapons across the ballroom. The scream of metal against stone rang in Jahn's ears before the swords came to a halt a good distance away in this cavernous chamber.

Alix drew his own sword with strength and grace, and Jahn wondered if the man his brother had become would kill these unarmed men. He was certainly capable. But Alix did not swing his blade. His voice was a low rumble as he said, "If you cared at all about protecting Sanura, you would've used those weapons on the men who claimed to own her as if she were a pretty jewel or a strong horse. You would've used those blades to cut out the hearts of women who would rip her insides apart in the name of some damned man's convenience. If you cared for her at all, you would not allow any man to *own* her!"

The two unarmed guards took a step away from Alix, and Jahn couldn't blame them. The man they faced looked capable of anything.

"Go home," Alix said, his sword remaining steady. "Sanura is now mine to protect. Be assured that if any other man ever touches her, I will do what you could not."

The guards both looked to the blue woman as if for direction, and she nodded. One of them foolishly made a move toward his weapon, which lay several feet away, but Alix stopped him. "Leave the swords. You don't deserve them."

Without a word of argument, the two foreigners backed toward the Tryfynian soldiers and the doorway. Alix waved his sword in their direction, directing them all out of the room. He quickly closed the door behind them before he turned to face his brother.

Jahn had the sinking feeling the night's drama had just begun.

"Now, on to our business."

To watch Alix take care of the Tryfynians and Sanura's protectors had been fascinating and even amusing, but Jahn was not amused to have those dark eyes turned on him with such hatred. As he'd watched and listened to events unfold, his mind had occasionally wandered elsewhere, most often to the woman who so ardently refused to forgive him. He wanted Morgana to remain at his side the way Sanura remained with Alix. He wanted the close bond these two so obviously shared—though he did prefer the natural color of Morgana's fair skin to anything so outrageous as Sanura's blue.

The bond Jahn desired, the loyalty Sanura showed to Alix, could not be forced or bought; it could not be decreed. Such a treasure could only be given. As emperor he could command much, but he could not command a woman's forgiveness; he could not order Morgana to love him as she once had.

Jahn waited calmly, wondering what was to come, realizing that anything was possible. He held Alix's gaze steadily, and was surprised by the depth of the fierceness he saw there. Something within Alix had broken loose, just as Sanura had claimed. Jahn had to admit that he'd been foolish to believe that his brother's struggles were behind him. Had this angry man always lurked behind the prince's steady face?

The brothers were surprised when Sanura placed herself between them, the dagger in her hand pointed at Alix's heart very near to the place where he had stained himself with her blue paint. She whispered something Jahn could not hear, though he strained to catch her words.

Alix responded, a cutting pain in his voice. "You would kill me to save him?"

"No," the blue woman replied. "But I would kill you to save you."

"That makes no sense."

Jahn sighed. None of it made any sense to him, either. His patience was at an end. "Cut my brother and I will kill you."

"I know," Sanura said confidently and clearly. "I understand completely."

"I don't," Alix said. "I don't understand this at all." He took his gaze from Sanura and looked squarely at Jahn once again. "If she does manage to kill me, you will not harm her and you will not imprison her. Do you understand?"

"Not at all," Jahn mumbled. When it came to women, he understood nothing. That fact became clearer to him every day.

Again, Sanura spoke softly, her words for Alix alone. Jahn could not understand—and perhaps he didn't need to. The woman had spoken of releasing Alix's dark side and of trying to contain it. At the moment, it appeared she was failing miserably when it came to containment. Her voice rose slightly and Jahn heard one statement very clearly.

"You won't survive if you murder your own brother."

"Let him go," Jahn ordered with confidence. "Alix won't hurt me. We've been through too much together. He's my brother, for God's sake. He's my *twin*." No matter what demons Alix battled, no matter what traitorous thoughts might've clouded his judgment, their brotherhood was stronger than any dark influence. Wasn't it?

"You're a fool," Alix said, for the moment paying no mind to the woman and the knife she held on him in such a threatening manner. All his attention was for Jahn, now, and the darkness, the hatred, was palpable. "I *will* kill you, if I get the chance. I will take the throne, this palace, everything you possess."

Jahn experienced a flash of anger, a rush of hurt, and all the frustration of the past days flooded through him. Apparently he'd been wrong to think that in the end brotherhood would mean more than ambition or hatred, as he had been wrong about so many other things. How had he gotten himself into this mess? He had gotten himself into it by starting the contest for empress, by lying to Morgana, by refusing to believe that his brother could ever be a threat.

"Do you want the empress I'm supposed to pick?" he snapped, thinking of the one woman who had thus far arrived for his consideration—the intolerable Lady Danya. "Trust me, you can have her!"

"I don't . . ." Alix began, and then his words died away. For a moment he looked lost, confused, uncertain, and

Jahn saw a hint of the man Alix had once been flicker across his face.

"Yes," Sanura whispered.

A moment later, Alix easily and fluidly moved the threatening dagger away from his flesh, as he could've done at any time. He pulled the blue woman into his arms and gasped as if the blade had found its mark. The expression on Alix's face was one of pain and release and sorrow, and he seemed to fight for every breath. For a moment Jahn wondered if the blue woman had somehow poisoned the man she claimed to love, and then . . . everything changed.

Sanura dropped the knife so that it clattered to the stone floor, and she jumped into Alix's embrace, wrapping her legs around his waist and her arms around his neck. She laughed and cried, and together the two of them dropped to the floor, where Alix knelt with the woman caught in his arms.

So, who was getting killed here tonight? Anyone? Jahn walked toward the entwined lovers. "I'm so fucking confused." Did the blue woman intend to kill Alix or make love to him here and now? It was impossible to tell. "Is this woman yours?"

"No," Alix responded. "No one can possess something so bright and beautiful as Sanura. No one can own her. But I am hers, heart and soul. I belong to her in every way possible."

Jahn sighed. Good Lord, how sentimental his brother had become. A menace one minute, a softhearted fool the next. He half paid attention as the two declared their love for one another and Sanura made it clear that the darkness which had driven Alix to plan to take Jahn's life would never be entirely gone—*great*—but was under control.

And then, in a moment of clarity, Jahn realized what had happened. This change in the situation—the change in Alix—had not come out of nowhere, as it had appeared to. Alix and Sanura had communicated silently. There was no other explanation for what he'd just seen. They had shared minds, shared hearts perhaps, and the result was a startling

change in the man who had apparently been considering—
no, *planning*—to murder his brother and take the throne
for himself.

Alix and Sanura were happy and in love, and Jahn tasted
bitterness in his mouth, felt that bitterness in his heart.
This was what he wanted from Morgana. Love. Forgiveness. A willingness to start again and look to the future. He
wanted her to think about the days to come, not the mistakes of the past.

Though in his opinion the past had been very fine. It
had just been tainted with a few lies and deceptions. He
hadn't planned to kill anyone or take over a country, he'd
just wanted a few days or weeks as a normal man without
the responsibilities of an emperor. Was that too much to
ask? Apparently it was, at least where Morgana was concerned.

Alix's words came back to taunt Jahn, and he could not
help but wonder if those words applied to Morgana as much
as—or more than—Sanura. *No one can own her.*

RAINER held Danya long after she fell asleep. She was
exhausted, shaken from a long bout of crying and confession. And what a startling confession it had been. No wonder her attitude had changed during their trip to Arthes! It
all made sense now. The fear, the anger, the way she had
sent Fai away and had attempted to send him away—more
than once.

If he'd thought for a moment that Jahn might choose
Danya as empress, he'd be obliged to share what he knew.
He certainly could not allow her to become empress, not
when there were plans to take over the throne through a
traitorous bride and an as yet unconceived child. As it
stood, he had time to consider how best to handle the situation.

If not for the child Kristo held prisoner, Rainer would
spirit Danya away from the palace tonight and they'd start
anew somewhere far from this place. But there was Ethyn

to consider. Poor Danya, she had done nothing but consider
the child for weeks, afraid of what might happen to him if
she disappointed Kristo. What hell she had been living in.

Danya woke with a start, perhaps due to a bad dream.
She threw herself into Rainer's arms and held on tight,
then slowly calmed herself as she realized where she was
and that she was not alone. She cuddled into his chest and
her arms went around his waist.

She still wore the undershift she'd stripped to when trying to seduce him. He had taken off his shoes and his
jacket, but nothing more. He couldn't remember ever wanting a woman as much as he wanted Danya, but he wouldn't
take her this way. He wouldn't allow her to think she owed
him anything, or that sex was the only comfort she could
find with him.

"I dreamed about Ethyn," she whispered as she settled
more securely against his side. "Sometimes I see him in
my dreams as Kristo described him, and he's playing and
laughing. Other nights I have nightmares where he feels
Kristo's coldness and is horrified by it." She shuddered. "I
have to save my baby, no matter what it costs."

"I know."

"Even if it means . . ." Danya began, a hint of desperation in her voice.

"I will help you," Rainer said. "Together we will save
your son, and you won't have to do anything you don't want
to do in order for that to happen."

Danya tilted her head to look at him, even though it was
difficult to see much detail in the room dimly lit with the
little bit of firelight that remained. "Why?" she whispered.
"Why are you going to help me?"

"Because it's the right thing to do and because I love
you."

She sighed and then cuddled against him, and soon her
lips found his throat. Rainer groaned a little, unable to stop
the rush of sensation. He couldn't take much more of this
and remain distant, even though he knew it was what Danya
needed. She could not continue to equate declarations of

love with sex, not unless she was willing to put him in the same category as Ennis. That bastard.

"When this is all behind us, love," he said, setting her aside. "When you are entirely mine."

She looked at him oddly, as if she didn't understand. Rainer sat up and directed his hand toward the fireplace, sending a burst of energy to the flames in order to increase the heat and the light in the room. Danya was cold, and he wished to look upon her. The energy which flowed from his hand was not visible like Morgana's, but it was no less effective. It fed the fire, it caused the flames to leap and dance.

He did not use his gift often—there was usually no need for it, and to abuse any magical gift could lead to trouble. But at this moment he did not wish to leave the bed and Danya's side, even though he refused to do more than hold her.

Soon enough she would have all of him, and he would not allow her to be sorry that she waited.

"Angelo, will you stay the night?" she asked gently.

"Yes, I'll stay."

"Thank you," she whispered.

He used the same power he had used to fan the flames to gentle Danya's energy, to gently urge her back toward sleep. Soon she settled down and returned to sleep—and hopefully better dreams.

IT was the middle of the night when Morgana's door opened and a dark figure slipped inside. If she'd been sleeping, perhaps she wouldn't have heard or seen, but this had not been a night for sleeping. The light of the fire illuminated him well enough.

How many other nights had Jahn slipped into the room while she'd been sleeping?

She lay there, unmoving, while he shed his crimson robe and then very gently sat on the other side of the bed. He dropped his head into his hands for a long moment before lying down beside her, not reaching for her or speaking or making any demands, but simply lying there. He had not come bearing jewels or clothing or shoes tonight, he just brought himself. That was all she wanted, to be totally honest. She wanted the man she had fallen in love with. She wanted Jahn Devlyn.

It would be easy enough to pretend she was asleep, and just as easy to sit up in indignation and insist that he leave her bed and her room. But instead she asked, "What's wrong?"

"You're awake."

"Apparently so. What's wrong?"

"You're awake and you have not yet kicked me out of the bed," Jahn responded.

"Not yet," Morgana said, and then she rose up on one elbow. "How often have you sneaked into my bed since I threw you out?"

"Every night," he confessed. "Sometimes for a long while and other times for a few minutes. You're a deep sleeper," he added. "Usually. What's keeping you awake tonight?"

She could not possibly tell him all that was on her mind! Until she decided how best to handle the situation, she would have to keep her problems to herself. One thing was certain: if she told Jahn everything, Kristo would somehow know, and the man who called himself her father would not go away quietly if his plans were spoiled.

She would love to tell Jahn that she was carrying his son, but until she knew what tomorrow would bring, how could she? "I will ask you one more time," she said testily. "What's wrong?"

"Why do you think something is wrong?"

"The sigh, the way you hold your shoulders, the very fact that you are here—they all tell me that something is wrong." Why did she care? Why did she want to know why he gave in to that sigh?

"I have lost my brother," Jahn replied. "He's not going to murder me in my sleep, but . . ."

"I would hope not!" Morgana responded.

"But he's lost to me all the same. I think he will be happy, which is very nice, but he has another life now, a life which will surely take him away from here." Jahn turned his face to her. "I've also lost the woman I love, and I don't know how to get her back. Brothers should move on, I suppose, but wives should not."

"You don't have a wife," Morgana said, but with less anger than she'd said those words in the past few days.

"And speaking of wives," Jahn said, "someone is apparently killing the bridal candidates before they even reach the palace. All but one, and she is totally unacceptable. Then there's you, a woman I love who has refused to . . ."

"We've had this discussion," Morgana interrupted, hiding the horror that rose within her. She knew what Kristo wanted. Was he killing the women he would consider her competition? Was she the cause of yet more deaths?

"You asked what was wrong," Jahn said. "I tried not to answer, but you persisted."

"I did, didn't I?" She settled closer to Jahn than she should, glad of the companionship and the warmth, seeking her own sort of comfort. She knew she should remain angry with him, but compared to what her long-lost father wanted, Jahn's lies seemed almost insignificant. Almost.

It was easier to talk in the dark, easier to hide her heartbreak and disappointment. "Why did you lie to me?" she asked, trying—and failing—not to sound vulnerable.

Jahn sighed. "You called me fat and stupid and something else I've already forgotten, and then I overheard your stepfather vow to give you to the next man who walked through the door, and I could not resist. I thought it would be great fun, and I also thought that by the time we got to Arthes, you'd be begging for a chance to be empress."

"Great fun," she repeated.

"I did not plan to sleep with you, and I certainly didn't expect to find a real wife in you," he explained. "The deception started as a lark and it ended up being my *life*. I know I should've told you the truth sooner, but I was terrified of losing you."

She had no reason to believe anything Jahn said, but she believed him now. He did love her; this would be so much easier if she didn't believe that to be true!

Morgana found herself burrowing into his side, soaking up the warmth he had always offered, wondering how many opportunities like this would come again. A handful, if her father had his way. A lifetime, if Jahn had his way. None, if she continued to send him away.

What did she want? If she could learn to control her magical abilities, then she wouldn't be a threat to those around her—but she could not undo the fact that she had killed a man. If Jahn knew, if *anyone* knew, she could not possibly remain in the position of empress.

She certainly didn't want to be part of the chaos and betrayal Kristo had planned, but if she told Jahn all that she had learned, somehow Kristo would find out, and then what would happen? The man who had sired her would not be stopped easily, she suspected. He had planned his takeover for some time, and she and her child had always been at the center of his scheme.

"I will tell you this," Jahn said in a soft voice. "You think I pretended to be someone I'm not, but that's not true. I did not pretend with you, Ana. I pretend with everyone else, as I have every day of my life since coming here."

She didn't know what to do, so she nestled more closely into Jahn's side and wrapped her arms around him. She did still love him; she could forgive him anything, though that didn't mean he shouldn't have to pay for his deception.

He should not have to pay with his life.

"I have missed this so much," he said, throwing one arm around her. He had dropped his imperial robes before crawling into bed with her, and as usual had come to bed naked. She wore a thin nightdress that did nothing to keep his heat from her. This was much preferable to sleeping alone. Alone and afraid and uncertain.

"So have I," Morgana said.

"I'm sorry I didn't tell you the truth sooner," he said, and she could hear the truth of that statement in his voice. "I was afraid the truth would cost me everything we'd found, and I was right. If lying means I got to keep you for a while longer than I would've otherwise, then I'm not entirely sorry." He sighed. "I won't force you to stay. As soon as I'm certain you're not in danger, you can leave any time you . . ."

Morgana lifted her head slightly. "Shut up and kiss me."

He did, bringing his mouth to hers with hunger and passion. It was so sweet, after too many nights spent alone. So arousing, after too many hours lost in anger and suspicion. Emperor or not, she knew this man to the pit of his soul, and to hers. She didn't know what tomorrow would bring, but she already carried his son within her, so even if they had only one more night together, nothing would change.

One kiss, and she was able to dismiss everything else from her mind. It was a blessing to be able to think of nothing but the sensations coursing through her body. It was ecstasy to throb and ache and touch without conscious deliberation. She loved Jahn and he loved her, at least for now.

He pushed her gown higher and spread her thighs, and she opened for him. When he touched her, when his fingers found the center where she throbbed and ached, she almost cried. Her own fingers aroused and tested him as well, as together she and Jahn happily tumbled toward the only conclusion this night could offer.

Suddenly hot, Morgana sat up and whipped the nightdress over her head, impatiently tossing it aside so she could feel her skin against Jahn's. When that was done, she did not wait for him to come to her, but instead straddled him and guided his hard length to her, into her. She sank down, taking all of him and experiencing a moment of pure relief and satisfaction, before the need for more spurred her on and she began to move in an easy rhythm that was theirs alone.

Morgana reveled in the feel of Jahn inside her, so she moved slowly, prolonging the pleasure. She'd missed this; she'd needed it. Physically, she craved the pleasure and the release. Emotionally, she craved the inexplicable togetherness just as intensely. No matter who or what he was, no matter who or what he was not, Jahn was hers.

No matter what she'd done, no matter who she was or could be, she was his. Like him, she felt as if she pretended with the rest of the world—but not with him. He had seen all of her—all that counted.

Her body was starved for his, and the gentle movements soon turned fiercer, more demanding, until she broke and cried out in release and delight. Jahn came with her, burying himself deep and shuddering beneath her.

She dropped down and rested her head on his shoulder. They were still joined, and she did not want to leave; she didn't want to move.

"I love you, Ana," Jahn said, burying one hand in her hair and holding her close. He was not foolish enough to think that just because she had given in to him physically, all was as he wished it to be. He knew her better than that. "Can you forgive me? Can't we forget the lies that brought us here and simply start again?"

Morgana lifted her head and looked down at Jahn, studying his fine face in the firelight. "We can't ignore what's happened," she said, meaning every word. "And I would not want to forget what brought me here." She stopped short of telling Jahn that she loved him; she hesitated, wondering how much she could tell. There was so much to be said. There was a child he did not yet know of; the accidental death of a man at her hands; a plan that included lies which made his own look like child's play; betrayal and cold-blooded murder; and a child-emperor who would lead with the guidance of his vicious grandfather, if traitors had their way.

To tell all she knew might mean the end of everything; to ignore it might also mean the end of all she held dear—including the man beneath her.

But she couldn't let him go with so much unsaid, she couldn't let the man she loved continue on blindly, unaware of what had happened.

In order to smooth the way, she told Jahn the good news first. "I'm carrying your son," she whispered.

His reaction was immediate and extreme. Jahn shouted and rolled her onto her back, laughing as he lowered his head to kiss her stomach. A sharp knock on the door followed, and a familiar voice called, "My Lord, is all well?"

"Very well," Jahn responded in a voice loud enough for the sentinels beyond the door to hear. "All is very well," he said more softly, for her benefit.

He would soon think differently, she imagined, but she would not rob him of this moment. To be honest, for the first time the child she carried seemed real, a blessing, a result of their love for one another. This baby could mean the beginning of a family. Their family. "You sound happy."

"Of course I'm happy," he said. "I'm back in your bed and there's a child on the way. What is there not to be happy about?"

There was more, and she could not keep it from her husband. "Our son will have my abilities, I'm afraid."

Jahn was silent for much too long, and there wasn't enough light in the room for her to study his face properly. Was he disappointed? Horrified? His voice was calm as he finally asked, "How can you know? And how can you know that the child you carry is a son and not a beautiful daughter who will look like her mother? How can you know the child will inherit your magic?"

Now the conversation would become more difficult. "My father told me, and his magic is so much more powerful than mine that I cannot help but believe him."

"Almund . . ."

"No," she interrupted. "My . . . my real father. Oh, Jahn, I have so much to tell you, and I don't know where to begin."

"We have all night, love," he said, smoothing a strand of hair away from her face. "Tell it as you will. I'm listening."

She took a deep breath, trying to still her heart, unbearably glad for Jahn's closeness. "My father intends to kill you. More rightly, he intends for me to kill you."

At least he did not bolt from the bed as if he felt endangered. "What a night," he mumbled, and then he lay down beside her and caught her to his body, where she felt safe. "Tell all, love, and together we will plan for what comes next."

JAHN had always known that one day his brother would marry here in this ballroom where so many affairs of state took place, here where just last night Alix had confessed that he planned to kill Jahn and take the throne.

This was another day, a brighter and decidedly more unusual day. Jahn had quickly become accustomed to Sanura's blue skin, but to see Alix wearing the same paint was as startling as the knowledge that the struggle within the younger twin continued, and always would.

There were only a few ministers present for Alix's marriage ceremony, and most of them were in shock, thanks to the hue of the couple's skin and the fact that the bride wore a neatly arranged sheet as her wedding gown. Those who knew Alix well were surely as surprised by the change in his demeanor as Jahn had been, but they said nothing. Father Braen positively sputtered, but the red-faced priest did as he was told and said the words which declared this man and woman properly wedded.

When the short ceremony was over, the ministers and Father Braen all but scurried from the room. Word that Prince Alixandyr had lost his mind and painted himself blue and married a woman of no political importance would likely spread quickly. Jahn wondered if they would even bother to make note of the fact that the prince was happy and in love.

A properly wed Alix approached Jahn with a smile—a smile which looked decidedly odd against a blue face. It was more than the blue which made Alix look not entirely like the man Jahn thought he knew so well. The eyes were different, darker and more complicated. The set of his shoulders, the smile, the stride—all hinted at the hidden man Alix had been fighting all his life. This was the real Alix, Jahn knew it in a heartbeat.

"We're leaving shortly," Alix said in a lowered voice, perhaps so his bride would not hear.

"You're welcome to stay, to make this your home." Just because Alix had wanted to kill Jahn last night, that didn't mean he was no longer welcome here. "You are still a prince, and your bride is now a princess."

Alix shook his head. "Perhaps one day we'll return, but I have many things to take care of before I can settle down."

Jahn knew that if he told Alix all that Morgana had told him last night, the trip he planned to start today would be postponed. No matter what, Alix would not leave his brother in such a crisis. He would not ride away once he heard that there was a plan of assassination—other than his own. But Jahn did not tell. This was what Alix and his bride wanted, and he would not stop them from leaving.

There was an awkwardness between the brothers, as if an invisible barrier had been erected. The cause of that barrier was more than last night's excitement and threats, Jahn knew. This was a new man, a new brother. And yet, the old one had not entirely gone.

An expression of great contentment crossed Alix's face. "Sanura deserves more than I can ever give her."

"She's lucky to have you."

"I'm the lucky one." The set of Alix's features became slightly more solemn. "What of you, brother? Will you marry a woman you do not love for the sake of a country?"

Jahn hesitated. A magically gifted son, a traitorous plot, a wife who gave him her body but had not admitted that she loved him and forgave him for his deception. How to explain all that in the mere minutes they had? "My marital fate is . . . complicated."

Alix moved closer, but Jahn felt no fear. The man who'd threatened him was gone—for the most part. "I have advised you often since you became emperor, and I will do so once more, brother. The right woman is worth more than a country, more than a throne. Don't let anyone make you take the wrong woman as your wife. If you are so foolish, you will soon regret your sacrifice."

"What if I've found the right woman and she will not have me?" It was a question Jahn could ask no one else.

Alix's smile reappeared. "You have always been persuasive where women are concerned. Call on all your charms."

"My charms have failed me," Jahn confessed in a lowered voice.

Alix laughed harshly. "I doubt that." He glanced back to his bride, and a contented expression passed across his face. "We must go. We have a long way to travel today."

"You won't stay until the First Night of the Summer Festival? Just a few more days." Again, Jahn considered telling Alix what was coming . . . and again he did not.

"No. The decision is yours. I've said all I can on the matter. Knowing you, I suspect all will be well."

Jahn made a scoffing noise under his breath. It wasn't his decision he was worried about. His decision had been made, but he wasn't at all sure about his wife's intentions. If they got past the excitement her father had planned, if they worked together to fight this foe who had risen up to threaten them both . . . then what?

The brothers had never been prone to hugging, opting instead for hearty handshakes and the occasional slap on the back. This parting was different from others. Alix and Jahn moved toward one another without hesitation for a long, hard embrace.

Their lives had changed dramatically when their true parentage had been unveiled, and those lives were changing again. "Good luck," Jahn said as they parted.

"And to you." Again, Alix grinned, reaching into his pocket and pulling out the thick leaf of a succulent plant. "Break the leaf and use the gel inside to clean off the blue." He tossed the leaf and Jahn caught it, noticing as he did so that everywhere he'd touched Alix's skin, he was stained with blue paint.

"Something to remember you by?" he asked sharply, and then they both laughed.

Jahn was certain he had never heard Alix laugh with such honesty. His eyes had never been so alive.

He looked forward to getting to know this man his brother had become when Alix and Sanura returned to Arthes one day.

The ballroom was horribly large and empty after the bride and groom made their escape. Jahn stood there for a long while, his mind spinning. A son, a reluctant wife he was not sure he could keep, a wizard who wanted him dead . . . the next few days were going to be very interesting. For the first time in his life he wished for a few hours of sweet, blessed boredom.

Chapter Sixteen

✺

The First Day of the Summer Festival

DANYA didn't know whether to be relieved or concerned that she hadn't seen Kristo in a few days. Having Angelo Rainer in her life as a friend, as a promise of what the future might be, was more than she'd ever hoped for, but there was still much to be decided before they could move on. Where was her son? When would Ethyn be brought to her?

How on earth would she escape doing exactly as Kristo demanded?

She forced herself to make her way to the level where Kristo was housed. It was an arduous climb, to lesser quarters. He planned to demand better housing as soon as she was wed to the emperor, but until then these secondary quarters on a level which required much climbing of steps would have to do. It wasn't difficult to find out which room her "uncle" had been assigned. She knocked upon his door with determination. Angelo had told her to leave the evil man alone and let him handle matters, but she could not. Her son's life was at stake, and she couldn't step aside and do nothing. She couldn't ask Angelo to endanger himself because of the foolish decisions she had made. What could she have done differently to save herself and Ethyn?

Kristo answered her knock quickly, even though it was early in the morning and Danya had thought she might awaken him. He was dressed in gray robes that hung on his thin frame, reminiscent of the way he had been dressed when she'd first seen him. He was very much awake. His hair had been combed, his face freshly washed. Either he had not slept at all or he was a very early riser. He wasn't happy to see her. She almost wished he wore the hood which would hide his features from her.

"What do you want?" he asked sharply.

Danya found herself wringing her hands. "Time grows short, and we have not finalized plans for tonight. Will you be there when the emperor makes his choice? Since he thinks you to be family, will you be present for the ceremony?" She swallowed hard, then finally asked the question which brought her here. "When will I see Ethyn?" *Where are you keeping him?*

"Go away," the cold-eyed man said. He started to close the door in her face, but Danya shot out a stilling hand and forced the door open, taking Kristo by surprise.

"I have agreed to do everything you ask," she said, her voice sounding much braver than she felt inside. "I am here, and I will marry the emperor if he chooses me, as you say he will. I'll have his child and, God help me, I will even stand by and let you take his life, when the time comes." She had been falling helplessly toward this moment, out of control and with one end in mind. Ethyn. "I've given everything of myself to your plans, all for the sake of my son. Now it is your turn to keep your promise. Where is Ethyn, and when will he be delivered to me?"

Kristo's hand shot out as if he intended to grab her, but Danya quickly stepped back out of his reach. She wasn't foolish enough to make demands and then step into the monster's private chambers. Here in the hallway they were not entirely isolated, not as they would be if she allowed him to drag her behind that door. Other doors lined this

hallway, and there were people close by, sleeping or preparing themselves for the day. She would not allow herself
to be alone with Kristo Stoyan, not ever again.

An unconcerned Kristo smiled and stepped into the
hallway, moving so forcefully forward that Danya had no
choice but to move a few steps more away from him and his
cold breath, until her back was against the stone wall and
she could go no farther. "I had hoped to avoid this confrontation until much later, but you have forced my hand with
your insolence." He leaned down and placed his face too
close to hers. The chill that touched her came not only from
his breath but also from his flesh, and a wave of what felt
like ice enveloped her. "You are no longer necessary. Another woman will be chosen empress tonight. Another will
give birth to the next emperor and assist the current one to
an early grave. You were never strong enough to do what is
required. If you were, Rainer would be dead by now."

Danya was hit with a heady mixture of relief and despair. There had been a time when being empress was all
she cared for, but what she wanted from life had changed
dramatically. She might actually have what Angelo offered—happiness beyond this terrible palace, a life with a
man who loved her. But if Kristo no longer needed her,
what would become of her son?

"I don't want to be empress," she said. "Not anymore. I
don't care about your plans for the emperor." She didn't
care who ruled, as long as he left her alone! She gathered
all her strength, finding a rush of bravery inside her that
she had buried for too long. "I won't spoil your plans by
warning the emperor or any at his command, but I want my
son. If you wish me to remain silent, you will bring Ethyn
to me immediately."

Kristo grinned, and Danya shuddered, as she always did
when he dared to look pleased with himself. "Your child
died as a baby, just as the old witch who delivered him informed you."

Danya's head began to swim. Her knees went weak.
"But the birthmark . . ."

"The memory of that birthmark was plucked from your weak brain as I searched for your vulnerabilities," Kristo whispered, his unlined face too horribly close to hers. "You had so many weaknesses to choose from."

Danya saw Ethyn in her mind, just as Kristo had described him. He was real! He had her eyes and he laughed well and often, and someone, somewhere, was caring for him until they could be reunited . . . "But my Ethyn," she argued weakly, her legs feeling less than steady.

"Ethyn was a dog I had when I was a boy," Kristo said coldly. "It was the first name to come to mind as I spun my story for you."

Danya's legs gave out and she sank to the floor, no longer able to stand. The crinkle of her full skirt was unbearably loud as she dropped, and the sound filled her head as if it were thunder or the rush of a raging river. For a moment she could hear nothing else.

Sitting on the floor in horrid silence, once the sound of her descent was through, she was completely hollow inside, empty and alone and in excruciating pain. She'd lost her son again, but this time her loss was much more excruciating than it had been two years ago, when her selfish mind had been on hiding the baby's existence—and her folly—from her family and from Ennis. In past weeks she'd learned to love the child she'd been so willing to give up at his birth. He'd become real to her, and she'd made great sacrifices to have him in her arms again. And all the time it had been a lie.

A great rush of cold washed over her, and she had just enough strength to look up and see that Kristo was pointing a thin, pale hand at her. It seemed as if the air he sent her way was washed in blue and green swirls that were pretty and evil at the same time. He kept smiling, and she wanted only to wipe that awful smile from his face. The cold that surrounded her was aching and dreadful, and she dropped her head into her lap, hiding her face, hoping that Kristo was killing her, hoping that the pain would soon be gone.

I'm sorry, Angelo, she thought. *I'm sorry I'm not the woman you think I could be.*

The wave of cold stopped, and Danya became vaguely aware that she and Kristo were no longer alone. Another resident of this hallway was leaving his quarters for the day and had been drawn to the couple. Danya wanted to scream at the boy to escape while he could, to run for his life, to save himself, but words would not come to her. She was numb. She was frozen.

"My niece has been taken ill," Kristo said, his voice filled with false concern. "Poor girl, she's never been quite right," he whispered, as if she could not hear his words.

Danya made herself small. She tried to disappear into the volumes of fabric suitable for an empress that made up her skirt. She tried to melt into the stone hallway so that perhaps the pain would go away. Her heart was beating so hard, it was about to burst through her chest.

And then it seemed that her heart did not beat at all.

The stranger pledged to fetch the palace physician, and when he was gone, Kristo leaned down and whispered to Danya once more. "You can tell everyone what you think you know, I suppose, but no one will believe you. You are weak. You are worthless. You are nothing."

And Danya tried even harder to disappear, because she knew that, evil or not, Kristo was right.

ALMUND Ramsden had traveled through the night in order to arrive at the palace early on this day. He was concerned about his daughter, worried that he had not made the right decision when he'd allowed Morgana to leave home with the emperor in his disguise. The man who led this country had sworn that no harm would come to Morgana, and Almund had believed him. So why had he not heard from her in all this time? Where was she on this important day, when the emperor would choose his bride?

Difficult or not, Morgana would make a good empress. And if that was not to be, she would make some other man a good wife. Still, Almund had been almost certain there had been a spark, of sorts, between the emperor and his beloved daughter as they'd argued on that fateful day. Reminded him somewhat of the day he'd met Morgana's mother . . .

Gaining entry to the palace was not an easy task, but with his connections—and his bluster—Almund finally managed. Soon it was evident that his rush to arrive had been for nothing. Morgana was not in the palace, he was told. She'd refused to be included in the emperor's contest; that was all anyone here knew.

He requested an immediate audience with the emperor, and was denied. He was informed that in five days Emperor Jahn would once again make himself available for audience with his subjects. Five days! Impossible.

Almund was furious. When he'd agreed to the emperor's plan—for what choice had he had?—he hadn't intended for his daughter to go missing. Like a fool, he'd hoped that spark he'd seen between the two would turn to more on the journey and Morgana would have the fine life she deserved. He'd hoped she would finally give up her foolishness in finding every man unworthy—as well as her impulsive declaration that she would never wed. Apparently that had not happened, since the palace was hectic as preparations were made for a feast and the emperor's important choice, and Morgana was nowhere to be found.

Everyone was mum about who the bride might be.

Obviously he'd made a mistake in allowing Morgana to leave home with the emperor. As he was grudgingly shown to his quarters, Almund realized that he should've denied even an emperor. Indignant and worried, he was not going to wait five days for his meeting. There would be great fanfare when the emperor chose his bride. Somehow, some way, Almund would be there, and he would demand to have his daughter returned to him.

And she had better be returned to him in the same untouched condition she had been in when she'd left home!

* * *

TURNING Danya and the young man who had stumbled across an unfortunate confrontation to stone would cause a commotion and perhaps raise an alarm, and Kristo could not have that. He had almost taken care of the girl in that way, teasing her with the iciness of his destructive power, pondering whether or not he should take her life and scatter the remains about the palace. He did wish to be rid of her, but it didn't matter. He was not worried about the lifeless lump of bones and flesh and tears Lady Danya had become as he, the young interloper, and the palace physician escorted her to her quarters. It would be a waste of his precious energy to start transforming those who did not matter to stone, when he might have need of all his energy on this night.

Besides, there was nothing left of Lady Danya. No strength, no hope, no ambitions. She was almost as cold as he. It was good that he had found Morgana. This one would not have lasted a year before breaking under the pressure of his demands.

Kristo and the other two men carried Danya into her bedchamber and carefully placed her upon the bed, ridiculously inappropriate and voluminous gown and all. The physician checked her heart and found a weak beat. He was concerned with her lack of color and her weakened heart, as any physician should be.

Looking at her, Kristo felt a surge of confidence. Danya wasn't going anywhere. She wasn't going to tell anyone what she knew. By the time she recovered, it would be done. He could deal with her tomorrow. Perhaps he would make Morgana turn this one to stone, in order to be certain that his daughter was entirely aligned with his purpose—a purpose which should also be hers in entirety. A murder in the palace would assure him that Morgana had the strength that he required—that she was the strong woman he thought her to be.

The young man who had come across the two of them in the hallway was glad to make his escape, once Lady

Danya was safely in her bed. The physician didn't look as if he planned to leave anytime soon. Kristo had much to do. It was going to be a busy day. He leaned toward the physician.

"She was talking nonsense before she collapsed. I fear something may have gone wrong with her mind." It wouldn't hurt to plant doubts, in case Danya recovered before the day was done. "Poor girl, her mother was never quite right in the head, but I had hoped this pretty child would not inherit the family weakness."

The physician turned his head and glared at Kristo. "Did anyone inform the emperor that Lady Danya has a family history of mental weakness?"

"No," Kristo said simply, "but I believe he knows. She's been behaving quite erratically since arriving here."

The physician nodded and returned his attention to the girl on the bed. Not only was she pale and cold, but her breath came so faintly it was as if she were almost dead. With any luck she would quickly die from a broken heart, devastated by the loss of a child who had never truly existed, mourning a baby she had buried years ago. Women were so weak.

His daughter would not be weak. He would not allow it.

"Perhaps you can give my niece something to help her rest more comfortably," Kristo suggested, feeling the need to be cautious as this important day unfolded.

"I could," the physician agreed.

"Lovely," Kristo said with a touch of relief. "A few days of rest and Danya may be her old self again."

The physician reached into his tapestry bag to fetch some remedy which would render Lady Danya insensible, and Kristo made his way from the room. This was the day—his time had arrived at last—and there was much to be done. But just to be safe, he turned in the doorway and watched as the physician spooned a dark concoction into Danya's lifeless mouth.

He felt a wave of relief that he had found his fine, strong daughter and did not need to rely on this damaged female in order to see his plan succeed.

TRINITY rode toward the palace at a leisurely pace, still uncertain of what he would do when he got there.

His time with Lady Rikka had been unsatisfying and much too short, but thankfully he had recovered from his affliction before she'd passed into the next life. Terrified of what he might do to her, she'd frantically told him how it had been Kristo's idea to rid the world of the competing bridal candidates before the emperor made his choice. Trinity wasn't sure that he believed her—there was no innocence in the woman, after all—but there had been some truth in what she said to him before she'd died.

"Besides, the man turned me to stone," Trinity said to the ghost that walked beside him. He did not know if the specters that haunted him were real or a figment of his imagination, but he did remember killing this particular man—a very long time ago. The ghost was tall and thin and still wore the ragged clothes he'd been wearing when Trinity had taken his life for some crime—real or imagined.

There were others, the haunting ghosts of those Trinity had killed in his innumerable years as an assassin, and if he looked closely, he could and did remember killing them all. That was the purpose of the curse, was it not? In days past, this particular ghost had always been close at hand, walking or running beside Trinity, standing over him as he became human again and took his first agonizing breath as his lungs turned from stone to flesh. Taunting him.

Instead of screaming and crying, as he had in early days, Trinity had come to consider the ghost or illusion or whatever it might be a friend. Not a close friend, but an escort, of sorts. Thinking of the visions around him as companions made him feel more in control than he had in the early days.

"It hurt terribly to be stone. I felt as if shards of glass were cutting through me."

"Yes, yes, so you have told me many times," the ghost said harshly. "It rather hurt when you killed me, so you'll get no sympathy here."

Trinity glanced to the rear, and as usual there was a long trail of bloody bodies walking behind him, some looking solid, others misty and insubstantial.

"You won't get sympathy from them, either," his personal ghost said.

"No, I suspect I won't."

Since Lady Leyla had laid her hands upon his body and cursed Trinity, ghosts of his victims had haunted him constantly. He wasn't quite as mad as he had been in the early days, but his mind was less than steady, that was for certain. The witch had made it impossible for him to harm the innocent, but she had done nothing to keep him from dispatching the less-than-innocent, as he had dispatched Lady Rikka.

The man who had turned Trinity to stone, in a futile attempt to take the life of a man who was cursed to immortality, was certainly not innocent, either.

Trinity worked the fingers of his right hand. "It's been many days since I recovered, but I swear, I feel as if there is still a bit of stone in my bones."

With Arthes and the palace rising before him, Trinity reined in his horse and stopped. What awaited him there? Another act of vengeance, another battle. At his heart he was tired of battles, tired of killing. Lady Leyla had ruined him with her curse, and he was in need of a long rest. Perhaps it was time to retreat once again to the Mountains of the North, where he could be alone for a hundred years or so—just him and his many, many haunting companions.

"It truly did hurt," he said again, and then, his decision made, he turned his horse to the north and rode away from Arthes.

The ghost at his side, determined to offer no sympathy, began to sing a dreary song. Soon they were all singing the tune of sacrifice and love lost and, finally, hell. As the capital city grew smaller behind him and the mountains which were weeks of travel away beckoned, Trinity—who knew he could not make the ghosts of his violent past shut up—sang along.

AFTER days of being determined to take nothing from Jahn—he called it stubborn to a fault, but she much preferred the word *determined* to describe her state of mind—Morgana chose and donned a dress suitable for an empress, one of the many Jahn had had delivered to her in way of an inadequate apology.

The gown she decided to wear on this important day was made of a fine, pale green silk and was minimally embellished. It was modestly cut in the bodice, compared to the frocks she had seen on Melusina and Anrid, but was certainly not prudish. She brushed out her hair and left it down and unadorned, in a style Jahn seemed to prefer.

She steeled her heart for what had to be done.

Her morning lesson with Deputy Rainer had been a short one, and had been conducted within the confines of her room with a watchful Blane present as chaperone. She had not forgiven the sentinel, who'd been present when Jahn had spun his lie, and he knew it. Smart man that he was, Blane was a little bit afraid of her.

Soon everyone would be afraid of her. One way or another they would all know what she was, they would all know that a witch once again resided on Level Seven.

Rainer had been absentminded and distracted, and so had she, so after a short lesson on gathering calmness as if it were a palpable thing, she'd dismissed him. Usually he liked to drag out their lessons as long as possible, but on this day he'd obviously been anxious to leave her. When Rainer and Blane had gone, Morgana practiced gathering serenity to and into herself. It was difficult when she could not find much calm in her life, much less gather it to her, but she needed control today more than ever.

She was not surprised when Kristo arrived, bearing tea as he had on other occasions, in order to explain his presence in her chamber. As she had learned to do when in his presence, she brought childhood memories to the forefront of her mind. She worked diligently to gather that calmness she so desperately needed, and set all other thoughts and emotions to the side. Kristo could not see what was truly in her mind; he could not know how she felt about him and his plans. She worked very hard to hide her thoughts from this horrible man who was, heaven help her, her real father.

She had never appreciated Almund Ramsden more than she did at this moment, as she looked into cold, evil eyes and remembered how she had so often—and so foolishly—longed to know and embrace the man who had given her life.

She took the opportunity to ask many questions about the power they shared, trying to learn as much as she could about the curse that had so taken her by surprise, the curse that had changed her life in an instant. Her interest was real, and Kristo mistook her questions for those of a woman who wished only to hone her own skills. In truth, she would gladly give her curse away—but she could not let this man see that. Not now.

Talk of the deadly weapon they shared could last only so long, and all too soon Kristo turned his cold eyes on Morgana and asked, "Are you ready?"

"Yes."

She could tell that he was trying to tap into her mind, trying to read her thoughts. She could also tell that he failed and was frustrated by the effort. "If you do not do exactly as I say, then everyone will know what you have done. Everyone will know that you killed that poor man with your magic. They will not be as forgiving as I have been, I trust."

There was much she could hide from Kristo, but he saw Tomas's death too well, too clearly. Perhaps she could not hide the murder from him because they shared the curse which he did not consider to be a curse, or perhaps it was because the guilt of a violent death weighed too heavily upon her heart to be entirely hidden.

"I understand," Morgana responded.

"Together you and I will make the emperor pay for all that he has done to you."

"Good," she whispered, thinking intently of a lengthy and dreary poem a long-ago tutor had made her memorize.

Kristo's brow wrinkled. "Do you understand what is required of you?"

She understood all too well. "What you have asked of me is very easy to understand," Morgana responded. "I make Jahn think that I have forgiven him, we marry, I give birth to his son, and then I kill my husband and make my baby an emperor who will rule with you, his doting grandfather, at his side. It's a simple enough plan, Kristo, and I am not a simpleton."

"Father," he said. "You should call me Father, my child."

The calm Morgana had tried so hard to gather seemed to fly away, breaking from her body in horror. The icy hint that she was on the edge of destruction, a destruction she was learning to control, grew. But she stopped the growth; she controlled the curse and filled her mind with senseless, simple thoughts. "Father," she whispered.

RAINER had been thinking of Danya since he'd left her very early this morning. She was more fragile than she'd allow anyone to know, and she'd do anything in order to save her son. He knew she would not be chosen as empress, and therefore would not be called upon to murder the emperor once a child had been conceived, but what else might Kristo ask her to do? Who else did he have on his side as he planned for a revolution which would begin in the emperor's bed?

He could not imagine that Lady Morgana would do

what Kristo had asked of Danya, but he couldn't be sure. What he did know was that Kristo, a man who had gone to great lengths to get what he wanted, would likely not walk away from his scheme if all did not go as planned. Tonight, when the emperor named the woman who would be his bride, something might very well happen, something which would harm the emperor and all of Columbyana.

Rainer requested—then demanded—an audience with a tense, fidgeting emperor whose mind was elsewhere. Emperor Jahn paced as the deputy minister warned that he suspected there was a treacherous plan in play, without revealing Danya's part in the scheme. He tried to make it appear that his magical abilities to read energy led him to believe that something was very wrong, rather than telling all that Danya had revealed to him in confidence. The emperor only half listened, even though Rainer's words were alarming.

"My Lord," Rainer finally said hotly, "I believe your life is in danger!"

Emperor Jahn looked at Rainer then, ceasing his pacing and giving all his solemn attention to the bearer of bad news. "Yes, I know."

"Perhaps you should postpone making your choice."

The emperor shook his head. "I can't do that. I set a deadline and I will stick with it, no matter what might occur on this night."

"But, My Lord Emperor, we cannot know who is involved in the scheme. You can trust no one. *No one*," he repeated for emphasis.

"That will be all," Emperor Jahn said crisply. "Your warning will be taken into consideration."

Rainer left the emperor, confused but certain that he had done all he could without breaking Danya's confidence and her trust. Was it enough?

He could not help but remember how nervous Morgana had been this morning. She'd been nervous for as long as he had known her, which in truth was not all that long, but today she had seemed different, somehow. Rainer won-

dered if that condition was normal for her or if somehow
Kristo had drawn Morgana into his scheme, just as he had
Danya. Blackmail, promises of power, a twisting of the
heart and soul for his own purposes. The man was truly
evil and would stop at nothing to get what he wanted.

But to tell all would put Danya's son in danger, and he
could not do that. Somehow he had to find the child and
make sure Ethyn was safe before a move was made on
Kristo. There was not much time! It would all begin tonight.

Rainer all but ran to the level where Danya's room was
located. At first he was heartened to see that she was still
in bed. She needed her rest. But then the man in the corner
of the room stood, and Rainer was startled.

Tol Whystler, palace physician, looked grim indeed.
"She's resting well," he said. It seemed that thanks to their
evening walks in the garden, everyone knew he and Danya
were friends, and Whystler was not surprised to see him in
her quarters.

"What happened?"

Whystler picked up his physician's bag and walked toward the door. "I believe she's had some sort of mental
breakdown. Her uncle said there's a family history . . ."

"Her uncle?" Rainer snapped as Whystler passed him,
headed for the door.

"Yes. He and Minister Calvyno's nephew helped to
move her from the upper level, where she collapsed, to her
own chamber, so she would be more comfortable. She was
nonsensical, so I gave her a spoonful of sleeping potion to
help her rest." He shook his head and glanced at the bed
and a resting Danya. "The emperor should know she is not
fit before he makes his decision. Not that she's likely to be
able to make an appearance tonight, when the choice is
made." His voice turned oddly cheerful, for a moment. The
physician didn't want to see Danya as empress any more
than other palace residents did.

"How long will she sleep?" Rainer asked, wondering
what had happened to bring Danya to this low point.

"The drug affects people differently, but it's unlikely she will stir before morning." With that the physician nodded and left the room, closing the door behind him.

Rainer moved to the bed and looked down on a pale, trembling Danya. He covered her with the blanket which had been kicked to the end of her bed, and then he lay down beside her, attempting to keep her warm. He wanted to track down Kristo and throw the man into a small cell on Level Twelve. Men like this one made Rainer wish Level Thirteen was still in use. If ever a man deserved to be thrown into a pit not fit for humans, locked away forever, it was Kristo Stoyan. But until Danya's son was returned to her, nothing could be done about the man who had stolen the child and secreted him away, using an innocent child against a loving mother.

Rainer placed the length of his body along Danya's, attempting to warm her. She was so cold! Her face was white as snow, and her skin radiated a chill which was entirely unnatural. He could not identify the energy, but was quite sure it had originated with Kristo. He ran his hands along her arms, he breathed warm air against her neck. Still, she remained too cold.

She would never forgive him if he did anything to endanger her son, but what was he to do? How could he save Danya and her child and the emperor, too? How could he do what was right?

A wave of sharp sadness radiated from the sleeping woman; it was unlike anything he had ever felt from Danya before. Rainer smoothed a strand of dark hair away from her snow-white face.

"What has that bastard done to you?"

Chapter Seventeen

EVEN though it was early in the evening and the partying had just begun, the sounds of revelry reached Jahn's ears, muffled through stone walls and his own distraction. Those who were ignorant—and those who were not—celebrated the coming of summer, when the sun was at its peak and the goddesses were heavy with child. Masked dancers had already begun to gather in the ballroom, where in a short time Jahn was expected to choose his empress.

It had seemed like such a simple, harmless contest on that First Night of the Spring Festival, when he had been tired of the constant nudging to take a wife, tired of the responsibilities that came with the small gold crown which sat so heavily upon his head tonight.

Thanks to his foolish contest, everything in his life had changed. Alix had taken a wife and was gone, no longer the steady and ever-present rock Jahn had always leaned upon. They would always be brothers, and perhaps one day they would be friends, as they had once been, but at the moment Jahn felt only a loss.

He'd had the very real concept of betrayal revealed to

him in a startling and disturbing way. Perhaps he had not asked to be emperor; perhaps he had not fought for his throne, as Arik before him had fought. But no matter how he had come to be here, this was his place in the world, and he could never again forget that there were those who would do anything to have the power that came with this position. There would always be those who would kill for what he had been born to.

Not only his life had been changed by the events he'd set into motion. Princess Edlyn was dead, as was Lady Leyla, whose body had been found with what remained of her traveling party. An attempt had been made on Lady Verity's life; he could hardly blame her for walking away from the palace and his contest for the simple life of a sentinel's bride. There was still no word from General Merin and the woman he had been sent to fetch, the Turi barbarian Lady Belavalari. And Morgana—her life had most certainly changed.

Almund Ramsden had arrived in Arthes this very day and, to hear Calvyno tell it, was working diligently to gain an audience. Jahn had been able to avoid the man, as well as many others, but sooner or later he would have to face them all. What would he say to the man when they finally came face to face? Jahn was emperor and by law entitled to anything he desired, but Ramsden was a father, and he had rights of his own.

Lady Danya was the only one of the six women who was apparently unaffected by the events of the past three months. From what little he had seen of her, she already considered herself empress. Was she working with those who wished to take this country from him? Or was she simply lucky in avoiding whatever sad fate might've been planned for her? Tonight would be a shock for her, he imagined, since as far as she knew, she had no competition and would soon have the position she craved.

The door to his office burst open, and Jahn's hand instinctively dropped to his sword. After all he had learned, he could not be unarmed when he faced what was to come.

He relaxed when he saw Minister Calvyno and behind him General Merin, in the company of two women and a young man Jahn had never seen before. Since Merin had been sent to fetch one of the potential brides, at least one of these women must be Lady Belavalari. Judging by the ladies' dress and attitude, it was clear which one was the barbarian.

"My Lord," Calvyno said, paler than usual and obviously shaken. "These ladies are . . . dare I say it . . . potential brides for your consideration."

Merin opened his mouth to say something but Calvyno continued.

"Rather, they would be potential brides if they had not already *married*."

There followed a convoluted and almost amusing account, told in turn by all four newlyweds. What it came down to was that Merin had married Lady Belavalari, and his brother Savyn Leone had taken Lady Leyla—miraculously not at all dead—as his wife. The body found had been that of her chaperone, Calvyno explained. He was flustered and apologetic, but Jahn found himself amused for a blessedly peaceful moment.

Perhaps he had not ruined too many lives—other than his own—after all.

Of course, this night was not yet over.

"I'm glad you're here," Jahn said as he approached the weary travelers. "You will be needed for the ceremony which is soon to take place."

Merin's shoulders squared. "My Lord, in case you did not fully understand, Bela is my wife, and Lady Leyla is . . ."

"Yes, yes, you're all happily and blissfully wed. That does not mean I cannot put you all to good use before the night is done."

He had some explaining to do, he supposed. Judging by the confusion and even anger he saw on the faces around him, those explanations were going to take some time.

"Minister Calvyno," Jahn said, turning to the weary man, "fetch us some wine."

"Gladly, My Lord." The man all but ran from the room, and Jahn wasn't certain poor Calvyno would ever return. It didn't really matter. It was possible he had all the help he needed right here before him.

"Ladies," Jahn said in his most charming voice, "please sit and rest. I'm sure it's been a tiring day."

And it was about to get more tiring.

MORGANA allowed herself to be collected by two solemn sentinels and escorted to the noisy ballroom where soft music played and wine flowed. The grand chamber had been decorated with crimson banners and depictions of the sun in all its glory, bright and shining down upon them all, as well as a number of statues and statuettes of goddesses large with child. Morgana tried not to look too pointedly at those statues. She herself was not yet so large, but she would be, one day soon. She was no goddess, but she was—or would be—mother of an emperor.

Kristo kept his distance, but was never too far way. His eyes bored through her. She felt them, like daggers in her back. Did he know what she was going to do? What Jahn was going to do? She tried to tell herself that Kristo was only one man, that he could not destroy a country with his hate, but she knew in her heart that her father was much more than simply one man. He was an ambitious monster.

Jahn was not yet here, and she longed to see him. She needed to see him! Even though the ballroom was crowded and she could not see everyone, if Jahn was here, she would know. She would feel his presence, she was certain of it. Where *was* he? The ballroom swirled with color and light, with laughter and music, until Morgana felt dizzy as she searched for crimson and gold and distinctively streaked hair.

Her initial idea, when she'd told Jahn of Kristo's plan,

had been to lock the horrid man away. It was quite a risk, even if he could be spirited away quickly and imprisoned. Like her, he used his hands to direct his destruction, so if those hands could be quickly restrained, perhaps they could avoid disaster. Kristo could do too much damage in a short period of time, and that wasn't even taking into consideration that he'd tell everyone about Tomas's death. Worst of all, he'd tell Jahn. She had confessed many things to her husband as she relented to him, as she'd surrendered so much, but she had not been able to bring herself to tell him that she'd taken a life. That wasn't necessary for what needed to be done. Perhaps it would never be necessary!

Jahn didn't think locking Kristo Stoyan away would do them much good. First, they needed to know who was working with the traitor, how many and where they were. Getting one conspirator out of the picture would be only a temporary solution. No, they needed to unmask all those who worked with Kristo, preferably tonight. How else were they to move on?

When the crowd stirred and murmured, Morgana thought that perhaps Jahn had arrived. She turned, and saw with disappointment that it was a strange, tall man in official clothing who'd entered the room, escorting two women. One of them was a strikingly beautiful brunette who studied the crowd meekly, and the other was a pretty woman with chestnut hair in a long braid, a masculine manner of dress, and an attitude. She was not at all meek.

A lady dressed in gold and wearing a feathered mask loudly and drunkenly greeted the newly arrived man as Minister Calvyno. Calvyno spoke softly to the woman, and she shook her head. He spoke to several other people in the area, and got the same response. Finally, he found and spoke to Anrid. Morgana's heart dropped. She had not seen Anrid or her friend Melusina before now, but they'd been here all along, lost in the crowd. Anrid smiled and pointed to Morgana, and when that was done, Calvyno caught Morgana's eye and held it strongly. He waved her over, and after taking a deep breath Morgana headed that way. The crowd parted. It had begun.

Morgana was very aware that Kristo carefully watched her every move. One misstep, and he could use his power to cause the chaos he craved. He could turn a man to stone—or he could tell everyone what she had done on the last seasonal first night, and her life would be over as surely as if he had transformed and shattered her.

When she reached Calvyno, he gave her a tight smile. "I was so happy to hear of your *belated* arrival, Lady Morgana. These two ladies also arrived quite recently. Lady Belavalari and Lady Leyla," he said with a casual and somehow distraught wave of his hand, "if you three will follow me."

There was no time for introductions, and even if there had been, Morgana didn't know what she would say. Keep your hands off my husband? You should've stayed far away from this place? Duck?

Calvyno led them all to the front of the room, where they were directed to a raised dais which was much too long for three women. Like horses at auction, they were to stand there, close but not too close together.

Morgana's heart rate increased and her mouth went dry. This was not the plan. She and Lady Danya were to be the only ones here. Jahn would choose Morgana and she would refuse, which would spur Kristo into action. Only then would they know how deep this treachery went. Morgana looked out over the crowd, catching many a curious eye. There was no other way, she knew that, and still she was afraid. Jahn thought they would be able to handle whatever Kristo did, but she could not be certain. If Jahn choose her and she said yes, then there would be no violence here tonight. They would have time to come up with another plan, to find another way to uncover the traitors.

While she stood upon the dais, fighting panic, the emperor arrived.

Morgana could only imagine that Jahn caused this kind

of stir whenever he entered a room. People stepped aside. They bowed and curtseyed. They stared after him with awe and admiration and respect—and even fear. He was a powerful man. She had never been more aware of that fact than as he walked toward her. Since learning his true identity she'd seen him in his crimson robes, but tonight he was dressed differently—though the color of his clothing remained the same. Trousers fit snugly atop polished boots. A perfectly fitted jacket was adorned with gold thread and buttons. His golden crown and polished sword caught the light. He smiled, but it was not the true smile she knew and had come to love.

He studied all three of the women who awaited his arrival, but his eyes lingered only on her.

And then he turned to look out over the crowd. "You have all come here tonight to dance and eat fine food and drink wine and, oh yes, to watch me pick an empress from among a special half dozen who have been deemed worthy. Sadly, Princess Edlyn lost her life on the journey, and Lady Verity of Mirham ran off with one of my sentinels. I'm not sure if I should imprison the rascal who stole her or offer him a higher rank."

There was a smattering of uncomfortable laughter.

"Still, I did say I would choose from six women, and I am a man of my word. Ladies?"

At that, Melusina and Anrid burst giggling from the crowd and took their positions on the dais. Morgana suffered a moment of pure horror. Had this been his plan all along? Was he going to publicly humiliate her? No, there was too much at stake. What was he doing?

Jahn turned and looked at each of the women in turn, then spun about. "Kristo Stoyan, I saw you here a moment ago. Where is your niece? It seems I am a bride short."

Morgana held her breath as the man Jahn had called by name stepped from the crowd.

"My Lord, my niece is unwell and unable to leave her bed," Kristo said.

"Impossible. Have her brought here immediately."

She should not be surprised that Jahn was such a good actor. He showed no fear as he addressed Kristo; he revealed no anger at all, no hint of his knowledge. Yes, he pretended very well.

"Lady Danya is truly unsuitable and unable . . ." Kristo began, but he was interrupted by a weak voice which managed to carry through the crowd.

"I am here."

The crowd parted once more, and a pale, disheveled woman who looked as if she'd just rolled from her bed was revealed. Deputy Rainer assisted her. It appeared as though without him she would surely drop to the floor, but she moved toward the dais with determination, her eyes unerringly forward.

The woman wore a plain gray dress that had seen better days, and her hair was simply pulled up and back. Her face was ashen, and she seemed decidedly unsteady.

"Lady Danya," Jahn said with a curt bow. "So happy you could join us."

Kristo was very obviously *not* happy to see Lady Danya.

DANYA walked toward the front of the ballroom, her eyes flitting from the women on the dais to the emperor she had once thought she'd desired above all to an enraged Kristo. She wanted to fly into the man who had stolen her dreams and effectively killed her son—or, rather, the memory of her son as he might've been, if he'd lived. But she could barely move, and without Angelo she would be no more than a heap on the floor, so she could only move forward slowly, one small step at a time. She clung to Angelo; he held her firmly.

When she'd awakened in her bed to see the darkness of night beyond her window and Angelo at her side, she'd immediately known what she had to do. After taking the time to comb her hair back and change into one of the simple dresses she'd brought from home—taking the time to tuck

Angelo's handkerchief in her bodice—she'd made her way here, to this fateful place and night. And she'd arrived just in time.

Angelo placed his mouth close to her ear. "Something is going on here. The energy is . . . interesting, and dangerous."

"Much is going on, I imagine." She looked at Kristo, the man who had all but killed her hours earlier.

"No, something else," Angelo said. "Don't confront Kristo. Not yet."

"But . . ."

"Not yet, love. Trust me."

She did. She trusted Angelo Rainer with her secrets, her weaknesses, her very life. "Fine. I suppose I should join the others."

There had been a time when she'd considered these women to be her rivals, threats who might take from her the extravagant life she'd imagined for herself. A life of privilege, of power. A life where she'd be given all she desired; and, more important, a life where she could escape the mistakes of her past.

Until she'd met Angelo, she had never even considered that she might deserve and want love. He helped her to the raised platform where five other women stood, and he held her hand until she was steady. Only when she nodded her head did he let her go. Rumpled, light-headed, angry to the pit of her soul, she stood there and waited. Kristo, the hooded man who had ruined her heart and ripped apart her soul, looked confused, then relieved. He obviously thought her so foolish as to think she still had a chance to claim the position of empress.

Let him think what he would, for now.

JAHN tried to appear nonchalant as he glanced about the ballroom. Those who were with him on this night were in place. When Kristo was denied, what would he do? He, General Merin, and a few others carried lengths of rope with which to bind Kristo's hands when the time came. Would that be enough to stop Kristo's destructive power? Morgana said he used his hands to direct his cold ruin, but that didn't mean binding them would stop it. Who would the man call forth, and how many would come to his aid? Were there traitors among the revelers, or were the revolutionaries awaiting a call from somewhere outside this room? Where was General Hydd, who had suggested Morgana as empress?

Merin stood in one corner of the room; his brother Savyn was positioned in another. Blane and Iann had the door, and other sentinels whose loyalty was beyond question were posted about the ballroom—and beyond.

When Jahn had found out that two of the potential brides were present—married or not—he'd come up with this new, better plan of attack. It was a plan that did not put Morgana in the middle of the action; it was a plan which would turn Kristo Stoyan's anger away from her.

He jumped onto the dais and walked behind the six women who were on display. He felt ashamed and equally annoyed that his plan had called them here months ago, when he had not considered them human beings, when he had not thought of them as fine women with feelings, but saw them only as necessary brood cows for the heir he was required to produce.

But he could show no shame now. Melusina and Anrid stood together at one end of the platform, each of them smiling widely and occasionally waving at their new husbands. Their bosoms were not as exposed as he was accustomed to, and yet they were far from prim ladies. "Beautiful as always," he said, leaning in close. Melusina giggled. "Would you make fine wives?"

"You should know, My Lord, since you recently made us wives of other men," Anrid said casually.

Jahn waved a hand. "Marriage can be undone as easily as it is done. I probably should've wed you two long ago, when I realized a wife would be required."

"Both of us?" Melusina asked.

"I could not bear to separate you."

"I rather like my new husband," Anrid said, as if a ball-room full of people didn't listen in.

"And I like mine!" Melusina said.

"I'm not sure that we would have you now," Anrid added with another wave to her husband, who shyly waved back.

"Pity," Jahn said as he moved down the line. There was a smattering of uncomfortable laughter in the ballroom, where masks had been lowered and the dancing had stilled.

Lady Belavalari—Bela, Merin had called her—looked none too pleased, even though she knew the plan well enough and did not consider herself in danger of being chosen as empress. "You look like a woman who can hold her own in any situation." He glanced at Merin, who did not smile. At all. "Do you know how to use that sword, Bela?"

"Yes, My Lord, I do," she answered in a strong and steady voice. "Would you like a demonstration?"

"Not really." He studied her muddied boots and messy braid. "Interesting," he muttered as he moved to Lady Leyla.

As Jahn studied the stunning woman who had married Savyn Leone, he did not let on that he knew her secrets. Witch, some called her, and knowing what she could do with a touch, he might call her the same. Then again, what was he to call Morgana if he called this lady a witch? They had both been born with unearthly powers. Did that make them witches or goddesses? Unnatural women or the most natural of females who called power from the earth and the sky?

"You're a fetching woman," he said.

"Thank you, My Lord," she responded meekly.

"The goddesses who are with child as the summer season of the sun begins are likely jealous of such beauty. Would I dare to insult them by taking a wife who would challenge their beauty?"

"I am only a woman, My Lord," Lady Leyla responded.

Jahn shook his head. "Why do I doubt that simple statement?" Then he moved to his wife. "Lady Morgana. I imagine everyone here knows that you refused my initial invitation to participate in this contest."

"I did," she responded.

"Why?"

"I refused because I had heard that you were gluttonous and foolish and irresponsible and likely quite portly. I was also under the impression that you had no chin."

"Don't forget stupid. And now that you have met me?"

"You are not portly," she said simply.

Again there was uncomfortable laughter throughout the room.

"You would be a troublesome empress, I have no doubt."

"And you would be a difficult husband, to any so unlucky as to be chosen."

Jahn chanced a quick glance at Kristo, who was red-faced and confused. This was not in his plan, so what would happen next? Whom would he call to his side?

Jahn moved to an unsteady Lady Danya, who looked more dead than alive. Only her eyes revealed life, and they seemed to burn with fever.

"You are a pretty girl, but you have a sharp tongue that has pierced many of the palace residents in weeks past. You ask much and give little. Do you have any redeeming qualities beyond your beauty?"

"No, My Lord," she said softly, "I do not."

He nodded his head. "Well, you're honest. That is a fine quality in an empress." For a moment Jahn held onto her arm, as she seemed to need the support. She swayed and then steadied. "I suspect there is more to you than meets the eye, Lady Danya," he said softly, this time his words for her alone and not for the amusement of the crowd and the enragement of Kristo Stoyan.

She looked him in the eye and answered just as softly. "Perhaps tonight we will find out if that is true."

Jahn released Lady Danya when he felt she was able to stand alone, then once again studied the six women before him. He occasionally touched a shoulder or a length of hair. None of them looked him in the eye; they kept their gazes straight ahead. Even Bela, who seemed ready and even anxious for a fight. He was happy to see that Morgana had given in and donned one of the new gowns he'd given her. She had chosen the green frock that complemented her eyes, but he could not afford to comment on that fact.

Finally he stood before the six women with his hands in the air. "I can't decide. I certainly don't want to send any one of them home rejected. Perhaps I should marry them all and see who gives me a son first. I can always put the rejects out to pasture when that is done."

Merin's Bela placed a hand on the hilt of her sword. Melusina stuck out her tongue, and Morgana's lips went thin and tight. Jahn was supposed to choose her and allow her to reject him, which would send Kristo into a rage and into action. If the rejection was *his,* no anger would be directed at the woman who carried his child.

"Then again, perhaps I won't marry any one of them."

Kristo was backing toward the far side of the room, rather than moving closer to his daughter and his emperor. With any luck, the plan was working. The man who had tried to manipulate both Danya and Morgana would gather whatever assistance he had waiting, and then they would know precisely what they were up against. Kristo and his cohorts would be defeated in short order and then, only then, could Jahn claim Morgana as his own—if she would still have him.

Jahn shrugged his shoulders. "This is all too much for a simple man like me." He looked at Morgana. "A gluttonous, irreverent simpleton cannot be expected to make such an important choice. This contest was a mistake. It's over. I will remain unwed."

Moans and a few squeals broke from the crowd that had gathered to watch the proceedings. And then an unexpected voice rang out in indignation. "There you are! What's going on here? Where have you been?"

Jahn locked eyes with Almund Ramsden, an angry and

rightfully affronted father who had arrived just in time, or so it seemed. Gone was the obedient servant who had willingly—if reluctantly—handed over his daughter many weeks earlier.

The man stalked toward Jahn. "What the hell have you done with my child?"

KRISTO turned and made his way to the window of the ballroom, grabbing an oil lamp from a table as he passed. He had not thought it would come to this, but he would not be denied. Not now. The emperor was playing games. He would play as well. He lifted the oil lamp and waved it across the open window three times.

His men, the mercenaries Rikka had hired and the general who would lead them, were watching and waiting. They were itching for a fight—hoping that all would not go well. The army was small, but they would have the element of surprise. Hydd insisted that Emperor Jahn was weak, and he and his men would not be prepared to fight.

Kristo didn't know what had happened, but this was not how the evening was supposed to play out. The emperor was supposed to choose Morgana and they'd be married immediately. Soon everyone would know about the child the empress carried, and, as Morgana's father, Kristo would be an important part of palace life. Soon enough the time would come for the emperor to be dispatched.

But the idiot emperor had not chosen Morgana. He had not chosen any of them! Rikka's plan to connive and cheat herself a place in the palace had failed. Now Kristo would do things his way. The emperor and those closest to him would be killed, and Kristo would claim the throne himself—with the blood of the emperor in his grandchild to soothe those who could not be convinced by force alone. He would have both military strength and an imperial bloodline on his side.

His men were close; it would not take them long to get here.

"My Lord Emperor," Kristo said as he left the window after signaling his army. It would be best if the emperor was here when the attack took place, lightly guarded and a part of the crowd. Hydd would know what to do. "If you will indulge me, I have some information to share." He placed himself between Emperor Jahn and Ramsden, a man who had arrived much too late to save his daughter.

"Don't listen to him!" Morgana shouted from her place on the dais.

Did she think he would give her away now, when no matter what had happened, she continued to carry the emperor's only child in her belly? The threat that he would tell others how she had taken a life was one he could hold over her for a very long time—for as long as she continued to be useful, in fact.

"I'm not finished with the emperor," Ramsden said. "He owes me an explanation about what has happened to my daughter!"

Kristo looked at Ramsden, and he was tempted to stone the man, here and now. "Lady Morgana is not your daughter," Kristo said coldly. "She is mine. Morgana has always been *mine,* just as her mother was *mine* long before she was yours."

Ramsden went pale. "She said you were dead."

"I am not dead, obviously," Kristo said, his voice lowered and meant for Ramsden alone. "I was simply discarded years ago for a man more easily manipulated than I allowed myself to be." He smiled, and Ramsden took a step back. "That would be you. Go away, you are no longer necessary. Morgana has her real father now. She no longer needs you."

Kristo dismissed Ramsden and turned again to the emperor, raising his voice so all could hear. "My Lord Emperor, I am a powerful seer, and I can tell you without question that on this night when we celebrate the fat bellies of the goddesses and the bright rays of the sun, five of these women are with child. One of those children is yours." He looked at Morgana. "And one of these women is a murderer. Yes, there is a vile murderess among your potential brides."

He held Morgana's unsteady glare. She was terrified that he would tell all that he knew. Though he would need to hold that threat over her for some time to come, he also needed that power now, as he reminded her to do her part. Kristo was concentrating so intensely on his daughter that he did not realize Danya had left the dais and stood very near.

"Let's make that two, shall we?" she said, as she shoved a dagger into his flesh, very near to his heart. He looked into her eyes, eyes which were suddenly stronger than they should be, eyes which were determined and sad and as cold as his own. "For Ethyn," Danya said, as Kristo's legs went weak and he dropped to the floor.

Chapter Eighteen

RAINER ran toward Danya, but he was too far away and
much too late. His hand dropped to his side, where it fell
upon an empty sheath. That was his dagger she'd driven
into Kristo—she had lifted it from him somewhere between her bedchamber and the ballroom. She'd planned
this all along. No wonder she had insisted upon coming
here tonight! As Kristo fell to the floor, he lifted a hand
and directed an evil, icy energy toward Danya. Rainer
could feel that evil power from a distance. He screamed,
"No!" But it was too late. Danya was instantly transformed
into a statue of dark stone shot with streaks of crystal.

Even in lifeless stone her face remained peaceful, as
though she had known all along what the sacrifice would
be for attacking Kristo and she had been willing to make
it.

Kristo was wounded, but he was not dead. Not yet.
Rainer could feel very strongly that the life was draining
from the man who lay bleeding on the ballroom floor, just
as he could feel that there was still life in what Danya had
become.

But not for long.

He could move water and air, sense power, give plea-sure and pain—but he did not know how to bring Danya back.

As Rainer reached out to caress what Danya had be-come, Lady Morgana screamed, in a screeching voice that carried throughout the ballroom, "Don't touch her!"

At that moment Rainer made the connection between the power that had turned Danya to stone and the power he had been teaching Morgana to control. Both were cold; both were powers of transformation, though this stone was very different from the crystal Morgana created.

"Can you undo what he's done?" he asked.

"Even if she could, she would not," Kristo said, badly wounded, bleeding, and yet still confident. "My daughter would not betray me that way; she would not save the woman who dared to try to kill me." He looked down at the wound in his chest, and perhaps at that moment he realized that Danya had not just tried to kill him; she'd succeeded.

Calmly, Morgana looked down at the dying man. "You are not my father," she said with a confidence that more than matched Kristo's. "My father is Almund Ramsden, the exceptional man who raised me, spoiled me, fed and clothed and housed and loved me all my life. You are noth-ing. You mean nothing." She turned to Danya—what was left of Danya—and studied the stone carefully. "Is she alive?"

"Yes," Rainer said, "but not for long, I fear. Can this be undone?"

"I don't know," Morgana whispered. "Warmth always stopped the rising of the curse for me." Her eyes flitted to the emperor, as she spoke those words. "But I don't know that it will help at this point. Also, this stone is very differ-ent from my own ."

It was the emperor who first noticed that Kristo had lifted his hand and was directing his dastardly energy at Morgana. A handful of men were trying to work their way to the emperor, but the crowd was thick and did not make

way. General Merin shouted for those in his way to *move*.
They were slow doing so. Without a second thought, Emperor Jahn threw himself between Kristo and Morgana,
shielding her body with his own, wrapping his arms around
her and protecting every inch of her from the man who
would do to her what he had done to Danya.

JAHN waited for the cold to pierce through him. There
had not been time to grab a rope and bind the wounded
man's hands. When he'd realized what Kristo was attempting to do, he could think of nothing but saving Morgana,
no matter what the cost. For a moment he did feel that cold,
and it hurt. It shot to his core and lingered there.

"I love you," he whispered.

And then the unearthly cold was gone.

"Jahn, no!" Morgana screamed, trying to extricate herself, trying to protect him the way he protected her. He was
stronger than she was, and did not allow her to move.

With the cold threat gone, he turned cautiously to see
that Rainer had kicked Kristo's deadly hand aside and
stomped upon the wrist, and that Almund Ramsden had
finished the job Danya had begun, running Kristo through
with his sword.

Deputy Rainer looked at what remained of Lady Danya
with terror in his eyes. Terror and love. Jahn recognized
that expression. He recognized the fear of loss and the love.
Three months ago he would not have, but tonight he knew
both too well.

"Can you do it?" Rainer asked.

"Not alone," Morgana said.

"Hurry," the agonized man whispered.

Jahn reluctantly released Morgana, ready to step back
and let her do whatever it was she could do. But she grabbed
his hand before he could take more than a single step away.
"Make me warm, Jahn," she commanded.

"Here?"

She smiled a little. "Just wrap your arms around me and hold me close."

"I can do that." He stood at her back and circled his arms around her. At Morgana's instruction, Rainer stood beside them. She created a warm transforming energy Jahn could feel pouring off her in sunlike waves, and Rainer, using his own magical powers, helped her to direct that energy gently toward the statue that had once been—and perhaps still was—Lady Danya. It was not a quick and easy task. Morgana and Rainer both trembled, and the partygoers who had not fled the ballroom backed away until there was a large empty circle around Kristo's body, Lady Danya, and those who were trying to save her. Only Merin and his brother dared to move closer rather than away, and they first made sure that their wives had been escorted to safety.

Almund Ramsden could not be moved. He occasionally stared at Kristo's body as if he were afraid the man would leap back to life, but for the most part he kept loving eyes on his daughter.

Morgana and Rainer worked hard, in a way Jahn did not entirely understand. He had begun to think that in spite of their efforts, the transformation could not be undone. And then he saw a sign of life. A single tear trickled slowly down a hard stone cheek.

LADY Danya's resurrection seemed to take forever. Morgana sucked up Jahn's heat, and with Rainer's assistance she worked to undo what Kristo had done. She gave off a wave of life in the same way she had, on occasion, given off a wave of cold death. If Rainer had not taught her the art of control, this would not be possible, but gradually Lady Danya came to life. Stone became flesh, an uneasy and ragged breath was taken, and in what was likely a shorter amount of time than Morgana realized, Danya and Rainer were in one another's arms.

And she was in Jahn's.

"I can't believe you would throw yourself between me and Kristo!"

"I can't believe you'd consider for one moment that I would not," he responded.

People were moving close again, now that Kristo was dead and Danya had been saved. Jahn ignored them all as he dropped to one knee and said, in a voice that carried throughout the large room, "Lady Morgana, will you marry me? Again?"

"Jahn, not here," Morgana whispered. "Stand up."

"Not until I get my answer."

"But you don't know everything!" She had been able to tell him about Kristo's plan and the child within her, but she had never gathered the courage to tell him what had happened to Tomas on the First Night of the Spring Festival.

"I know all I need to know."

She couldn't allow him to go on believing she was someone she was not. "Jahn, I killed man."

"Yes, I know," he responded calmly.

Morgana blinked hard and would've backed away, if he had not taken her hand and held on. "You can't know . . ."

"Tomas Glyn, who, I have no doubt, earned his fate. Don't look so surprised, love. First there is the tale of a man turned to glass by a witch, and then I see with my own eyes that you have that power. I also know that you have no malice in you, and that if he roused that power, he deserved his end."

"But . . ."

"I have killed in war," Jahn interrupted. "I have taken the lives of monsters and not lost a moment's sleep over their deaths. Your heart is better than mine, if you torture yourself over the death of a man who intended you harm. He did intend you harm, did he not?"

"Yes," she whispered, and a weight was lifted from her shoulders.

"If you had not killed him, I would've. Now, will you be my empress?" He asked. Then, in a lowered voice, he added, "Please. I beg of you, forgive me for my mistakes and make me your husband again."

"I promised my mother I would wait for love."

"And did you?" he asked expectantly, as if he did not know.

"Yes," she said again, smiling down at the man on his knees before her.

She had thought the evening's excitement was over, but a half dozen sentinels rushed into the ballroom. "My Lord," Blane called, "you were right. A small army approaches from the west. General Hydd is in the lead."

Jahn rose and quickly kissed Morgana's hand. "How many are there?"

"Fifty, perhaps," Blane answered.

"We have men in position, as I directed?"

"Yes, My Lord."

"My horse and shield are waiting?"

"Yes, My . . ." Blane began.

Just as Morgana said, "No!" Surely it wasn't necessary that Jahn put himself in danger!

Her husband smiled down at her. "A fine woman once told me that I had never fought for this palace and all that comes with it."

"That woman was a thoughtless idiot."

"That woman was right, and tonight I will fight for the palace, the country, and my empress, just as I ask my sentinels to fight. Don't worry, love. We have them outnumbered and we are prepared in a way Kristo never expected."

"Come to my bed wounded, and I will be *very* unhappy," she responded, not showing the fear for his safety that grew in her heart, so close to the child they had created.

"I'll keep that in mind." With that Jahn bowed to her, then turned on his heel and joined Blane and the others.

* * *

SHE was so cold. Danya tried to melt into Angelo's arms, but she could not. She still felt like stone. "I thought I was dead."

"So did I," Angelo said, and she could hear the fear in his voice.

Danya lifted her head and looked him in the eye. "Why did you save me? I deserve death for all I've done."

"You've done nothing," Angelo responded.

"I aligned myself with an evil man and promised to . . ."

"You promised to do as he asked to save your son," Angelo said sharply, "and yet you harmed no one."

Tears filled her eyes. "I aligned myself with Kristo because of a lie. Ethyn . . . there is no Ethyn. There never was." Her heart broke for the son she'd lost, and she wished, for a moment, that she was still made of stone. Then perhaps her heart wouldn't break.

Angelo took her face in his gentle hands. "That is all behind us. Marry me, Danya. We'll have sons, one day. Daughters, too, I expect."

The pain in her heart faded a bit. This man was the only one she'd ever trusted. The only one who'd ever loved her . . . the only man she had ever truly loved. "I look terrible," she said, raising a hand to her mussed hair.

He smiled. "You look beautiful, as always." And then he kissed her, and Danya was able to let go of the pain of her past mistakes. There were a lot of them, so she could not say they were gone for good, but still, for the first time in a very long time, she saw her future as real and bright.

AFTER a few hours, Jahn returned, sweating and aching, but victorious. Kristo's army had been defeated and General Hydd—always so anxious for a fight—was dead. He'd been quite surprised not to be attacking those who were unaware, and even more surprised to see Jahn's sword raised against him. General Merin had been appointed minister of defense, though he said his term would be a short one. He had other plans, apparently.

Tired as he was at this hour of the night, Jahn leapt up the stairs to Level Seven and Morgana's chamber, only to find it empty. For a moment he surveyed the dark, lifeless room in horror, and then, with hope in his heart, he raced to his own imperial chambers, where he found his wife waiting for him. He'd never known such relief, such solace. She remained dressed in green, and her eyes were wearier than he liked to see them.

"Victorious and not a scratch on me," he said with a grin, holding his arms wide.

Morgana did not smile as her eyes fell on a nasty tear in his jacket, a rip caused by a blade which had swung too close. "Don't ever joke about putting yourself in danger, Jahn. It isn't funny." She sounded very much like a wife, and he liked it.

"I could use a bath," he said, reaching for the buttons of his imperial crimson uniform.

"Not yet," Morgana said, taking his hand in hers and looking into his eyes. "Tell me you're sure. Tell me you really love me and you don't care that I have a power I might not always be able to control. Tell me that you would want me as your wife even if I wasn't carrying your son."

"I'm sure of all of that and more."

Morgana relaxed. "I had to be certain. Let's go."

"Go?"

He allowed her to lead him away from the bed and the bath he craved, down the stairway to the ballroom which had been the site of such excitement earlier in the evening. Four tired sentinels followed, as ignorant of Morgana's plans as Jahn himself was.

"Last chance to change your mind," Morgana whispered.

"Never."

She opened the doorway to the ballroom and revealed a small but important crowd. Father Braen stood upon the dais, with Ramsden nearby. A battle-weary Blane was there, as were Iann and Sorayo. Even Calvyno, with a bit of color in his face, was present.

"It might not look like much, My Lord Emperor," Morgana said, "but this is a wedding fit for the ruler of a country."

"And his empress?" Jahn asked as he walked toward Father Braen with Morgana's hand caught up in his.

"Yes."

He glanced around the room. "Where is Rainer? I thought he might be here."

Morgana lifted her chin. "While you foolishly fought even though it was not entirely necessary for you to do so, Rainer and Lady Danya were married by Father Braen. They are much too busy to attend *your* wedding."

"I imagine that's true."

It took a short while for preparations to be made, for Morgana to say a word to her father, for Father Braen and Calvyno to arrange papers and signatures and such. Soldiers, tired and in some cases wounded, continued to trickle into the ballroom as preparations continued, and soon the chamber was filled. These men should be having their wounds tended to or claiming much-needed rest, but instead they came here in droves.

The sun was rising before Jahn and Morgana stood before Father Braen and said their vows, making what was already in their hearts official. The light that poured into the room was warm and filled with life. It was a new day. When Jahn turned about, determined to take his bride to their bed as quickly as possible, he was shocked to see that the room was filled—and that when he faced them, every man in the room dropped to a knee and lowered his head.

Jahn stood there for a moment, stunned at the response.

Blane made his way forward. "Most of them have never seen you fight before," he said in a lowered voice, "and they were impressed."

"I didn't do anything extraordinary," Jahn said. He had fought like the others, no more, no less.

"My Lord, you rode at the front of the line and you fought well. You did not hide behind others or cower upon a hilltop directing others. You drew blood, and more than once you came to the aid of a soldier in need."

Morgana *tsk*ed in concern for a battle which was now over. "Honestly, Jahn, you could've hidden or cowered a little!"

He looked down at her. "No, Ana, I could not. Emperor or not, that's not who I am. No more pretending, not with you or anyone else."

"No more pretending," she whispered.

They walked toward the ballroom entrance, where people made way for Jahn with respect and awe. When they were away from the others and climbing the flight of stairs to their chambers, Morgana added softly, "Next time there's a fight, I'm going with you. Once I have my abilities under control, think of what an asset I might be."

"You are . . ."

Before he could say "not," she broke away and ran from him, laughing. He chased her up the stairs, and just before he caught up with her, Morgana looked up at the ceiling— or beyond—and said with a smile, "Mama, you were right."